BORGIA ROSE

In memory of my Mama,

KD Allbaugh

BORGIA ROSE
A NOVEL

The Poisoning of Richland County

K.D. ALLBAUGH

Battle Ridge Rising Sun Press

Printed in the United States of America

ISBN paperback: 978-1-7360809-2-4
ISBN eBook: 978-1-7360809-3-1

Book Cover and Interior Design: Creative Publishing Book Design
Cover Art: Bogdan Maksimovic

This book is dedicated to the memories of loved ones who will never be forgotten: My Ghastin and Newkirk ancestors who came to Wisconsin to find new lives for themselves and for their families. Uncle Charlie, a man of music with an unforgettable laugh who was loved dearly by his family and friends especially Aunt Cheryl. Little Sofie, who made the world a better place by just being in it, your mom and dad keep your memory alive. Silas and Bernice Allbaugh, Will and Laura Ghastin, and Willard and Dora Maude Newkirk for being the loving grandparents that John and I now aspire to be to our beautiful grandson. My dad, Bob and my stepdad, George for being good fathers to a feisty kid.

In special memory of my grandmother, Dora Maude Newkirk. You loved without judgement and encouraged me to chase my dreams. Whenever I create a character who is strong, loving, and wise, she is a reflection of you.

PROLOGUE

The story of Rose Zoldoske has remained a mystery to this day. This young woman was either a scapegoat mistreated by the popular opinion of a small-town hierarchy or she was, in fact, a cold-blooded murderer.

Rose's life began simply in the rolling hills of beautiful Richland County, Wisconsin. She was born in Ithaca, a tiny hamlet just a few miles from the county seat of Richland Center. Rose was determined to leave the impediments of near poverty and make a better life. While some people would admire her industriousness, others would condemn her for her ambition. This fictional account inspired by real-life events attempts to reveal the mystery beneath the public case, hidden away.

Many of the facts of the narrative have been revealed over time and much speculation has been added to the facts. Few people know what really happened to the innocent people who died and to Rose herself. If these deaths were murders, they were murders by poisoning, cold and calculated, like the infamous Borgia family of old Italy.

"I was born with a stain. A mark, like the mark of Cain. But it is the mark of my father, my family, The mark of Borgia."

—Cesare Borgia

CHAPTER 1

MONDAY, JANUARY 4, 1897, WAUPUN, WISCONSIN

The January morning dawned gray and gloomy. The rising winter sun had attempted to pierce through the overcast skies, causing momentary glimmers from its position low in the sky. At each attempt, it was met with heavy-laden clouds, pushing it back into obscurity and submission. The sun continued its endeavors, undaunted by the seeming futility of the efforts.

Rose Zoldoske sat in a straight-back wooden chair staring out a window at the winter sky. Her dark, observant eyes apprised her of every endeavor made by the sun to break from the oppressive bonds of gloom surrounding it. Instead of experiencing a sense of melancholy at the dreary sight, Rose was encouraged by the sun's tenaciousness to overcome its plight. She felt a solidarity with the daystar, as if the celestial object reflected more of her own state-of-affairs than it reflected its brilliance.

Rose shifted her gaze from the window to the gray cotton material of the dress covering her lap. She smoothed the various wrinkles in the coarse skirt with her slender hands, attempting to flatten them into a neater semblance. The bristly fabric caught at her fingers, callused from work and exposure to cold, causing a slight rasping noise in the silence of the room around her.

Rose inspected the fraying edge of the cuff on her sleeve. She would have to mend it soon. Each tiny snag needed to be addressed before it accumulated into a larger rip of the thread-bare fabric. Rose learned from Mrs. Wilson, the best of milliners, that it pays to be meticulous when trying to keep an older garment from showing its wear.

Rose flipped her arm over and examined the inside of her wrist. She squinted to see the miniscule delicate embroidery she had placed at the cuff when she first arrived at Waupun. Though ornamentation of any sort was strictly forbidden, Rose sewed the tiny embellishment there so she could abide wearing the distasteful gray sack she had been given. No one could see her handiwork, but Rose had the satisfaction of knowing it existed.

The sound of the door being unlatched and opened echoed in the barren room. Rose shifted her gaze back to the window and the winter morning outside. She refused to turn her eyes to meet the person standing in the doorway, though a slight curiosity sparked her interest as to why she had been brought to this room and who might require her as their audience.

The clearing of a raspy throat told Rose who her visitor was. Edna Barnett, an older woman in her sixties with a tall stature and broad shoulders, entered the room. Edna walked with a small limp, dragging her right foot, the result of a bout of polio as a young child. She approached Rose holding a woolen shawl in front of her, extending it towards the younger woman.

"They informed me I might find you waiting here. I thought to bring an extra shawl as they keep these offices as cold as ice." Edna laid the covering across Rose's hands which were demurely folded in her lap. "And not a moment too soon, I'll wager. You look like an iceberg already."

Rose turned her gaze towards the woman only a few feet away. She did not welcome close proximity from any of the staff members, but Edna was the rare exception. Though Edna had the bearing of a military general, she was also the one person who possessed a sense of compassion for the girls in her care. Rose learned that while Edna brooked no nonsense from anyone under her watchful eye, she would not tolerate the mistreatment so prevalent among the other guards.

"Yes, they woke me at dawn and brought me here without explanation." Rose leveled her gaze into Edna's eyes, something she rarely did since coming to Waupun. Instead of finding a challenge in the green eyes, Rose found interest in what she stated.

"Well, they are being confidential about this then, as I have not been notified of why you were escorted to the offices. Before you borrow trouble, Rose, remember, they address bad tidings right away. I guess we shall wait together to see what the day brings." Edna settled herself into a chair across the room and took out a newspaper to read. "I see the news reporter in Wausau has brought you up in his column again. I am surprised you have not decided to tell him your story. It might not hurt." The matron peered at Rose on top of the copy she held open. "It just might help to tell your side so people could understand what occurred."

Rose grimaced as her gaze turned back to the winter morning sky outside her window. "To tell a story you have to know what happened yourself." Rose whispered quietly to the sun, still trying to break through the gloomy haze. How could Rose explain to others what she did not understand herself? Her best possible course of action was to think back to when it all began.

CHAPTER 2

WEDNESDAY, SEPTEMBER 5, 1888. ITHACA, WISCONSIN

(NINE YEARS EARLIER)

A faint breeze swayed the tall stalks of wheat as their prickly beards shimmered in the morning light. The humid Wisconsin summer continued relentlessly and the taste of the transformation in season was a welcome environment. Soon the colder autumn breezes would gust and then usher in the winds of winter, but this seasonal moment was one of perfection.

Rose waited outside in the family wagon, eager to travel the eight miles leading to Richland Center. While it seemed a small destination for such a great journey, one accomplished in less than half a day, Rose was excited to begin her new life. Born to Polish immigrants, Andrew and Elizabeth Zoldoske, she was the third child of nine children.

Like most families, there were always plenty of mouths to feed and often not enough to give them. Andrew traveled from Poland in 1850, arriving in New York and making his way across half of this gigantic country to the beauty of the Midwest. He dreamed of farming his own land but did not have much success in producing anything but more offspring.

The rich black soil and the gentle rolling hills were what drew Andrew to the county from Steuben, New York in 1863. His young wife Elizabeth hated leaving the security of their home and family behind, but she packed up their first daughter Amelia and left for Wisconsin to pursue her husband's dream of being a wealthy farmer.

While the Civil War created a demand for wheat and the first few years of farming were successful, Andrew did not foresee the sudden decline in the need for wheat at the war's conclusion in 1865, nor did he invest in other crops. Garden produce became important, but Andrew invested everything in his wheat fields and, whether because of pride or determination, he refused to diversify, thus losing all the profits he had accumulated.

Meanwhile, eight more children were added to the family. After Amelia there came, Clara, Rose, Willie, John, Henry, Frank, George, and Edward. Willie died at the tender age of eighteen only two years previous. Rose felt the loss of her younger brother keenly, as they had been so close in age and almost inseparable. Rose saw life literally being drained from her mother by the day and knew if she did not escape, her own life would also be in peril.

When an opportunity to travel to nearby Richland Center and hire out her services as a seamstress transpired, Rose leapt at the chance to leave her family and the farm. She had a deep affection for her parents and siblings, but she had always felt the need to aspire to a life of greater culture and comfort. Rose was bright, capable, and comely. She knew she could make a much better life for herself if she were only given the smallest of chances.

The family gathered around Rose to see her off; Rose hugged each one as she made her way towards her parents at the end of the line. Rose saw the weary eyes of her mother, noticing the sheen of unbidden tears there. Elizabeth sighed as she embraced her daughter tightly.

"Be careful, Rose. You are not used to the ways of city folk. I am sure you will work hard for Mrs. Wilson and make me and your papa proud of you. Go to church each week and say your prayers every day. Remember, you can always come back home again." Elizabeth smiled at her daughter with resignation. In her estimation it would have been a better idea to dispatch Amelia or Clara to town as they were shy and; sensible girls, but fiery Rose insisted she be the one to go and her two older sisters happily agreed to the arrangement.

Rose grinned at her mama, her dark eyes sparkling with her excitement. "I won't forget, Mama. I am going to work hard and send back the money to help you and Papa save the farm. I will make such a good name for myself that people will remember me long after I am gone. Just wait and see."

Rose turned to her father and took his hand to climb onto the wagon seat. Andrew nodded at his pretty daughter with her wavy, dark hair arranged into a style Rose had copied from a picture in the Ladies Home Journal. Rose sewed her outfit herself including the delicate embroidery on the sleeves of her blouse and matching short jacket.

Rose sat with her back straight and focused unswervingly ahead as they jolted forward. She felt an unexpected lump in her throat at the thought of separating from her family, but she commanded herself to put away any sentimentality. Rose believed a new life awaited her in Richland Center, and she was determined to make it a life worth living, no matter what she must do to attain it.

CHAPTER 3

LATER THAT DAY, RICHLAND CENTER, WISCONSIN

Laura Mitchell sat staring out her parlor window as the afternoon sun danced in tiny arcs along her Persian rug. The bustle of colorful clientele arriving and departing from the Center Hotel across Church Street distracted her from the deep melancholy she suffered since the death of her daughter Nellie on this day one year previous. Her beautiful girl had been only fourteen when she was taken by illness and Laura's heart still grieved her loss.

Laura held an embroidery hoop in her hands, but many months passed since she had the clarity of mind to work on the finery. Her grief combined with the tonics her husband George, a doctor of homeopathic medicine, administered to her left her in a haze of despondency. There were days when she could not even rise from her bed and now she regretted having vacated the cloistered shelter it provided on this terrible anniversary.

Overcome by her emotions, Laura did not notice George had entered the parlor and stood staring at his wife with consternation. Dr. George Ray Mitchell was a prominent physician in the city. Having graduated from the University of Chicago medical school, he carried the social standing of his surname as well as the prestige of his profession.

George's appearance was meticulous in his dark gray suit. His black shoes, polished daily to avoid the constant dust of the hard-packed dirt streets of the rural town, gleamed in the rays of the afternoon sun. He tapped one foot impatiently upon the Persian carpet as he reached inside his vest pocket and withdrew his gold watch. After checking the time, he glanced again at his wife. Either Laura did not realize that he had entered the room, or she did not care, and George surmised it was the latter rather than the former.

"It is almost two o'clock by my watch. Mrs. Wilson said she would be arriving at two with her new girl. I asked Annie if you ordered tea to be served, but she said you had forgotten. I told her to bring it in right away. Really, Laura, is it too difficult for you to remember to serve a guest some tea?" George's derisive tone made Laura wince, but her eyes remained on the scene outside the parlor window.

The housekeeper, Annie Hoskins, a pretty young woman with fiery auburn hair, entered the room with a tea tray. She set the tray upon a small side table and smiled at George as she exited the room. George walked to the service and poured the steaming fragrant liquid into a delicate porcelain teacup.

He reached into the vest pocket opposite of the watch pocket, withdrew a dark colored glass bottle, removed the stopper, and administered several drops of the reddish-brown liquid into the tea.

The sound of a spoon clinking against the expensive china brought Laura out from her stuporous state as George approached her.

"Here, take this and drink it." he commanded, as he replaced the embroidery hoop in Laura's hands with the teacup and saucer. Laura mechanically lifted the cup to her lips and took a small ladylike sip.

The bitter taste of laudanum mingled with Earl Gray tea would have made anyone else reject the concoction, but Laura immediately took a larger drink, allowing the opiate to alleviate the crushing pain in her soul by numbing all her senses.

George watched as his wife sipped the tea. Seeing this pallid, thin woman before him, it was difficult to recall that Laura was once the voluptuous blonde beauty who turned every head in Chicago society just fifteen years prior. The moment he laid eyes upon Laura Douglas he knew he would claim her as his own. George was dashing and willing to woo the young woman (and her huge trust fund) to add her to his promising future as though she were a piece of art added to a collection.

Laura succumbed to George's charms and a whirlwind courtship, engagement, and marriage took place within months. Their first daughter Nellie arrived not long after, causing more than one raised eyebrow among the high society of the Chicago elite.

George wasted no time spiriting Laura and her financial assets off to rural Richland County. He set up his practice and Laura made a beautiful home in the little brick house located on the corner of Church and Haseltine streets which also housed George's medical office.

A few years later their son Frederick was born, and Laura was in her element as the wife of a popular doctor and the mother of two adorable children. Laura was part of every important charitable organization in town and the epitome of the perfect wife and homemaker. She basked in the glory of adoration from even the most stoic of the gentle women of Richland Center. It had been a small piece of heaven on earth for Laura until tragedy struck and rendered her unable to cope with her shattered dreams and broken heart.

Annie reappeared in the doorway accompanied by the milliner, Mrs. Dora Wilson, and a pretty raven-haired girl with a brilliant smile. Laura felt as if a breath of fresh air washed over her when she turned her attention to Miss Rose Zoldoske, the young woman hand-picked by Dora to apprentice in the millinery. It had been prearranged by Mrs. Wilson and Dr. Mitchell that Rose would be a boarder in the Mitchell home.

Laura sensed a sudden break in the clouds of her despondency as Rose came to sit beside her on the settee, taking Laura's slender hand in greeting. The two women were soon chatting as if they were old acquaintances instead of newly met strangers. Mrs. Wilson stood smiling at the pair and nodded to George in approval. Perhaps this Rose would be the saving grace Laura needed to reclaim her life once again.

CHAPTER 4

TUESDAY, JANUARY 15, 1889, RICHLAND CENTER, WISCONSIN

The January morning was cold but not bitter as Rose walked along the edge of Church Street towards Mrs. Wilson's millinery shop on Court Street. She knew to stay off the wooden sidewalks as the fog from the night before had frozen to every surface, making them treacherous to navigate. Many people had broken a limb falling on the sheen of ice as it collected there, and she did not wish to be the next victim.

Rose was enraptured at the vision in front of her. The same rime ice that made the sidewalks so treacherous gathered in the trees, making each tree resemble a masterpiece of art. It left the surfaces decorated with feathery spicules of pure white, giving the land-scape an ethereal quality in the haze of daylight. She could imagine gossamer winged fairies hiding among the wispy branches as they laid in wait for unsuspecting humans on which to perpetrate their hijinks.

Rose's life had changed so dramatically in the four months since she had come to work for Mrs. Wilson and to live with the Mitchells. Dora was an excellent seamstress and expected Rose to learn quickly and work hard. She was also a mother figure for the pretty young woman of twenty-one years.

Rose could discern the compassionate heart of the widow towards her, and it made her more determined to please her employer and mentor with her labors and her comportment. Rose's industriousness and talent turned a profit for the milliner, and she shared her financial gain with her protégé.

Rose sent a portion of her earnings to her parents, but she was able to purchase some fabric and notions to sew a Sunday dress for herself. Mrs. Wilson insisted she make a matching hat. As the assistant to the town milliner, she needed the appropriate chapeau.

When Rose was not at work in the millinery shop, she spent time with Laura and the Mitchell family. She blossomed under the tutelage of the former Chicago debutante. Laura helped the young woman learn the niceties of conducting herself as a proper lady and exposed her to the cultural worlds of art, literature, and music. Rose was so brilliant she advanced quickly in all the amenities. Soon it was difficult to tell that she had been born without all the education and advantages of the other more prominent young women of the town.

Laura made certain that Rose became a member of the same First Methodist church that the Mitchell family attended. With encouragement from her mentor, Rose was soon asked to teach in the Sunday School, join the church choir, and become a member of the most prestigious charities and ladies' societies, including the secretive Women's Club founded by Julia Bowen and Laura Briggs

James. The famous suffragette, Susan B Anthony, visited the club in 1886 causing quite a stir amongst the town folk.

Rose was greatly influenced by these female pioneers of change, while Laura felt the club was worthwhile for social status only. Laura pointed out to her repeatedly that Mrs. James would be better off staying at home and raising her young daughter Ada than trying to influence the entire world outside little Richland Center. Rose felt Mrs. James was accomplishing both goals at the same time.

Rose reached the millinery shop on Court Street just as a group of young ladies arrived for their fittings. Mrs. Wilson welcomed the girls into the store as she nodded her good morning greeting to her. Rose hurried to take off her coat and hat and don her apron so she could assist Dora with her work. The gathered young women chattered amongst themselves, reminding Rose of a gaggle of geese swimming about on the mill pond at the edge of town.

"What do you girls think of this color?" asked Mae Hyndman, the self-appointed leader of the group of friends. "I think one must be careful with certain colors or one will be sallow like others we know." She giggled and a couple of the other girls, Rena Allen and Alice Berryman, joined her. Mae's comment was far less about the hue of the fabric and far more about the disparagement of an unnamed young lady.

"I think it is a nice shade of blue, Mae. If the color is appealing to you, then that should help you determine you like it. It really should not matter how it would appeal to someone else." Ella Maly smiled as she spoke gently to her friends. She picked up the blue cloth and held it against Mae's golden tresses. "See? It is quite beautiful when I hold it next to you. I can just picture a gorgeous hat for spring made from this fabric."

"Oh, Ella. You silly goose! I wasn't thinking of this color for me. It is just like you, Ella, to think of the sweetest things to say." Mae smiled back at Ella with a smile that did not reach her icy blue eyes. She turned with a flounce to face Mrs. Wilson and asked, "Are we ready to measure Mrs. Wilson? I haven't got all day. I have an appointment to see Dr. Mitchell in an hour."

Dora nodded grimly and began to arrange items for the fittings. Rose hurried to bring out the hat blocks of various sizes and a cloth tape measure for sizing. She placed a chair behind the young ladies where each could take their turn and sit as she took the measurements, dictating them to Rose. Mae took her place in the chair first, having the audacity of deciding her time was the most valuable of those assembled. She sat upon the chair like a regal princess with her attending court surrounding her.

"It is imperative I see Dr. Mitchell right away as I have been afflicted with the most torturous of headaches and only Dr. Mitchell is capable of relieving them." Mae sniffed slightly to heighten the effect of her suffering while the other girls murmured their sympathies. Only Mrs. Wilson and Rose remained silent, which Mae, in the midst of her contrived wretchedness, noticed immediately.

"Well, I would wager that if I suffered any affliction, one peek at Dr. Mitchell might cure me." Alice Berryman nodded knowingly, twittering like a bird in laughter. The other young ladies bobbed their heads in hearty agreement, causing only Ella and Rose to blush at the shocking reference to the doctor's physique and dashing handsomeness. Mrs. Wilson cleared her throat abruptly in disgust, but the young ladies continued their discussion without acknowledging the censure.

"Dr. Mitchell is the finest of physicians and would make the best of husbands. He is so attentive to my needs. He is always telling me

I have only to call him day or night and he will come immediately to attend to me. I don't mind saying that he is underappreciated by Mrs. Mitchell who barely acknowledges his existence, since their 'tragedy'. Such a heartbreaking thing to see how she treats him." Mae's pronounced judgment of Laura Mitchell caused Rose to see a red haze of anger. How dare she speak this way of Rose's dearest friend? She began to rise from her seat in the corner to address the audaciousness of this claim.

"I believe Dr. Mitchell is attentive to all of his patients, regardless of who they are." Ella spoke up quickly as she saw the thunderous expression on Rose's face. "As for Mrs. Mitchell, she is a generous and gracious lady who has endured a great tragedy and deserves our prayers." Ella watched as Rose stilled beside her. She intervened before Rose could spout out the vehement thoughts swirling in her head, that could cause Miss Hyndman to revile her and make an enemy of her. In a small town like Richland Center, it was important not to make enemies of the influential, even the odious Mae Hyndman.

Rose nodded silently at Ella and returned to her seat in the corner where she could regain her composure once again. As Rose watched the beautiful young lady still standing between her and the ostentatious girl seated in the chair, she knew she had found a new friend in Ella Maly.

CHAPTER 5

LATER THE SAME DAY

George Mitchell sat at his desk watching the people walk up and down Haseltine Street. He had a short reprieve from patients whom he received in the medical office attached to his home.

George was keeping a careful watch so he could intercept the next person before Annie Hoskins, Mitchell's hired girl, could answer the door. Normally, he would have allowed Annie to answer the side door and show the patient back to the room where he would await them, but this situation was anything but normal.

George glanced at his reflection in the small mirror attached to the wall on his right. He was always fastidious in matters concerning his office and especially in matters concerning his person. His dark brown hair was always groomed to precision with a perfect part on the left side.

He appeared youthful for a man of forty with nary a gray hair or wrinkle; he assumed it was his superior genetics and careful maintenance that caused this phenomenon of physical and intellectual distinction, when it was more likely it was his ease of circumstance compared to the hardships of the laborers surrounding him.

George's thoughts turned to the past few months and the changes wrought upon his household by the presence of Rose Zoldoske. He agreed to take the young woman as a boarder so she could distract his wife Laura, as she had become a tiresome burden to him. Rose surpassed all his expectations by not only distracting Laura, but also drawing her from the deep melancholy in which she had been immersed.

Rose provided companionship and an opportunity for Laura to trifle with the young woman as though she were a living doll, molding her into an impeccable imitation of a woman of refinement. Rose seemed eager to allow her mentor the power to make the transformation, clinging to every word Laura spoke and making every change Laura suggested.

While George expected others to treat him as a Rasputin of sorts, he did not appreciate Laura being given the same deference, even though the situation worked to his advantage. The fact of the matter was that George was envious not of Laura's attention to Rose, but of Rose's attention to Laura.

He did have to admit that Laura's health and her appearance had improved dramatically, making her appear less like a frump to him. She regained some of her youthful stamina and her former beauty even though it was as faded as an old slipper. George could not abide what he saw as physical defects in himself or in others.

George glanced up from his musings to see Mae Hyndman approaching the side door of the house. He slipped down the corridor towards the door and opened it with a brilliant smile before Mae took the opportunity to ring the bell and announce herself as a visitor.

Mae was resplendent in hues of muted red, including a red bonnet balanced upon the cascade of golden curls trailing down her slender neck. She cast her blue eyes downwards, batting her eyelashes, in an effort to feign demureness, but George caught the response of avid interest there. He tried to refrain from chuckling to himself, this girl made all this much too easy.

"Good afternoon to you, Miss Hyndman. Right this way please. Take my arm so you do not stumble on the steps." George held out his arm to her and Mae grasped it, pressing it to her body as she ascended the stairs towards him. He led her down the narrow corridor to his office and settled her in a chair, closing the door behind them. He turned and knelt at her feet, looking into her eyes as he gently touched her cheek with the back of his hand. Her sigh was audible and rather unladylike. George smiled as he attempted to appear concerned.

"I am so sorry to hear your headaches have returned. I assure you I will do my utmost to alleviate any discomfort. It is indeed unfair someone so fetching should be troubled so grievously." George continued to stroke her porcelain cheek with the back of his hand while he grasped one of her gloved hands resting in her lap with his opposite hand. He could tell that her shallow breathing increased rapidly as she closed her eyes.

"Thank you, Dr. Mitchell. I rely upon your expertise as my physician. I seem to have run out of the headache remedy you prescribed, and I knew only your assistance would take this wretchedness from me." she whispered, attempting to draw him forward so he could hear her. George complied. Mae could feel the exhalation of his breath brush against her face and hair. She opened her eyes and tilted her head forward.

The three short knocks on the wooden office door sounded like the staccato report of a gun as it echoed loudly in the small room. George stood to his feet quickly as Mae touched the place on her cheek where his hand had just been. The doctor crossed to the door and yanked it open with an expression of murderous rage on his visage.

Annie Hoskins, the hired girl, stood on the other side of the door, her hands perched on each hip and a cast of defiance in her green eyes. She tossed her head in anger, her auburn curls spilling down out of the scarf tied about her head. Annie stepped inside the office without being bidden. When she saw Miss Hyndman and the tableau before her, she narrowed her green eyes even more as she announced in a clipped tone,

"Pardon me, Dr. Mitchell. I was not aware of a patient being there with you. I always get them and bring them back here for you." Annie's shrill voice grew louder, obvious jealousy dripping with each word. "Mrs. Bailey just came to the door asking for the rheumatism tonic for Mr. Bailey and I told her I would come and ask you about it. I had no idea." Her tone was accusatory as she glared at Mae and back at George.

"Tell Mrs. Bailey I will take it to Mr. Bailey at the store this afternoon. Thank you, Annie, that is all." George's dismissive tone caused Annie to gasp and take several steps backward into the hallway. He closed the door on her abruptly and turned back to Mae, still seated in the chair.

"I really must be going, Dr. Mitchell. My mother will be concerned about my whereabouts. Will you please call on me at your earliest convenience?" The previous mood broken, Mae stood and took her leave, forgetting her debilitating migraine and the essential curative she sought only moments prior. George watched her exit back down the corridor, out the side door, and briskly up Haseltine Street.

Later that evening, as George readied for bed, he was still seething over the afternoon interruption followed by an overcooked dinner served with hostile glances from Annie. The only bright spot in the dreadful evening had been the amiable presence of Rose. She teased young Freddie, chatted with Laura, and even showed modest interest in him. He was still in doubt as to whether Rose's presence in the house was beneficial for him, but he had more pressing matters to attend to.

A light tap on his bedroom door alerted him to Laura's entrance into the room. Laura smiled at him as she came and kissed him, taking her long vacant place on the other side of his bed. George grinned to himself as he turned to extinguish the lamp. This was unexpected albeit not unwelcome. Perhaps Rose could stay after all. This line of thought prompted him to address his wife as he approached the bed in the darkness,

"My dear, I believe it is time to hire a new housekeeper."

CHAPTER 6

SUNDAY, AUGUST 11, 1889, AVOCA, WISCONSIN

The brilliant sun was high in the azure blue sky over Lake Avoca, part of the lower Wisconsin River waterway, nestled in the small village of Avoca. Tiny white clouds floated lazily along as though they were buoyant in the tranquil lake that mirrored them below. Dragonflies skimmed the water and flitted in the tall prairie grasses growing in the savannah just beyond the lake. Enormous burr oak trees stretched their limbs to the heavens outlined by the green hills surrounding the area, creating a peaceful paradise for a Sunday afternoon outing.

The Mitchells joined various members of the community in boarding the train at the depot in Richland Center and riding the trek by railway to Avoca. Laura insisted Rose accompany them, declaring she was now a part of their family since the two women were almost inseparable. Rose had never had the opportunity to experience traveling anywhere by train, so even the short distance to Avoca was a great adventure for her. She was so happy she had finished a new summer outfit for herself just a few days before.

Rose had fashioned a new dress from a piece of light blue India mull that Mrs. Wilson had left over from a previous order. The mull was a less expensive imitation of the fine lawn material that composed Laura's summer finery, and she was pleased with what she and Mrs. Wilson were able to create from it. Rose matched the frock with a light blue straw hat. It was a perfect color against Rose's black hair and dark eyes, and she felt as attractive as Laura kept asserting that she was.

The thirty-passenger railway car was nearly full as it pulled into the Front Street depot in the small town of Avoca. The beautiful summer day beckoned various residents of Richland Center to enjoy the pristine beauty of the placid lake and the only prairie lands east of the Mississippi River. The train was filled with the sounds of laughter and talking competing with the clickety-clack of the track, the sound of the steam engine winding down to a halt, and the intermittent whistle alerting everyone to the train's impending stop at its destination.

Rose followed Dr. Mitchell with Laura on his arm as they disembarked from the train. Young Freddie, only a lad of eleven, darted around excitedly with some of the other town lads, causing his mother concern for his welfare. When Laura voiced her concerns to George, he dismissed them, reminding her he had been a lad of only fifteen when he joined the Union Army and fought in the Wisconsin Fifth Regiment. This reminder did not ease Laura's concerns for her son, especially after seeing him nearly run down by a nearby pony cart.

"Frederick. Come here. You are distressing your mother." George barked the order as though young Freddie were under his military command rather than his paternal guidance. Rose noticed Freddie's face redden as the other lads with him started to chuckle about the reference to his mother. He glared at his mother, placed his hands in the pockets of his trousers and walked back towards his parents, kicking at the dirt as he went.

"Freddie, what were you telling me about your favorite fishing hole?" Rose stepped in front of him and placed her hand on his shoulder. "Do you think you will be able to catch enough fish for a wonderful fish fry this week?" Rose attempted to rescue Freddie's wounded feelings while distracting him from the other boys still laughing at his expense.

Freddie lifted his forlorn eyes to meet Rose's eyes and flashed her a smile that was dazzling. "I should think I would make a fine mess just for you, Rose. I have a secret bait I use, and it works better than just about anything." Freddie fell into step beside Rose as they followed George and Laura down the street towards the lake. He gave a smug glance at his companions, letting them know the beautiful young woman beside him chose him for an escort while ignoring the rest of them. If there was anything to distract a boy from his shenanigans, it was the presence of a pretty girl.

Soon, the group had a picnic area set up on the shore of the peaceful lake. An immense tree provided shade for the party as the ladies sat down upon the quilts spread across the ground. The Mitchell's new housekeeper, Annie McClaren, joined them on the excursion for the purpose of setting up the afternoon feast.

Annie smiled at the reception for the cold ham sandwiches, fried chicken, potato salad, watermelon slices, pickles of every sort, and, of course, various kinds of cheese. She had even baked a multi-layered chocolate cake which she insisted upon holding herself on the train to keep it from toppling. Annie knew she had done a service to her employers from the reactions of the families around them.

"I don't know how we ever got along without our new Annie." Laura glanced at George as she praised the new housekeeper who had been recommended by Mrs. Wilson and chosen by Laura rather than her husband. "She came to rescue us from our previous unfortunate situation and has made herself invaluable to the entire family."

Laura referenced the dramatic scene created by Annie Hoskins when she was told they no longer required her services. The fiery redhead shouted obscenities at George and even hurled several dishes in his direction. She was immediately packed away on the next outbound train to an unknown destination, causing the murmurs of the town gossips to resonate like the cicadas and tree frogs on a summer evening.

George cleared his throat and nodded his silent agreement, knowing that the less he commented on the circumstances, the better. The new housekeeper was unattractive, a plain daughter of a huge farm family nearby. She resembled a cookie-cutter replica of all her siblings, both female and male. She was industrious and kept an immaculate house along with preparing appetizing meals, things the former Annie had not achieved.

After enjoying their repast, the members of the party gathered into smaller groups with varied interests, the small children were herded to lie down in the shade for afternoon naps, and the older children enjoyed wading and fishing in the placid lake. An atmosphere of relaxation and repose settled over the matrons, including Laura, as she leaned against George and sighed with satisfaction.

"I think I shall go and check on several rowboats to entertain the young ones after they tire of swimming." George rose from his position beside Laura and stretched his limbs. "You and Rose should enjoy your tranquility before Frederick descends upon you once again." He walked away but not before Rose noticed that he headed in the opposite direction of where the rowboats were moored.

Laura smiled as she leaned against her friend and closed her eyes. "I was waiting for an opportunity to tell you something, but I want your promise that it must be a secret between us." Laura left her eyes shut as she whispered so no one else but Rose could hear her. "I trust you with my secrets, Rose."

"Yes, of course." Rose felt a sense of satisfaction that this young, beautiful woman of such a high social station trusted her as a confidante. She knew hers was a place of distinction many in the small-town hierarchy believed was undeserved by an uncouth, uneducated outsider. Rose felt a strong loyalty and gratitude to her benefactress, mentor, and friend. She would take Laura's secrets to the grave if necessary.

"It has been so long that at first, I was unsure of the symptoms I have been experiencing of late. I had given up all hope of ever conceiving another child again, but it appears, yet another miracle has occurred since your arrival in our lives, Rose." Laura opened her deep blue eyes and the joy mirrored in them made Rose's heart swell with happiness for her friend.

"This is wonderful news, Laura. There is no person more deserving of these good tidings after all you have endured. I will be happy to keep your secret, but wouldn't it be wise to at least inform Dr. Mitchell?" Rose took Laura's slender hand in her own and held it as she smiled.

"Yes, all in good time. I just wanted you to know first as I will rely upon you to help me in various ways. May I count on you as my dearest friend?" Laura's eyes held a plea Rose could not quite comprehend.

"I will be only too happy to help you in any way. Do not worry about a thing as I shall endeavor to make this maternity as delightful as possible for you." Rose pledged her assistance with a resolve that would not be abandoned, regardless of the cost to her.

Later that afternoon, as the sun cast long shadows across the shore, the group gathered to return to the depot for their departure. Frederick caught a substantial passel of panfish and walleye, receiving a lot of praise from Rose in front of his contemporaries, much to his satisfaction. George reappeared after a lengthy absence without the previously mentioned rowboats, forgetting his initial errand. Laura and Rose walked arm in arm, enjoying the camaraderie of their new confidence.

As they waited to board the train, Rose noticed Ella Maly in the company of a young depot agent. The couple seemed oblivious to the clamor around them as they spoke to each other in hushed tones. An occasional melodious laugh would escape Ella and drift across the space to Rose like the tinkling of tiny bells. Ella's eyes crinkled in the corners, expressing her enjoyment, and Rose felt delight for her new friend and a sense of longing for herself.

The sun began to set as the train bound for Richland Center carried its load of passengers to their destination. Rose overheard the snippets of conversation from the same group of young ladies who patronized Mrs. Wilson's shop months prior, their self-appointed leader, Mae Hyndman, being the loudest voice among them.

"Did you see her cuddling against the doctor's wife as though they were the dearest of friends? Honestly, I don't know who she thinks she is."

"Did you see her dreadful dress and hat? I suppose it is the best someone like her can do. I wouldn't be caught dead in it." Mae's hushed whispers were loud and harsh, followed by the sniggering laughter of the other two girls, Rena and Alice.

Rose attempted to shut her eyes and ears against the cruel words, but her heart had been pierced with their poisonous barbs. Even while Laura showed her the utmost kindness and acceptance, she knew that with other parties she would never belong.

CHAPTER 7

MONDAY, AUGUST 12, 1889, RICHLAND CENTER, WISCONSIN

Rose arrived early at Mrs. Wilson's millinery shop the following morning. She spent the previous night tossing and turning, her memory replaying over and over the acerbic remarks uttered by Miss Hyndman. She rose before dawn, taking the dress she had just worn for the Sunday outing at the lake, and embroidering delicate flowers upon the cuffs of the sleeves. The painstaking needlework done in such dim lighting had caused a ferocious headache, but Rose persevered with what she set out to accomplish.

Dora was pouring a steaming cup of tea as Rose entered the shop. The kindly lady could see the pain etched across the face of her young protégé as she poured a second one for her. She sat down in her comfortable sewing rocker and just waited, understanding sometimes a person in distress needs companionable silence more than they need unnecessary conversation.

Rose picked up the teacup and saucer and took it to her chair situated next to her employer's. The fragrance of the Oolong tea suffused over Rose's aching eyes, throbbing temples, and stiff neck, easing the intensity of the discomfort within minutes. The wretchedness of her inner wounds remained, as though a thorn pierced her heart and left her without remedy.

"It's always nice to begin the day with a good cup of Oolong tea." Dora Wilson spoke to the setting around her, the piles of fabric and the notions, the hat blocks that held partially formed hats, and the sleeping black cat stretched out upon the wooden floor, basking in the rays of morning sun.

"I once read that Oolong tea was discovered in an ancient Chinese province by a humble tea grower. Unlike the great tea farms of the nobility who dominated the trade, this simple man made an honest living by working hard and selling his tea for a fair price."

"One evening after a day of plucking tea leaves, this farmer was distracted by a beautiful deer roaming the forest and he forgot some of the valuable tea leaves he harvested. The next morning, he returned to find a brown, wilted mess instead of the tea leaves. He decided to try a new process on the leaves and attempt to rescue his entire day's wages."

"Some of the more prominent farmers criticized him and mocked his efforts, but he persisted and what resulted was a sweeter, more fragrant tea that became far more valuable than the black tea leaves he initially plucked. He named the new tea Wu Long after himself and to this day it remains costly. People knew this tea by his name when the more powerful people were entirely forgotten. We shouldn't ever give anyone else the authority to determine our value for us." Dora sighed as she sipped the last bit of tea from her cup and stood to gather her supplies for the day, leaving Rose to ruminate.

Her words were the balm that soothed Rose's wounds and fortified her spirit. Rose knew some people such as Mae Hyndman would always attempt to make her feel inferior, but she did not have to allow it to determine her value. She stood and crossed to Dora, embracing her surprised employer in a tight hug.

"Land sakes, we should get started before half our day is nearly gone." Dora Wilson cleared her throat and nodded at Rose as she bustled about the room, but not before Rose noticed the sheen of tears in the older woman's eyes. Rose put away the teacups and brought the projects for the day to the worktable.

The two women immersed themselves in the task in front of them. The clock in the adjacent sitting room struck noon when Rose raised her eyes to the sound of the bell on the shop door jangling, announcing a customer's entrance. She squinted at the bright light streaming through the open door to see a familiar figure standing in the doorway, his worn hat in his hands.

"Papa. You have come to visit." Rose announced more to herself than to the two other individuals in the shop. "I didn't know you were planning to come to town." Rose walked to the door and hugged her father as he stood part of the way inside the room. She pulled her father's arm, looking at Mrs. Wilson across the room.

"I come to talk to you about something real important, Rose. Good afternoon, Mrs. Wilson." Andrew Zoldoske added the latter comment, nodding at Dora while he grasped his daughter's arm and led her out the door onto the sidewalk. He turned to close the door behind them as Rose stared at him, her mouth open, aghast at his ill-mannered behavior.

"Papa, what in the world! Why were you so rude to Mrs. Wilson?" Rose's voice was mixed with anger and embarrassment. She stopped when she saw the expression on her father's pale face.

"I told you already. I have something important to tell you and not much time to tell it. So just hush, girl and listen to me." Andrew's loud voice was uncharacteristically harsh, causing Rose to glance around them, hoping no one was nearby.

"Your mama and I are packing up our belongings and heading out for Oklahoma right away. There is an opportunity there I just can't pass up and things still aren't doing good here. I came to get you and bring you along with us." Andrew delivered his news in a matter-of-fact tone.

"Papa! I can't just pick up and leave! What would Mrs. Wilson do without a helper when she has been so good to give me this job and this is her busiest time? I have responsibilities to her and to the Mitchells". Rose thought of the promise she made to Laura just the day before and knew she would not break it so soon.

"Those folks ain't your blood family, Girl. We need your help there in Oklahoma just like you've been helping us the last year." Andrew came to his real point; he needed his daughter's finances rather than needing his daughter. Rose knew she had a choice to make, one affecting the rest of her life.

"Papa, I am now over the age of majority with a life of my own to live. I choose to stay here and honor my commitments to Mrs. Wilson and the Mitchells. I will still send you part of my regular pay so you will have the benefit of it and not have my room and board as a concern. I'm sure you will see this is really the best plan." Rose fixed a determined guise upon her face as she stared back at her father.

"Your mama will be upset about this. She made me come to get you without delay." Andrew's admission caused Rose a moment of hesitation regarding her mother. She knew Elizabeth would be heartbroken to move away without her daughter, while Andrew seemed to have overcome his parental sentiments.

"Tell Mama I am working hard, and I will visit her sooner rather than later." Rose knew if she expressed any stronger tenderness in her message that her father would not relay it. She trusted her mother to be able to read between the lines.

Andrew stood looking at his daughter, then turned and began to walk away without another word. Rose understood the finality of his actions as she watched him cross Court Street towards his waiting horse and wagon.

Rose walked back to the door of the millinery shop. She opened the door, realizing that the door to the next part of her life had just been opened as well. She would enter through it and not look back. She was, after all, Andrew Zoldoske's daughter.

CHAPTER 8

THE SAME DAY, THE H.T. BAILEY STORE, 194 COURT STREET

Ella Maly sat at her desk in the Bailey Dry Goods Store watching the mid-morning sunlight stream through the front windows. The red brick building built in the Italianate style housed the store on the first level and an opera house and the Masonic Temple on the second level.

Ella had been hired six months earlier by H.T. Bailey as a book-keeper for his thriving business. Mr. Bailey was well known in the city for being an astute and somewhat parsimonious businessman, his miserly ways even causing Mrs. Bailey to label him as a Scrooge more than once. While he was frugal, Mr. Bailey was a good employer and trusted Ella with his financial empire.

Mr. Bailey would have scolded his young employee if he had realized she had been reliving her Sunday afternoon spent in Avoca rather than recording the number of calico bolts presently available on the stockroom shelves. Ella jotted the occasional numeral into the ledger, then returned to chewing the end of her pencil as she tried to determine the exact shade of brown that described Joe Bohan's eyes.

Joe Bohan was the assistant to his brother, Dan, the depot agent for the Milwaukee & St. Paul Railroad in Avoca. The Bohan brothers built a lumber and implement business in the little town by the lake to complement the booming building trade established by the arrival of the railroad.

Joe was often sent to Richland Center to trade for dry goods with the illustrious H.T. Bailey. He met Ella during one of his visits soon after she started her job as the bookkeeper for the dry goods store. The two began their relationship as good friends and realized that affections much deeper than friendship were burgeoning between them.

Ella, at the age of twenty-one, was a fair beauty. Her complexion was like fine porcelain, complementing her naturally curly brown hair and hazel eyes. Even fairer than her physique was her disposition. She was a kind, humble, honest, woman who valued others more than possessions and social position.

The mixture of her outward attributes and inner character made Ella one of the rarest forms of belles and many of the young men of the community tried to gain her attention to no avail. Though Ella knew she could marry to advance her prospects in life and her social standing, she wanted to spend her life with someone she loved if she decided to wed at all.

The previous four months she had spent in the company of Joe convinced the young woman that waiting for the right man had been a good decision. They enjoyed the same hobbies: singing, reading, and hiking outdoors. Joe shared his aspirations of owning and operating a bank with Ella and she shared her dreams of writing poetry and short stories with him.

While seeing each other on a regular basis, they both decided it was best to keep their romance quiet until they made it more formal. Only Ella's younger sister Lillie knew about the deep attachment her sister and dearest friend had formed with the dashing young depot agent from Avoca.

The clock on the store wall striking noon brought Ella out of her reverie. She glanced guiltily down on the scarce number of items she had entered in the ledger that morning and determined she would work through her lunch as well as stay late to compensate for her morning's musings.

As Ella reached for an apple sitting on the nearby window ledge, she noticed the door opening across the street at Mrs. Wilson's millinery shop. An older gentleman with the garb of a farmer led Rose Zoldoske outside to the sidewalk where he turned and began an animated discussion with her. While the occurrence was nothing out of the ordinary, the expression upon Rose's face made Ella take note of the exchange.

Ella observed that Rose seemed shocked and somewhat dismayed as she glanced around the street and then cast her eyes downward during the older man's harangue. Ella felt a pang of sympathy for her and silently prayed the news being delivered to the young woman was not of a tragic nature. It was not uncommon to have someone arrive with bad tidings from a distant state or even another country.

After a few minutes more, Ella noticed that Rose's disposition took a sudden turn. Rose straightened her shoulders, raised her head, and made direct eye contact with her visitor as she spoke with an almost expressionless countenance. Rose's courage in the face of a possible tragedy ignited an even deeper sense of compassion within Ella for the young woman.

The man walked away from Rose without a word, leaving her standing alone on the sidewalk looking abandoned. Ella watched in amazement as Rose closed her eyes and then turned to the door of the millinery shop, a brave smile on her face as she reentered the doorway. Ella could not hear a single remark that had been uttered between the two, but she knew deep down something significant had just occurred to Rose Zoldoske.

Ella stood and crossed to the store's front door as she devised a plan to go and ask Rose to come for dinner at her family's home in the coming week. Once Rose met the boisterous and gracious Maly family, she would feel less like a stranger in the small community. Ella made a promise that day to help Rose in the future so the young woman would understand she possessed true friends in Richland Center.

CHAPTER 9

WEDNESDAY, AUGUST 28, 1889, RICHLAND CENTER, WISCONSIN

The long shadows of a summer's eve descended upon the side porch of the Mitchell house as Rose and Laura sat together trying to catch the faint wisps of breeze in the oppressive heat and humidity. The tree frogs sang in loud choruses while lightning bugs lit up the dusk.

The occasional June bug buzzed and smacked against the screens, making Rose grateful for the protective barrier between her and the detested beasties. The physical appearance of the armored insect made Rose shudder, especially when she encountered one in the outdoor privy.

George had been called away on a medical visit and Freddie joined a group on an excursion to Miner Hill Bluff, a trek of the bluffs on the east side of the city earlier in the day, leaving Laura and Rose to a quiet respite at the end of a busy day.

Rose had worked extra hours with Mrs. Wilson to finish a trousseau for a prestigious client, Catherine Lee Tobin. Miss Tobin was engaged to marry a young architect, Frank Lloyd Wright, at the Unity Chapel he designed in Wyoming Valley near Spring Green. The groom's mother, Anna Lloyd Jones, descended upon poor Mrs. Wilson with numerous demands.

Wright had been born in Richland Center and his mother knew from experience Dora's work was far superior to any of the millinery shops in Chicago. Rose gave her employer as much support as possible, but both women had been exhausted by the amount of effort and by the irascible Anna Lloyd Jones.

Rose sat in a wicker chair with her bare feet propped up on a small ottoman, allowing air to travel up through the layers of restrictive, albeit fashionable clothing. Laura reclined on a wicker settee, she loosened some of the stays in her corset and fanned herself with a gilt-edged fan with a mother of pearl handle.

"I am beginning to notice the changes in my figure, and it won't be long until George notices as well." Laura sighed as she looked down at the small protrusion beneath the loosened corset. "I will have to make him aware of our joyous news soon. Before I do, I need to ask something of you, Rose. I truly need your help in a matter in which I trust only your discreet assistance."

"I will be only too happy to help you with anything, Laura." Rose lifted her head from its relaxed position so she could study Laura's face. "What can I do for you?"

"Sometimes in a marriage there are things a wife must address and other things a wife must ignore in her husband. I have found over the years that my husband has infatuations for various young women. It is something I choose to ignore as he doesn't seem to advance his attentions beyond an infatuation, and he is otherwise an excellent provider and father. The only time this frailty of George's has caused me concern is when I am expectant and cannot show him the fullest amount of attention." Laura shifted her position and clasped her slender hands in front of her abdomen as though she were protecting the babe nestled there.

Rose's face pinkened at the nature of Laura's conversation. While she thought that being a gracious wife was important, she did not see how Laura could overlook her husband's emotional infidelities. George did not have to seek physical intimacy with others to be unfaithful to his wife and she deserved so much more than this caddish behavior from her husband. Rose was unsure of what Laura wanted her to do. Maybe she wished for Rose to help her confront her husband?

"While I understand George will likely divert his attention to someone else, I thought perhaps this time I could control who receives his interest. If you were willing to distract him from other women by paying close attention to him during this time, I would know that he is not crossing a line into adultery. I trust your relationship with my husband, Rose. You are pretty and will serve as a distraction until after my baby is born. Will you please help me?" Laura finished the last two sentences rapidly as she understood the enormity of her request.

"What exactly do you mean by distracting him?" Rose's head was spinning from the implication of Laura's entreaty. While she was eager to assist her dear friend, she would refuse to play the harlot in a sordid affair. Rose could envision her mother's look of despair if she found her daughter had abandoned all the spiritual and moral training, she had instilled in her since childhood.

"Oh my, Rose! Please do not misunderstand me. I am only asking you to pay extra attention to him by comments. He is an extremely vain man and can be easily manipulated by anyone willing to flatter him. It has become apparent to me the odious Miss Hyndman has flattered my husband to no end and George imagines himself to be smitten with her. What has not occurred to either of them is the fact they are both self-admiring creatures and will soon compete with the other for flattery. On the other hand, you are a sweet young woman who does not require all the exertion this conceited little chit of a girl does. He is as lazy as he is vain, so he will welcome your attention without having to expend himself to reciprocate. I will have the ease of mind knowing no other women are in the picture, and you will be helping to rescue our dear little family of which you have become such an integral part." Laura nodded her head sagely as if asking another woman to flirt with her husband was the most natural thing in the world.

"I don't know what to say. You know I would do anything to help you, but is this really the best course of action? What if George misunderstands my attention? What if other people think ill of me because they don't understand the situation?" Rose's words were stumbling over each other as she tried to form them in a mouth gone dry.

"I will be right here to make certain he will not make advances and I would never allow anyone else to speak ill of you for any cause Rose. On the contrary, as I esteem you, so will all the others. What do you have to say?" Laura stood and came to put her hand on Rose's shoulder in a gesture of supplication.

Rose could think of a million reasons to refuse, but the one reason to accept was standing in front of her pleading her case to her dearest friend. If Rose could not help Laura with this, she knew her mentor would feel betrayed and possibly abandon their friendship, something she needed now more than ever.

"When do we begin?" Rose asked with trepidation, knowing she would need to proceed with great caution and prudence, hoping Laura's goal could be achieved without causing irreversible adulteration to one and all.

CHAPTER 10

SATURDAY, SEPTEMBER 28, 1889, SEXTONVILLE, WISCONSIN

The mid-afternoon sun luxuriated in the vividness of gold, red, orange, and purple hues reflected from the trees near Nourse Bluff. The crisp air was spicy with the fragrance of green pines interspersed among their flamboyant deciduous counterparts. It was an ideal day for apple picking, a hayride, and eventually, a bonfire later in the evening.

Rose accepted an invitation from Ella Maly and her sister Lillie to accompany them to the home of Albert A. Ghastin in the small village of Sextonville, just a few miles from Richland Center. A gathering had been planned to celebrate the fall harvest at the Ghastin farm with A.A. and his pretty wife Mary hosting, along with A.A.'s father, Albert Sr., who was a well-known veterinarian in the county.

Rose had enjoyed the invitations from Ella to join her family for dinners and the occasional outing. The affable members of the

Maly clan made her welcome in their company. Ella was gracious to Rose, making her feel like a valuable integrant in the various group meetings Ella attended. She even paved the way for Rose's acceptance by some of the most exclusive young women in the town, including the uncharitable Miss Hyndman, who now professed Rose as a "dear friend".

The ladies of the party were asked to gather beneath a small clump of apple trees, each of them standing beside an individual tree with her apron fanned out and held up with her hands. The gentleman would climb ladders into the apple trees, pick the apples, and toss them into the waiting aprons.

It was common for couples who were "sweet on each other" to pair up for this activity. Ella was claimed by Joe Bohan before anyone else could even ask her and the two headed for a tree off in the distance. Rose watched as Lillie was soon asked by Frank Nourse, Mary Ghastin's youngest brother, to assist him with the apple picking.

Rose felt a sense of dread begin to grow in her stomach. What if everyone paired off and she was left to stand there by herself, embarrassed and alone? So many of these people had known each other since birth, while she was once again the outsider. Perhaps she could find Mary and offer to help set out the refreshments or supervise the young Ghastin children, Harry, Will, and little Floyd, keeping the rambunctious little boys from mischief.

"Well, it seems to me you might be willing to help a stranger out?" A pleasant looking gentleman spoke, causing Rose to turn to her right and peer at him. Van Buren McCollum smiled at Rose's reaction. He was a dashing figure, with dark hair and dark eyes.

Ella had mentioned that Van Buren McCollum was an adventurer and a poet; he had just returned to his parent's farm in Sextonville from years on a remote South Pacific Island. Rose could hardly believe someone so sought-after would ask her to be his partner.

"I would venture to say that I am a stranger in this group as you seem to be quite well known to everyone, Mr. McCollum. I would be honored to be your partner, however." Rose smiled back at Van as he offered his arm to her. They strolled towards one of the larger apple trees. Van scaled the waiting ladder and nimbly positioned himself on an upper branch of the tree, poised to begin picking the apples and tossing them to Rose, who waited below.

"I admit I miss racing the indigenous boys of Nuku Hiva to see who could be the first to climb the trees, although the trappings of shoes and a suit are considerable disadvantages in the undertaking." Van chuckled as he tossed the ripe McIntosh apples into Rose's waiting apron. The crimson red apples with splotches of green smelled sweet and fresh, the scents making Rose's mouth water.

Rose carried the gathered apples over to a basket on the ground and transferred them, returning to her spot beneath the tree. "I can't imagine traveling all the way across the ocean and seeing the things you have seen. What made you think of venturing there in the first place?" Rose tipped her head back to see Van hanging upside down from the high branch by his knees.

"My love for the island came from my love for reading about distant, faraway places. When I was only a boy, my family lived in Leicester, Massachusetts. I was sent to school under the tutelage of Clara Barton, who later left teaching and took up a role as a nurse in the Civil War. Miss Barton encouraged me to read all kinds of books and I was rarely seen without a book in my hand."

"After a few years, we moved to this little spot of heaven on earth in Wisconsin and while many of my brothers were content to settle down and farm this rich and fertile ground, I felt my destiny called to me from far away. I read a novel by Herman Melville entitled *Typee, a peep at Polynesian life.* It was all about Melville's memories of the people on Nuku Hiva, part of the Marquesas Islands, and I knew I needed to see it for myself. I worked my way from California on whaling vessels until I reached this island paradise, and I knew it was my new home."

Rose listened, enraptured with Van's story of his adventures. "What about the people there?" she asked. "Were the people civilized at all?" Rose imagined the cannibals described in the penny dreadfuls circulated in every small town.

"I guess it would depend upon your definition of civilized, Rose. The indigenous Polynesians are an industrious tribe of people. Everyone has a place in the tribe, and all are respected equally among them. The elderly and the young are cared for with compassion and honor, creating a strong sense of community. There is no pride, greed, or selfishness." Van swung up and straddled the branch he sat on, still tossing apples down to Rose as he continued.

"It was when the outsiders, the "civilized", came that things changed for the little village. Some members of the tribe were taken and sold off as slaves, some were introduced to a new religion and taught to hate others without religion, and a system of oligarchy was introduced to the tribesmen, ruining the sense of community that stood for generations."

"Though the people lived for hundreds of years without the benefits of our society, they were decimated by the societal tide of individualism and the influx of diseases invading such as smallpox and measles. Soon, in an effort to survive, they pick up the remnants of their village and move away from the intruders. When these intruders aggressively pursued them, they were met with the resistance of a native people desperate to live without their influence. And yet, in all the accounts, it is the indigenous natives that are called savages. I believe the wrong group has been labeled as savage." Van looked down to see most of the young people surrounding him, listening intently.

Rose stood there with tears in her eyes as she heard the plight of the native Polynesians. "What has become of them? Have they survived?" she asked with an earnestness that made Van smile at her compassion.

"Yes, despite the scourge of civilization, there is a remnant that remains, and these are the people I call my own." Van descended from his place in the tree with an easy grace and landed beside Rose. The others in the party applauded at what they considered Van's performance; only Rose seemed to understand the true significance of his words. It was often difficult to distinguish the civilized from the savage.

Mae Hyndman approached Van with a dramatic flourish, "Mr. McCollum, Mary told us you met Robert Louis Stevenson and exchanged poems with him. Please come and give us some of your poetry as we thirst for cultural enticements." Mae led Van away, leaving Rose still standing beneath the apple trees pondering the people of Nuku Hiva.

On the wagon ride back to Richland Center later in the evening, Rose sat between Ella and Lillie and listened to the heedless chatter around her. Van McCollum's story still settled upon Rose like a cloak of heavy wool, her heart grieving for the tribal people of the tiny island at the unmerciful hand of those who considered themselves their betters.

George awaited Rose's arrival in the parlor. Laura's contrived plan had worked over the course of the past month. George, being quite taken with Rose and her attention to him, forgot all about Mae Hyndman. As Rose entered the darkened Mitchell house, she was accosted by an angry, demanding voice.

"Just where have you been all evening and who have you been with?" George asked. His question sounded more like a demand and it frightened Rose with its intensity. George's moderate interest in Rose quickly transitioned into passionate jealousy. Rose felt trapped in a situation not of her own making, much like the people of the Nuku Hiva tribe. She also felt the first pangs of desperation to escape this small town and venture to where the "savages" were civilized.

CHAPTER 11

TUESDAY, DECEMBER 24, 1889, RICHLAND CENTER, WISCONSIN

A fluffy light snow floated to the ground like small feathers released from the evening sky as Rose walked with Dr. Mitchell and Freddie towards the First Methodist Church. A Christmas Eve program was scheduled to begin at 7 p.m. and most of the town planned to attend. Laura, being in a delicate condition, had been directed by George to remain at home with Annie to look after her.

Rose offered to stay with her, but George insisted Rose accompany him and Freddie instead. Freddie was slated to perform in the program, and George assured Rose that the boy would be disappointed if she were to miss his debut in the boy's chorus. It seemed odd to Rose that Freddie was far more nonchalant about her attendance in comparison to his father. She realized a boy of Freddie's age was often lacking sentimentality; she comforted herself with that opinion, to cover for George's eagerness towards her.

Rose donned her new wool coat and matching hat in a deep cobalt blue, an early Christmas gift from Laura, and took George's arm when he offered it. More than once, Rose noticed the occasional stare from the ladies in the entourage traversing along the sidewalks with them towards the church.

Rose recognized the malicious stares of the busybodies of the town who assumed everything without knowing anything. Moreover, Rose understood the disparaging gawking was fueled by scurrilous words exchanged like currency, hidden under the premises of "prayerful sharing" among the same people who claimed to have a religion of love and charity to others as its centrality.

A girl with less tenacity than Rose would have ended the charade Laura had begun for the sake of saving herself from the clutches of these black-garbed magpie matrons, but Rose was not easily deterred. Each time she witnessed the stares or heard a wisp of the whispers, she straightened her back and threw back her shoulders in silent but open defiance.

"Good evening, Dr. Lovering. Good evening, Mrs. Lovering" Rose smiled at the distinguished couple ascending the stairs to the church vestibule. Dr. Lovering tipped his hat to Rose and returned her cheery greeting, while Mrs. Lovering offered her the slightest polite nod.

"I am hoping we will enjoy a beautiful selection of the cello from you this evening, Mrs. Lovering. I always look forward to hearing you play." Rose tried to engage the stoic woman again with a compliment.

"Thank you, Rose. I have been invited to perform and I chose *The Ode to Joy* as a duet with Jimmy McAvoy on his violin. It pleases me that you have begun to appreciate the finer points of music." Mrs. Lovering nodded her approval at Rose and moved to take her husband's arm as he escorted her towards the front pews in the church.

"Alas, poor Jimmy McAvoy," George whispered close to Rose's ear. "Mrs. Lovering's renditions are often mistaken for alley cats fighting." He led Rose and Freddie to a pew and allowed them to sit before sitting down next to Rose. Rose struggled to maintain her composure, trying not to giggle at George's description of Mrs. Lovering's musical abilities. It did not help that George kept glancing at her out of the corner of his eyes and imitating a quiet mewling sound.

The church program began, and Rose was enthralled at the recitation by the Richland Center High School's champion student, Pearl E. Doudna. Rose was amazed at the young man's eloquence. Mrs. Lovering and Jimmy McAvoy played their duet while Rose struggled not to laugh at George's continuing imitations of the unmelodious sounds of the cello. Then Jimmy played *Silent Night* as a solo on his violin and Rose nearly cried from the dulcet music the hometown virtuoso created.

Finally, it was time for the boy's chorus and Freddie rose from his place beside Rose to join the other boys at the altar. Rose noticed the trembling of Freddie's hands as he passed over her in the pew, so she reached out to give his hand a gentle squeeze of reassurance. He smiled brilliantly at Rose and walked down the aisle with more assurance.

"My son has excellent taste in young ladies." George leaned closer than he needed to whisper in Rose's ear. "I appreciate your attention to him on my behalf, Rose. I hope you know I will never forget your kindness." He sat pressed lightly against Rose's side, his presence distracting her from the young boys' performance. Rose was startled to hear the polite applause signaling the concert had come to an end.

Soon Rose was outside, the cold air bracing her warm cheeks. Rose took the arm George offered her, concerned she would stumble in the state of mind she currently found herself.

Freddie scrambled to catch up with the pack of boys ahead of them; now their dignified performance was completed, the rambunctious lads were sliding along on the icy street. Freddy left Rose to make her way home with the romantic overtones of George's attention increasing with their every step. Rose tried to increase their pace, but George increased the pressure on her arm, slowing her even more.

"I wanted to take this opportunity to tell you how beautiful you are tonight, dear Rose." George slipped his arm around Rose's waist, causing her to slip on the ice so he could steady her again. To onlookers it only appeared that the kind doctor had prevented the silly young woman from falling on the ice, but Rose knew the actual intentions were far more inappropriate. She would have to scramble to escape George's attention without ruining the façade she and Laura had established. The answer came instantly, and Rose proceeded without thinking about the future consequences.

"I am pleased you have noticed me, George, but what can really come of it when Laura is certain to find out that we have strong feelings for each other? If only you were not a married man and able to pursue the obvious affection that is present. I have no intention of becoming your consort and yet I cannot stand the thought of leaving this place and never seeing you again. I am afraid we will have to continue to esteem each other from afar, at least for the time being, and hope for a better future." Rose sighed and feigned wiping a few tears from her eyes with her handkerchief as he nodded in silent agreement.

"You may be right, Rose." George held Rose's hand to his heart, and they continued in the darkness towards the haven of Laura and the Mitchell home. Rose sighed inwardly, congratulating herself on her extrication from the current predicament, not realizing she had just caused a much larger one and possibly a course of action that could alter her life forever.

CHAPTER 12

WEDNESDAY, DECEMBER 25, 1889

Christmas morning dawned with brilliant sunshine sparkling across the fresh snow from the previous evening. The sun's rays splashed on Rose's face as she lay in bed listening to the sounds of Annie beginning the preparation for dinner. Rose sat up and smiled, feeling the excitement of a child who eagerly anticipates Christmas and realizes it has finally arrived.

Rose dressed and completed her ablutions, paying careful attention to her hair, styling it in a fashion Laura had chosen from the latest ladies' magazine from Paris. She knelt beside her bed and reached under it, bringing out the gifts she had wrapped for Laura, Freddie, Annie, and George. A second small bag held presents for Mrs. Wilson and Ella and Lillie Maly that she would deliver in the afternoon.

Rose left her room quietly, not wishing to wake Laura, who had difficulty sleeping. She went down the stairs and towards the kitchen where Annie was stuffing the goose for dinner. The smell of fresh cinnamon rolls and hot coffee beckoned to Rose from the sideboard in the dining room. George and Freddie were seated at the table as Rose placed a roll on a china plate and poured a steaming cup of coffee from the silver pot. She carried her breakfast to the chair nearest Freddie, leaving the other place next to George for Laura.

"Merry Christmas, Rose!" Freddie greeted Rose cheerfully with a mouth partially full of uneaten roll. George looked up from the newspaper he was reading with an expression of chagrin and opened his mouth to chastise his son's table manners.

"Wesolych Swiat Bozego Narodzenia, Freddie. This is how you tell someone Merry Christmas in Polish." Rose spoke quickly, attempting to prevent George's harshness from ruining the young boy's exuberance. Rose patted Freddie's shoulder, winked, and gently reached to close the mouth still partially open. The boy grinned as he obediently shut his mouth to chew the remainder of his food and even used his napkin to wipe his lips afterwards.

Laura appeared in the doorway of the dining room looking pale and tired. Rose stood and reached for Laura's arm, guiding her to the chair, Freddie flanking his mother's other side while George sat eating his breakfast and reading his paper without even glancing at his wife.

"Thank you, dear ones." Laura sat down in the chair Rose pulled out for her. Freddie brought his mother a plate with a cinnamon roll and Rose poured a cup of tea from the silver teapot, mixing it with a generous dollop of cream. Laura pushed the plate with the roll away and tried to take a sip of the tea set before her. She smiled weakly at the concerned countenances on the faces of her son and her friend.

"I think just the cup of tea will work best for right now. Darling boy, why don't you eat this for your mama?" Laura pushed the plate with the roll across the table towards her son. Freddie grabbed the offered roll and began eating it with a voracious appetite. George peered up from his newspaper and glared at his son.

"I think you have had more than enough breakfast, Frederick. Take the remainder of your plate and go and dump it in the scrap pail in the kitchen." George pointed at his son and indicated the door with a tilt of his head. He folded his arms in front of his chest, waiting for his son's obedience.

Freddie, dismayed at his father's instructions, looked at his mother for assistance. Laura closed her eyes and nodded her head at her son. Freddie stood, tipping his chair over as he stomped towards the kitchen door with his plate. Rose could hear his sniffling cries as he left the room.

"George, was that really necessary? It is Christmas morning after all." Laura reached to put her hand on George's arm next to her on the table. The pain in Laura's eyes was almost more than Rose could bear, but George did not seem likewise affected. He shifted his arm, repelling the hand of entreaty placed there.

"I would not have to do such things if you did not pamper the boy, Laura. You are making a weak, useless, sissy of him, and now you are adding obesity to it. Our son should be ready to enter military school soon and you will be the ruin of him if you persist. It is you who are cruel to the lad. You will cause him to be ridiculed by his peers for being the mama's boy that you have created. I have told you before to leave the discipline with me, as I know best what is to be done with him."

Rose stood and gathered her plate and cup, heading for the kitchen before she lost all control and began shouting at the brutish man. She entered to see Annie hugging a crying Freddie, who overheard every cruel word his father spat out. The housekeeper started in alarm at the swinging sound of the kitchen door, then relaxed when she saw Rose enter instead of George.

Rose set her dishes on the worktable and went to the stove where the leftover cinnamon rolls stood, still warm in the pan. She scooped up another roll and took it to Freddie, urging the boy to take the offering. He peeked at the kitchen door in hesitation, not wanting to incur more of George's scathing remarks.Rose placed herself between Freddie and the door as a physical barrier but more importantly, as an emotional buffer for the vulnerable young boy. Annie gave her a quick nod and a lopsided grin to show her approval and patted Freddie's shoulder in encouragement.

Freddie tried to smile at the two young women who had just become his champions and allies in the Mitchell household. He ate the cinnamon roll to rid himself of the evidence of their miniature mutiny and left out the back door without a coat to avoid another encounter with his deprecatory father.

"There ought to be a law. To treat his own child in such a way. He parades around the town as the most gentile of citizens. If people only knew what goes on in this house they would feel differently about the good doctor" Annie whispered her vehement declarations to Rose as she banged the pots and pans in the basin.

Rose nodded in agreement and steeled herself to walk back into the dining room. Laura was sitting alone at the table, her head in her hands as she cried. Rose looked for any signs of George's presence and when she found he had taken his leave, she headed for the front door, picking up her coat and a wool blanket from the hall closet on her way.

Once outside, Rose took a sharp left turn, heading for the back-yard and the small treehouse Freddie built in the oak there. She scaled the ladder, lifting her skirts to prevent herself from tripping.

She pushed the blanket ahead of her into the treehouse and towards the boy crumpled into a ball in the corner.

"My grandmother always insisted the best way to get a chill is to go out in the cold without a coat. I would not want to see anyone get sick on Christmas Day of all days." Rose spoke in general terms so the boy would not feel he was being ordered about like a soldier. She crawled across the crude wood floor of the treehouse and placed the blanket over Freddie, who was shivering from the exposure to the Wisconsin winter morning.

"I don't think they would care if I got sick and died. In fact, I think my father will be relieved and my mother will soon have a new baby to replace me." Freddie's words were whispered but earnest. Rose saw the anguish reflected in the young boy's eyes as she shook her head.

"No, Freddie. Your mama loves you very much and I think your papa does, too, in his own way. I know I think of you as a dear friend, and I would miss you if you were gone from us. I am sorry you heard those hurtful words. The pain they cause in your heart is real. I'm not telling you to not feel pain but to realize the words spoken about you were really about the person who said them. Hurt people hurt other people for the oddest reasons. I have had people do the same to me, and I will either accept their words and be miserable or realize their words are their reflections and not my own, so I can be free of the harm intended." Rose spoke quietly and slowly, letting the truth of her words cover the boy like the wool blanket he had wrapped around him.

"So, you see, you have the choice to accept or reject those words. I think you should reject them and come back inside to enjoy the rest of your Christmas with me, Annie, and your mama." Rose patted the boy's shoulder and started to crawl back towards the ladder leading down to the ground. By the time she descended the ladder and glanced upwards, she saw Freddie's grinning face looking at her from the top. He descended the ladder and landed beside her in the snow with a plop. The two of them walked hand in hand back towards the kitchen door at the side of the house.

The Christmas dinner and opening of gifts was a somber occasion for the Mitchells and Rose. George reappeared in the parlor with gifts for Freddie, Laura, and Rose. He did not speak of his earlier words, or hint at an apology, but chose to ignore the outburst altogether, expecting everyone else to do the same.

George had become a master at inflicting deep wounds on his family and then acting as if nothing had occurred. If the offended party dared to speak to him later, then he treated them as though they were the aggressor. Laura learned silence was the better way to forge peace in the situation.

Late in the afternoon, Rose and Freddie bundled up against the winter chill taking Rose's gifts to Mrs. Wilson and the Malys. The cold air made the snow crunch under their feet as they walked along Church Street towards Mrs. Wilson's shop. Rose could not resist taking small bunches of the snow in her hand, packing them, and throwing the snowballs at Freddie, encouraging him to reciprocate. The two were breathless and laughing by the time they arrived at the back door of the shop. Freddie stepped up to rap the door knocker placed in the center of the wood door.

"Why, look at the two of you! You look as if butter wouldn't melt in your mouth." Mrs. Wilson laughed at the mischievous pair who still had bits of snow sticking to their hats and eyelashes. "Come right in and warm yourselves by the fire. Merry Christmas!" Mrs.

Wilson's exuberance in greeting Rose and Freddie made the Christmas exchange at the Mitchell house seem even more dismal in its lack of genuine affection.

Soon Rose and Freddie were seated by the fire with Mrs. Wilson enjoying a cup of hot chocolate and Christmas cookies along with her warm, inviting conversation. Rose loved to see as well as hear Mrs. Wilson laugh at Freddie's jokes. Mrs. Wilson's laugh went all the way up to her eyes, which warmed in hue with her congenial chuckling and the creases at the end of each eye crinkling in delight.

Rose could tell Mrs. Wilson was the exact tonic that had been needed for Freddie's hurting heart. She was amazed at the capacity of some people to harm and wound with their words and the capacity of others to heal and restore.

"Oh my, Rose, this is far too grand a present for an old lady." Mrs. Wilson held the beautiful shawl Rose had sent away to New York City to give to her mentor and friend. The older woman's work-worn hands felt the silky smoothness of the cloth in her lap as she smiled at Rose. It was worth every penny of the dear price Rose paid for the finery, to see the smile on Mrs. Wilson's face.

Soon Rose and Freddie took their leave of Mrs. Wilson to make their way towards the Maly house on North Park Street. They could hear the shouts and laughter coming from Maly's yard as Ella, Lillie and many of their siblings and friends were assembled in the yard building snowmen. Joe Bohan had just finished gathering a massive heap of snow that he shaped into a block so Ella could sculpt frozen statuary. Joe's eyes flashed with admiration every time his hands touched Ella's hands as they worked together.

Rose noted again the budding romance between the couple. She was genuinely happy Ella had found a person who adored the sweet, gentle, young woman. Rose and Freddie watched for a few minutes as Ella sculpted and Joe teased Ella. Rose decided she and Freddie would need to return to the Mitchells before Annie waited for them for their supper. Rose left little parcels of chocolate creams for Ella and Lillie to unwrap later and made her way with Freddie along the six blocks towards their home.

"That seemed like a lot of fun, Rose. I wish we could have stayed longer and helped build the snowmen." Freddie peeked at Rose wistfully. She knew he did not look forward to returning to their home when they had experienced such pleasant company since leaving the Mitchell house.

"The wonderful thing about snow is it is also available in our yard, Freddie. What do you say we let Annie know where we are and build a couple of snowmen of our own?" Rose giggled at the eager nodding of his head in affirmation. Freddie hummed a Christmas carol as they finished their walk and arrived at the house.

Freddie set about gathering sizable amounts of snow in two tall heaps while Rose went into the house to tell Annie of their plans. Laura was so delighted to hear of their activity she sent out hats and an old shawl with Rose along with coal and carrots from Annie in the kitchen. Soon Freddie and Rose were sculpting a dapper man and a fashionable young woman, laughing, and throwing the occasional snowball at each other.

Within an hour there stood two impressive snow sculptures. Freddie appeared extremely satisfied with their labors. Annie came out to see the elegant couple and Laura watched from the parlor window, clapping her hands in appreciation of their efforts. Freddie's face, tinged red from the cold air and from the slight blushing at Annie's effervescent praise, showed his delight.

Rose gazed up from their entertainment to see George crossing the street from the Central Hotel. His nose was red from imbibing spirits rather than exposure to the cold. He walked slowly as if trying to maintain his balance in the slushy street. George stopped at the gate leading to the yard and squinted to see the snowmen.

Rose, Freddie, and Annie gathered in the yard. All three seemed as frozen in place as their snow counterparts, Rose internally willing George to pass by without commentary. George never seemed to heed external cues of any sort, made a snorting sound as he shook his head.

"Just what we needed in our front yard for the whole town to see, replicas of your mother and me." George chuckled at his own unintended rhyme and made his way towards the front door, leaving Freddie, Rose, and Annie staring after him.

As soon as George gained entrance to the house, Rose heard the telltale sound of snow falling in masses. Before she or Annie could stop him, Freddie pushed both snowmen over, demolishing both to smithereens.

CHAPTER 13

TUESDAY, JANUARY 7, 1890, RICHLAND CENTER, WISCONSIN

The bitter cold of a Wisconsin January settled upon the city of Richland Center. Subzero temperatures prevailed for days without an end in sight. Many of the citizens, being of hearty stock and raised for generations in countries like Germany and Norway, went about their daily lives without disruption from the arctic conditions.

Rose tried to look out the parlor windows but the heavy frost on both the inside and the outside of the glass pane made it difficult to see. She glanced back at Laura who was bundled up in several blankets on the parlor settee. Laura was within one month of giving birth to her child and her swollen face was now matched with swollen feet and hands that were not only distended but bruised with mottled colors of gray and blue.

Laura experienced daily dizzy spells and shortness of breath, things that made Rose and Annie concerned for her, but George insisted Laura was healthy and strong and no one should mollycoddle a woman just because she was about to have a baby.

Laura had begun to struggle with episodes of mental anxiety and feelings of impending doom, so much so that she often sequestered herself in her bedroom with all the shades drawn against the sunlight, insisting the bright lights made her dizziness and headaches worse. Rose knew the continual isolation combined with the seasonal lack of natural sunlight was a bad combination of Laura's increasing despondency.

A few days prior, Rose devised a plan with Annie to invite a few of the ladies of Richland Center to tea that afternoon as a surprise for Laura. The ladies offered to bring some refreshments and a few gifts for the coming baby, to cheer up Laura and help her through this difficult time.

Rose helped Laura to wash herself and styled her hair in a becoming fashion, telling her a little pampering would make her feel better. Rose and Annie carefully guided Laura down the stairs with Freddie's help and made her comfortable on the settee.

Just as the parlor clock chimed two o'clock, there was a knock at the front door. Laura looked alarmed, as she hadn't expected any visitors. "I hope that isn't someone bringing bad news." Laura shuddered. "I keep feeling as if someone is going to die."

Annie almost dropped the silver tea service, "Please don't say that Missus! I can't stand to hear folks talk of death and such. It is very bad luck indeed." Annie righted the tea service that had tipped slightly in her frightened state and set it upon the parlor table. She then crossed to the front hallway door and thrust it open with a distraught look on her face.

Mrs. Wilson, Mrs. Lovering and several other of the town's matrons stared at Annie's sudden appearance and distressed visage. Mrs. Wilson led the group of ladies indoors past the housekeeper who stood at the open door, staring at them with her mouth still agape. Rose shook her head silently at the housekeeper as she welcomed the ladies and assisted them with removing their heavy coats in the hallway.

"My goodness sakes! One would think Annie had just seen a hobgoblin." Mrs. Wilson chuckled to Rose as she handed her a dish of applesauce. "I was practical in my choice for Laura's refreshments, as a good applesauce is better for her right now than cakes and treats."

Rose nodded her head in agreement with her employer's wisdom. "Yes, perhaps I can get Laura to eat some of it. Her appetite has not been good as of late. Thank you for thinking about it."

Rose heard the small collective gasps from the women as soon as they saw Laura lying on the settee. These were women who experienced multiple childbirths and they were distressed to see Laura's condition. Rose was now convinced this pregnancy was not of an ordinary nature, no matter what Dr. Mitchell tried to say to the contrary.

"Laura, dear. Would you be more comfortable with a few more pillows?" Mrs. Wilson and the other ladies gathered around Laura, adding pillows under her feet and adjusting the pillows located behind her back. Rose admired the ability of the small group of women gathered to nurture one of their own without pomp and pageantry.

Soon Laura was looking better than Rose had seen her in several months. Laura accepted a small dish of applesauce Mrs. Wilson made and when she had finished, she sipped some bone broth Mrs. Lovering warmed up in the kitchen herself, much to Annie's surprise that such a "grand lady" would be able to do so menial a task.

Laura then opened small gifts as the ladies gathered around her complimenting the handiwork of each contributor. Laura's eyes shone with tears as she ran her fingers across a tiny lace cap made by Mrs. Wilson.

"Such a precious bonnet for my little one. Every stitch is simply perfect. Thank you all so much." Laura met the encouraging eyes of each woman and nodded her appreciation for something given far more valuable than the gifts or refreshments, the intangible benefits of care and compassion.

Two hours passed by, and the women were soon gathering their things to return to their homes. Annie had been summoned to assist them. She added warmed stones from the oven to each pocket to keep hands and fingers from frostbite. Annie was so relieved to see the dramatic change in her employer in only two short hours, thankful the former morbidity had been assumedly forgotten. Just then, Annie caught the tidbit of conversation between Laura and Mrs. Lovering.

"I have no doubt if something happened to me George would remarry our Rose within a few months. She is so dear to him and to us all." Laura assured the shocked Mrs. Lovering, in a hushed tone, that what she said was quite true.

Later that night, in the comfort of her own tiny attic bedroom, Annie vowed to say extra prayers in the coming days to ward off all the bad tidings she was sure Laura had just proclaimed in the Mitchell household. An ominous sense of foreboding permeated the darkened house and its inhabitants; intensified by the chiming of each hour on the parlor clock signifying the days were numbered for some who dwelled therein.

CHAPTER 14

SUNDAY, FEBRUARY 2, 1890, ROCKBRIDGE, WISCONSIN

The February sun shone brightly, illuminating the ice formations on the massive rock edifices bordering the Pine River near Rockbridge. The snow, which had accumulated through January, was in the process of thawing during the daylight hours only to be captured in ice formations as the temperatures decreased with the setting of the sun.

As the melted snow ran over these natural rocks, it dissolved minerals within the rocks and colored the ice formations into works of intricately brilliant art. People from far and wide would make the trip to see the beautiful ice sculptures flowing off the rocks in the small hamlet of Rockbridge.

Joe Bohan and his brother Dan rented sleighs and, with the assistance of Ella and Lillie, gathered a party for a sleigh ride to Rockbridge. Ella invited Rose to accompany them, but Rose had declined because she grew more concerned about Laura's health by the day. Mrs. Wilson heard Rose had turned down the offer to enjoy the afternoon sleigh ride with the other young people. She tried to convince Rose to change her mind.

"A baby won't come just because you keep watch over it, Rose. Laura will be in good hands with Annie and myself to watch after her while you take an afternoon and enjoy yourself. You have been either working with me at the shop or cooped up in Laura's room for almost a month now. It won't hurt anyone a bit for you to take a few hours of fresh air and sunshine. In fact, if I were still your age and the Bohan brothers asked me to go anywhere, I would probably outrun the horses to catch up with them." Mrs. Wilson nodded emphatically as she urged Rose to go and change her clothes before the party left town.

Rose glanced at Laura in concern. Laura had been improving in physical and emotional health until they received the devastating news of her father's sudden death two weeks prior.

The shock mixed with her grief at the loss and her inability to travel to her mother and siblings had taken a considerable toll on Laura's wellbeing. George increased the dosage of tonics he administered, and Rose spent countless hours with Laura, even sitting at her bedside many nights until Annie or Mrs. Wilson would force her to go to her own room and rest.

Finally, Rose, persuaded by the cogent arguments of Mrs. Wilson, went to change her dress quickly, while Freddie was sent ahead to delay the sleigh party from departing without her. Rose donned her heaviest coat and a red woolen hat, mittens, and scarf, a Christmas gift sent from her mama, and left with a wave to Laura and Mrs. Wilson. The brisk air embraced her, and she breathed it in a deep inhalation, allowing it to refresh her, chasing away the mental cobwebs of her self-isolation.

The party departed for the several mile trip to Rockbridge, Ella leading the others in songs as they glided across the snow; the bells of the sleigh adding a melodious tune to the voices lifted in chorus. Rose sat quietly for the first part of the journey, listening in appreciation to Ella's sweet soprano voice.

Gradually she felt the weight of the last few weeks lift from her, chased away by the gaiety and camaraderie of her companions. Ella squeezed Rose's hand in encouragement when Rose began to sing with the ensemble, adding her alto harmony.

Soon they arrived at the natural rock bridge that gave the little town its name. Massive boulders of sandstone layered and blocked, jutted sixty feet into the air in a half-mile long narrow configuration. The west branch of the Pine River connects to the central branch of the Pine River underneath the rock outcroppings forming a natural bridge over it and a tunnel through the rocks to the one side of the river.

The deep green pine trees growing on the top of the sandstone formation were still flocked in pure snow glistening like scattered diamonds in the afternoon sun. The icicles formed over the orange, red, and yellow sandstone in a pendent mass gave the impression of a time in ages long past. The sheer beauty of the picturesque scene took Rose's breath away as she tilted her head back further to take in the encompassing view.

"I wish I were an artist so I could attempt to capture this beauty in a painting, but I wonder if something this beautiful cannot actually be captured in still life." Rose mused as she hugged Ella next to her. "Thank you for inviting me along with you. This is healing to the soul. I will store up a memory to try and take home for Laura. I only wish she could see this for herself."

Ella returned Rose's embrace. "Is Mrs. Mitchell really in a bad way? I feel so sorry for her, as she was so delighted about this baby and now, she seems almost worse than after she lost Nellie."

Rose nodded in agreement with Ella's expression of sympathy for Laura and the baby. "There are days when I wonder if she will hold on long enough to see this baby. She is just so weak, and she still needs the strength to deliver this child. She seems to have given up after learning of her father's passing."

"What of Dr. Mitchell? Does he seem upset as well?" Ella whispered her questions to keep the others in the sleigh from hearing.

"It doesn't seem to upset him at all. He keeps insisting she is fine, and all will be well. I hope for Laura's sake he is correct." Rose lifted her eyes from her friend's face to the captivating vista before them. Her eyes wanted another drink of the serenity displayed in the natural beauty before their departure.

"Since it is just the two of us, I thought you should know Mae Hyndman is leaving Richland Center soon. She is being sent away to her aunt up north in Barron County. Her mother became aware of some rather unsavory associations and wanted to keep her from harm's way. Mae is very distraught over being sent off in this manner, even though Mrs. Hyndman told everyone she was being sent for more schooling to cover over the matter. I know there have been times that Mae was less than kind to you, but if you could help me by being kind to her in her distress, I would count it as a personal favor." Ella squeezed Rose's mittened hand in supplication.

"Why, of course I will be kind to her, Ella. I can only imagine how painful that might be. You are such a sweet friend to all of us, none of us deserve you, Ella Maly." The last sentence of Rose's declaration caught the attention of Joe, who was seated ahead of them in the sleigh. He nodded his head in vehement agreement.

"You are correct, Miss Zoldoske. I think only the angels in heaven deserve Ella's company. None of the rest of us here on earth are near good enough." Joe turned the sleigh towards Richland Center and returned home. Ella reached out and playfully tipped Joe's hat from the back, so the front brim banged his nose. A snort of laughter was emitted from deep within Joe as he adjusted the hat back to its proper place.

The group enjoyed the fast pace of the horses and sleighs as they flew across the snow towards home. Singing could be heard from blocks away as the group approached the city limits again. Joe stopped here and there, allowing various members of the party to disembark. Soon he stopped in front of the Mitchell house, jumping down to help Rose from the sleigh. Ella was the only remaining passenger.

Rose waved to Ella and Joe as the sleigh darted down Church Street in a clamor of bells. She made her way to the front door where Freddie appeared at the door looking terrified.

"I am so glad you have come home, Rose. Mama was feeling very poorly, and Papa said to come for you because the baby is on the way. He said you should go to sit with Mama right away. Please hurry Rose!" Freddie ran back up the stairs with Rose close behind him, taking off her coat and outer garments as she went.

Apparently, Laura's baby had not listened to Mrs. Wilson's sage advice about when babies should or should not arrive and so it decided to begin its arrival early. Rose said a quick prayer as she paused outside Laura's door. Hopefully, this baby would heed Dr. Mitchell's motto that "All will be well."

CHAPTER 15

TUESDAY, FEBRUARY 4, 1890, RICHLAND CENTER, WISCONSIN

It was three o'clock in the afternoon when Rose stumbled into her bedroom and closed the door behind her. Exhaustion coupled with the tension of the previous forty-eight hours of Laura's labor and delivery made Rose's fatigued legs wobble and her foggy brain whirl with confusion. Rose could not even hold her blood-shot, swollen eyes open long enough to remove her dress, still spattered with blood, before she fell upon her bed.

Three hours later, Rose awoke with a start to the sounds of Annie preparing a meal in the kitchen below. Rose's eyes still felt as if a bucket of sand was abrading in each one and her mouth was parched from being partially open as she slept.

There were tremors of pain in her lower back and legs from sleeping in a single position for so long. Rose rolled to her side to try and alleviate the discomfort. Rose was still exhausted, but her mind began to replay the events she had witnessed as if they were being depicted again in slow motion.

George had overseen the delivery of his child, being assisted by Rose, Annie, and Mrs. Wilson. Even now Rose ground her teeth at the recollection of George's reticent demeanor as Laura's birthing pains increased and her distressed cries rang throughout the house. He would come and check on the progression, then retreat to his office on the first floor. Rose was certain she smelled alcohol on his breath more than once throughout the night.

As the grueling night passed into the early morning hours and then into mid-morning and afternoon, Laura continued to suffer through each wracking contraction. Her body was limp and lifeless from exhaustion, sweat poured off her body, drenching the bedclothes and giving the stuffy bedroom a fetid, sickly odor.

Laura's skin was almost translucent with dark purple splotches of blood vessels showing through it. She had ceased to cry out with each labor pain and her eyes were partially rolled back when she attempted to open them. Only an occasional faint ragged breath of air assured the others she still lived.

At the beginning of each hour, George would enter the room, check Laura's progress, and leave again. Rose had not experienced childbirth herself, but she was strongly beginning to question George's medical expertise and his love for his suffering wife. Finally, as the second day began to wane and give way to the early morning hours of the third day, Mrs. Wilson began to question George about sending for Dr. Haskell to assist him in this strenuous birthing.

"Perhaps all of us need some respite, including you, Dr. Mitchell. You have gone without rest and Dr. Haskell could attend to Laura while you rest." Mrs. Wilson chose her argument for calling for assistance wisely, basing it on George's needs rather than those of his poor wife.

"Call for Haskell for all the good it will do. This child will be the death of her." George's flat and emotionless voice matched his air of indifference, making Rose's blood boil. Rose prayed that Laura was in a delirious state so that she no longer understood his declaration and the manner in which it was delivered.

Annie was dispatched to ask Dr. Haskell to come in haste. Soon the physician was standing at Laura's bedside assessing his new patient with great concern. He sent for a local midwife to relieve the very weary Mrs. Wilson, but Rose refused to leave her post beside Laura. Dr. Haskell performed an examination to determine the position of the baby. His face paled as he glanced up from his examination to glance at the midwife. Her face mirrored his shocked horror.

"This poor woman has been mutilated beyond repair. There are injuries that are common in childbirth, but I have never witnessed anything to this degree. It is little wonder she has such difficulty. The child seems to be down in position and ready, but it cannot proceed any further. We will need to operate immediately and take the child by the cesarean method. Hopefully, we will still be able to spare both the mother and the child, but it has been far too long already." Dr. Haskell shook his head in dismay at the neglect of his colleague, Dr. Mitchell.

The midwife bustled about the room readying it and Laura for the surgery. Rose swallowed the bile heaving in her throat as she saw the tools the doctor took from his bag and sanitized them.

The heavy, sweet scent of the chloroform administered by a cloth placed over Laura's face caused Rose's head to spin until she thought she would fall from the chair she sat upon. Dr. Haskell took a position at the side of the table and motioned for Rose to hold the cloth containing the chloroform.

"There then, Rose, we need your help if we are to save her. That's right, hold it steady and don't breathe it in yourself. Did anyone see where Dr. Mitchell went? Never mind, we don't have time to wait for him. God help us all."

The next hour was filled with sights and sounds Rose never knew existed. She tried to concentrate on administering the chloroform the way Dr. Haskell had shown her and prayed Laura would survive the ordeal. Dr. Haskell delivered the baby, and the room was deathly still. The tiny form was the color of an eggplant and laid motionless in the doctor's hands. Rose felt the pressure of the sobs building in her chest until she felt she could not breathe.

In a moment, there was a sputter, and a frail cry pierced the silence. Dr. Haskell was bent over the little figure, rubbing it vigorously with a towel and hanging it upside down by its ankles. There were larger gasps and soon more vigorous cries emanated from the tiny person. Both Dr. Haskell and the midwife were relieved as the baby began to wail with vigor. When Rose dared to inspect the baby again, she was as pink as could be, her little arms and legs were thrashing wildly, pummeling the good doctor who had just saved her life. A beautiful baby girl with dark hair and dark eyes was thrust into Rose's arms by Dr. Haskell as he turned to try and revive Laura as well.

Laura still lay on the table, unconscious and in a terrible state. Dr. Haskell went to work stitching the incision he had made, while the midwife took over the chloroform duties from Rose. Annie and Mrs. Wilson crept into the room to stand beside Rose and peek at the Mitchells' new daughter, who was still wailing.

"Perhaps we should take the child down to her father and leave Dr. Haskell to his work?" Mrs. Wilson suggested as she relieved Rose of the tiny bundle in her arms. Mrs. Wilson began to coo and hum to the child, rocking side to side as she wiped the little face.

"I would leave the baby here for now." Dr Haskell looked up from his work to the ladies gathered around the baby. "I have known more than one woman who would revive when they heard their own baby. A mother will do anything for her child, including thwarting her own death at times. Why don't you bring the baby close to her head as she may be waking up shortly and will want to see her fine daughter. Dr. Mitchell can come and find his wife and child if he cares to do so." Rose could hear the disdain in Dr. Haskell's voice when he mentioned the absent father.

George appeared in the room as if he had been summoned. His eyes darted from the carnage of the delivery to the tiny bundle in Mrs. Wilson's arms.

"Is she alive?" George whispered the question in a flat tone. Rose could see his eyes were fixed on the slight rise and fall of Laura's chest.

"Both your wife and your daughter are very much alive, Sir. I am just finishing the last of the sutures so I will need your assistance in moving your wife back to bed. Hopefully, she will wake up soon, and I don't wish for her to see herself in the current situation." Dr. Haskell motioned to the stained table and mess on the floor. "I would also suggest calling for one of the new mothers in town to help with nursing the babe until your wife is stronger."

Mrs. Wilson handed the baby back to Rose and bustled about the room setting things straight and helping to freshen Laura and change her nightgown. The midwife was dispatched to call upon one of the neighbors and ask for assistance with nursing the baby. Soon Annie and Mrs. Wilson had the room cleaned.

Rose stood at the side of Laura's bed holding Laura's newborn daughter and silently pleaded with her friend to open her eyes. Rose placed the babe next to Laura on her pillow. The tiny girl's mewls grew louder as she stuffed her tiny hand in her little rosebud mouth, the sure sign of hunger.

Rose bent over to scoop up the crying child when she noticed the flutter of Laura's eyelashes. Laura let out a low moan and then a louder one as her still unfocused eyes flew open. Laura blinked several times then focused her eyes on the little figure next to her still wailing from hunger. A slow smile spread across Laura's face as she gazed upon her new daughter.

"Charlotte. Her name is Charlotte. We'll call her Lotte" Laura whispered to Rose before she passed out again from the overwhelming pain.

Hours later, as Rose lay on her bed after a brief respite, a realization struck her like a lightning bolt; George Mitchell had never even asked to see his newborn daughter.

CHAPTER 16

TUESDAY, FEBRUARY 18, 1890

Two weeks had passed since tiny Charlotte Mitchell made her first appearance in the Mitchell household. There was a constant stream of people entering the house with parcels of food and well wishes for Laura and the baby. Mrs. Nona Hendy, an older, widowed woman, was hired to take care of the infant until Laura could recover. The entire household had all the trappings of a three-ring circus, just because a baby had arrived.

George had taken to hiding from all visitors by staying long hours in his office. He had Annie make the horsehair couch in the corner into a makeshift bed and even had his meals delivered there instead of eating in the dining room. He pretended to be busy with his medical practice, but it was easy to see through his ruse as very few patients showed up to be treated by Dr. Mitchell since the night of Lotte's birth.

George blamed the sudden diminishment of his practice on the blathering tongues of Dr. Haskell and his wife. Haskell had the nerve on the morning after Charlotte was born to take George aside and ask him about the birth injuries Laura sustained bearing Nellie and Freddie. Haskell dramatized the circumstances of Charlotte's birth and had even gone as far as informing George that Laura should never again consider bearing another child.

Haskell informed George as a husband he must release Laura from all future "wifely conjugal duties". George was certain the old charlatan had taken his fraudulent version of the events home to his gossiping wife and the upright Mrs. Haskell had made it her virtuous duty to inform the whole town. While George had absolutely no proof any character assassination was perpetrated by Dr. Haskell or his wife, his own nature assumed two primary things: the evil machinations of his own heart would be the intent of others and he himself could not be at fault, so it had to be someone else's fault.

George sat staring out his frost-covered window, plotting his revenge against Dr. Haskell, while sipping on a brandy from a crystal cut Waterford snifter. A slight tapping on the office door made George grimace as he watched to see who dared to enter his domain.

Freddie stood in the doorway holding a parcel of letters and newspapers. The boy glanced nervously at the floor and shifted back and forth as if he were unsure whether to enter and possibly incur his father's wrath. George nodded his permission for his son to enter the room.

"Papa, the post office sent this batch of mail over to the house. They said no one had been there to pick it up for weeks and there might be important items. I thought I should bring it all to you right away. Some of it is for Rose and for Mama but I wanted you to see everything first." Freddie blurted his mission out and stood waiting for George's response.

George reached for the pile of mail as Freddie dumped the load onto the desk, nearly upsetting the open decanter of brandy. Freddie reached for the crystal decanter, rescuing it, while glancing at George with a terrified expression on his face.

"Be careful, Frederick." George's voice was low and gravelly but without vexation. "Is there anything else?" George wished to return to his ruminations without being disturbed.

"Papa, Annie said to ask you about doing something with the mice. They have been really bad, and Annie is worried about exposing Lotte to disease." Freddie stood at attention with his hands behind his back as though he were George's soldier instead of his only son.

"It's probably all this blasted food lying about. Can't people just mind their own business? It is not as though I cannot provide food for my family. We are not a charity case!" George's voice raised in volume. The final sentence was yelled as an exclamation at his son.

George's outburst was soon followed by the howling cries of his newborn daughter in the bedroom directly above them. Freddie winced as he listened to the frightened cries of his baby sister. Soon they heard Rose's voice responding to the babe, followed by the melodious sound of Rose singing to calm the tiny infant as she carried her back and forth across the floor.

"Go ask Annie for some cheese. I will show you how to put grains of strychnine in the pieces and soon we will be rid of our pests." George dispatched his son to the kitchen as he sorted through the piles of mail. He noted four of the letters were addressed to Rose from the same sender, A. Zoldoske.

George knew he would have to send Freddie with the letters to Rose after they finished lacing the cheese morsels with the lethal poison. He shoved the letters aside and picked up the brandy snifter to empty its contents. Silence from the room overhead indicated Rose had been successful in quieting the squalling child, returning the house to a noiseless quagmire that was diametrically different from peace.

Freddie returned in short order with the pieces of cheese. George rose from his chair and crossed to the cabinet of glass jars, choosing the jar of white grains of strychnine. George put a glove on his hand and pressed the small granules into each piece of cheese as Freddie watched his father.

"You must be careful not to touch it, inhale it, or ingest it as you will not know you have been poisoned until it is too late. These mice will think they have found a feast when they have found their own destruction." George finished the work and replaced the lid to the glass jar, taking it back to its designated place in the cabinet. He handed the tray of cheese to Freddie.

"Take these to Annie and tell her to be careful. Tell her I will have supper in my office." George dismissed Freddie and turned back to his desk and chair. Freddie was gone by the time George noticed Rose's letters still on the corner of the desk. He decided he would remember to give the letters to Annie or Freddie later so he would not risk the caterwaul of the crying infant again.

George could return to his musings without bothering himself with the guilt of his egocentric sentiments by blaming the innocent tiny infant sleeping in the room above him.

CHAPTER 17

WEDNESDAY, FEBRUARY 19, 1890

The February clouds hung low in the sky as Rose made her way to Mrs. Wilson's millinery shop. The air was dense, it felt like a shroud wrapped tightly around Rose's body, attempting to suffocate her whenever she took a deep breath.

It had been two weeks since Rose had worked with Mrs. Wilson, the kindly lady insisting Rose was needed at the Mitchell home after the birth of little Charlotte or Lotte as she had been nicknamed by the family. Rose felt as suffocated in the house as she did by the air around her. She welcomed the opportunity to return to Mrs. Wilson and the busyness of the shop.

Laura had shown small improvements since Lotte's birth, but she was still very weak, unable to get out of her bed for more than a few minutes at a time. Rose spent most of her days helping to care for Laura and the baby while managing some of the household duties Laura did not have the strength to do.

Annie was very helpful with all the actual chores and Mrs. Hendy was helpful with caring for Lotte, but the daily decisions that needed to be made to manage a household had been laid aside by George when Laura did not make them. Even the mail had been neglected, as was evidenced by the huge pile of missives thrown onto the dining room table this morning.

Rose attempted to sort some of the letters into piles and in doing so she found several letters for herself. She scooped her letters up and put them in her reticule so she could read them during her lunch break. She did not want to take the time to read them, making herself tardy for work when her employer had been so gracious towards her.

"Welcome back!" Mrs. Wilson greeted Rose as soon as she stepped through the door of the shop. The usually tidy shop appeared disheveled with bolts of fabric left about and hat blocks stacked on chairs. Obviously, Mrs. Wilson had worked many hours by herself trying to keep up with all the orders and had not the time nor energy to put things away in their proper places.

Rose took her coat and hat off, storing them with her reticule on the shelf behind the counter. She was determined to have this shop tidy again before lunchtime as well as help Mrs. Wilson with the long list of new orders.

The two women worked together in companionable silence. Mrs. Wilson would point out the occasional directions for an order as Rose cut fabric. When Rose would cross the room to retrieve a new bolt of fabric, she would fill her arms with items to put away as she went and soon the little shop was looking like its well-ordered former self. Rose was amazed when she saw the small clock on the wall, and it was one-thirty.

"Let's put some water in the kettle for tea and make some sandwiches." Mrs. Wilson rose from her chair and stretched before attempting to walk towards the kitchen in the back. Rose noticed the weary bearing of the older woman's frame as she moved. Mrs. Wilson had been doing far too much by herself the last several weeks without a word of complaint to anyone.

Rose hurried to cut out the fabric she was working on while still being careful not to ruin the pattern. She put the fabric pieces aside and scurried to put away the rest of the tools not being used, getting the feather duster out and dusting the countertops and shelves as she went. Gathering dust was a constant hazard in the millinery trade as it could easily ruin the expensive fabrics. Rose felt a sense of accomplishment when Mrs. Wilson returned with their simple repast.

"Oh, how I have missed you, Rose. You always seem to know exactly what to do." Mrs. Wilson's eyes glimmered with appreciation and relief as she took in the results of Rose's efforts. "Now come over here and sit with me. You need to eat to keep your strength up."

Rose surmised it was Mrs. Wilson who needed the strength from the meal more than she did, but she came to sit across from her employer at the small parlor table in the corner. She knew Mrs. Wilson would eat more and take the time to rest if she did, so she was happy to take a break from her labor.

"I have missed you and your Oolong tea." Rose wrapped her fingers around the cup and sniffed the fragrant tea appreciatively. She found the aroma of the steaming tea awakened her appetite that had been dormant since Lotte's birth. She reached for the sandwich made from thick slices of wheat bread and a generous slathering of apple butter. Her stomach growled loudly in anticipation of the first bite, causing her to blush and Mrs. Wilson to smile.

"How goes it at the Mitchells'?" Mrs. Wilson asked after they had both eaten a good portion of their sandwiches. Rose knew Mrs. Wilson asked with the kind concern of one who witnessed some of the events surrounding the delivery of the baby. Had it not been for Mrs. Wilson's intervention in asking for Dr. Haskell to come, both Laura and Lotte might have perished that night.

She also witnessed George's odd demeanor throughout the birthing process and then his apathy towards his wife and child afterwards. There would have been many women of the community who would have told these strange tales to the entire town afterwards, but Mrs. Wilson kept it to herself, knowing gossip did not remedy any situation.

"Mrs. Mitchell is still so weak. She seems very happy about Lotte, and she loves it when Freddie is nearby. Freddie has been so good to his mother, he even learned how to give his mother the dose of Nux Vomica Dr. Mitchell has prescribed for her." Rose appealed to the older woman for guidance. " Does Mrs. Mitchell still need so much medicine two weeks later?"

Mrs. Wilson paused before she answered. "She had one of the most difficult deliveries I have ever witnessed, so it may be appropriate, but what did Dr. Haskell say about it?"

"Dr. Haskell has been dismissed." Rose glanced down at the floor as she heard the small gasp escape from her employer. Both women knew Laura would be much better off under the care of the dismissed physician. Both women also knew it would be impossible to suggest this fact to the arrogant Dr. Mitchell.

"Lotte is growing quickly, she has almost everyone in the house wrapped around her little finger." Rose did not need to mention which family member ignored the tiny newborn as Mrs. Wilson already knew. "It has been difficult to get even some of the basic tasks accomplished. In fact, no one had even been picking up our mail for a few weeks. I have several letters in my reticule to be read when I have a few spare minutes."

Mrs. Wilson nodded her head in concern for Rose. "Why don't you take a few moments to read them right now as you finish the rest of your tea? I need a few minutes to find an item I stashed away for later and now, for the life of me, I can't remember where I put it." She chuckled as she stood from her chair at the small table and exited the shop through a connecting door into her home next door.

Rose knew her kindly employer was giving her a few minutes of privacy to read her letters as Mrs. Wilson was an immaculate house-keeper and there was a minute chance of anything being misplaced in her home. Rose went to fetch the letters from her reticule and brought them back to the table to read.

She sorted the small pile of letters by the post date on the envelopes and was shocked to find several were from mid-January. While there were a couple of different scripts in the handwriting, the two final letters were the familiar scrawl of her father. Rose could only imagine that her father needed more money sent for his next great opportunity. She found herself chagrined as she set his letters aside, hoping for more pleasant subject matter from the first two letters in the pile.

The first letter was from her sister, Clara, describing a severe bout of typhoid fever that had infected a huge number of people in their small community in Oklahoma. Clara complained of the lack of social events so close to the Christmas and New Year holidays. Clara taught school in Everton and was angry so many families removed their children from school until the danger of the outbreak had passed.

Clara was even unable to host the school Christmas program after she had made a new dress and hat to match the occasion. Rose shook her head at her sister's priorities when so many people were in peril. At least Rose was able to glean from Clara's ranting that none of their family had taken ill.

The second letter was from Rose's younger brother, George. His hurried printing described how Clara had taken ill after being exposed to her remaining students at the school and now Rose's sister Amelia and her brother Henry, along with their father, had all fallen ill with typhoid fever.

George was worried about his mother, who spent all her time trying to care for the desperately ill family members. George's final sentence was a simple statement, "Please pray for us all, dear sister, especially Mama." The letter was dated early January and mailed later.

Rose felt the cold prickles of fear climbing her spine as she opened the third letter, the first one written by her father. Several bills of paper money fell into her lap as she unfolded the letter with shaking hands.

"Rose, we have many of us taken sick. We need you to come right away to help. Your mama is doing poorly after tending to us all. Please come right away."

The third letter had been dated over two weeks ago. Rose's hands shook as she opened the fourth and final letter from her father and began to read its contents.

Rose's loud shriek brought Mrs. Wilson back to the store front from her home next door. Mrs. Wilson found Rose passed out on the floor with the letter still in her hand. The short, direct note written by Andrew Zoldoske told the entire story.

"Amelia, Clara, and Henry are all dead. Your mama died early this morning. Rose, why did you not come to help us?"

CHAPTER 18

THURSDAY, FEBRUARY 20, 1890

Rose woke up in her own bedroom at the Mitchell home. Her mind grappled through a thick fog of thoughts and emotions, trying to comprehend how she had come to be here, safe in her bed. There was a nagging feeling of doom and pain as she tried to recall what had happened.

Mama. The memory came back sharply, like a knife stabbing into her heart. Was her mama dead along with her sisters and her brother? How could it be true? She remembered reading the letter from her papa, but it seemed almost as if it had been a dream. Certainly, it was a dream since she found herself in her bed once again and not at the millinery shop where she had read the horrible news.

That was it. It was only a dream. Rose opened her eyes again and struggled to sit up. The light was faint in the room. It was early morning, and the house was eerily quiet. Rose ran her hands through the tumbled mess of her hair. As she threw off the covers and leaned to put her feet on the floor, she noticed she was still partially dressed, as if she was going to work. Why would she have gone to bed in such a state? Confusion and dread battled for the primary response to her current state.

A soft tapping on the bedroom door and the entrance of Mrs. Wilson and Annie caused the dread to rise in Rose's throat until it choked her. Her breaths came in short rapid bursts trying to navigate around the huge lump forming in her throat.

Rose opened her mouth to speak, to ask what had happened, and only heard the strangled moans of someone in anguish. She wondered who was making the noises until she realized that no words could form upon her lips and the moans were the release of the overflow of the depths of her grief.

Mrs. Wilson sat beside Rose on the side of the bed. She hugged Rose to herself and laid the young woman's head upon her shoulder while stroking her hair. Annie knelt in front of the pair. Rose could hear the gentle trickle of water as Annie lifted a cloth from a basin of water and wrung it out. Annie placed the warm cloth on Rose's forehead and face, the smell of lavender permeating the cloth and bathing Rose's face in a tranquil aroma.

It was not a dream. Henry, Clara, Amelia, and Mama were all gone. Mama. Rose realized she would never see her mother on this earth again. She had not wanted Rose to leave the family and come to live in Richland Center, but Papa had insisted Rose could help their finances by taking the job with Mrs. Wilson.

Mama had sent Papa to get Rose and bring her with them to Oklahoma, but Rose had refused to go. Mama had needed her help to care for their sick family members, but Rose had not responded to their letters. Mama had died thinking Rose was ignoring her.

The tears coursed down Rose's cheeks as the sobs began to shake her body violently. Mrs. Wilson rocked side to side with Rose in her arms while making a crooning sound like the one Rose made for baby Lotte when the infant cried. While comforting, it could not hold against the waves of grief that crashed against Rose's soul. Rose struggled to breathe over the lump in her throat, the tears filling her nostrils, and the excruciating pain overwhelmed her mind. She felt certain she would suffocate soon.

Another knock on the bedroom door brought George's entrance into the dark room. He cleared his throat as he took in the sight of the three women, the one in the first stages of overwhelming grief and the other two comforting her to the best of their abilities. George considered the scene as though it were a tableau, a practice he had developed as a young boy of only fifteen when the horrors of war were thrust upon him.

George walked to the side of the bed where the women huddled together and cleared his throat again, (a nervous tic when he was uncomfortable and could not control the situation).

"Here now, Rose. Drink this." George held out a glass tumbler of his preparation of Sydenham's Laudanum; the reddish bitter opiate had been mixed with saffron, cinnamon, and cloves, then placed in a pint of sherry wine. The bitter miasma mingled with the heavily pungent scent of the spices created an aura that could almost be glimpsed as well as sniffed.

Rose lifted her head from Mrs. Wilson's shoulder and Annie removed the cloth from Rose's face so she could look at the doctor standing in front of her. George was impeccably dressed, as usual, with his hair and beard groomed. The scent of his pomade wafted across to her and Rose found it unusually comforting. He held the glass up to her lips as his eyes locked with hers, a small smile playing about his mouth.

Rose attempted to sip from the glass but the lump still present in her throat caused her to gag and choke. Fear slammed against her as she struggled to catch her breath, perhaps she too would die. Perhaps dying would be what she deserved as a negligent daughter, allowing her mama to die without her.

George leaned over and swept Rose to her feet, wrapping his arms around her and applying several hard pats to her back. Rose gurgled and caught her breath, the relief overtaking her as the much-needed air whooshed out of her lungs and then back in again. She began to cough, which caused George to rub her back as he still held her there upright against him.

George waited a few moments for her coughing to subside, took the tumbler back from Annie, and turned Rose in his arms so he could offer it to her again.

"Try again. This will help you to rest." George held the glass steady in Rose's shaking hands. Rose hiccupped and cautiously tried to sip the medicine again. This time it went past the lump in her throat and almost immediately a warmth spread over Rose's body, numbing the incredible pain as it traveled through her system. The lump in her throat began to subside as the delicious warmth traveled onwards to her limbs.

George and Mrs. Wilson laid Rose down upon her bed. The fluffy feather pillow and cool linen sheets caressed Rose as she began to drift into unconsciousness, into a world where grief could not touch her. Rose shut her eyes, hoping when she awoke again, she would find it had been just a terrible dream after all.

CHAPTER 19

FRIDAY, FEBRUARY 28, 1890, H.T. BAILEY STORE, 194 COURT STREET

The late afternoon sun cast long shadows through the front windows of the H.T. Bailey store. It had been a warmer than usual day for Wisconsin, the sun and mild temperatures melting the remaining snow on the rooftops, causing the cold water to run off every surface and drip incessantly from the eaves of each building into the street below. The unpaved street quickly became a quagmire of mud that each customer entering the mercantile tracked in with their shoes.

Ella had been hard at work wiping up the floors to keep ahead of the mucky mess, but a faint vestige of mud remained on the wooden floorboards. Ella sighed and pushed wisps of her curly brown hair from her forehead, leaving a small streak of dried mud unnoticed by her there.

The tiny bell perched above the door jingled as it opened and yet another mud-laden customer entered the store. Ella perched her mop against the wall and turned to see who stood just inside the doorway.

"The street is a god-forsaken mess!" Dr. George Mitchell stood on the sodden rug placed to catch the initial mess but had long since been quashed by the mud and now added to the soggy mire on the floor. "My shoes are covered, so I will stay over here if I might trouble you for just a moment, Miss Maly."

Ella nodded and walked to where the handsome doctor stood with his hat in his hands. She was amazed he thought of staying on the rug when so many people just traipsed right through, ignoring that she was in the process of cleaning the mud while they tracked more into the room.

She was also amazed Dr Mitchell knew her by name and that he wished to speak with her. While they attended the same church, they were far from being in the same social circles within the small town. Ella heard the bad news about Rose's family. She hoped the doctor was not there with more bad news about her grieving friend.

"I was told you have been playing the piano for church occasionally and that you also have a fine singing voice." Dr. Mitchell was direct in his comments but in a gentle way indicative of his manners and station. "I have been arranging some of the music for specials and I was wondering if you might consider singing this solo for a Sunday morning service?"

He reached inside his coat and withdrew some sheet music from his inside pocket, handing it to the blushing young woman. At the same moment, he glanced at Ella and his eyes widened at the smear of mud across her forehead. One side of his mouth twitched slightly in a grin, but he immediately put his hand to his mouth and cleared his throat to cover his indiscretion.

"You wish for me to sing a solo? I'm not certain I would be able to attain the level of performance of someone like Mrs. Lovering."

Ella knew the infamous Mrs. Lovering loved to be the soloist at the Methodist Church and almost no one else dared to volunteer to sing in her place.

"While no one performs quite like Mrs. Lovering, I am certain you would be well received by the congregation." Dr. Mitchell smiled his encouragement. "Please browse through the music at least before you make a decision. You could let me know what you decide next Sunday after church. My family has been absent from services for far too long and I plan to remedy that beginning next Sunday."

"I am sorry Mrs. Mitchell has been debilitated since Charlotte's arrival. I hope she is regaining her strength. She is such a kind lady to everyone, especially to dear Rose. May I ask how Rose is doing as well? I stopped by your home last week, but she wasn't receiving guests yet. My heart is broken because of her loss." Ella's eyes glistened with tears at the thought of losing members of her family.

"It was a tremendous shock to Rose, of course. She has been bravely trying to face her grief. I am sure she would appreciate another visit from you soon, as she has stayed in the house with Mrs. Mitchell and the baby. We sent a telegraph to her father as soon as she learned of her mother's and siblings' passing, but due to the delay in receiving the news, all the burials had already taken place. Rose decided to stay here and continue to care for my family."

Ella shook her head in understanding and absently swiped her hand at the brown curls on her forehead. She brought her hand down to see splotches of dried mud she inadvertently dislodged from the smear on her forehead. Ella blushed beet red from embarrassment as her mouth hung open and her eyes grew wide with shock.

"Here. If I might be of assistance?" Dr. Mitchell stuck his hand inside the same coat pocket and withdrew a pure white handkerchief. He smiled as he extended it toward Ella, urging her to accept his offering.

He then gave a slight bow and placed his hat on his head, exiting the jingling door as Ella stared after him with one of her hands on her burning cheek and the other hand holding the crisp linen handkerchief smelling of hair pomade.

Before Ella could recover, the bell on the door jingled again and she was face to face with her secret suitor, Joe. Ella shook her head in disbelief and consternation. Why was it these gentlemen did not show up on the days when she had her hair done neatly and her face freshly washed and clean?

Joe seemed preoccupied as he trudged towards her, his boots squishing with mud. He stopped within an arm's length of her and cocked his head to one side as he regarded her mussed hair, mud-streaked forehead, and brilliant red cheeks.

"Ella, did you know you have mud on your forehead?" Joe reached in his pants pocket and fished out a red bandana. He stepped closer to swipe the bandana on Ella's forehead. It smelled of coal mixed with a bit of sweat. He wiped the dried mud from Ella's forehead.

"I didn't realize you were coming to town today." Ella attempted to recover her composure as she stuck the white handkerchief in her dress pocket and smoothed her hair into some semblance of order. "I thought you were planning to come to church on Sunday." 'When I would have looked much better than this.' she thought to herself.

"I came on an errand for my brother and because I wanted to talk to you. Do you have a few minutes to walk with me?" Joe held out his hand to her in entreaty and Ella forgot her consternation. She went to get her coat and hat and soon returned to accompany Joe out the door and down the sidewalk.

The melting snow continued to drip off all the buildings, producing a shower at the end of each block, so the couple walked down to the corner and stood under the small porch of the boarding house. Joe stared out at the street while Ella watched Joe carefully and waited for him to speak.

"The real reason I came to town was to talk to you myself, Ella. I didn't want to just write a note and risk you misunderstanding the situation." Joe took Ella's hand in his own. "I won't be in church on Sunday because the railroad is sending me on a fact-finding trip."

"Oh, I see. How long will you be gone?" Ella smiled as she understood Joe made the trip to Richland Center to see her before his short trip for the railroad.

"That's what I wanted you to understand. The railroad is sending me to South Dakota to check on a number of their interests there. There are so many business prospects now that South Dakota has achieved its statehood. It may take a long time before I return to Wisconsin. If the prospects are very good, then I may not return at all." Joe squeezed Ella's hand gently.

Ella felt as if a rug had just been pulled out from under her. Her legs wobbled, tears flooded her eyes, and her hands shook with uncertainty.

"You are leaving me?" Ella's voice was no more than a whisper. The tears trickled down her cheeks.

"That is the part I didn't want you to misunderstand," Joe said as he grasped both of her arms, "If I stay there, Ella, then I want you to come and join me. I love you, Ella Maly. I want you to marry me and then join me in South Dakota." Joe looked earnestly into Ella's eyes, willing her to accept his proposal.

"You want to get married now?" Ella's emotions switched abruptly from misery to astonishment. What would her parents say to this sudden development?

"I would prefer to get married before I leave this week, but if you need some time, I will try to understand. I know this is a surprise, and you might need a few days to think about it. We knew we wanted to marry so this just makes it a little sooner than we planned." Joe smiled as Ella stared at him in amazement.

"I will need some time, Joe." Ella knew she loved him, but it felt so rushed.

"Let's get you back inside and I will come back tomorrow afternoon." Joe led Ella back down the block to the front of the Bailey store and quickly kissed her cheek. He stepped off the sidewalk into the muddy street and turned the corner out of sight.

Ella scrambled to wipe her tears before she entered the store. She reached into her pocket for a handkerchief and found the white linen handkerchief with the initials GRM embroidered in the corner where she had hidden it when Joe arrived.

CHAPTER 20

SATURDAY, MARCH 1, 1890

The wind blew bitter and strong as Ella made her way towards the train depot. What had been a mild February became a turncoat into a wintry beginning of March. The piercing wind pelted Ella with bits of ice as it tugged at her skirt and her coat. Ella wrapped a woolen scarf around her shoulders and head so that only her eyes peeked out from underneath.

Ella could hear the train whistle as she approached Seminary Street. She was grateful she would not have to wait long for Joe to arrive on the train from Avoca. The original Richland Center depot had been destroyed years earlier in an explosion of gunpowder stored within and now only a small shelter stood in its place.

Ella stepped inside the shelter and listened to the howling wind compete with the wail of the train whistle, leaving her feeling disconcerted. Shakespeare wrote, "Beware the ides of March" and while it was meant for the fifteenth of the month, the ominous connotation of foreshadowing made her shudder with more than the frigid air.

Joe jumped from the caboose onto the wooden platform as the train slowed. His eyes brightened as soon as he saw Ella waving her mittened hand in greeting. He increased his pace to close the distance between them and wrapped her in an enormous hug, not concerned that other people might witness the public embrace. Joe hoped Ella would become his wife by the end of the day, so the gossipy feathers of the small town's denizens could afford to be ruffled.

Joe felt Ella stiffen at his caress. He assumed it was a mixture of the frigid temperature emanating from her shivering body and the modesty of a virtuous young woman. He pulled away slowly to search into her eyes and felt a surge of dread form in the pit of his stomach. Ella's eyes glistened with tears, but it was apparent to him that they were not tears of joy. Joe knew he needed a moment to recover from this revelation.

"Well, it must be true that they say March comes in like a lion and goes out like a lamb." Joe chuckled, a rough, hesitant sounding laugh, as he looked down at his shuffling feet, unsure of what else to say. While glancing at the mud floor, he noticed Ella did not have a suitcase with her, the dread in his stomach expanding to a lump in his throat causing him to clear his throat several times. He felt Ella's small hand reach for his own, he glimpsed the face of the most cherished person in his life.

"Not yet, Joe. I love you with all my heart, so I am not saying never, I am just saying not yet." Ella's sweet voice trembled with emotion. "I want to marry you but eloping and leaving this way would hurt my family deeply. I want a ceremony with both of our families present so everyone in the world will know it is Joe Bohan that I love and choose. I will stay here to work and save while you go to South Dakota and find a living and a place for our home together.

Please don't leave me thinking I am sending you away without the hope of reuniting."

Joe felt the rush of heat burning his face despite the arctic winds that blew on the couple relentlessly. His mind reasoned that Ella was right, it was better to do it this way. He could return to her later after he made a home for her. They could be married in a church with both of their families present. Joe's heart struck down the reasonable arguments of his mind with the overpowering feelings of rejection and anger.

"Sometimes later never comes, Ella." Joe stepped back abruptly and felt the shock resonate through Ella's slim form before he could remove his hands from her shoulders. Joe turned his back, walking towards the waiting train, pretending not to hear Ella's sobs carried on the roaring tempest that matched the tempest in his heart.

CHAPTER 21

SUNDAY MARCH 2, 1890

The March wind continued to bluster, causing the glass window-panes of Laura Mitchell's bedroom to vibrate while emitting a prolonged, mournful howl like the cry of a wolf. The drafty room held a chill even though a moderate fire in the fireplace battled against the elements for dominance.

Laura instinctively tucked the blankets around baby Lotte tighter and held the sleeping infant close, Lotte's downy head of dark hair snuggled against her mother's chest. In the repose of slumber Lotte resembled a doll more than a human, her perfect porcelain skin with the faintest touch of rose color on her chubby cheeks and perfect little mouth drawn up in a tiny pink bow.

Laura glanced from the sleeping babe in her arms to Rose, who sat in a chair next to Laura's bed. She noted Rose's pale complexion and the obvious loss of weight that left Rose's dress overly large and hanging from her frame. The most notable feature in Rose's appearance was the vacant, lost expression on her face and most especially in her eyes that had always sparkled with vibrancy. Rose stared out the window without seeming to see anything there.

Laura shifted Lotte, freeing her hand to reach out and take Rose's hand dangling beside her. It was frigid to the touch. Laura rubbed the top of Rose's hand to bring extra warmth before placing it inside the coverlet with her own. Rose stirred slightly at the sensation of human contact and turned her gaze towards her friend.

"Your hands are like ice, Rose. Do you want my shawl? It's over on the bureau." Laura's words of concern caused the faintest glimmer of a smile to play across Rose's face.

"I hadn't really noticed. I guess it is chilly today, isn't it?" Rose stood and walked to the bureau across the room, picked up the shawl and brought it back to her chair beside the bed. "Are you certain you don't need your shawl for you and Lotte?" Rose gazed at the beautiful little girl snoring in Laura's arms.

"No, we have all the blankets we need to keep warm in the little nest you have created for us. I am much more concerned about you. Either put the extra shawl on or crawl in here beneath the covers with us so that you will be warm." Laura smiled at the thought of Annie's expression when she walked in to see all of them huddled together in the four-poster bed. The housekeeper was easily shocked at some of Laura's ideas and Laura felt certain that Annie would regale the entire town by nightfall if she found them so.

Rose wrapped the soft cashmere shawl around her shoulders, tucking her hands inside the shawl. It still amazed her that her friend would be so generous, sharing her extravagant wardrobe with her as though they were of equal status and not the wife of a prominent physician and the shop girl who boarded with them. Laura and Lotte had been the only bright spots in Rose's bleak existence since the death of her mother and siblings.

George had also been of assistance by offering dosages of laudanum since the first night of her distress. He made up the same concoction and left it on Rose's dresser each day. She came to depend on the powerful drug and felt its dissipation from her system as it wore off. Rose was grateful that George continued to supply it, knowing she needed a buffer between herself and the reality of her substantial loss.

George also helped Rose send a telegram to her father, explaining the delay in communication and asking if she could return for her mother's funeral. The short reply came back that the funeral had already taken place, but Rose should pack immediately and take the train to Oklahoma. Rose's father wanted her to cook and keep house for him and her brothers now that her mother and sisters were gone.

A week passed after the curt response by telegram and Rose received another letter from her brother George. Her hands shook with fear at the tidings it might bring. George wrote that yet another brother, Henry, had fallen ill and died of Typhoid fever.

George, unlike their father, begged Rose to stay where she was, hoping she would be spared from succumbing to the illness. He told Rose it was their mother's dying wish that Rose would be spared from it. Within the folds of the letter her brother enclosed a lock of their mother's hair for Rose to keep in her memory.

Rose knew she had a decision to make. She could return to the remnant of her family and live out her days in servitude to her father or she could remain where she was and live out her promise to care for her dearest friend. It did not take her long to decide that she would stay with Laura and help her regain her health while helping to care for Lotte and Freddie.

"Rose, would you mind fetching my box from the top drawer of my bureau?" Laura's question broke through Rose's ruminations.

Rose nodded, crossing back to the bureau. She opened the top drawer and lifted the silk-covered box of Laura's most prized possessions. She took the box back to the bedside and placed it on the coverlet to not wake the still-sleeping Lotte.

Laura used her free hand to open the box and lift several items out as she searched through it. She lifted out a small silver locket, a cluster of seed pearls forming a cross on its cover and placed it on the coverlet beside Rose.

"I bought this on a trip to Chicago a number of years ago. I intended to give it to my Nellie on her sixteenth birthday." Laura's voice trailed off in the remembrance of her lost daughter. "I never thought I would have survived her loss; it was so devastating. But then you came to live with us and brought new hope to me, Rose. I want you to take this and keep the lock of your mother's hair in it so you will always remember the love she had for you and the love I have for you too. It doesn't have a chain but perhaps you can get a nice pendant so you can clip it on like a brooch or a watch chain." Laura placed the locket in Rose's hand, smiling through the tears that shimmered in her eyes.

"Laura, I can't take this. It is so remarkable. It should be saved for Lotte instead." Rose gazed down at the silver locket and back at her friend. "It is you who has been so good to me and there is no way I can ever repay you." Rose lifted the locket to give it back to her friend.

"Lotte will have her own locket someday. This one is yours." Laura shook her head at the offering of the locket. She moved her hand over Rose's and closed Rose's hand around the locket, patting it as confirmation of her intentions.

Both women sat in silence for a few moments realizing the deep bond that irreparable loss forged between them. Their quietude was interrupted by the sound of whistling coming from the sidewalk below, the whistler being loud enough to drown out the intermittent wails of the wind. Rose crossed to the windows to peer out and see who was creating such a racket on a Sunday morning.

George approached their home from the direction of the Methodist Church where he decided to resume attending services after a long absence. Rose pressed her face against the chilly glass pane to make certain she heard his whistled tune correctly.

George was returning from a house of worship with not a hymn of praise but a tavern ballad from the Civil War called, "Lady Mine" on his lips. Rose shuddered as the telltale connotations of the song mixed with the plaintive howling of the wind. In more ways than one, the wolf was at the door.

CHAPTER 22

TUESDAY, MARCH 18, 1890

The rays of the springtime sun stretched through the front windows of Mrs. Wilson's millinery shop creating a path for the dust motes to flit in the air like tiny fairies dancing. Mrs. Wilson and Rose worked in companionable silence preparing for an important customer to arrive within the hour.

The days since the deaths of Rose's mother and siblings stretched out like those rays of sunshine until Rose became uncertain of how long a time had passed. The more days that elapsed, the hazier the memory of the events became for her until Rose could barely distinguish between what had actually occurred and what she thought she remembered.

Rose continued to take the daily doses of laudanum prepared by George. She dreaded the feeling of being without the medicinal effects that kept her overwhelming grief at bay. She resumed her daily activities, but she often had "black periods" of memory loss where she could not account for what occurred.

The always astute Mrs. Wilson noticed the abrupt change in Rose's demeanor and tried to ferret out the cause without upsetting the poor girl who endured such a tragedy. Mrs. Wilson felt it was best to keep Rose as close as possible, to keep a watchful eye over her protégé.

"Land sakes, it's almost one o'clock! Mrs. King and little Sofie will be here any minute now." Mrs. Wilson displayed bolts of fabric on the worktable for the affluent Mrs. King to choose from while she whisked away any stray items scattered across the massive oak table. "Rose, will you be a dear and fetch the new hat blocks from the storeroom?"

Rose stared up at her employer and nodded. Her legs felt wooden as she moved slowly across the room towards the small storeroom in the back. Her eyes felt as if there was wool stuffed behind them. The small hat blocks made to fashion a child's hat were stored on a shelf near the door, but Rose had difficulty remembering where they were.

She searched the shelves several times before locating them. Once she located them, Rose stood holding the hat blocks in the center of the storeroom until she heard the ringing of the shop bell announcing the arrival of their guests. She turned and headed towards Mrs. Wilson at the front of the shop.

An elegant lady dressed in a beautiful plum gown and matching cape entered the store, leading a little girl by the hand. While Mrs. King was a beauty to behold, it was her little daughter Sofie who took Rose's breath away.

The four-year-old little girl with dark ringlets had almond-shaped eyes framed with thick black eyelashes and a fair complexion sprinkled with a tiny smattering of freckles across her pert little nose. She was dressed in a pink smock with a pink coat and bonnet that highlighted her beautiful coloring. The most breathtaking aspect of the little girl's appearance was the obvious sparkle of mischief in her eyes and the sweet grin that played about her little mouth as though she constantly knew a secret.

Sofie was immediately drawn to Rose as well. Mrs. Wilson chuckled as the tiny girl took off her coat and hat, placed them on a nearby chair, and danced her way towards where Rose stood. Sofie tilted her head back to gaze into Rose's eyes as she took Rose's hand into her own. She led Rose back to her mother, nodding her little head wisely as she spoke.

"Look! Mama, I have found Princess Irene from our stories!" Sophie beamed as she presented Rose to her mother. "She is still sad from losing her mama, but she will be happy again because the story said so." The little girl nodded her head emphatically, shaking the dark curls up and down.

Mrs. Wilson gasped as Rose paled before them and grasped the table at her side. How did this little girl whom she had never met know so much? Rose blinked as she peered into the soulful eyes of the sprite before her.

"It's good to hear I will be happy again. I believe it because you say the story you read said it was true, and fairytales never lie". Rose felt the tears pooling in the corner of her eyes, threatening to cascade down her cheeks. She breathed in deep, regaining her composure so as not to alarm Sofie with her emotions.

Sofie released Rose's hand and twirled before her with her hands extended upwards, the exact replica of a tiny ballerina at the top of a music box. Once her revolutions were complete, Sofie reached for Rose's hand, once again leading Rose towards the mountain of fabric piled on the other side of the table.

"Sofie loves her fairytales. She is always finding characters from them when she accompanies me." Mrs. King glanced at her daughter whispering to Rose on the other side of the table. "I hope she has not caused offense."

Mrs. Wilson watched the pair giggling and whispering back and forth like old friends. "No offense was intended, and I am sure none was taken. Rose has suffered some great losses, but it seems your little girl was just what Rose needed."

The afternoon passed quickly as Mrs. King selected various fabrics and allowed Sofie to choose from her favorites as well. Mrs. Wilson and Rose placed the little girl upon a stool and took all the measurements needed to make her new hats while Sofie imagined aloud that she was being fitted for her crown of gold and rubies. As soon as Sofie was allowed to step down from the stool she flitted about the shop, her tinkling laughter trailing behind her.

Rose stared at the child in marvel, expecting to see fluttering fairy wings sprouting from her tiny shoulders as her feet seemed to barely touch the floor. Sofie left a lightness in her spirit that had been absent through the haze of grief. Rose heard her own laughter again, a foreign sound that had been gone for too long.

"Sofie, we must go soon. Please gather your things and tell Mrs. Wilson and Rose goodbye." Mrs. King guided her daughter to the chair where she had placed her coat and hat. Sofie grimaced but obeyed her mother and began to put her arms in the coat.

Rose crossed to where Sofie stood and knelt to help her fasten the coat and tie the ribbon of her hat under her chin. Sofie closed her eyes for a moment as an angelic smile turned her lips upwards, her dark eyelashes fluttering lightly. Suddenly, Sofie opened her beautiful dark eyes and leaned to whisper to Rose.

"Don't be sad anymore, Princess Irene. Your mama loves you very much and she wants you to be happy again until she sees you in Heaven." Sofie's hand gently caressed Rose's cheek as a tear trailed down it. Rose caught the girl's hand on her own and kissed it with gratitude.

Sofie's soft giggle followed her from the shop as she danced through the door and down the sidewalk with her mother. Mrs. Wilson dabbed at the corner of her eyes as she saw the beautiful smile on Rose's face and the expression of hope returned to Rose's eyes. Rose had just recalled something her mother always said.

"You never know when you are entertaining an angel unaware."

CHAPTER 23

MONDAY, MARCH 24,1890

Laura Mitchell stared out her bedroom window, opened to allow fresh air into the room. She could hear the song of a robin in a nearby tree and she smelled the earthy scent of the thawing ground. The clamor of wagons and carriages rumbling up and down Church Street towards the shops on Court Street and the hotel across the street from the Mitchell home reminded her the world outside continued to exist. Laura sighed as she plucked at the lace on the sleeve of her dressing gown. It seemed ages ago since she had ventured forth from her bed and her room.

Her beautiful daughter Lotte was now seven weeks old, a chubby-cheeked, healthy babe. Laura could hear her baby beginning to fuss and the gentle response of Mrs. Hendy in the room down the hallway. She wished she could recover enough to take over nursing her baby.

Laura had not experienced this degree of difficulty in recovering after the births of Nellie and Freddie. She knew this birthing had been grueling on her body, but her frustration at her continual state of weakness grew day by day.

It was all Laura could do to be moved from the bed into a chair for a short period of time before the wracking coughing and uncontrollable shaking of her entire body began. Sharp, stabbing pain seared from the region of her abdomen and below, causing Laura to lose consciousness after her wails rent the silence of the house.

Laura glanced back out through her window at the sidewalk below. George appeared from the side of the house where his office was located, accompanied by a comely woman with a modish sense of style.

She was dressed in a brilliant blue dress, cut to accentuate her curves while still maintaining the propriety of daytime dress. A tiny blue hat perched at an angle on her coiffed auburn hair, peacock feathers adorning the side and a dark veil extending over part of her face giving her a mysterious air. Yet, there was something familiar about the woman to Laura.

This mysterious woman walked alongside George while holding his arm, which to the casual observer was an ordinary gesture between the gentlemanly physician and one of his patients, but Laura sensed otherwise. The way the woman held George's arm was possessive, as though she had a claim to stake (one that should only belong to Laura).

Laura could not hear their conversation so she knew it was being held at almost a whisper, but she could hear George's occasional laugh, the same charming laugh that once captured her attention.

George could be the epitome of an alluring gentleman when he had the proper inducement. He seemed to revel in procuring the interest of the fairer sex as though he were collecting seashells or butterflies to add to his caches, doting upon the oblivious quarry until she was absolutely smitten and then shelving her interest like one would pin a butterfly to a mounting board before moving on to the next conquest.

A dull pain surrounded Laura's heart. She was all too familiar with the process and had in fact made allowances for George's infatuations in the past. "It's just part of his nature" became an excuse for her husband to abandon her emotionally while he sought his conquests. Laura was ashamed she had begged poor Rose to distract George while she was in confinement. The hapless young woman had been used as bait for the appetites of her fickle husband.

Laura determined that she needed to rise from her helpless state and as soon as she recovered, she would set about confronting George. She would also make certain she remedied her situation with Rose, releasing her from the arrangement they previously made and making certain that Rose's reputation remained without blemish. A new strength of conviction surged through Laura, causing the sensation of strength in her limbs to return with it.

After a moment of hesitation, Laura scooted to the edge of her chair and used her arms to push herself upwards onto her wobbling legs. She straightened her back; the muscles having forgotten how to work after weeks of disuse. A small thrill of victory surged through her before the first wave of excruciating pain doubled Laura over, causing her to lose her balance and fall forward onto the windowsill and then to the floor.

The tumultuous sounds of Laura falling against the window caused George to look up from his vantage point on the sidewalk to see his terrified wife. Mrs. Hendy and Annie came running from different rooms to find Laura crumpled up on the floor unconscious.

Laura awoke in her bed to the stinging stabbing of a needle in her arm as George injected her with a powerful dose of morphine.

Freddie and Rose stood on the other side of the bed with Annie, all three of them looking affrighted. Laura opened her mouth to speak and encourage them to take heart, but she could not form words.

She knew what to say but for the life of her she could not get her mouth to say it. The haze of the potent medicine began to take effect and the waves of stillness overtook her mind, still struggling to speak. Laura realized she would have to wait to set things right until she woke up again.

"We will have to take turns sitting with her. Someone must be here to give her a dose of medicine if she begins to stir in the night. She mustn't try to get up again or the next fall might kill her." George gave the directions to Rose, Freddie, and Annie as they stared at Laura's pale, listless face. The three nodded silently in agreement, knowing this duty would fall upon their shoulders as the illustrious Dr. Mitchell quitted the room in search of his office and the brandy decanter.

CHAPTER 24

TUESDAY, MARCH 25, 1890

The early morning sun trickling through the windows of the Mitchell's dining room mocked Rose as she sat alone at the oak table. Usually Rose welcomed the light, it reminded her that the day was just beginning and held limitless possibilities. After the long night she spent at Laura's bedside watching her dearest friend writhe with numerous convulsions, Rose felt drained of any vestige of hope. The usual messenger of hopeful tidings seemed to pierce her skull with pain in its intense brightness and deride her for being foolish enough to expect anything but more tragedy.

Rose sat with a cup of tea that was growing more tepid by the moment. Annie had placed a steaming cup in front of her when she stumbled into the dining room and collapsed into a chair almost an hour ago. Rose spent most of the night watching Laura, giving her doses of Nux Vomica and holding her rigid body as she shook with convulsive fits.

Finally, Freddie came to relieve Rose around five o'clock in the morning. Rose felt conflicted about leaving the boy to watch his mother alone, but she knew she was nearing the state of collapse herself, which would only frighten the young lad even more. She gave Freddie the dosing instructions for the medication and the admonition to call for her or Annie if his mother went into a convulsive state again.

Rose knew she should have gone straight to her own bedroom for a nap but the longing for a cup of tea and the need for a dose of laudanum drove her downstairs, where Annie was bustling about in the kitchen. Rose took a small bottle of the laudanum with her into Laura's room, but she had refrained from using the medication so she would be alert enough to help her friend.

She nearly drained the small bottle of its contents after sitting down at the dining room table and the reddish-brown liquid ran like quicksilver in her veins, causing a hazy stupor that relieved Rose of the enormous weight of pain and fear she carried.

She stared at the teacup on its delicate saucer placed in front of her. Her hand moved to grasp the thin handle but instead she clumsily bumped the teacup, causing the amber liquid to slosh over the side of the cup into the saucer. Rose attempted to lift the teacup again only to fail and spill more of the tea into the saucer and onto the snowy-white linen tablecloth covering the table.

Inwardly, Rose winced as she knew Annie would rail about the stain on the tablecloth, but outwardly Rose watched in fascination as the brown stain spread, seeming to eat the tablecloth in its wake. She wondered how far the small brown patch would stretch without anyone to inhibit its progress.

Rose heard screams from Freddie upstairs. He sounded as if he were a million miles away rather than just the floor above her. Rose watched in fascination as Annie ran from the kitchen through the dining room and up the main staircase towards Laura's bedroom. Rose wondered why Annie would use the stairs reserved for the family and their guests instead of the staircase for the servants at the back of the house?

After what seemed like an extended period to Rose, Annie's wails joined those of Freddie's which had become almost constant. Rose grew irritated with the pair as she knew that soon they would awaken tiny Lotte in her nursery down the hall. Rose knew she should get up and go back upstairs to caution them, but she did not have the ability to stand, her limbs felt lifeless and even her head became almost too heavy to hold upright.

Rose stared at the brown tea stain on the white tablecloth. Her head felt cumbrous as it pulled at her neck sharply from one side to the other. She fell forward onto the table, her head connecting with the hardwood beneath the tablecloth. The rest of the tea came gushing from the overturned teacup pooling onto the tablecloth and dampening Rose's hair.

It was an indeterminate amount of time before Rose came to again, the sharp bite pinching her upper arm cutting through her insensate state. Annie stood beside her continuing to pinch Rose as well as slap Rose's face while pulling Rose into an upright sitting position. Annie was yelling, her face was red as tears coursed down her cheeks.

Rose struggled to keep her eyes open. Annie continued to pinch her hard. Rose began to register the words that Annie kept repeating to her.

"Wake up you foolish girl. The Missus is dead, and you lie here like an old drunk. Get up, I say Rose, or I will strike you hard. Do you hear me?"

CHAPTER 25

SUNDAY, MARCH 30, 1890

The Mitchell house on the corner of Church and Haseltine streets was ornately adorned in black crepe. A wreath with numerous black bows was fastened to the front door and swags of black crepe were draped from the lower portion of the roof and around each window.

A local farmer brought hay in from his farm and spread it across both streets to muffle the sounds of wagons and horses outside. Even the passersby from the hotel across the street and the shopping district of Court Street one block away passed by the Mitchell house in subdued quiet out of respect for Laura Mitchell's family.

Inside the house, the black crepe seemed to cover almost every surface. From the inside, the windows had black drapes covering them from floor to ceiling as well as each mirror on the walls. A picture of Laura on her wedding day hung in the parlor and it too had the customary black crepe draped above it. All the clocks, including the grandfather clock in the hallway, had been stopped, each bearing the time of 6:33, the time of Laura's death.

The black spilled over onto the garments of the people assembled inside the house as if an inkstand had been spilled and the ebony liquid had penetrated everything in its path. Laura's sister, Mary, arrived the day after Laura's death, as well as George's brother John, along with George's father, Cyrus, and Cyrus's third wife, Amanda. The house seemed to overflow with human beings all dressed in the customary black except for tiny Lotte who had been dressed in her pure white christening gown as the fashion of the day dictated.

While the inkinesss cast a bleak and ominous aura over the assemblage, it was the silence that seemed to torment Rose the most. From the moment she bestirred during Annie's tirade and realized what had occurred in the bedroom upstairs there was a silence that had descended upon the household, suffocating her in its heaviness.

Rose went through all the appropriate motions of the bereaved household, including being a "watcher" over Laura's remains for the required three days before her funeral and burial on Saturday. She assisted Annie and Mrs. Wilson with draping the black crepe inside the house, while neighbors assisted with the outside adornment, since the family and servants could not be seen in public until the funeral.

Rose answered the front door for scores of friends and neighbors who brought copious amounts of food and came to pay their respects to the woman the whole town had come to admire. Rose had woodenly responded to the same comments over and over.

"What a fine lady. She was much too young."

"Heaven has gained another angel. She is at peace."

Rose knew many of the people arriving at the home were there from morbid curiosity thinly disguised as compassionate concern. A young mother and prominent community figure had died, and all the busybodies had their own theories as to what occurred. While none of them obtained any real facts to formulate their opinions, it didn't stop the onslaught of whispered notions behind gloved hands while standing in the parlor where Laura laid in state.

Saturday morning dawned bright and fair. Rose could not help thinking how much Laura would have enjoyed being outside in the fresh spring air as the crowd assembled at the cemetery. Robins sang from the oak tree positioned on Park Street where it met with Eighth Street.

Laura had loved to hear the sharp peek of alarm followed by the repeated chirrs that sounded like a chuckle from the perky brown bird with a bright red breast. The robin had always been a harbinger of the approaching change of season, transforming the bare brown trees and the brown ground into shades of emerald and a reminder that life was renewed again.

With a sharp pang of grief, Rose realized this would no longer be true for Laura. It seemed surreal that they would return to the house and Laura would never be there again, her gracious laughter and gentle presence leaving a void that seemed insurmountable. The minister spoke of Laura's new life in heaven and Rose hoped it was true. If anyone deserved heaven, it was Laura Mitchell.

The rest of the day became a blur of masses of people and the daily routine of chores that needed to be accomplished even in the face of death. Rose worked in silence alongside Annie, as the housekeeper was still in shock from the sudden turn of events.

Rose wanted to ask questions about how Annie had found Laura and Freddie in the room upstairs, but the pinched face of the young servant let Rose know that conversation would not be welcome. After working late into the night, Rose retired to her bedroom and laid down upon the bed with her clothes still on.

Rose woke up to the rain pelting against the windowpanes as if suddenly the heavens poured out its grief over the family's loss. She roused herself enough to get off the bed and wandered across the room to the window draped in heavy black material. She drew back the material and pressed her forehead against the cold glass to revive herself.

She could feel the cold wind pressing against the window and the pressure of the rain drops as they hit against the pane. Rose wished the rain could penetrate her spirit and flood it, pushing out the heaviness of sorrow until it left her completely.

A motion in the yard below caused Rose to look towards the back door, which was positioned at an angle from her bedroom above it. George stood just outside the door in the pouring rain without his hat or coat, lifting his head towards the leaden skies and allowing the rain to cascade upon his face. His clothing dripped with the excess water as it pooled around his feet. Rose wondered if George wished for the same purging by water as she did.

A carriage pulled up to the walk on the Haseltine corner of the house. George was pulled from his reverie by its sudden appearance. He marched towards the carriage door, waving the carriage driver off as he opened the small door himself. A beautiful young woman leaned her shrouded head outside the door and spoke in hushed whispers to George, who remained standing outside the carriage door in the rain. A heated exchange occurred, followed by George slamming the carriage door and signaling the driver to leave.

George still stood in the rain with his hands running through his soaked hair, a gesture Rose recognized as one of frustration and anger.

He marched towards the back door but glanced upwards to see Rose standing in the window staring at him. The chills Rose felt from his returned stare could not be attributed to the cold wind blowing the rain against the pane.

Rose rushed to repair her disheveled state of dress by splashing used tepid water from the basin in her face and attempting to comb the frizzy mess of tangled hair. Her black dress was wrinkled from sleep, so she threw more water on it, attempting to straighten the worst of the wrinkled masses. She found an apron, dyed a dull gray, so she tied it on over the wrinkled dress as she made her way out the door and down the hall to the back stairs.

Annie was in the kitchen preparing trays of food for the breakfast buffet. The smell of black coffee, usually so inviting, made Rose's stomach lurch with queasiness. Rose looked at the tray of scrambled eggs and sausages that had just been prepared, the smell of the food causing the bile in her throat to rise involuntarily.

She wanted to turn and run back up the stairs but instead she picked up the tray and headed for the swinging door leading into the dining room. Annie gave her a curt nod of acknowledgement from the stove where she stirred a kettle of oatmeal.

Rose carried the tray to the sideboard and placed it there beside the trays of biscuits and muffins and a pitcher of country gravy. The mixture of smells made Rose's eyes water as she tried to hold back the gagging sensation she felt. She knew she needed to make a quick escape into the main hallway before she lost any contents remaining in her stomach.

George's father, Cyrus Mitchell, sat at the head of the table with his young wife to his right and his other son, John, to his left. Laura's sister Mary sat further down at the table sipping a cup of tea. Rose could feel Mary's eyes on her back as she placed the tray on the sideboard, causing an even greater feeling of distress.

Rose turned to make her escape as she heard Cyrus clear his throat and hold his plate of half-eaten food up, expecting her to come and take the plate from him.

"I will have some of those eggs and sausages, young lady. It took long enough to get them out here." His sharp gaze tore through Rose. "I asked the other gal for some oatmeal and have yet to see it either." He cleared his throat again and extended his arm further towards Rose.

Rose stared at the older man. His white beard held bits of the biscuit he had just consumed, making her stomach roil. She hesitated a moment, wanting to rush out of the room, but she knew such behavior would have disappointed Laura, who was always the most gracious of hostesses. She leaned forward, taking the proffered plate with a trembling hand, and turned back to the sideboard.

"Cyrus, I don't think she is one of the servants." Cyrus's wife Amanda whispered loudly at Rose's turned back. Rose felt a rush of embarrassment begin to compete with the nauseousness.

"Well, what is she then if she isn't one of the helpers? Be quiet. If I wanted you to have an opinion, I would give one to you." Cyrus barked at the quiet woman who flushed with her own embarrassment.

Rose's hand trembled as she spooned the eggs and sausages onto the plate. She continued to feel Mary's stare creep up her torso and neck like a wave of heat.

"What is she? That is a very good question. I would imagine she is another one of Laura's hopeless charity cases. My sister was always rescuing someone. I noticed she wore black to the funeral when everyone knows only her immediate family is allowed to wear it. What is she indeed?" Mary's voice dripped with acidic sarcasm as she discussed Rose as though Rose was not standing right there in front of them.

The silver spoon clattered back onto the platter as Rose whirled around to place the China plate in front of Cyrus with a loud plop. Rose was seething with anger at the callous treatment from the extended members of the family. A myriad of things that she wished to tell them swirled in her mind like a flock of angry black birds. She opened her mouth to spew the angry invectives on the tip of her tongue when she noticed Freddie standing in the hallway staring at her. His red-rimmed eyes caused a deep pain in Rose's heart.

"Freddie, what can I get for you? Is there anything you would like to eat? Annie has made some of your favorite things." Rose forced a smile on her lips as she crossed to the boy and led him to the table, seating him across the table from his waspish aunt. Rose turned back to the sideboard, grabbed a plate from the pile stacked there and selected foods she knew Freddie liked. She took the plate to the boy and sat down in the chair next to him, ignoring the gasps and staring by the rest of the assemblage.

Freddie picked up the silver fork at his side and attempted to take a bite of the food. He coughed as he tried to swallow, his pale face turning red with the effort. Rose understood the sensation of a huge knot in his throat causing difficulty in swallowing. She patted his back.

"I will go and get you a nice cold glass of milk. I know Annie has some in the icebox. That might help a little." Rose stood and ignored the rest of the adults seated at the table as she walked towards the kitchen door.

Annie was standing just inside the kitchen door, her face red with anger. "They had best not speak that way to the boy or they will find themselves without any more meals in this house." Annie crossed to the ice box, picked up an earthen pitcher pouring frothy white milk into a glass and handed it to Rose. "The sister was up with Mrs. Hendy this morning telling her to get little Lotte's things ready to leave this afternoon. Just where in the world does she think Mrs. Laura's baby is going to go?"

Rose gasped at this bit of news. The last thing Laura would want would be for Lotte and Freddie to be separated from each other. She could not imagine the sweet little girl living with her nasty aunt who disparaged her mother after burying her only yesterday. Rose knew what needed to be done.

Rose returned to the dining room with the cold glass of milk for Freddie. George entered the dining room in the interim and seated himself at the opposite end of the table from his father. He had dried his hair and changed his clothes.

Rose placed the glass in front of Freddie while looking straight into Mary's eyes. Rose straightened her back and took a deep breath.

"As to the question of who I am? I am honored to have called Laura my dearest friend on this earth, closer than any sister. Laura did have compassion for me and took me into her family as she was superior in every way to me. She was also superior in every way to all of you, so that makes us more alike than any of you care to realize. I will stay here to make certain the very best is done for Freddie and Lotte, the way Laura herself would have done it and no one needs to ask anything more about what is to be done with them. I made a promise to Laura, and I intend to keep it." Rose left the silent dining room before she lost her nerve.

Later that afternoon, two carriages were lined up on Church Street to take Mary and John away to the train station and Cyrus and Amanda back to their home outside the city. George smiled to himself as he watched them leave. Rose had single handedly taken care of the strenuous situation and left no room for dissent.

He decided then and there Rose would be kept on as part of the Mitchell household for as long as she proved herself helpful to him. He didn't know what promises Rose made to Laura, but that didn't concern him if it benefitted him at the moment. George knew their situation would change but he would worry about how to send Rose away when it was time to do so, just as he had sent his most recent paramour away only that morning.

CHAPTER 26

FRIDAY, JUNE 27, 1890

The front door of the Bailey store stood wide open, catching the wisps of a June breeze and a horde of flies from the horses tethered to the hitching posts outside. Ella sat at her desk swatting the pesky intruders. The long slant of the afternoon sun stretched lazily through the open door and the front windows as if it were beckoning Ella to leave her dreary numbers in the ledger and follow it outside.

Ella stretched in her chair and yawned, trying to remain at her work until the five o'clock whistle could be heard from the mill. Her thoughts kept wandering to the busy plans of the weekend ahead. The time had come to dedicate the new courthouse standing just two blocks from where Ella sat. Most of Richland Center would be involved in the festivities, including the actual dedication ceremony on the courthouse steps, a community picnic, and most exciting of all, a masquerade ball.

Ella looked up from her ledger to see her sister Lillie entering Baileys. Lillie's face had a determined look and Ella knew her sister

would try to get her to leave work and accompany her to the millinery shop. Ella looked back down at her ledger just as determined
to finish her work before she called it a day.

"Ella! Are you still at it? I waited at the Cheap Goods store
hoping you would come and help me pick out some scraps to finish
our costumes; two birds of a feather. You know that Mrs. Wilson
promised to let us choose from some of the feathers she has in stock,
and I don't want them to be all picked over by the time we arrive. I
saw Mae Hyndman walk towards Mrs. Wilson's and you know she
won't leave anything for anyone else." Lillie looked pleadingly at her
sister, willing Ella to leave with her in haste.

"Knowing Mrs. Wilson and Rose, they will set some special
ones aside for us and not let Mae have all of it for herself. I am just
about finished with the ledgers and then I will need to help with the
dusting in the shop. You are welcome to go over to Mrs. Wilson's
right now and wait for me there if you like." Ella smiled at her sister
and continued to write in the ledger. She pretended not to hear Lillie's
sigh of exasperation.

"I waited at the Cheap Goods store for you and little good it did
me. Mr. Bailey has left for the day and wouldn't even know that you
weren't here and I'm sure Uncle Charlie would be glad to finish up
on the dusting for you." Lillie pointed to the sweet older gentleman
everyone in the town called Uncle Charlie who was currently on the
rolling ladder, dusting the upper shelves while whistling a spritely
tune. He smiled at Lillie as he continued to work.

"I would be happy to finish the dusting on my own, Lillie, but
I think your sister has a problem with leaving her work unfinished,
even for a good reason, like the dance. She has the honesty to give
Mr. Bailey a full day's work for her pay whether he knows she did

or not. Sometimes doing the right thing isn't easy, but it's still the right thing." Uncle Charlie looked down from his perch on top of the ladder and winked at Lillie below.

"I tell you what Lillie, if you leave your sister at her work, I will make sure the first song we play tomorrow night is one of your favorites. Which one would you choose?" Uncle Charlie was a brilliant musician who played multiple instruments with the local dance band. Lillie knew it would be an honor for her to choose the first song.

"Uncle Charlie, you have yourself a deal." Lillie beamed. "I think you should start the dance with 'Listen to the Mockingbird'. It's one of my favorites and when you start whistling like a mockingbird at the end, no one can keep from dancing."

Uncle Charlie's chuckle, warm and resonant, warmed both girls' hearts. He began to whistle the requested tune as Ella and Lillie listened in pure bliss to the beautiful tune by the skilled musician. Lillie remained until he finished and then waved to Ella as she turned for the door, singing the song to herself. Uncle Charlie stepped down the ladder with an agility that disregarded his seventy years of age, bowed to Ella, and continued towards the back storeroom whistling the merry tune.

Ella, grateful for Uncle Charlie's encouragement, continued with her work for the next half an hour. She had just put her pencil down when she heard someone clear their throat. She had been so preoccupied with finishing she hadn't heard George Mitchell enter through the open door.

"I'm sorry, Dr. Mitchell. I didn't notice you standing there. Uncle Charlie went back to the storeroom, but if you need to find something I am sure I can help you." Ella stood, smoothing her dress as she walked towards the doctor. "What can I get for you?"

George smiled at the young woman before him. She possessed such a natural beauty and grace, something out of the ordinary for the affected female population of the small, rural town. Ella was definitely the fairest of the fair, but she did not seem to be arrogant about the fact.

"I came to see you about the music for the church service this Sunday. I understand you have been very helpful during my absence the past few months. I am planning to rejoin my services with the choir and special music, and I wondered if we might work together?" George noticed the tiny gold flecks in Ella's beautiful brown eyes.

"I would be happy to work with you, Dr. Mitchell. It has not been the same choir since…" Ella's voice trailed off, realizing she shouldn't bring up Laura Mitchell's passing to her bereaved husband. "I am certain everyone in the choir will be happy for you to lead us again."

"Yes, well, it is time to get out and do things again. Probably some of the matrons in our town will think it's too soon, but I need to do something outside the four walls at home. I appreciate your help with the music, and I insist you call me by my first name as we will be working together and do not need to be so formal."

Ella nodded her acceptance. He was very handsome in his dark suit and tie. The black armband he wore on his left arm still signified that he was in a stage of mourning, but he was right to think he could not just sit at home for months on end. Involvement in the Methodist church seemed a very appropriate option.

"I plan to see you bright and early on Sunday morning although I am told there is a community celebration tomorrow night and you may not wish to be such an early riser the next morning?" George heard about the masquerade ball, but he knew it would be inappropriate for him to attend a social event just yet. Otherwise, he would have been sorely tempted to press his advantage and ask Ella to allow him to be her escort. The thought of waltzing with the beautiful Ella Maly in his arms made George feel a new vigor for life.

"Early Sunday morning will be perfect. I will meet you then, George." Ella pivoted as she heard a loud gasp coming from the doorway. Lillie had returned with her hands full of bright-colored feathers. She stood in the doorway with her mouth open, her eyes wide with shock. She had obviously walked in and overheard the last part of the conversation, hearing her sister refer to the prominent town doctor and recent widower by his first name.

Ella did not have time to feel chagrined with her sister. She immediately noticed that standing right behind her gaping sister, was Rose holding an armful of feathers as well. Ella was not disconcerted by Rose's presence, but rather, the very peculiar look on Rose's face as she stood staring at the pair.

A few tense moments that felt like a year ticked by before the spell was broken by the arrival of Uncle Charlie, still whistling as he came upon the scene. Uncle Charlie would later describe to others that he had seen battlefields with more joviality than the day he witnessed Rose Zoldoske catch Dr. Mitchell with Ella Maly.

CHAPTER 27

SATURDAY, JUNE 28, 1890

The bustling of wagons and carriages outside on Church Street rattled the dining room windows inside the Mitchell house. Most of Richland County was gathering just one block down on the corner of Haseltine and Central streets for the dedication of the newly finished Richland County Courthouse. Rose could hear a local band tuning their instruments in preparation for the ceremony as she sat at the dining room table writing some correspondence and finishing her second cup of tea.

Freddie stood at the windows, watching several of his companions walk past, their happy-go-lucky voices reminding him of his own circumstances that were far from carefree. Freddie had not enjoyed being the center of attention following his mother's death, everyone looking at him with pity and speaking in hushed tones.

Three months had passed, and the public response changed from the intense outpouring of sympathy that overwhelmed Freddie to an uneasy apathy bordering on avoidance. Most people wanted to move on to the next interesting thing and the reminder of the Mitchell tragedy, while unfortunate, was depressing and better forgotten and unmentioned.

Freddie tried to be courageous and not show his emotions to anyone, especially to his father, who had not shown any emotions of his own. This left Freddie frustrated and angry as the toll the grief took on his mind and soul became too big for him to bear. He felt frustrated that he was expected to withdraw from public life as he knew it to mourn when he was not allowed to grieve his mother's death in a visible way.

Freddie's sigh was loud as he leaned his head against the glass windowpane. He could feel an unnamed rage boiling behind his eyes, threatening to spill in liquid drops down his cheeks. He bit down on the inside of his cheek, distracting himself with the sharp pain to keep himself from recognizing the worse pain emanating from his heart.

The metallic taste of blood pooled in his mouth, but he drove himself past the trauma of watching his mother die right in front of him, knowing she would have been the first one to comfort him if only she were still there.

"It looks like just about everyone will be at the courthouse today." Rose's calm voice came from behind Freddie's back. He sensed that she stood near him without touching him in any way. He could not stand the sensation of anyone touching him since the morning he held his mother's hand as her life left her body.

"I think we could manage a look at the ceremony without attracting too much attention, don't you? We could be rather lost in the crowd, so to speak. That is, of course, if you had any interest in seeing it?" Rose suggested an outing, an escape from the gloom of the dark house with its black crepe still draped everywhere.

Freddie wanted to be at the courthouse ceremony like nothing ever before in his young life. He nodded his agreement with his eyes still watching the people pass by outside. He heard Rose walk to the table and gather her things.

"I will go upstairs and get my hat. On my way back down, I will drop into the office and tell your father where we are going. Why don't you go and find your cap?" Rose left Freddie standing at the window as she left the dining room for her bedroom upstairs. She pinned her black hat to her dark curls pinned up at the back of her head and pulled the short black veil forward over her face.

She still cringed at the contempt Laura's sister had shown her for wearing the black mourning clothes, but Mrs. Wilson quickly reminded her that she also wore black for the deaths of her mother and siblings as well as the friend she had loved like a sister.

Rose took the back staircase downstairs as it led towards George's office in the back of the house. She tapped lightly on the door that was standing ajar. A huge whiff of strong spirits assailed her as she pushed the door to open it.

The black shades were still drawn, leaving the room very dark. A light clink of glass being set upon the desk helped Rose locate George in the dimness of the room. Rose knew George would wait for her to speak first.

"I am taking Freddie out to see the courthouse ceremony. It isn't good for him to be pent up inside all the time. He needs some distractions."

"Who doesn't need some distractions?" George's harsh laugh rang out in the stillness. "Yes, fine. Mrs. Hendy is upstairs with the little one?" George still refused to use Charlotte's name, or her nickname given so lovingly by her mother.

"Mrs. Hendy is in the kitchen, but Lotte is napping right now so she will be close by." Rose's eyes were adjusting to the darkness of the room, and she could see George's disheveled appearance, his uncombed hair, and wrinkled clothes that he slept in. He looked nothing like the public persona of Dr. Mitchell, the dashing, young, dedicated doctor. Rose wondered how many people would consult the good doctor for medical advice if they knew his private situation instead of the public one that so many rushed to believe. She realized so many things were determined by public opinion, and one could hide many things if they hid them behind a façade.

The clink of the glass on the desk again let Rose know the conversation was over, and she had been dismissed. She walked back down the corridor and through the back kitchen door. Annie and Mrs. Hendy were sitting at the worktable with mugs of coffee and freshly baked sugar cookies on a plate. Rose smiled at the pair as she picked up two sugar cookies and headed towards the hall and the front door.

Freddie was waiting for her at the front door. His pale wan face lit up briefly at the sight of the offered sugar cookie. He opened the door with his free hand to allow Rose to pass through before him. She paused in front of him, her eyes glancing at the black armband the boy still wore on his left arm.

"I think you have worn this in public long enough. The rules for all of this are quite rigid for adults but are not so much for younger people. You do what you want, but I know she would not want you to feel out of place among your friends." Rose was careful not to mention his mother by name, knowing Freddie's hurt was still deep.

Freddie paused for a moment. The black arm band reminded him of all the unexpressed emotions he felt and the rules that society and his father had about them. He shoved the sugar cookie in his mouth and removed the arm band, shoving it in his pants pocket.

The band was playing a march by Sousa as Rose and Freddie crossed Haseltine Street and then Church Street. Hundreds of people were gathered surrounding the massive stone and brick building festooned in red, white, and blue garlands. Rose and Freddie paused at the corner of Haseltine and Central streets, staying at the outer perimeter of the crowd.

Freddie stood beside Rose, his hands shoved into his pockets, his eyes looking at the ground at his feet. One of the neighborhood boys, Robby, came to greet Freddie, punching him in the shoulder. Rose held her breath waiting for Freddie's response to the unwanted contact.

To her great surprise, Freddie grinned and punched Robby back in the shoulder. Robby indicated with a slight nod of his head the passel of boys collected a few yards away waiting for them, having sent Robby as the emissary to collect their chum. Freddie, understanding their mission, looked hopefully towards Rose, who stood beside him.

Rose nodded her head as it was hard to see her expression under the veil on her hat. Freddie turned to Robby and disappeared into the crowd with the group of boys. Rose felt alone and vulnerable without Freddie's company next to her.

Rose sensed someone near her before she turned her head to see Anthony Hellar, a young man who worked at the lumber yard, standing next to her. Anthony removed his hat, nodding at Rose as he shifted his weight from one foot to the other.

He came precariously close to banging into Rose's shoulder as he swayed from side to side, and Rose was grateful for the veil hiding her expression. She could not help but smile as she thought of how he looked like Freddie when the young lad waited too long to go to the privy and needed to hold his water.

"Tis a fine day, yah?" Anthony's distinct German accent was pronounced, but it sounded so much like the Polish accent of her father's, it gave her a start. Rose nodded, wanting to be polite, but not wanting to draw attention to herself in the company of the young man. The town busybodies would probably excuse Rose's attendance at the ceremony, but they would be relentless if they thought Rose was flirting with the young man while she was in mourning.

Anthony did not take Rose's lack of a verbal reply as a deterrent in their conversation. "All of the stone used to build this courthouse was quarried right here in the county. It took years to get it all here. It was nine years past when a boy of fifteen years was hanged using the stones that had been gathered to build. He was caught as a thieving murderer of young Mrs. Coleman and a crowd came and took him from his jail cell and hung him right over that huge pile of stones." Anthony pointed towards the huge stone arches in the front of the courthouse edifice as he spoke.

Rose felt a chill run up her spine and bile began to rise in her throat as she looked in disgust at the building that interested her only moments before. She knew she needed to escape this man and his ugly version of justice.

She withdrew her fan from her reticule and pretended to be overcome, fanning herself and backing away from him. She turned to head back down Haseltine Street and the refuge of home when Anthony reached out and grasped her upper arm.

"I came over here to see if you would be going to the dance tonight. A lot of folks say you think you are too good for the likes of us regular guys because you live with the Mitchells. I guess I had to see if it was true for myself. Just remember, your people are just like mine, coming here with nothing but the clothes on their backs. Living among fancy people don't make you fancy." Anthony's German accent raised his natural speaking voice into almost a shout. Other people standing around them looked to see who was speaking so loudly as the crowd started to quiet for the first speaker.

Rose pulled herself free of his grasp and all but ran the entire block towards the Mitchell house. She did not stop until she was inside the front door, shutting it behind her as if she were barricading the entire population of Richland County out on the other side. Her breaths came in heavy gasps, her lungs burning from exertion mixed with the humiliation she had just endured at the hands of Anthony Hellar.

Rose made her way up the stairs to her bedroom, seeking the vial of laudanum stored in her top dresser drawer. She took a sip of the bitter liquid, willing it to numb her body, mind, and soul. Rose put the stopper back in the vial and carried it to her bed where she laid down without bothering to remove her shoes or hat.

The last thought that came to Rose before she succumbed to the haze of opium was perhaps, she and George Mitchell were not so different after all.

CHAPTER 28

MONDAY, JULY 21, 1890

he July heat covered the small town of Richland Center like a woolen blanket. Mrs. Wilson's millinery shop door stood wide open as well as all the windows in an attempt to catch any stray breeze available. The air hung heavy with humidity and the dust of the street outside. Rain had eluded Richland Center for weeks and the grass had withered, turning brown and crisp.

Rose sat with Mrs. Wilson attempting to see the delicate stitches she sewed into yet another one of Mrs. Julia Bowen's hats. Sweat cascaded down Rose's forehead into her eyes, stinging them with its saltiness. She blinked as she wiped the sweat away with her kerchief, praying she would not soil the expensive fabric she held with her sweat.

Mrs. Wilson stood slowly from her chair, stretching her cramped muscles as she walked towards the door connecting the shop to her small house in the back. Rose heard her open the door and walk through it, though she did not look up from her needlework.

Mrs. Wilson returned with two glasses filled with ice and cold lemonade. The heat and humidity immediately worked on the glasses, making droplets of condensation on the sides. She crossed to the small table in the back and beckoned for Rose to join her.

"Come and drink this while it is still cold, Rose. We will have to enjoy it away from our handiwork to preserve the fabrics." Dora Wilson sank into a small rocking chair and held the cold glass to her temple.

Rose looked longingly at the cold treat offered to her. She was determined to finish the embroidery she had begun three days ago before she left today. She looked at the older woman enjoying the glass of lemonade and knew ice was a rare treat. The fact Dora Wilson would share this with Rose spoke volumes about her kindness and generosity. Rose decided she would not waste the ice that had been so graciously proffered.

Rose could feel the cool liquid sloshing inside the glass and hear the faint clinking sound of the ice chunks as they brushed against the sides. Her mouth thirsted for the first delicious sip of the tart lemonade. She held the glass against the side of her face, enjoying the coolness of the glass and the condensation. Rose closed her eyes as she held the glass to her lips and sipped the cold lemonade, the tangy taste rolling over her parched tongue, refreshing her.

"I hope we get some rain soon. My garden has turned into a desert even though I water it every evening. I don't remember the last time we have gone this long without rain." Dora repeated the sentiments of nearly every citizen of the town.

Rose nodded in agreement while envisioning her older friend trudging with heavy buckets of water from the outdoor hand pump to her garden. Rose knew she needed to beat Dora to the garden watering that evening. Perhaps she could convince Freddie to come back in the early evening with her and help in the endeavor. Freddie was always eager to help the kindly widow who offered love and attention to him and Lotte as though they were her own grandchildren.

"I wonder what will happen to the Ringling Brothers circus next week. They always bring the animals to feed and bathe along the Pine River and the water is so low right now it will be difficult to handle those enormous elephants." Rose delighted in the annual circus show performed by the circus company of five brothers who resided in Baraboo, approximately forty miles east of Richland Center.

"They always bathe the elephants just below the mill dam so there will be more water there." Mrs. Wilson nodded as she reminisced. "At least it won't be as exciting as last year when Eph Williams and Joe Sherbeck brought their one-ring circus into town. Dashing Mr. Sherbeck swept our Ida Dix off her feet and by the end of the week she was walking a tightrope in the show. The town talk was that Ida was set to run off with Joe and the circus, so, on the final night, her pa showed up with a shotgun meant for Joe. Ida was walking on the tightrope and fell off it when she saw her pa. Good thing the lads had a canvas stretched out below to catch her." Dora chuckled out loud at the memory.

Rose listened wide-eyed as Dora's story continued. "It turned out Ida had no intention of running away and the gossip of the rumor mill creating reactions in her father could have been the cause of Ida's death if not for the quick thinking of the local boys who caught her." Dora stood, collecting Rose's empty glass with her own. She took the glasses back to her kitchen while Rose resumed her embroidery work.

Later that evening, Rose lay upon her bed in her shift. The intense heat made the prospect of donning a nightgown seem impossible. Earlier, Rose had returned to water Mrs. Wilson's garden with Freddie's assistance, the efforts causing her to require a bath afterwards. She appreciated the cool water in the metal tub Annie prepared for her in the lean-to attached to the kitchen. Annie used the lean-to as a summer kitchen to keep the heat of the stove away from the house.

The buzzing of the cicadas droned outside the open windows. Heat lightning snapped in the distance without the promise of the much-needed rain. Rose thought about the story of Ida Dix. Ida's narrow escape from death brought chills to Rose's spine as though it were a harbinger of a future course of events.

Rose smoothed calamine lotion on her wrists and ankles. Red angry welts appeared there, a result of her continued use of laudanum, but even this uncomfortable side effect did not deter her from taking multiple doses each day. She desired the numbing effect that took away her troubling anxious thoughts, allowing her to drift into an altered state where the pain could not follow her. Rose hid numerous bottles of laudanum in various locations and kept a small vial in her bodice.

She had just finished applying the lotion, then taking her nightly dose of laudanum and extinguishing her lamp when she heard the slight tap at her door followed by the sound of a slow push from the other side.

Rose attempted to lift her head from the pillow, but the powerful drug began to take effect, making her efforts futile. She rolled onto her side towards the door instead, wondering if Mrs. Hendy needed assistance with Lotte, who had been fussing with teething for the past several nights.

Rose stared at the door, now slightly ajar, then shut again with the sound of the lock being slid into place. She willed her eyes to focus on the figure approaching silently to the side of her bed. She blinked several times in the dim moonlight, hoping she was not seeing the ghost of one of the people she had lost in the past year. Her heart began to beat erratically at the thought of a poltergeist encounter.

"It's too hot for anyone to sleep. This time of night is always the hardest for me, anyway, and now it is as if we are in an inferno. I came to see if you were struggling to sleep too." George approached Rose's bed, speaking in a low whisper tinged with drink. Rose felt his hand gently move her dark hair that fell across her face when she rolled to her side.

Rose did not reply. She was unsure that what she was seeing was real. She experienced several other hallucinations over the last few months, and she supposed at least this delusion was less frightening than the appearance of a ghost. In fact, if Rose were being honest with herself, she was attracted to George. She dreamed of him on other occasions, and she would happily dream of him that night too.

Rose was drifting away as his arms surrounded her from behind, his face leaning on her face, the whiskers of his beard tickling her as he kissed the back of her neck. Rose sighed in contentment.

"That's right, Rose. Just close your eyes," George waited as he watched Rose slip into unconsciousness once again.

CHAPTER 29

SATURDAY, SEPTEMBER 6, 1890

The blistering heat and drought of July and August had capitulated to the cooler temperatures and torrential rains of September. The last week of August saw a break in the heat in the form of tempestuous storms. The rolls of thunder shook the window-panes of the Mitchell house until Rose was certain they would break.

Saturday morning dawned fair and bright, the brilliant early morning sun chasing away the remnants of stormy weather, leaving only puddles of rain in its wake. Freddie and his buddies splashed about while digging for nightcrawlers in the yard. Rose watched them spatter mud all over themselves and grinned at herself. She was sorely tempted to go outside and join the rambunctious group.

"I declare if that boy tracks more mud in this house, it will be the end of me." Annie sighed dramatically as she entered the dining room where Rose sat watching the boys' escapades from the dining room windows. "I just cleaned everything so I could take this afternoon off for the County Fair and there he goes messing things up again."

Rose grimaced at Annie's scolding tone. It had been far too long since Freddie enjoyed the antics of a young boy his age. Rose was determined that Freddie would return to his regular schedule and enjoy his friends and hobbies. Laura would have wanted that much for her son and Rose knew she would be one of Freddie's only advocates as his father did not hide his lack of interest in either of his children.

"Let him be, Annie. It is good for him to laugh and play again. I will help you clean any mess he tracks in the house." Rose lifted her teacup to her lips and sipped the last bit of Earl Gray mixed with milk and honey. "I suppose it is time to get Lotte ready for our outing at the fair today." Rose stood, picked up her teacup and saucer, and started to make her way towards the kitchen. Annie intercepted her, taking the teacup and saucer from her hands.

"I suppose you're right about the boy, Rose. He has had a tough time of it. I am just looking forward to an afternoon's entertainment and I don't want anything to delay me." Annie turned towards the kitchen door. "Mrs. Hendy was down a while ago with her breakfast dishes, so she has probably started getting the baby ready to leave. I will set some water to warm up for Freddie to wash up in if he can just come in the backdoor instead of the front hall this time." Annie looked at Rose, hoping she would give Freddie the instructions, as he was far more likely to listen to Rose than anyone else in the house. Rose nodded her silent agreement to the errand.

Rose made her way through the parlor towards the front door when she heard the loud laughter coming from the front steps just outside. She whisked the front door open to find a very muddy Freddie about to open the door with a group of four more boys right at his heels. Rose shuddered at the reaction Annie might have to the entire muddy troop entering through the front door and traipsing across her immaculate floors.

"Whoa there! How did the hunt for nightcrawlers go?" Rose smiled at the boys, knowing it was a mistake to begin by giving them the command to not enter the house, but rather suggest it might be better for them to use the other door. At the same time, she calculated to herself how much cleaning it was going to take to get these boys ready to attend the social event of the season. She hoped Annie had put two kettles of water on to heat.

"We didn't have to dig very far and there were just oodles and oodles of them!" Freddie nodded his head emphatically, causing a clump of mud to fling from his person and land next to Rose's slipper. Freddie noticed the mud and looked at Rose sheepishly waiting for her reaction.

"That's wonderful boys! All those nightcrawlers will help you land some nice trout when you go to Rockbridge with Mr. Ghastin." Rose smiled. The boys were planning a fishing trip with the local veterinarian who was an outstanding angler.

The banks of the Pine River near the marshy areas and rocky outcroppings of Rockbridge were one of the best fishing areas in the region and many of the locals took the secrets of the coveted areas to their graves with them. Mr. Ghastin volunteered to take the boys camping and fishing with him the following day as there was no school on Monday because of the fair weekend.

"We decided to go in and get a snack before the fair, "Freddie looked at Rose with anticipation, hoping she would not humiliate him in front of his chums as his father often did.

"I think that is a great idea. Why don't you wait out in the back-yard, and I will ask Annie to bring out something for you? I know she is heating up some water so you can get the mud off and be on your way to the fairgrounds. If you have a snack first, the water should be ready for you in no time at all." Rose kept her voice light without a tone of command so the young boys would think the arrangement suitable. From the agreeable looks on their faces, Rose surmised her subtle method worked.

The boys headed for the backyard while Rose shut the front door, latching it in case Freddie had a sudden change of heart and came tracking through the front. She walked back through the parlor into the dining room where she found George sitting at the dining room table drinking a cup of coffee.

He was freshly shaven, and his hair done with pomade, his light gray suit and white shirt were immaculate, his black shoes gleaming with polish. He was ready to attend the fair himself, making the event one of the first social gatherings he attended since Laura's death. Rose caught her breath at the sight of him; he cut a dashing figure and he knew it.

"You are very fetching yourself, my dear." George's voice was husky as he assessed Rose. He recognized her reaction to his transformation. George was accustomed to attracting females and he immensely enjoyed the power he held over them.

Rose's left hand shot to her hair, smoothing it, while her right hand adjusted the wrapper she wore. She knew George was toying with her, like a cat with a mouse between its paws. She was chagrined at herself for her blatant reaction to his attentions. She passed by him on her way to Annie in the kitchen. She could hear his low laughter as she left the room.

"I have the boys waiting outside in the backyard for you. All it will cost you is a few cookies and glasses of milk while they wait for the washing water." Rose distractedly touched the hair at the nape of neck. "I am going upstairs to check on Lotte and to get myself ready to go."

Rose's choice of her best dress and hat became of the utmost importance to her. She would take the extra time to wash herself, apply some bergamot and lemon oil cologne, and fashion her hair in a becoming style. Rose was determined to turn heads in appreciation today, especially the one with the meticulous gray suit waiting downstairs.

CHAPTER 30

SAME DAY, RICHLAND COUNTY FAIRGROUNDS

The road leading north of the city was packed with carriages and wagons as most of the county headed towards the Richland County Fairgrounds for the annual county fair. The pastureland beyond the city cemetery and just before Bowen's Mill had been purchased in 1873 by the Richland County Agricultural Society to host the event. Every man, woman, and child anticipated the celebration, the Maly family being no exception.

Ella sat in the back of her father's wagon with her younger siblings, Willy, Lillie, Amelia, and Charlie. She clutched a basket of items she intended to enter in the fair, praying the bumpy dirt road filled with potholes would not break the contents: glass jars of strawberry/rhubarb preserves, a picture with wood violets and lace pressed into muslin, and a painting of the picturesque cranberry bogs at Steamboat Rock

Charlie bounced from person to person in the wagon, pointing at the scenery along the way. Ella rescued the young boy from going over the side of the wagon more than once, reminding him to sit down so he wouldn't fall. She couldn't blame her little brother for his excitement, she felt the same way even though she was an adult. The only point at which Charlie fell silent was when their father passed the city cemetery on Park Street.

"Ella, do you think it is haunted?" Charlie whispered in his sister's ear as he glanced over the side of the wagon at the tombstones laid out in rows advancing up the steep hill on Eighth Street. "Willy said the spooks could turn you into a spook too just by looking at them."

"I am certain Willy is wrong, Charlie." Ella comforted her little brother with a pat on his back while casting a stern eye on her brother Willy, who sat opposite them looking sheepish. "When a person dies, they don't become a spook, as Willy said. In fact, it is much like my glove on my hand." Ella raised her free hand to let Charlie see the ivory lace glove there. "A person who has died does not need their earthly body anymore, their spirit leaves it behind, much like when I take my hand from my glove. It is only the glove that is left behind and not the person. You have nothing to fear from it, just as you have nothing to fear from my glove." Ella smiled at her youngest brother reassuringly.

"Apparently, Willy is afraid of gloves!" Lillie snorted, smacking the back of Willy's head for emphasis. Willy, in turn, pushed Lillie into Amelia, who let out a clamorous squeal of protest.

"Mama! Willy is pushing! I almost dropped my picture for the fair!" Amelia's shrill protest rent the silence surrounding the cemetery, causing Catherina Maly to turn from the front seat of the wagon and glare at her tumultuous brood in the back.

"And Amelia is squealing louder than the piglets at the livestock barn." Willy stuck his tongue out at Amelia, earning him another slap to the back of his head from Lillie.

"That's enough." The two calm words spoken by their father, Anton, were all that it took for the sibling hijinks to cease immediately.

After peace had been restored, Ella attempted to change the subject back to the previous excitement of the fair. "Mr. Bailey was telling all of us at the store there would be an Edison phonograph on display in the pavilion tent by the amphitheater. Can you imagine hearing a recording?" Ella smiled at her wide-eyed brothers and sisters.

"What do they listen to with this Edison phonograph?" Charlie was fascinated, and even Willy looked mildly interested in his sister's story.

"Mr. Bailey said it plays recordings of music and of people telling stories," Ella explained.

"Why in the world would you need a recording when you can just hear a band play, or a person tell a story right in front of you? I don't think it will ever amount to anything." Catherina shook her head in disgust at the newfangled contraption. She had been raised in the old country and did not trust many of the newer ways of the United States, including modes of technological advancement.

"But Mama, Mr. Edison has also helped to develop the telegraph and the incandescent light bulb. Before too long, people can have electric lights in their houses instead of kerosene lamps or candles. I can't wait to see what will happen next." Ella was excited about a future that held the promise of dreamers like Thomas Edison.

A short clearing of Anton's throat let Ella know she should change the subject again or risk drawing the ire of her mother. Ella looked out upon the fairgrounds as the wagon reached the crest of the hill. Brightly colored tents were sprawled everywhere around the grounds and people were swarming in masses.

Anton slowed the wagon and pulled off to the side of the road before the driveway to the fairgrounds. The county fair officials were known to charge up to twenty-five cents to park an entire wagon with two horses, so it would be less expensive to park the wagon and walk the extra distance carrying all the fair entries with them.

Ella climbed down from the wagon, smoothing her dress, and adjusting her hat while holding her basket of fair entries. She waited for her mother's final inspection of the younger children before setting out along the side of the road.Shouts of greeting came from neighbors who walked with them towards the fair entrance. Ella could not help feeling the excitement bubble up within her at the thrill of attending the county fair.

The entrance fees were paid, and the entire family began to separate into groups to take their entries to the various tents for judging. Catherina took Amelia with her to the ladies' pavilion while Charlie stayed with Anton in the livestock barn. Willy was permitted to seek out his friends and wait for his older brothers, John, and Anthony Jr. to meet them at the greased pig-catching pens. Ella and Lillie left the group together, heading for the ladies' pavilion where the household entries were located.

"Let's get our fair entries registered and then get over to the phonograph," Lillie suggested. Ella could tell her sister shared her excitement over the exhibition. Lillie stopped in front of the ladies' pavilion.The line for fair entries stretched all the way out of the tent. By the time they registered their entries, it might be almost time to meet their parents at the wagon for their noon meal.

"Why don't we take turns waiting in line? One of us can wait here and the other one will go see the phonograph demonstration and then we will switch?" Lillie suggested. "There should be plenty of time for both of us to see it that way."

"I will wait here, and you can go first." Ella knew her sister was silently hoping she would volunteer to wait in line first while Lillie went to see the phonograph. Lillie hugged Ella and set her fair entries on the ground beside her sister's feet as she hurried off towards the amphitheater.

Ella passed the time waiting in line listening to the music of the bands in the music pavilion competing with the noise of the animals in the livestock barn mixing with the clamorous sound of many voices. The occasional shrill cry of a rooster drowned out all the noises combined.

"Hello, Ella," Rose stood a few feet away with Mrs. Hendy and Baby Lotte. Rose looked hesitant to approach closer, as the two girls had not spent time together since the day Rose walked into Bailey's store. They had not fought that day, but they maintained a distance because of the awkward situation.

"Rose! It is so nice to see you." Ella tried to set Rose at ease with her warm greeting. She wanted to end the unnamed awkwardness between the two friends. She noticed the faint blue circles beneath Rose's eyes and the paleness of her skin. It seemed almost translucent in the midmorning sunlight. Rose had always been so hearty and robust, she seemed like a shadow of her former self. Ella's empathetic nature surged with compassion for her friend and all discomfiture was forgotten at once.

"It seems most of the county is here as well. Lotte was alarmed by the noises of the animals near the barn, so we decided to move nearer to the ladies' pavilion." Rose reached to take the squirming baby from the tired nanny. Lotte's tiny hands reached to grasp Rose's face as Rose dropped a kiss on her forehead. The two appeared as a sweet tableau of mother and child to anyone who did not realize the existent circumstances.

"I know there are shade trees near the creek. A few of the older folks are gathering there as the heat of the day increases. They are serving cold lemonade near there as they use the creek to keep the lemonade cold. I am looking forward to a cold lemonade once Lillie and I are done registering our entries." Ella rambled as she shifted her basket to pick up Lillie's entries and move forward in the line.

"Here, let me help you." Rose bent to pick up Lillie's basket at Ella's feet, shifting Lotte to her opposite hip. "Mrs. Hendy, would you take Lotte to the shade trees and see if she will nap for a bit? I will wait with Ella here and join you after a while." Rose handed the baby back to Mrs. Hendy while still holding Lillie's basket for Ella.

Mrs. Hendy and Lotte were soon dispatched to the shade trees with the promise of lemonade for the tired Mrs. Hendy while Rose kept Ella company in line. A surprised Lillie returned to see her sister visiting with Rose. She took the basket from Ella's hands and then turned to Rose to receive her basket as well.

"Lillie and I were taking turns standing in line so we could both see the phonograph demonstration before lunchtime. Would you like to come with me to see it, Rose?" Ella offered.

Rose agreed to Ella's plan and the two left Lillie staring after them as they made their way towards the amphitheater. An enormous, colorful tent with closed sides had been set up and a sign indicating "Edison's phonograph" marked the entrance to the tent. They had just entered the tent in time for the demonstration.

The small player with the fluted horn sat upon a velvet-covered table. The small crank was turned slowly and soon the melodious words of 'Mary had a little lamb' were sung amid the loud crackling noises of the player. Ella and Rose, along with the rest of the crowd gathered, stood in amazed silence. There was thunderous applause at the conclusion of the demonstration. Ella followed Rose from the tent.

"There you are, Rose. I sent Freddie in search of you and came to look for you myself. The Ladies Aid Society is giving a memorial to the fairgrounds on behalf of Laura, and they requested we be present in the amphitheater to receive it before the races. We have a few minutes to return before they begin." George tipped his hat in greeting to Ella as he hurriedly ushered Rose towards Freddie who was waiting a few yards away. Ella noticed there was something almost intimate and possessive about the way George held Rose's arm. She felt surprised at the pinch of jealousy she experienced.

"Thank you, Ella. We will talk again soon?" Rose's smile erased some of the pallid features that had been so prominent. Ella nodded her agreement as she waved goodbye.

Ella turned to make her way back to Lillie in line at the Ladies' pavilion. The crowds were growing denser around the phonograph pavilion, making it difficult for Ella to navigate while attempting to walk in the opposite direction. Suddenly, Ella bumped into someone and felt herself falling backwards when a hand shot forward, grasping her arm, to keep her from hitting the ground.

"Whoa there! Are you alright Miss?" Strong arms supported Ella, guiding her to the outside fringe of the crowd and safety. Ella glanced up into the face of her rescuer and shock reverberated through her like a bolt of lightning. A face so familiar and dear to her and yet slightly different, the face of Daniel Bohan, Joe's older brother.

"Ella?" Daniel's face registered some of the shock that Ella felt. "I didn't realize it was you. Are you hurt?" Daniel brushed at some of the dust near the hem of Ella's skirt that dragged in the dirt during her near fall.

"Thank you, Dan. I am fine. How are you and your family?" Ella tried to gather her wits together quickly as she noted again how similar Dan was to his brother in looks and mannerism.

"I am well. Everyone else is…" Dan paused. He knew Ella wished to know about one member of his family, and he didn't know how to tell her. Dan knew Joe left after Ella refused him. He decided the best course of action was to be direct with her.

"Everyone is well, Ella. I assume you have not heard from Joe since he left Wisconsin?" Dan paused briefly, but when Ella remained quiet, he resumed. "Joe loves his new job and his new home. He met a young woman there and they were married last month. It was a whirlwind courtship."

Ella felt the ground swaying under her. She nodded her thanks and left Dan standing in the crowd as she made her way back to Lillie.

"Ella, you look as though you have seen one of the spooks that frightened Charlie," Lillie looked at her sister with concern, "Are you okay?"

Ella's face was drained of color and drenched with perspiration. She felt as though a huge black chasm opened and threatened to swallow her whole. She wanted nothing more than to go to sleep and wake up when this nightmare had passed. Joe was now lost to her forever. The pain of this heartbreak came to her in waves.

"Only one of my headaches," Ella lied. "Let's get these entries registered and head towards the amphitheater. I know Dr. Mitchell went there with Rose a few minutes ago. Perhaps he will have something to give me to help with the pain?" Ella prayed that George Mitchell would be able to come to her rescue.

CHAPTER 31

THURSDAY, OCTOBER 2, 1890

The chill, crisp air and the brilliant leaves adorning the maple trees lining Haseltine Street gave a spring to Rose's step as she walked towards Mrs. Wilson's shop on Court Street. She loved this time of year even though it meant the passing from the warm, humid weather into the frigid iciness of winter.

As she walked along, Rose reflected on the time she had spent with Ella since their reunion at the county fair last month. They attended several society and church meetings and had gone once again to Nourse Hill near Sextonville to pick apples with the other young people.

Like Rose, Ella seemed a more somber version of herself, but some of the old activities had reestablished a sense of normalcy again in Rose's life, making the pain of all the tragedy she endured lessened to a degree. Rose once again looked forward to the future.

As Rose entered the millinery shop, she noticed that while the front door was unlocked, Mrs. Wilson was not in her customary place behind the counter. A moment of dread seized Rose as she called out for her friend.

"Mrs. Wilson! Are you here? It's me, Rose." Rose's voice shook involuntarily as she approached the door leading to Mrs. Wilson's home in the back of the store. She was relieved when she heard the handle of the door turn, saw the door open, and saw her employer standing in the doorway.

"Land's sake! You frightened me! I can't think of what I would do if something happened to you," Rose exclaimed, her relief at seeing Mrs. Wilson was standing healthy and whole in front of her. It was then Rose noticed the empty vials in Mrs. Wilson's outstretched hand.

"Rose, can you tell me about this? I found all these vials hidden in various locations in the storeroom and the shop. Most of them are empty but this one has a few drops left in it. What would anyone need with this much laudanum?" Dora Wilson looked at Rose with concern. She noticed small things here and there, but she had not suspected Rose had been consuming so much of the medicine.

"Oh, those silly old things? Dr. Mitchell gave those to me a long time ago when I first lost my mother. I brought a small bit of the medicine with me wherever I went at the time, but I guess I was careless in not disposing of it after I had no use of them anymore," Rose's lies were skillfully mastered as she had been telling herself the same falsehoods to justify her use of the powerful drug for a long time.

She hated to deceive her dearest friend, but her dependency upon the laudanum overrode all else, including the relationships that mattered most to her. Rose once read a quote by Montaigne, "Habituation puts to sleep the eye of our judgment". It was ironic she had once felt judgmental towards those who were weaker than their influences, ones who could not or would not overcome their foibles, for now she appeared to be that hapless soul.

Dora Wilson's face showed her doubts. "Rose, there are too many vials here to have been such a long time ago. Are you certain the usage hasn't been more recent? I understand how much you need relief from the immense pain you endured, but I am concerned if you continue to use it. I don't want this to be the cause of the next tragedy in your life." Dora laid the vials down on the small table beside her to take Rose's hand in her own. "You only have to tell me you need help, my dear girl, and you shall have it."

Rose was stunned into silence. She did not want to lose Mrs. Wilson's friendship, but she was not able to admit that she needed the help so freely offered to her. She stared back with a look of defiance.

"I don't know why you would doubt what I have told you. Have I ever done anything to make you accuse me of such behavior?" Rose switched to the ploy of making the transgression belong to another instead of owning it herself. She winced inwardly at the look of hurt flashing across Mrs. Wilson's face, but she held her moral ground tenaciously.

"No, you have not done anything, Rose. I only wish to help you." Mrs. Wilson's face showed her distress, but she disengaged from her line of questioning, leaving Rose feeling relieved once again, as though she had evaded the issue. Rose promised herself she would be more cautious with laudanum in the future and perhaps even decide to stop taking it altogether.

"I know you are only the most helpful and kindest person in the world," Rose wrapped both of her arms around Mrs. Wilson in a tight hug. "You are always so concerned about everyone else when we should be more concerned about you. Now, let me get to work and cut out all the fabric pieces so your hands don't cramp up with rheumatism."

The rest of the day passed with Rose in a congenial mood. As she walked from the shop to her home, Rose reflected on the possibility of going without the dosages of laudanum.

Mrs. Wilson had always been a very wise lady and if she saw bad tidings connected to the continued use of medicine, then Rose should take that into serious consideration. By the time Rose reached the house on Haseltine Street she had decided to discontinue her use of the laudanum without delay, not understanding the side effects of breaking her addiction cold turkey.

The side effects were not long in making themselves known. By dinnertime, Rose suffered a headache and nausea, making the baked chicken on her plate unpalatable. She excused herself from the dinner table and made her way upstairs to her bedroom. Splashing water on her face and neck from her wash basin alleviated the symptoms momentarily.

Rose was distressed. She had made plans with Ella to attend the singing school conducted by Mr. Henry Gordon at the Presbyterian Church that evening and she had looked forward to it all week.

Perhaps if she took only a small dose of the laudanum, half of what she normally took, she might feel well enough to attend the social gathering. Rose made her decision as she crossed to her dresser and reached inside the top drawer for the bottle she knew was hidden there.

An hour later, Rose was finishing her toiletries and readying to leave to meet Ella. She was surprised at just how quickly the laudanum relieved the illness. Certainly, it could not be so harmful when it was so helpful. Rose collected her blue hat and coat and headed down the stairs as she heard Ella knock on the front door.

The two girls walked the short distance to the church, the autumn leaves cascading around them as they walked along the boarded sidewalk. Rose felt a rush of vitality and was grateful she had not missed this outing. The church was filled with people. Rose and Ella found some seats near the back row.

Dr. Lovering and Mrs. Lovering sat in the row just ahead of them. Mrs. Lovering turned as the girls took their seats and spoke in a hushed tone that carried throughout the church.

"Hello, girls. I am sure you heard about the unfortunate happenings at the high school overnight? `` The woman spun her web of gossip, knowing Ella and Rose were uninformed of her story. Both girls shook their heads and she continued.

"It seems someone took Mrs. Sweet's milk cow in the middle of the night. The cow was found amid a mess of dung still chewing its cud on the top floor of the high school building this morning. It is beyond me how disrespectful young people are nowadays." Mrs. Lovering shook her head in disgust as Rose and Ella struggled not to laugh at the thought of the cow in the classroom.

"Well, I tell you, since Mr. Sweet is the Superintendent of the School and Mrs. Sweet's father is Judge Fries, someone will be in a mess of trouble when they are caught. I am certain I could tell them just who was involved already," the matron nodded her head knowingly.

"No, my dear. You have an opinion of who you think did this, but you do not know who did it. There is a difference between the two." Dr. Lovering interrupted his wife as she was about to reveal the names of her suspects. Mrs. Lovering glared at her husband.

"Is this seat taken?" Rose had been so enthralled by the exchange between the Loverings she did not notice that George was standing in the aisle next to her seat. He had groomed and smelled of his hair pomade and cologne. Rose smiled in appreciation as she nodded.

George stepped across to where Rose sat in the pew and settled himself between Rose and Ella. Rose furrowed her brow at his choice, but he leveled her with a dazzling smile, and she smiled back. Ella shifted her position in the pew to make more room for George, as his long frame barely fit between the two girls. George turned the same dazzling smile on Ella and Rose could hear a small sigh escape her friend.

"Annie mentioned you were both attending tonight, and I thought you might not mind if I joined you at the last moment. I have heard these singing sessions are quite good. Mr. Gordon was trained in London, and we have the privilege of his expertise here in Richland Center." George nodded at Dr. Lovering and Mrs. Lovering, who was still turned in her seat staring at the good doctor sitting between the two pretty girls.

Mr. Gordon stepped to the front with Alice Berryman to accompany him on the piano. The evening progressed pleasantly, the entire audience participating in the singing. Rose enjoyed listening to George's deep, rich baritone as he sang next to her.

Towards the end of the evening, Mr. Gordon asked George to come forward and sing a selection for the audience. Rose beamed with pride as George rose from his seat and walked towards the music teacher who held the music sheet in his hand. George looked at the music and smiled as he gestured for Ella to join him at the front.

"This is a song we have been practicing for special music together," George explained as Ella stood from her seat beside Rose and shyly went towards George and the piano. Ella sat at the piano, took the music sheet from George, and began to play the introduction. George's voice blended perfectly with Ella's as they sang together. There was a moment of hushed appreciation before the audience broke out in applause at the conclusion of the duet.

"Wasn't that just perfect? It's as if they were made for each other," Mrs. Lovering gushed as she whispered loudly to Rose. The nausea returned immediately as Rose tried to gulp down the hot bile rising in her throat. It was now apparent to Rose and all the city that Dr. Mitchell and Ella Maly were becoming an item.

Ella returned to her seat beside Rose, blushing becomingly. George stood beside Mr. Gordon, as the music teacher, dismissed the assembly for the evening. Friends gathered around Ella and Rose to congratulate Ella on her outstanding performance. Each comment sent another stab of pain into Rose's abdomen as the bile continued to boil and rise from her stomach into her throat.

Rose was grateful for the short distance on the walk home as she attempted to converse with Ella in the same light banter that had begun their evening. Ella seemed completely unaware of Rose's discomfort as she relived the story of the milk cow in the high school. Rose could hear a giggle besides Ella's and assumed it was her own, she felt so far removed from the current situation.

Finally, Rose was standing on her front steps. She hugged Ella and fled inside the house and up the stairs to her bedroom. As soon as she closed her bedroom door, she walked to the top dresser drawer and the bottle awaiting her there. Hands shaking, she spilled some of the liquid as she gulped the laudanum. Taking the bottle with her, she threw herself upon her bed and hoped for oblivion to come and claim her tormented soul.

CHAPTER 32

FRIDAY, OCTOBER 3, 1890

The eastern edge of the night sky was just giving off a pale hue of pink when Rose bolted upright on her bed. The lingering effects of the sizable quantity of laudanum she consumed the previous night began to fade, leaving her confused and dazed.

Her dreams had once again been ardent and consisted mainly of George. Rose blushed deeply at the remembrance even though she was completely alone in her thoughts and in her room. In the twilight of her dreams there were passionate kisses that left her lips swollen along with physical contact that was deeply intimate even without the act of coupling.

Rose was left to ponder how her subconscious devised the occurrences in her dreams while her maidenly consciousness was unaware such occurrences existed. Even now, the thoughts made beads of sweat trickle along her spine, mixing with the crisp air in the unheated room that penetrated her thin cotton shift.

As the faintest light pierced the darkness of the room around her, Rose began to question herself about the previous night. She recalled the performance at the singing lessons, the pain of realization stabbing at her again. She recalled the dreadful walk home with Ella, who innocently knew nothing of her extreme discomfort. She recalled the rush up the stairs and to her dresser for the laudanum she had sworn herself off forever.

She recalled flinging herself bodily upon her bed with the laudanum bottle still in hand. What Rose could not recall, trying as hard as she might, was removing her shoes, her dress, and undergarments except for her shift, and removing the combs and pins from her glossy black hair that now cascaded down her back.

Rose swung her feet over the side of her bed, feeling the small woolen rug under her as she stood and squinted at the floor in the dim light of the room. She edged around the perimeter of the bed, keeping one hand on the bed's side to guide her. Her left foot struck the first object, the heel of her shoe. Rose squatted down to look at the shoe and found it was upside down so that it stood on the laces with the heel sticking upwards.

The other shoe was not next to the first, so Rose continued her search, crawling on her hands and knees in the grayness of the predawn light. Next, she found her dress wadded up with her stockings and undergarments inside its haphazard folds as though she had removed all of them before throwing any of them aside. As she crawled further, she located her other shoe against the far wall opposite the side where she normally entered her bed. This was not the oddest part of the shoe's discovery, however, as Rose found all her combs and hairpins crammed inside the discarded shoe.

Rose sat on the cold wood floor with her back against the wall holding her shoe full of hairpins. She wracked her brain for any remembrance of how she disrobed the night before, hoping some

small snippet of memory would come back to her mind. Nothing
came to her save the vivid scenes of her dream in the night. She willed
her mind to dwell elsewhere no matter how tempting she found them.

A new realization struck Rose, causing a shiver to surge down her
spine and reverberate in her limbs. In the midst of her vivid dream
was the recollection of George removing the combs and pins from
her hair, running his fingers through her tresses, and placing multiple
kisses upon the thick dark strands.

The initial recollection was not what caused such grave concern
for Rose. She also recalled that she protested George might lose her
valuable combs, so he placed them in her shoe as she giggled at the
sight of it.

A hard knot formed in Rose's stomach. Numerous recollections
of the dreams over the past months came flooding back to her mind.
The dreams felt so real to her because they had not been dreams after
all. How could this be? Certainly, her mind was playing tricks on her.
Rose would never have given herself over in such a way. While she
felt an intense attraction to George, she did not love him.

Rose forced herself up the rough wall to a standing position
despite the outcry from her shaking limbs. She staggered to the
dresser to look at herself in the small mirror positioned in the center
of the wall above it. The gray light was giving way to the light of
dawn as Rose gazed at the reflection staring back at her.

Her face was pale and drawn with dark circles under eyes that
gaped with an air of emptiness within. Her still swollen lips mocked
her naivety. Rose realized that while the laudanum she had been
taking all this while had taken the pain of her situation away momentarily, it also took a far greater toll upon her, one that could change
the course of her life forever.

It was several hours later that Dora Wilson looked up from her work to see Rose standing in the doorway in front of her. The girl looked affright, her hair tumbling about her in every direction and tears streaming down her reddened cheeks. Dora rushed to take hold of Rose in fear the poor girl would fall over where she stood.

Rose lifted her reddened eyes to look directly into Mrs. Wilson's face. The only words she could manage came straight from Rose's heart.

"Please help me, Mrs. Wilson. We must save me from myself."

CHAPTER 33

FRIDAY, OCTOBER 24, 1890,
LOYD, WISCONSIN

The sun was just rising over the hilltop on the farmstead of Isaac and Louvenia Newkirk, leaving pale hues of light to bounce off the dazzling reds, yellows, and oranges of the tree leaves surrounding the farmhouse. Rose made her way out into the chilly air to collect the eggs from the henhouse. The hens were already cackling loudly, protesting the lateness of their breakfast.

Rose walked towards the henhouse scattering feed as she went, luring the hens from their perches and reducing the chances of being pecked as she removed the eggs from the nests.

She knew better than to disturb a hen sitting on a nest, as the tiny creatures were famous for their pugnacious ferocity in defending their young. Only one small banty hen remained in the henhouse. She eyed Rose with suspicion, making the soft clucking sounds of warning.

Rose gathered the eggs from the surrounding nests while trying to watch the banty hen as the sound of her clucking increased in intensity. She shifted the egg basket to her hip and walked past the hen, trying not to make sudden movements. The banty hen stood in her nest, ruffling her feathers before flying off with her sharp talons bared towards Rose's legs. Rose rushed for the safety of the door as the hen shrieked, pecking at her heels.

Isaac Newkirk, Rose's host for the previous three weeks, stood in the yard grinning at the fleeing girl. He had been up for hours, long before the sunrise, tending to his farm animals and daily chores. His wife, Louvenia, had risen at the same hour that morning. Her daily chores involved caring for their brood of four children, keeping house, and preparing wholesome food for her family, along with her additional farm chores. Her endeavors often caused Isaac to claim, "a man works from sun to sun, but a woman's work is never done."

"Looks like that little banty is dead serious about her young'uns." Isaac remarked to Rose as she lifted the hem of her skirt slightly to reveal the bloody scratches left by the attack. Isaac shook his head at the sight of the scratches.

"You should go find Lou in the house. She has a balm for everything. Next time, let Horace go to the henhouse. That boy is as stubborn as the banty." Isaac pointed to his thirteen-year-old son who was working near the barn on a leather harness. Horace snorted in laughter at his father's comment, though he did not comment himself as he was already a man of few words, just like his father and grandfather before him.

Rose nodded to Isaac and carried the basket of eggs back towards the old farmhouse. She could hear the chorus of voices from within as the Newkirk children spoke to each other, laughing as they started their chores. Ten-year-old Aletta corrected three-year-old Arthur who had found the maple syrup in the pantry.

"Arthur, you don't need more syrup for your porridge." Aletta chided her little brother as she held her infant brother, Noble Sylvester, whom the family nicknamed Vester. She watched Arthur's small hand dripping with the amber syrup onto the spotless wood floor beneath the table and turned to get a washrag from the bucket in the corner.

Rose entered as the scene of sibling banter played out before her and she was struck with the similarity to her own childhood. Her younger brother Willie had been a rascal, always finding mischief. Her older sisters were like Aletta, always chiding him for mischief.

A wave of longing for her family washed over Rose, causing her to wince from its potency, making her forget the immediate pain of the bloody scratches covering her shins. Most of those family members were now gone and the realization Rose would never see them again caused tears to well up in her eyes.

"Oh law! What has that nasty banty done this time? Just wait and see if she doesn't end up stewing in a pot yet." Louvenia Newkirk, lovingly referred to as Lou by her adoring husband, took Rose's arm as she surveyed the damage done to Rose's legs. The scarlet blood from the scratches flowed freely down Rose's legs, pooling onto the floor already covered with the sticky maple syrup. Rose looked down at the floor, concerned about the mess she was making, while Lou seemed entirely oblivious of anything but Rose's wounds.

"Aletta, fetch my healing basket." Lou guided Rose to a bench next to the wooden kitchen table. Without warning, Lou threw Rose's skirts up over her knees so she could get a better look at the bloody wounds. Rose blushed at being so exposed in the main portion of the house, hoping Isaac and Horace would remain outside.

Lou crossed to the woodstove and poured water from a kettle sitting on the back portion into a bowl. She picked a few linen scraps from her bag of fabric scraps, bringing the material and the warm water to where Rose sat. Kneeling at Rose's feet, Lou immersed a piece of the material in the water and began to clean the wounds.

A sharp stinging caused Rose to gasp momentarily. Aletta brought the basket of herbs and medicinal bottles to her mother. She gave Rose a look filled with sympathy, as she had been a previous victim of the same banty hen. Even little Arthur stopped stealing maple syrup from the jug on the table long enough to lean over and pat Rose's arm in sympathy, his sticky face covered in syrup as he smiled at Rose.

Lou worked diligently, cleansing the wounds over and over to reduce the risk of infection. She applied an ointment made of yarrow root to staunch the bleeding and wrapped both legs in clean linen strips. Her hands were gentle and quick, reminding Rose once more of her own mother, causing her tears to well up again. Lou looked into Rose's eyes, glimpsing the pain that went far beyond her physical wounds there. Lou pulled Rose into an embrace.

"There, just let the tears do their work, Rose." Lou's gentle reminder caused Rose's tears to increase as Lou rose to the bench and sat with Rose, holding her hands. Aletta set little Vester in his cradle and crossed to the stove to stir the oatmeal bubbling in the pot. Aletta instinctively knew her mama needed her help so that her mama could in turn help Rose.

Lou was a healer. Each injured person, each vulnerable creature was brought to Lou for her gentle ministrations. Three weeks prior, Mrs. Wilson had realized Rose needed help far beyond the usual practices of the town's physicians. She knew Rose needed to heal from the inside out and that took a healer like Lou. Mrs. Wilson brought Rose to the Newkirk's in the little hamlet of Loyd, trusting that Lou and Isaac would help without asking questions and without judgment.

The first few days of Rose's stay had been strenuous. Lou took Rose to the small, single room homestead cabin in the woods, away from the rest of the family. Rose's physical addiction to laudanum caused her to have violent tremors and fits. Lou held Rose through each one, mopping her forehead of the profuse sweat and keeping Rose from hurting herself in her convulsions.

After several days of numerous seizures, Rose began to improve physically, her body responding to the nurturing care she received. Lou realized Rose's healing had only just begun as there were also deep emotional and mental wounds that were obscured by the administration of the laudanum. Lou knew from experience opium did not heal mental wounds, it only buried them deeper, making them more difficult to heal.

Lou had witnessed all of Rose's current side effects in Isaac when he returned to her from the Siege of Vicksburg in July of 1863. Isaac served in the Union Army with the 11th Wisconsin Infantry Regiment and fought courageously during the siege, being wounded twice. Isaac returned to Wisconsin addicted to the laudanum they had given him to ease his pain.

Most of the Newkirk family thought that Isaac would not endure, but his cousin Lou, a beautiful young woman with a miraculous gift for healing, came to tend him. Lou brought Isaac back from the brink of death and the two fell in love and married despite the objections they received due to their kinsman relationship.

Lou waited patiently, offering to listen to Rose speak her grief aloud, but Rose denied any remnants of grief. She gradually transitioned through the various stages of her grief: denial, anger, bargaining, depression, and a gradual acceptance as Lou encouraged that each stage was perfectly natural, and no one should be skipped.

Rose came to the realization that her overwhelming grief had not diminished with her use of laudanum; it only increased. While she was far from being completely whole in only three weeks, Rose was well on her way to a new beginning without the burden of overwhelming grief and without the addiction to laudanum.

Lou encouraged Rose to let the tears flow as they were now, sitting in the middle of Lou's kitchen with her skirts pushed up over her knees and Lou's tribe of children surrounding her in sympathy and puddles of maple syrup. Tears were the body's way of washing the soul of the poisons built up within it.

Rose went from being annoyed at the sudden tears that seemed to overcome her out of nowhere to being relieved she could experience genuine feelings once again. Rose knew she was one of the many creatures who owed their lives to the healer, Lou Newkirk.

CHAPTER 34

FRIDAY, OCTOBER 31, 1890

The October wind blew the remaining leaves from the almost barren trees as the darkness of night surrounded the city of Richland Center. The leaves swirled together down Haseltine Street as the unseen wind pushed them along, creating an eerie sense of an unearthly presence on this night of Halloween. The moon loomed in the sky, casting its glow over the landscape below and over the children gathering to attend the bonfires at the end of the street.

Rose walked along the street accompanied by Freddie and his gang of cohorts. The boys carried clubs dipped in kerosene and lit so that the torches bobbed along as the carriers walked, creating the sensation that the shadows cast upon the ground around them moved under their own volition. More and more children carrying torches joined the procession to the end of Haseltine Street, each torch adding more to the spectral ambiance.

Rose shivered from the chill in the wind, she wrapped her scarf tighter to protect herself from the cold and to add to the general anonymity that each person adhered to during the bonfires. She smiled at Freddie who was wrapped in a ragged blanket, his face covered in ashes from the kitchen stove to conceal his identity.

An old derby hat full of holes was perched at a jaunty angle upon his head. Freddie insisted he found the hat near the train tracks and informed the other lads that its original owner had most likely been a bonafide tramp from one of the trains. Rose felt certain she had seen the same hat blow off Postmaster Jim Key's head one day and be trampled under several teams of horses, causing Mr. Keys to throw the hat out, but Rose would never reveal her suspicions and lower Freddie's prestige in the eyes of his friends.

Rose had returned from her stay with the Newkirk's to the Mitchell household only a few days earlier. She was amazed at Mrs. Wilson's ability to guard her privacy by creating "an errand of importance". Mrs. Wilson announced unapologetically and privately to Rose that her recovery was of the utmost importance and therefore the created story was not an untruth. Rose appreciated Dora Wilson's faithful friendship more than ever as she returned to the Mitchell house without a barrage of questioning from Annie and Mrs. Hendy about her absence.

Freddie had been particularly happy to see Rose again. He asked Rose to accompany him on Bonfire night, as each group of children were required to have a single young adult as their chaperone to prevent injuries and vandalism amongst the frenzied mass of young-sters gathering in the darkness. Rose knew just how important the event was to Freddie and it was an honor that he would ask her to go with him rather than seeking out one of the single young men from the high school.

The ground had been cleared at the end of the long street with the nearest houses being several blocks away, safe from catching fire. Piles of wooden objects were placed out in front of numerous homes in the town so that "hooligans" and "hobgoblins" could come and take them for the bonfire's incendiary materials. Two stacks of wooden objects loomed in the moonlight waiting for the many torches to come and unite as one.

Long tables had been set up on one side of the street with refreshments and entertainment for the children once the bonfires were ignited. The parents of the children labored for hours to set up the activities for their progeny even though not one of the parents was permitted to attend the festivities. This annual Halloween tradition became the perfect irony of organized chaos and safe jeopardy.

Rose was pressed on every side by the mob of children gathering around her. She was grateful that several older boys had taken charge of those carrying torches, keeping them to one side, a safe distance from the smaller children. Angry shouts arose from gruff voices without any malice intended. The children holding the torches circled the two enormous piles waiting for the signal to light the bonfires.

A boy stepped forward with a tin whistle and a hush fell upon the noisy crowd. Rose could distinguish from her vantage point the ragged blanket from their basement rag pile and the jaunty hat upon the signal giver's head. Freddie had been chosen by his peers to give the signal to light the bonfires. Rose's heart warmed to see him as he stood so proudly on the platform and blew the shrill whistle that pierced the darkness around them.

The torches were thrown upon the piles and sharp cracks in the fuel-soaked wood resounded as the fire ignited it. The children gasped in awe and then began cheering wildly as the fire raced up the piles, shooting out the top as though the fingers of the flames attempted to reach out to the skies above them. An intense heat chased away the coldness of the October night until many moved farther away from the flames to escape the heat. Rose drifted to the outside perimeter of the crowd gathered while keeping a watchful eye on Freddie and his friends.

The tantalizing scents of apples and pumpkins hung heavy in the air, causing Rose's mouth to water. She walked towards the refreshment tables, overflowing with pies and cookies and tarts laced with apples, pumpkin, spices, cinnamon, and sugar.

Rose's appetite had returned once her addiction to the laudanum was broken. She selected a hearty piece of apple pie with a decadent caramel sauce poured over the top and walked back to her vantage point to make certain Freddie had not fallen into the fire.

"Oh, hello Rose! I am so glad to see you!" Ella's voice was close by as Rose turned to see Ella standing next to her. "Or are we supposed to pretend we don't recognize each other?" Ella laughed as she watched the disguised children cavort around them.

"I believe we can be recognized as we are not the actual hobgoblins." Rose returned Ella's smile while she took another bite of the pie. "We are only the chaperones."

"I have missed seeing you, Rose. Mrs. Wilson explained to all of us at the Sunday School that she sent you on an important errand and that you wouldn't return for several weeks. I hope your errand was successful?" Ella looked wistfully at the pie Rose held.

"I think it was very successful indeed. Mrs. Wilson is the kindest employer as she chose this errand for me. Would you like one of the pieces of pie before the children gobble them up?" Rose laughed as she led Ella to the refreshment table to get one of the few pieces of pie left. They stood together by the table enjoying the treat to the last bite in companionable silence. Freddie reappeared to collect Rose for a "very important mission". Giggling, Rose followed him with a wave to Ella.

Alice Berryman approached Ella, holding out her hands to her as she spoke. "Come get your fortune told! It is the funniest thing ever!" Alice took hold of Ella's hands and led her towards a tent erected for the occasion. The tent was draped in scarves and bright colored beads, it looked just like a gypsy marquee from a penny dreadful. Ella hesitated at the opening of the tent.

"Who on earth is in there?" Ella peered into the dimly lit tent at the figure disguised as a gypsy princess, her face covered with veils. Golden bangles jingled as she moved her arms to beckon Ella to enter.

"She said her name was Minnie Braddock, but we all have different guesses about who she really is. It's all just in fun, Ella." Alice gave Ella a small push, propelling her through the tent opening. The heavy scent of jasmine hung in the air from the burning incense stick, leaving wisps of smoke that curled upwards.

"How much for a fortune reading?" Alice took Ella's hand in reassurance as she stepped forward. Ella gripped Alice's hand and stared at the veiled figure before them.

"No charge. No charge." The raspy voice was masked to further obscure the mysterious woman's identity. "Come. Peel the apple in one piece and then wait until I tell you what to do next." Minnie Braddock handed an apple and a paring knife to Alice while nodding her head in encouragement.

Alice had years of experience of peeling apples for a big family, so she was able to peel the apple, leaving it in one long, red strand. She held out the peel along with the apple and the paring knife to the gypsy. Minnie took the peeled apple and the paring knife and set them aside, leaving the peel in Alice's hands.

"You must turn around and then throw the peel over your left shoulder. The peel will form the initials of the one you are to marry.

You have your heart set on it, don't you, dearie?" the woman cackled, sending shivers running up Ellla's spine.

Alice felt silly but she did as the woman instructed. She winked at Ella then turned to face the girls with her back to the gypsy. She threw the apple peel up in the air over her left shoulder. Rena and the other girls giggled in excitement as the gypsy knelt to examine the apple peel on the ground.

"Let me see. Oh yes, this looks as if it could be the letter "G" or possibly the letter "C". Does this make sense to you, Alice?" Minnie's voice was in a whisper beside Ella's ear. "Beware of the letter "G". Find yourself a good, upstanding, "J" and make a quiet life with him, Ella."

Ella pondered several things. Minnie Braddock must be someone she knew as she had not given her name and none of the other girls present had used it. Minnie also knew Ella should be wary of a name beginning with the letter "G", but how would she know anything of Ella's present situation? Before she could ask any questions, Minnie turned to Ella and offered her the apple and the paring knife.

Ella hesitated before accepting the apple and the knife. She began to peel the apple, ending with one long, red strand dangling from her fingertips. Alice smiled encouragement as she turned Ella to face the group of grinning girls and away from the gypsy waiting impatiently. Ella sighed and threw the apple peel into the air over her left shoulder while Alice clapped her hands in anticipation of Ella's fortune.

The room was silent as the gypsy peered down at the peeling on the ground. There was more silence as the gypsy knelt and stared at the peeling, standing up again beside Ella, abruptly turning her towards the opening of the tent.

"That's all we have for tonight, girls. It is late and the children need to be gathered up and taken home." Minnie ushered Ella, and the rest of the girls out of the tent, then walked rapidly down Haseltine Street, leaving the group of astonished girls standing there bewildered.

"Whatever is the matter with her? I would bet anything, Ella, that you got the initials of her beau, and she is flying off to make certain he is at home where he is supposed to be." Alice patted Ella's shoulder in consolation at the loss of Ella's fortune-telling. Ella laughed at Alice's version of events, following the others to gather her brothers and sisters and head for home.

Rose returned to the entrance of the tent the other girls had just vacated. She looked at the apple peeling still lying on the ground where Ella had thrown it. It had flown apart and landed in jumbled pieces, a tangled mess with no beginning and a blunt, short end.

Rose shivered once again, telling herself it was the cold in the air and not the eerie sensation that prickled the hairs on the back of her neck. She went in search of Freddie and his friends to hurry them homewards where she could ponder the aberrant occurrences of the evening from the safety of her own bed.

CHAPTER 35

MONDAY, NOVEMBER 10, 1890

The six o'clock whistle at the mill blew just as Rose entered the Mitchell home. She and Mrs. Wilson worked for hours on an order that was to be shipped to Chicago and Rose insisted on staying past her usual time of five o'clock to help finish the order. Rose could feel the strain of the fancy needlework she had done in the pain in her eyes and the cramps in her fingers, but she was grateful she felt the pain of her labor instead of the dreary haze of the laudanum.

Annie was just setting plates on the dining room table as Rose entered the hallway. Rose could tell from the loud thumps as the place settings hit the table that Annie had experienced a difficult day and she was destined to hear the details. Rose straightened her stiff shoulders and managed a pleasant smile to greet the disgruntled housekeeper.

"Tis nice of you to finally show up. Himself was in search of you an hour ago and in as terrible a mood as I have ever seen. He starts shouting at me as though I am in charge of your comings and goings.

Then the young lad came in like a whirlwind and his mood was also as black as pitch. The two maelstroms collided and such carrying on, loud enough to wake the dead or at least wake the babe upstairs so she too joined in the screaming. I tell you, Rose, I have worked in service before, and other civilized houses never behaved in such a way." The volume of Annie's voice increased so much throughout the telling of her story that she was on the threshold of screaming, though Rose felt it best not to mention the fact at this juncture.

"I am sorry for the trouble, Annie. Why don't you pour a cup of tea for yourself? I brought some fresh chocolate creams home, and you should help yourself to them." Rose held out a confectionary bag filled with the treats as a conciliatory gesture.

Annie looked like an angry bird with ruffled feathers who did not want to be appeased, but the treaty offered was beyond her willpower to refuse. She let out a final huff as she reached into the paper bag Rose extended towards her and selected several of the chocolate creams. Annie gave a curt nod of acknowledgment and turned to exit through the door to the kitchen.

Rose placed her hat and gloves on the mantle of the dining room fireplace and headed for the back door with the chocolate creams still in her hand. Rose sought out Freddie first and did not have to think twice about where the boy had gone. Rose quietly opened the back door as she knew George was probably sitting in his darkened office just down the hallway and she did not wish to encounter him yet.

Once outside, Rose headed for the treehouse in the tree in the corner of the yard. She knocked on the board at the base of the tree as she looked upwards.

"Freddie, it's me. May I come up?" Rose waited in the silence as dusk settled around her. Instantaneously, the rope ladder came inching down from the dark treehouse above, indicating that Rose's request had been received and granted. Rose hitched up her skirts, grateful the tree was hidden from the view of the people on Church Street. She climbed the rope ladder skillfully while holding her skirts and the paper bag of chocolate creams in one hand. Rose climbed onto the floor of the treehouse with as much grace as she could muster without falling.

As Rose's eyes adjusted to the dark, she could hear Freddie shifting into a sitting position in the farthest corner. Silence greeted her entrance as the boy stared at her from his vantage point. Rose knew she needed to proceed with caution. Without a word she opened the bag of chocolate creams and held it out towards Freddie.

The bag was snatched from her hand with a brusqueness unusual for the boy Rose knew and loved. Instead of feeling offended, Rose felt honored that she was one of the few people to whom Freddie would reveal his true feelings whether they were appropriate or not. Rose continued to wait in silence as she heard the bag rustle and then vigorous sounds of chewing commence.

Her patience was rewarded when Freddie moved to sit next to her and bumped her hand with the mostly emptied bag of chocolate creams. Rose reached into the bag, selected a piece of candy, and popped the entire thing into her mouth, thinking that her mother would have been mortified at the unladylike way she ate it.

She was rewarded with a slight chuckle from Freddie and another bump with the bag offering another chocolate cream. Rose took another from the bag and popped the second one into her mouth as well. Freddie's response to her tomboyish antics was a loud laugh, including a snort through his nose that made Rose laugh, causing her to choke slightly from a mouth crammed with chocolate.

Freddie gave several hard slaps to Rose's back that stung her skin but helped her to stop gagging long enough to spit the bolus out upon the floor. A few seconds of silence were followed by gales of laughter from both. Freddie laughed so hard he leaned his head against Rose's shoulder. She could feel the tension in his body begin to wane and he allowed her to put her arm around his shoulders as he rested his head in her lap.

"I hate school. I don't ever want to go back again. Father said I was being a foolish baby. Please don't let him make me return." Freddie poured his soul out with his words into the safety of the comforting arms Rose placed around him. Rose knew better than to ask why Freddie hated school or to remind him he must attend school. She stayed quiet, knowing Freddie would tell her.

"The teacher made all of us present our family lineages today." Freddie continued while Rose waited for him. She knew Freddie had worked exceedingly hard on his own family lineage. She cringed inwardly. Had the teacher criticized Freddie's work? So many children were crushed by the careless words of the adults in their lives and Freddie endured more loss than most children at his tender age. Rose felt a fierce defensiveness rise in her heart for the boy she held in her arms.

"The teacher commended my work in front of the whole class, and I was very proud of it until Annabelle pointed out that I don't have a mother anymore." Freddie paused and Rose felt a pain searing in her heart.

"Freddie, you do have a mother and though she can't be with us anymore she will always love you. There is nothing that can take her away from you." Rose felt tears pooling in her eyes. "I can see why this would make you so upset."

"Annabelle is just a dumb girl. She says things and I have learned not to listen to her. It was what Mary said that made me so mad. Mary was laughing and telling everyone I will probably have a new mother by next year. Mary's mother has been telling everyone that my father is courting someone and there will be wedding bells." Freddie blurted out the real reason for his outrage at the school.

"Rose, I don't want a new mother. I want all of us to go on as we are now. What if she doesn't like me or Lotte? What if she thinks that you should go and live somewhere else? I don't want you to go away. You are the only person who reminds me of Mama." Freddie dissolved into tears as Rose sat shocked at his revelation. She had never thought of the scenario Freddie just presented and she most certainly did not intend to leave Freddie and Lotte in someone else's care. She would have to find an alternate solution to this possible dilemma.

"We mustn't borrow trouble before it happens." Rose spoke to Freddie with a confidence she did not feel. "I don't intend to go anywhere, so you don't need to worry about it. As for school, I will ask your father about allowing you to assist Mr. Ghastin in his veterinarian calls for a few days. It will be a good learning experience for you and soon your classmates will move onto other things to discuss." Rose ruffled Freddie's hair as he sat up and looked at her with excitement. Freddie loved the kindly man and looked for ways to spend time with him.

"Let's go into the house before Annie begins shouting about our missing dinner," Rose suggested. She waited for Freddie to scramble to his feet and then she rose from her seated position on the treehouse floor. "Don't worry about not being very hungry, as I would imagine that Annie is feeling full herself and dinner may be lighter than usual." Rose remembered the handful of chocolate creams Annie took to the kitchen earlier.

Rose was correct about the dinner. Annie served them lighter fare, including a beef vegetable soup and some slices of fresh bread instead of the usual three to four courses. Rose and Freddie ate at the dining room table alone, as Mrs. Hendy ate upstairs in the nursery and George was nowhere to be found.

Rose took it upon herself to write a quick note to Mr. Ghastin asking if Freddie could help him for a couple of days. She knew she should probably ask George first, but at this point she would rather ask for forgiveness than for permission.

Rose left after dinner to dispatch the note and get Mr. Ghastin's agreement with her plan. When she returned, the parlor lights were all ablaze and the sound of the piano came to Rose as soon as she opened the front door. Rose removed her hat, gloves and coat and hung them up in the hallway closet. She crossed to look into the parlor and found Freddie sitting glumly on the settee.

George stood at the piano while Ella played, and they both sang. The recollection of the singing class came back to Rose. She had been so distracted by all the events that had followed she had pushed the revelation of the evening out of her mind. Watching Ella and George sing together brought the realization back with a forcefulness that took Rose's breath. Was Ella the new mother as Freddie's classmate had inferred?

Rose stared at the pair as the song ended and George turned to see her standing in the doorway. "I was looking for you earlier this afternoon to tell you that Ella and I intended to practice special music this evening, but you were nowhere to be found." George was matter of fact as he motioned for Freddie to stand.

"Frederick, you can be excused now." George ushered his son towards Rose, who backed out of the doorway into the hallway.

Freddie followed Rose into the hallway as George closed the parlor door behind him. It was obvious George did not desire their company while he and Ella practiced alone in the parlor.

Rose was still stunned as she walked towards the dining room and pulled out a chair to sit down. Freddie took the seat next to her, glancing back towards the parlor door occasionally. They sat in silence for a few moments as Rose tried to collect her thoughts.

"Why don't you fetch the checkers, and we can play them at the dining room table tonight?" Rose suggested one of Freddie's favorite pastimes to distract the boy while she tried to figure out what to do next. Freddie's problem of a new mother seemed so remote only a few short hours ago and now it seemed a much likelier possibility than Rose could have imagined.

"The checkerboard is in the parlor. What do we do?" Freddie indicated with a nod of his head towards the parlor that he was unwilling to incur the wrath of his father even for his favorite game.

"I shall go and fetch it then." Rose sighed as she stood and crossed the dining room back into the hallway. She tapped at the parlor door and waited only a second for a reply before opening the door. If she expected to witness a love scene playing out before her eyes, she found it was anything but an amorous meeting. Ella sat at the far end of the settee and George sat in a chair on the opposite side. Ella held the sheet music they practiced, and they seemed to be discussing only the music and nothing else.

Ella smiled at Rose as she entered the parlor and crossed to the table where the checkerboard lay. Ella stood and came to stand beside her as Rose began to pick up the pieces from the table.

"I was just telling George that I needed to go so there's no need to move your game, Rose. I promised Uncle Charlie I would stop at Bailey's and pick up an order he set aside for my mother earlier." Ella crossed to the small chair where her coat and hat had been laid out by George and began to dress for her trip home.

"I will be happy to accompany you, Ella, and see you home." George smiled as he left the room to fetch his coat and hat from his office at the back of the house. George had become a gentleman when he let Rose travel the same route at night by herself numerous times. George returned in a few minutes and showed Ella to the door as Rose stood watching the pair from the table in the parlor.

Freddie heard the front door and came to find Rose still standing in the parlor as though she were frozen in her spot. He looked confused at the front door.

"Where did they go? What are we going to do now, Rose?" Freddie anticipated they would resume their normal checker game in the parlor, but Rose's response surprised him more than a little.

"I feel the sudden need for some fresh air. Would you like to walk with me Freddie?" Rose walked determinedly to the hall closet, donned her hat, gloves, and coat and motioned for Freddie to get his cap and coat in all haste. They were soon out the front door and on the sidewalk in front of the house traversing down Church Street towards the Bailey building.

Soon the objects of Rose's interest were in sight. George and Ella strolled along on the opposite side of the street laughing and talking until they reached the steps of Bailey's store. Rose and Freddie stopped a half block away, tucked out of sight by a tree as they watched what transpired between the couple.

George stood holding both of Ella's hands as he faced her. Suddenly, Ella's older brother, Anthony, came around the corner and nearly knocked them over before he could stop. Anthony had been sent by his mother on the same errand Uncle Charlie had dispatched Ella. He informed George that he could see his sister returned home safely, so George tipped his hat and turned to leave.

Witnessing the change in plans, Rose sprang from behind the tree, pulling Freddie along with her as the two ran back down Church Street towards home. They just made it back into the parlor when George walked through the front door. He looked into the parlor to see Rose and Freddie playing checkers as if they had been in that place since George left the house. He turned, without bidding them goodnight and walked towards his office, leaving Rose and Freddie breathless from the quick run back into the house to cover their covert walk outdoors.

Rose settled into her chair to play the game when her tumultuous thoughts were interrupted by Freddie's thoughts spoken aloud.

"I don't want a new mother, Rose, and I will do whatever I need to prevent it from happening." Freddie's threat was clear. Rose knew she would have to do something to save Freddie from making good on it.

CHAPTER 36

MONDAY, NOVEMBER 24, 1890

The tiny bell on the door of Mrs. Wilson's millinery shop seemed to chime incessantly as troops of children from the elementary school entered and exited the shop dropping off their packages of collected clothing to be donated to the less fortunate. The kindly shopkeeper volunteered her shop to be the collection area and donated her time mending any garments before they were put in baskets along with food donations by the Ladies First Aid Society.

Rose stood at the counter with Hattie Dove and Emma Brewer sorting the clothing into piles. She smiled as she saw Freddie approach her with a group of boys. The boys carried boxes of clothing too heavy for the smaller children to carry.

A parade of school children had been formed by Mrs. Haskel and Miss Jordan, one of the teachers at the school. Freddie was chosen to carry a box with the U.S. flag draped over it at the head of the parade of students. His face beamed with pride as he placed the box on the counter. He removed the flag from the box, careful not to let it touch the ground, and took it outside for a ceremony of folding the flag once again.

"Freddie is becoming so grown-up." Mrs. Brewer smiled as the boy exited with the flag in his arms. "I am so happy to see him doing so well in school. His mother would be so proud of him." Emma took a handkerchief from her apron pocket and dabbed the corner of her eyes at the memory of Laura Mitchell. Rose and Hattie nodded quietly in agreement.

"I am certain Laura is smiling down on him and on Lotte too. She has grown so quickly. She is such a happy baby and reminds me of her sweet mother every day." Rose's enthusiasm over both Mitchell children made Hattie and Emma exchange a knowing glance between them.

"I think of all the people who might be willing to mother those poor children, that the good doctor should remember who Laura wanted to take care of them. It was quite clear to all of us she only wanted you, Rose. It is also obvious how much you adore both. Has Dr. Mitchell spoken about any intentions yet, my dear?" Mrs. Brewer, who was known for her direct and yet kindly manner, posed the question with sincere interest.

"Goodness, no. Dr. Mitchell has been mourning his wife as is appropriate and he has not discussed any future plans with me or with anyone else." Rose knew the kindly matron meant well, but she did not wish to start any more rumors about George's interests.

"He may not have discussed it with you yet, but it might be a good idea for you to discuss it with him. Many widowers with small children remarry sooner than most and they often find a person who will make the best mother for their children. It would be a shame to see you pushed out of a good marriage because the two of you did not form a romantic attachment. Just remember, Rose dear, second wives are often not love affairs, but they can be faithful, solid, commitments because the fanciful flings of youth have already been quenched." Emma Brewer nodded sagely at the young women in front of her.

"Perhaps Rose is interested in one of the fanciful flings of youth? She hasn't been married before and most of us dream of marrying for love." Hattie patted Rose's hand as she answered Mrs. Brewer's suggestion that Rose marry George without hoping for a loving marriage.

"I haven't really considered anything except Freddie and Lotte," Rose admitted. "While I am not looking for romance, I don't think I could bring myself to the practicality of discussing a marriage possibility like it was a business arrangement." Rose tried to make herself forget that she and George had declared their love for each other while Laura was still living. Even though Laura asked Rose to distract her husband, Rose still felt remorse for acting the part of the jade.

"You wouldn't have to discuss the matter with him yourself, Rose, just ask a few well-placed friends to suggest the possibility of marriage with you. I am certain there would be several people willing to speak on your behalf. I know I am willing to do so or to send Mr. Brewer. Sometimes men take suggestions better from other men. All you must do is ask, Rose." Emma Brewer opened a possibility Rose had not considered. She could remain as a mother to Freddie and Lotte without the interference of a future Mrs. Mitchell. Rose knew Freddie would not consider her a threat and he would not act out in a harmful manner.

The shop bell chimed again as George walked through the door as if he had been summoned by their conversation. Hattie and Rose blushed as the topic of their recent discussion approached the counter. Emma nodded at Rose and turned a beaming smile on the unwitting young doctor.

George carried a box, placing it on the floor at the ladies' feet. He removed his hat to reveal his perfectly groomed hair, the scent of his hair pomade wafted over the ladies, causing Hattie to sigh softly. A slight grin tugged at the corners of his mouth. George loved the effect he caused in young women.

"Good afternoon, ladies. I brought some donations over myself as I did not wish to task Freddie with it." George uncovered the box to reveal a pile of Laura's dresses and shawls. "I felt these would be put to better use than just filling the closets and drawers. I would appreciate it if you did not mention the donation to my son." George looked into Rose's eyes, imploring her to help him. Rose nodded. George flashed her a brilliant smile causing another sigh to escape Hattie as Emma nodded in agreement.

George tipped his hat to the ladies and made his way back to the shop door. Emma waited until she was sure the good doctor was outside and at least a block away from them.

"I think you may want to consider asking for some recommendations, Rose. It seems Dr. Mitchell may be making room for the second wife to take up residence."

CHAPTER 37

WEDNESDAY, NOVEMBER 26, 1890

A bitter November wind blew against Rose's back as she entered the door to the medical offices of Dr. Lovering. Mrs. Lovering looked up in consternation from her chair beside the humble fireplace. Rose shut the door, blocking the offending wind from entering the sparsely furnished space, but not before she caught Mrs. Lovering shivering and pulling her threadbare shawl around her slight frame.

"What brings you out into the cold Rose? You wouldn't catch me venturing out on such an evening." Mrs. Lovering stood from her chair and turned to where Rose stood beside the door. "Did Dr. Mitchell send you out? He normally sends Freddie or one of the other town boys to fetch Dr. Lovering." Tiny black eyes peered back at Rose with curiosity, reminding her of the crows that perched in the cornfields at the edge of town.

"Good evening, Mrs. Lovering. Dr. Mitchell didn't send me out. I came to see Dr. Lovering for myself. Is he available for a few moments?" Rose approached the older woman while trying to manage her most engaging smile. The iciness in Mrs. Lovering's eyes matched the bitter chill of the wind outside as she motioned for Rose to follow her up the narrow back steps towards the tiny room at the top that served as the doctor's examination room and office.

Mrs. Lovering paused more than once on their ascent, causing Rose to fear the elderly lady might fall on the stairs. Rose knew better than to offer any assistance, as the one thing Mrs. Lovering still seemed to have in ample supply was her pride.

Dr. Lovering had come to Richland Center as one of the first physicians in the small town and the prestige associated with this position had been the height of Mrs. Lovering's social status. As the town grew, more doctors arrived, and the aging physician received fewer of the patients that once kept him busy into the night.

Dr. Lovering compensated for his loss of patients by making tonics of every sort and selling them as curatives. Dr Mitchell was one of his best customers, purchasing a tonic made of ground school chalk and soda water for stomach ailments, a salve made of laundry soap and Vaseline for aches and pains, and the most popular, the sugar pills, for anyone with a psychosomatic illness.

At that time, most mental illnesses were treated as oddities, ignored, or disguised as eccentricities. Extreme cases were incarcerated with criminals, left unclothed, chained, and beaten. If not for the efforts of reformists like Dorothea Dix, the mentally ill would have continued to be treated as the unheard and unseen victims of reprehensible medical treatment.

Rose entered the cluttered little office behind the very winded Mrs. Lovering and surveyed her surroundings. Boxes of small glass bottles were stacked upon each other, leaving a small aisle to walk between the stacks.

Rose heard from Mrs. Wilson that Dr Lovering paid the young boys of the town to go through refuse piles, collect the glass medicine bottles, and bring them back to him. He washed the bottles out and refilled them with his various tonics. Rose could see many of the "clean" bottles still had remnants stuck to the inside, making her cringe slightly.

"Well, Rose! What brings you out on such a bitter evening? Would you care for a hot cup of tea?" The kindly old physician gestured for Rose to take the one chair cleared of any boxes while he looked for a clean teacup among the stacked piles of items. His own teacup bore brown stains from a multitude of uses and the chipped teapot sat without a cozy.

Rose was inclined to politely refuse his offer, but she didn't wish to offend his hospitable nature. She nodded her acceptance and watched as Dr. Lovering emptied dried herbs from a teacup into a basket and wiped the teacup with his sleeve. He proceeded to pour a light brown liquid into the cup and extended it towards Rose with a kind smile.

"Thank you. I am sure this is just what the doctor ordered." Rose accepted the teacup and sipped, hoping the disposed herbs were not of a poisonous nature. The "tea" was stale, tepid water with a brownish tinge, but Rose sipped it appreciatively as if it were the finest tea straight from London. She did not realize what level of poverty the Loverings had been reduced to, as she had not the necessity to visit the doctor's office before that evening. Rose made a mental note to ask Mrs. Wilson about assisting the elderly couple without making them think it was charity.

Rose realized she had been lost in her mental ruminations for too long as she looked back into the expectant and inquiring faces of Dr. and Mrs. Lovering. She came here for a purpose, and she needed to get to it.

"Dr. Lovering, I wished to consult with you on a couple of matters. The first problem is that I have been plagued with a cough recently and our housekeeper, Anna, suggested I ask you about your cough syrup. She said it cured her cough as right as rain in no time at all." Rose devised a plan to see the doctor for a medical reason first before she asked him about the second purpose for her visit. She did not need the cough medicine now, but she knew it might be good to keep the tonic on hand for the winter months when grippe set in.

"Yes, yes, of course. We can fix some right now. Did you say there was more than one reason for your visit?" Dr. Lovering turned towards his cupboards to fetch the materials he would need for the tonic. He removed a jar of grated ginger, a tin of cayenne pepper, a jug of apple cider vinegar with the mother floating in it, and a crock of honey from his supplies.

Rose was relieved to see his ingredients were less drastic than the "One Night Cough Syrup" George often dispensed. Those ingredients included alcohol, chloroform, morphine, and cannabis. After her stay with the Newkirks, Rose tried to avoid all of George's remedies, knowing many of them contained the opiates that caused her addiction.

"Yes, I did have another reason to consult you. It has a more private nature to it." Rose glanced at Mrs. Lovering who finally caught her breath and stood just over Rose's shoulder taking in every word.

Rose knew anything discussed with Mrs. Lovering's presence might as well be announced in front of the City Hall and every church in the town, as the elderly woman was known as a gossip. Dr. Lovering had taken an oath of discretion in his profession, but it did not extend to his wife.

"What on earth does a young woman need to say to a doctor that can't be overheard by another?" Mrs. Lovering let out a snort of disgust as she saw her husband nod at the doorway indicating her exit. She spun on her heel and tossed her gray head in derision as she made her way to the doorway and down the narrow stairs. Dr. Lovering made his way over to the door, closing it to prevent Rose from being overheard by his wife perched at the bottom of the stairs.

"Continue, my dear. How can I help you?" Dr. Lovering took a mixing bowl to his gathered ingredients and began to measure out each one for the cough syrup.

"I was advised by several people, including Mrs. Brewer that I should ask for your assistance in a matter concerning Dr. Mitchell." Rose twisted the handkerchief she pulled from her reticule in her hands as she spoke.

"Is there something amiss? Dr. Mitchell has not been inappropriate towards you, has he?" Dr. Lovering put down the ingredients he was mixing and turned to take Rose's hand in his own as he looked directly into her eyes. Rose could see the measure of concern about George's behavior reflected in the depths of the kindly doctor's eyes. It made Rose wonder why Dr. Lovering was so apprehensive.

"No, it's nothing like that. I have been treated very well by Dr. Mitchell and all the household. I still miss Laura every day, but I take solace in the fact I am helping to raise Freddie and Lotte as Laura would have wanted. I hadn't really considered that Dr. Mitchell may start looking for a new wife to care for the children. Mrs. Brewer suggested I ask a few people to mention to him that I would be a suitable wife. I know I might not be considered as fashionable as other possible choices, but I would have his children's best interests in mind. I promised Laura I would take care of them. I know Dr. Mitchell holds your opinions in very high esteem and so I wondered if you might be willing to speak with him on my behalf?"

Rose hadn't realized she'd been holding her breath until she ran out of air and the last few sentences tumbled out very rapidly. She felt awkward about bringing up the subject, but she also felt relieved in a way she could not explain. She had been looking at the floor for most of her speech, but she ventured to look up at Dr. Lovering to gauge his reaction to her unorthodox request. She steeled herself to see a reaction of shock and displeasure.

His gentle eyes were filled with compassion and understanding. He simply nodded in agreement as he turned back to finish mixing the cough syrup. When the mixture was complete, he poured it into one of the glass bottles piled next to his desk. Rose was so relieved at Dr. Lovering's kindness towards her, she did not even care if the glass bottle was completely clean.

Rose took a five-dollar bill from her reticule and put it on the small, cluttered desk next to the doctor. Immediately he began to protest; her payment was far too great, but Rose knew it was much needed by the elderly couple and she would have to find a way to give them more in the future.

Rose descended the narrow stairs holding her cough syrup. She passed by Mrs. Lovering, who was perched on the bottom steps just as her husband predicted. Rose returned Mrs. Lovering's dark scowl with the sweetest smile she could muster, knowing the dour woman's reaction came from her insecurities about what the future might hold.

While it was tempting to return Mrs. Lovering's scowls and acidic barbs, Rose knew she would not stand in a place of judgment over someone who had lost so much, no matter how poor her behavior. Rose wrapped her coat and scarf around herself and opened the outer door to face the bitter November winds. As Rose pulled the door shut, she heard the old woman's threat over the noise of the howling winds.

"You will pay for your impertinence towards me, Rose Zoldoske. Just wait and see."

CHAPTER 38

SATURDAY, DECEMBER 6, 1890

Dusk was just descending as Rile Smith, the city's lamplighter, began his rounds down Court Street. The tall, slender man was garbed in a black oilskin Cape Ann Sou'wester hat and coat with some old rags draped over his shoulder and a can of kerosene in one hand.

Rile stopped at each intersection where wooden posts held the boxes that enclosed the kerosene lamps almost seven feet into the air. Most lamplighters needed a ladder, but Rile had been blessed with extraordinary height, which made his occupation very suitable as he could easily reach the kerosene lamps he lit.

The yellow glow of the lamps as they were lit gave the appearance of warmth to the cold, snowy darkness of the street. Near the end of the street, both floors of the Bailey building were ablaze with lights, beckoning the citizens of the town to the Opera House located on the second floor.

The lamplighter paused at the brilliantly lit window of Bailey's store to look at the assemblage gathered within before making his way around the corner towards Church Street. Rile knew the more prestigious members of the city would not welcome his presence in their midst as he was considered "odd" even by the groups of children who often gathered to taunt him and call him names as he went about his work.

One of the few people to extend genuine kindness to the ridiculed outcast was standing just inside the door of the Bailey building. Ella had noticed that Rile paused at the window, his face stern and immobile, but the look in his eyes betrayed his yearning for acceptance. More than once, Ella had chased away school children who gathered in groups to mock Rile, causing the older man to shout at them in anger. Ella did not understand the petty meanness of the children, but she did understand that children were often a reflection of their parents.

Lillie stood next to her sister chatting vivaciously with Rena Allen about the evening's entertainment, a variety show hosted by the Odd Fellows. There was a band ensembled, acrobats, dancers, and even a magician. The sounds of the band warming up their instruments, floated down from the floor above, heightening the excitement of those gathered.

"Can you believe Mae Hyndman has gone off and gotten herself engaged of all things?" Rena whispered loudly over the din of the people around them. "My mother heard it from Mae's mother, and it seemed Mrs. Hyndman was not very pleased about the arrangement. Mae is returning home soon for Christmas and to plan her wedding. It just seems very sudden if you know what I mean?" Rena winked at Lillie and Ella.

Ella blushed at Rena's inference of Mae's impropriety. She knew there were circumstances that led to hasty marriages, but she was not accustomed to hearing about the details. She glanced sideways at

Lillie who was still laughing at Rena's comments, quieting her sister with only a look.

"Mae has lived up North for almost a year and could have met her intended very soon after she arrived. It only seems sudden to us because we weren't aware of her every waking moment, like we are of everyone who lives here. It is exaggerated to think she has any other motives for her upcoming marriage." Ella defended the absent Mae even though she knew Mae would probably have assumed the worst of someone else in her situation. Ella was tired of the small-town gossip and the pettiness that accompanied it. She thought again of the people in the room who made Rile the lamplighter a persona non grata.

Lillie shook her head silently at Rena, who looked about to retort. Lillie knew her sister had an extremely compassionate heart and would become upset over the continuance of careless commentary regarding Mae, ruining the chance of enjoying their evening entertainment. She decided to change the topic of conversation entirely.

"Have you seen the new Sears and Roebuck Catalog? Isn't it amazing that you can send away for so many items and they will just mail them to you? I know almost all the pages are already dogeared at our house by our younger brother and sister. Just the other day little Charlie asked me if I thought Santa might use the Sears and Roebuck catalog?" Lillie laughed with Rena as she noted Ella's relieved and grateful expression.

The crowd gathering to wait for admittance to the Opera House was almost to the point of overflowing when the door finally opened. Ella and Lillie purchased their seats in the general section as the reserved seats near the front were much more expensive.

They made their way upstairs and looked for seats among the rows of benches that were quickly filling. Rena motioned for the girls to follow her to the spot where they could sit together. It was a tight squeeze as they chose the best seats that were not located behind one of the many pillars that ran from floor to ceiling.

"This looks like it will be standing room only." Ella turned her body slightly to make more room for her sister, who sat pressed against Rena on her other side. Ella had the advantage of sitting on the end of the bench, so she did not have someone to her left if she could keep herself from falling off the bench altogether.

"Good evening, ladies. It seems tonight's entertainment is very popular." George Mitchell tipped his hat to the girls while smiling at Ella. He wore a dark suit cut in the latest fashion and tailored to fit him perfectly. Ella could hear Rena sigh out loud at the sight of him.

"I reserved two seats for tonight and found I had use for only one. Could I interest you in using the other seat? The only downfall is you must sit beside me and bear my boring company." George asked the question of the girls while extending his hand towards Ella, indicating that she alone was the recipient of his invitation.

Ella was frozen in her seat as she stared back at him. She knew the polite thing to do was to decline his offer and stay with her sister and Rena, but she found herself wishing that she wasn't so polite.

A sudden nudge from Lillie almost sent Ella crashing to the floor before she caught herself with some assistance from George's extended hand. He grasped her shoulder to keep her from falling backwards over the bench. Ella could feel the warmth of his hand through the sleeve of her dress.

"What a nice offer, Ella. Don't worry about us. In fact, Rena and I will have more room to sit this way." Lillie was smiling up at George as she grasped Ella's other shoulder and stood, helping Ella to her feet.

Lillie sat again and slid over to the end of the bench, leaving Ella no recourse except to step out into the aisle and follow George towards the front of the opera house. Ella glanced back to see her sister and Rena grinning at her from their seats as she made her way forward.

George continued towards the front until he reached the first row. Ella knew the reserved seats there were very expensive. She wondered why George reserved more than one if he couldn't use it. Ella began to rack her brain for something witty and graceful to say but she was rescued by the music, the cue for the show to begin.

Ella enjoyed the entire show. She had attended many variety shows in this same opera house previously, but none of them seemed as spectacular as this one. She knew it was mostly due to her excellent vantage point, front, and center of the stage.

She was honest with herself; it was also due to the chivalrous attention paid to her throughout the entire show by her charming companion. George made her feel like a queen with an entire court to do her bidding. A stab of regret assailed Ella when the grand finale ended. The time flew by, and she found that she did not wish to return so soon to her sister and Rena.

"May I see you home?" George seemed to read Ella's thoughts about not wanting the evening to end yet. Ella's perfect complexion was tinged with a becoming blush as she nodded her assent. She stood and took George's arm as she followed him towards the stairs leading to the first floor. She waved at Lillie as she passed by, knowing her sister understood without having to discuss the arrangement.

A gentle snow was falling, the enormous flakes drifting to the ground like feathers, making the otherwise rough dirt street seem surreal in its beauty. Ella was aware there was a crowd around her, other people leaving the Bailey building in couples and in groups, but it seemed to her there was only the two of them walking down Church Street.

Her hand remained in the crook of George's arm as they walked together. George tipped his hat in greeting to several people they passed along the way. The crowd walking along the path with them thinned as they walked three more blocks before turning towards Park Street, leaving Ella and George to walk the remaining distance alone.

"I am so pleased you decided to accompany me." George waited until they were alone before initiating a conversation. Ella wondered if he did not wish for anyone else to overhear them. "I was hoping we might spend some more time together if you are willing." George placed his right hand over Ella's hand that was still in the crook of his left arm. He stopped on the walk below the pine in front of the Maly house.

The pine tree's branches obscured them from the view of the occupants of the house and anyone further down the street. The spicy scent of the pine needles mixed with the pleasant scent of George's hair pomade caused Ella to close her eyes for a moment in appreciation. Ella opened her eyes to see George's face very close to her own as he rested his chin against her forehead.

"Yes." It was the only thing Ella seemed capable of saying at that moment and yet it was all she really needed to say. She tipped her head back as George kissed her, holding her in his arms.

George stepped back slowly, breaking the embrace. Ella wanted him to continue but knew he was showing the restraint of a gentleman, not allowing things to progress too quickly. For the second time that evening Ella wished she had not been so polite. George chuckled softly as if he had read her mind again. He brought her hand to his lips, placed a kiss on her palm, and then curled her fingers around it, keeping his kiss there for her to hold. George turned to retrace his steps in the falling snow as Ella finally found her voice.

"George, who was in the other seat originally? Who didn't show up?" Ella told herself she had to know his answer and yet didn't want to know the other person's name. She feared his answer might change the course of their newly formed attachment.

George paused before answering. "Who said she didn't show up?" George's dazzling smile made Ella's heart race. She watched from her place beneath the pine tree as he walked away. Ella knew her life had changed in the heartbeat of a moment; it would never be the same again.

CHAPTER 39

MONDAY, DECEMBER 22, 1890

The fresh snow crunched beneath Rose's feet as she made her way towards Mrs. Wilson's shop in the early morning. The winter sun in a brilliant blue sky made its appearance after a lengthy absence over the last two weeks. Leaden clouds brimming with snow had dumped over three feet in that time, causing the city to halt to a standstill until it could be cleared away. Most of the shops, including Mrs. Wilson's millinery had closed for several days as no one could navigate the roads leading in and out of the city.

Rose spent her time entertaining Freddie and Lotte with activities in preparation for their Christmas celebration. She knew Freddie's first Christmas without his mother would be exceedingly difficult. George had made no mention of any thoughts of celebration.

Rose and Freddie created long strands of cranberries and popcorn to decorate a tree they would cut down on Christmas Eve and bring into the parlor. She enlisted the assistance of Annie and Mrs. Hendy in dipping small candles to place in holders upon the tree; the ladies had responded with unaccustomed eagerness, even dying the candles a beautiful deep crimson color to add to the festivity of the occasion. Paper and ribbon rosettes were fashioned from the scraps in the sewing basket to hang upon the branches along with small gifts.

Christmas cookies had been baked and decorated with icing and sugar, making the house smell divine, mixing with the scents of cocoa and peppermint. Oranges were hidden away in the cellar to be handed out as gifts to each member of the household. Annie purchased a goose from a neighboring farm to stuff and roast and serve along with sweet potatoes and a salad made from the leftover cranberries and oranges.

Rose had also stayed up late into the night making gifts for the children, a new red stocking hat for Freddie and a crocheted blue bonnet for Lotte. She purchased a set of tin soldiers along with a new bag of marbles for Freddie from the Bailey store right after Thanksgiving.

Last night she had finished a soft flannel rag doll for Lotte from the cut pieces of one of Laura's robes she rescued from the donation pile. Rose was determined that the children would be delighted with the small tokens of love she could bestow upon them.

Lotte entertained everyone with her antics, crawling from person to person and lifting her chubby arms up to be held and kissed. Her bright eyes sparkled with excitement as she watched the preparations, trying to place herself at the very center of the activities. She was even pulling herself up to stand alongside the settee. Rose was certain she would be taking her first steps early in the new year.

Freddie had been whittling something with his pocket knife, sending curls of wood shavings onto the Persian rug in the parlor, causing his sister to race after the wood shavings in an attempt to shove them in her mouth. Rose had pried the little girl's mouth open more than once to remove the shavings, prompting Mrs. Hendy to cluck like a mother hen about the imminent danger to the baby.

Neither Rose nor Annie had the heart to scold Freddie about the mess he made when they realized he was carving an angel for the top of the tree in memory of his mother. Rose made a note to herself to collect some white dove feathers from Mrs. Wilson's shop to adorn the angel's wings.

"Freddie and Lotte would make you so proud, Laura." Rose whispered to the gentle winter wind that mimicked the character of her friend as it caressed her face gently and caused the snow to swirl in a playful pattern on the path where she walked. "I know Christmas won't be the same without you, but I will make it the best I can for them."

The absence of other people on the street caused Rose to continue her conversation, "I asked Dr. Lovering, Mrs. Brewer, and Mrs. Hyndman to speak to George about the possibility of making me his second wife. I wanted you to know this only because I made a promise to you once and I am committed to making sure your children are raised in a loving home. I don't know how George has responded to their solicitations on my behalf, but I hope it is still your wish that I would be the one to care for them."

Rose paused at the corner of Court and Church streets where a mound of snow had been pushed to clear the streets. The snow was piled to a height over Rose's head, it stood like a majestic mountain obstructing Rose's view of anything further down Church Street. Rose listened for the clattering hooves of horses indicating a sleigh was headed in her direction. She was greeted by silence except for the sway of the gentle wind and the occasional twitter of a bird.

Suddenly, a bright red cardinal came from a nearby tree to perch on top of the snow drift. He stared at Rose with his tiny black eyes but did not seem concerned by the nearness of her presence. Rose gasped at the beauty displayed before her, the vivid colors of the blue sky, the white snow, and the red cardinal painted in a way no artist could capture. She stood motionless, drinking in the beauty of her surroundings, before the bird flitted off as quickly as it landed.

Rose resumed crossing Church Street when she was struck by the realization of an adage of her mother's: a cardinal was often a sign from someone in Heaven sending their love to those who were left behind. By the time Rose crossed the street and made her way to the shop's door, she had convinced herself that Laura sent the cardinal as a sign of her blessing.

Mrs. Wilson smiled her greeting as Rose entered the shop. Piles of various fabrics and half-finished orders were strewn on the counter, the time just before Christmas was one of the busiest of the year and they had lost several crucial days of Rose's assistance with the work.

Rose noticed plates and bowls with remnants of food stacked on the small work table. Mrs. Wilson had likely spent every waking moment working to fulfill the Christmas orders by herself. Rose felt a sudden pang of remorse that she had not been more help to her friend even though she would have been unable to even walk the distance in the near blizzard conditions.

Rose removed her coat and hat and stored them behind the counter. She hugged her friend and took the project from her tired hands as she led her towards one of the rocking chairs by the window.

"I would say a pot of Oolong tea is in order for you and then I will start on the most pressing of the orders. We will work through each one even if I must spend all night doing so." Rose went to the small stove situated in the corner, she stirred the embers of the fire and took the pot of water, moving it to the front burner to heat. She added the Oolong tea leaves to the teapot and returned it to the small table where Mrs. Wilson sat watching the hustle and bustle of her younger friend.

"I am so relieved you could make it in today. Mrs. Hyndman is bringing Mae in to fit her for several wedding items, and we still have several orders to fill for Christmas. I know the good Lord doesn't give a soul more than she can handle, but sometimes I wish he hadn't trusted me to handle quite so much." Mrs. Wilson chuckled as she watched Rose pour the boiling water into the teapot. The warm spicy scent of the tea filled the room.

"I didn't realize Mae was coming home for Christmas. Alice Berryman mentioned Mae was engaged to a nice young banker from Ashland. I am certain she and Mrs. Hyndman will tell us all about it." Rose laughed with Mrs. Wilson about the mother and daughter's propensity towards gossip as Rose worked diligently, waiting for the tea to brew.

Soon the tea was ready. Rose poured it with a generous dollop of milk in Mrs. Wilson's cup. Rose brought the tea tray to the table and sat in the opposite chair, taking up a small child's hat to work on while she sipped her tea. The red and green plaid fabric of the hat had been fashioned into a Scottish tam with a pom fashioned of golden yarn perched at the very top. Rose worked at fastening a small gold braid to the drawstring rim which reminded her of a crown.

"Won't that be perfect for little Sofie King? Her mother ordered it a while ago, but she hasn't been able to pick it up because Sofie has been so ill. Dr. Haskell says it was diphtheria and the whole family has been in quarantine for the last week. It sounds as though Sofie is improving, but I guess it was touch and go for a day or two." Mrs. Wilson shook her head as she picked up another project to work on.

Rose's heart began to beat rapidly, her breathing coming in short gasps. She couldn't bear to hear that sweet little Sofie was so sick and had come close to dying. "I will finish this today and deliver it to their doorstep myself this afternoon."

Rose would do anything for Sofie. She willed herself to remain calm and counted slowly to remove the terror of losing yet another person in her life. Rose knew she craved the mind-numbing effects of opium when this terror assailed her, but she also knew if she returned to the drug, she would be lost to it forever.

She finished the tam after embroidering Sofie's initials in gold thread on the side and turned to the next project in the pile. The two women worked into the afternoon until they heard the ringing of the bell at the shop's door. Mrs. Hyndman and Mae entered like a whirlwind, both women speaking simultaneously as they greeted Mrs. Wilson and Rose and took off their coats and hats.

Rose went to brew some more tea as Mrs. Wilson took careful notes on the Hyndman order. There were six hats total, including one with a bridal veil that Mae would wear for her wedding day. Mrs. Wilson looked exhausted at the thought of the work ahead of them. Rose put her hand on Mrs. Wilson's shoulder in reassurance. At least they had a month to complete the order as Mae was returning to Ashland in January. Mae excitedly told them all about her wedding and her fiancé.

"January weddings are very fashionable nowadays and I have been told they also bring good luck to the bride and groom." Mae nodded her head in affirmation as she spoke, and Rose nodded in agreement. The ill feelings of the past seemed to be behind the two girls and Rose found herself wishing the best for Mae's future.

"It sounds like there may be a March or April wedding here. I don't know if I will be able to return so soon after my own wedding, but I should at least try to attend the wedding of a childhood friend." Mae continued to prattle on about her own wedding, but she piqued Rose's curiosity about a local wedding enough to ask.

"Who is the local bride? I haven't heard of any recent engagements." Rose knew she had tripped into one of Mae's entanglements of local gossip, but she was surprised she had not heard that a local couple was so near the altar. She turned towards Mae and did not notice the uneasy expressions on the faces of Mrs. Wilson and Mrs. Hyndman beside her.

"Oh Rose, you silly goose! Certainly, you of all people realize what the whole town's talking about, Ella Maly is going to marry Dr. Mitchell!"

The room held the dim shadows of a late winter afternoon when Rose opened her eyes. She found herself stretched out on a small bed in Mrs. Wilson's tidy bedroom while her employer sat in a rocker nearby watching Rose with concern clearly written across her face.

Confusion clouded Rose's memory as to how and why she had ended up in Mrs. Wilson's private residence attached to the back of the millinery shop. All she could recall was a conversation with Mae and her mother about Mae's wedding.

Wedding. A sharp stab of pain assailed Rose with intensity. There was something about a wedding, but she could not figure out why on earth a wedding would cause her such distress. Rose stared at the ceiling above her, trying to bring to mind what had happened, but she drew a complete blank as though she were staring into an abyss.

"You passed out cold in the store. Fortunately, Rile Smith was right outside my shop, cleaning the streetlamps, and he assisted me in carrying you back here to my room." Mrs. Wilson's comforting voice drifted over the troubling waves in Rose's mind, calming Rose instantly. "Mrs. Hyndman wanted to call Dr. Mitchell, but I felt that wasn't the best idea in the current situation. You have been out for several hours, Rose."

George's name seemed to trigger another emotional response that Rose felt deep in the pit of her stomach, like a raging inferno, out of control Instantly, the inferno split her heart and mind in two as she remembered the conversation with Mae.

Wedding. George. Ella.

Rose heard the loud wails reverberating off the walls of the tiny bedroom, but it took her several moments to realize that she was the source of the mournful cries. She collapsed into Mrs. Wilson's outstretched arms as the hurt, betrayal, and fear for the future collided and cascaded down her face in a torrent of tears.

Mrs. Wilson sat, holding the shaking frame of the girl. She knew the violent tears had been pent up for months and needed to be released before Rose could move on to better things. She waited until the tears abated and there was only the sound of small involuntary hiccups like the patter of rain after a violent storm had passed. Her next words were of comfort and wisdom.

"Mae isn't completely correct about them. There hasn't been an official engagement announced, only a lot of small-town stories. I don't think Ella would ever try to deceive you, Rose, by not telling you about this. She just isn't that kind of girl." Mrs. Wilson was deliberate in only mentioning Ella's good intentions, as she was unsure of Dr. Mitchell's intentions towards anyone. "Don't blame Ella for any misunderstandings you may have with the doctor, she has always been a good friend to you."

Rose knew Mrs. Wilson was right. Ella had been kind to her, defending her when others had been so unkind. She also knew George was very adept at attracting young women and bending their wills to his own. It was possible Ella did not understand that Rose was the one chosen by Laura to take care of the Mitchell children in the event of her death.

Perhaps all Rose needed to do was address this to Ella and everything would be set to rights once again. She decided to wait until after Christmas so there would not be any distractions from the wonderful celebration she had planned for Freddie and Lotte.

Rose stood from the bed slowly with a firm look of determination set in her features. Mrs. Wilson's look of concern increased when she noted the expression on the young woman's face. The two women proceeded towards the front of the millinery shop together. Mrs. Wilson kept a firm hand under Rose's arm for support.

The small plaid bonnet fashioned for Sofie still sat on the counter, reminding Rose of her commitment to deliver it to the King's house that day. Rose picked up the bonnet to put it in her reticule when Mrs. Wilson stopped her.

"Let's wait until tomorrow to take the bonnet to Sofie. She may be asleep this evening and I want to see you straight home safely." Mrs. Wilson took the bonnet from Rose's hands and placed it back on the counter for safe keeping.

It was already dark with the yellow glow of the street lamps lighting their way as the two women progressed to the end of Court Street and turned right to progress the two blocks down Church Street to the gate in front of the Mitchell home.

"I can make my way from here," Rose assured Mrs. Wilson as they paused at the gate. "I don't want to cause any alarm over this little setback, and I am feeling much better. I am certain that you are right. I just need to talk with Ella, and we can work this out for everyone's good without what you call a 'tempest in a teapot.'" Rose laughed nervously as she hugged Mrs. Wilson.

Dora Wilson watched as Rose walked the rest of the way up the walk, climbed the stairs, and opened the front door. A sense of trepidation made her shiver more than the cold wind pulling at her skirts. She bundled her coat about her and walked away quickly as though she could outrun the feelings of disquietude that chased her into the night.

Dora credited her sentiments to her recent nightly reading of William Shakespeare's MacBeth, but she kept replaying a specific quote from the classic over and over in her mind.

"Something wicked this way comes."

CHAPTER 40

SATURDAY, DECEMBER 27, 1890

Snowflakes drifted lazily out of the sky like goose feathers released from a massive feather pillow. Rose sat in the dining room with Annie and Mrs. Hendy while they planned the meals and festivities for the coming week.

The celebration of Christmas Eve and Christmas Day had been a success in the Mitchell household, especially considering the amount of tragedy the family endured over the past year. Freddie and Lotte were treated to many of the sights, sounds, and traditions of the Yuletide, including a massive pine tree that had been cut down and delivered on Christmas Eve.

Lotte clapped her hands in delight at the sight of the sparkling ornaments and gifts left on the branches, and Freddie had carved a beautiful angel in memory of his mother for the top of the tree.

George surprised all of them by bringing gifts into the parlor on Christmas morning, a bicycle for Freddie, a porcelain doll for Lotte, new gloves and scarves for Annie and Mrs. Hendy and a beautiful gilt music box for Rose. Everyone had been taken aback by his thoughtfulness and generosity, Rose most of all.

George had not even mentioned celebrating Christmas, so Rose had not expected his cooperation, let alone his participation in the festivities. He led the singing of carols on Christmas Eve as they lit the candles on the tree and placed the angel at the top. He helped Freddie and Lotte place their stockings by the fireplace so Father Christmas could fill them with goodies. He even carved the roasted goose at the Christmas Day dinner table.

The children were delighted with their father's sudden interest in them. Freddie beamed as George praised his workmanship on the carved angel. He shouted in excitement when George wheeled in the most expensive bicycle from the Bailey Store and handed it to him. Little Lotte seemed more hesitant of her father's attention at first as she was unaccustomed to his presence, but she soon warmed up to George's charms and insisted on sitting upon her father's lap while opening her gifts, including an expensive doll with dark golden curls like Lotte's that had been in the Speidel Jeweler's window display only a few days before.

Rose felt embarrassed to give Lotte the rag doll she had made, it was so simple in comparison to the exquisitely painted doll with silk clothing that sat beside Lotte on her father's lap. Rose did admit some relief at Lotte's squeal of joy when she saw the rag doll and Freddie's grin when he recognized the material came from one of their mother's robes. Lotte even insisted on taking the rag doll with her when she was taken upstairs for her afternoon nap.

Rose smiled as she sat at the dining room table, remembering her joy at opening her gift from George. The small gilt box had a rose etched in the top and the delicate notes of "Fur Elise" played as the tiny handle was turned. Rose had never been given so beautiful or personal a gift as this in her life. She was certain the advice from Dr. Lovering and the others had hit their mark.

"Rose, you look like the cat that ate the canary. Have you heard a word that I am saying?" Annie's scolding tone broke through Rose's musings. "Should we plan on serving oysters or black-eyed peas and greens for New Year's Day? Dr. Mitchell loves oysters, but I don't think the children will enjoy them. Black-eyed peas are considered the luckiest of foods and I think we can use all the luck we can get." Annie nodded emphatically to prove her point about the selection she preferred.

Rose enjoyed the oysters, but she nodded her agreement with Annie's menu preference. She knew if Annie was happy with the main menu there was a good chance that the cook would add other delectable dishes to the fare. She made a mental note to buy some oysters for herself soon and make a special dish of them for George as well. Perhaps she could turn the special treat into a dinner for just the two of them to share. After his extravagant Christmas gift, she felt anything was possible.

Rose still intended to talk with Ella so there would not be hard feelings between the two of them in the future. She knew once Ella understood Laura's last wishes regarding George and the children that she would bow out of the attachment gracefully. With Ella's beauty and sweetness, it wouldn't take long for her to find a dozen new beaus if she was so inclined. In fact, Rose might be able to suggest a few eligible young bachelors who would be perfect for her friend.

It was in that moment of inspiration that Rose decided to combine her hankering for oysters with a small party including Ella and some of the other young ladies. She would play the hostess and even include Mae Hyndman to show the young lady that her original scenario involving Ella and George had been misguided, it was actually Rose who would be heading for the altar soon after the new year.

"I think the black-eyed peas are the perfect supper for New Year's Day, Annie. If you plan a dish of Hoppin' John along with leafy greens and cornbread, there should be a multitude of good fortune in store for us all. As a matter of fact, I intend to eat a double portion!"

CHAPTER 41

MONDAY, JANUARY 5, 1891

Dora Wilson sat in the small rocker at the front of her millinery shop as Rose entered the shop door. The brisk January wind broke through the door at the entrance and brought a sudden chill to the elderly woman's face and hands. Dora shivered, assuming it was only the natural reaction to the elements and not the continuance of the pervading sensation of ruination that had harassed her waking moments since the evening she had taken Rose home. Dora attempted to cast off the apprehensiveness by giving Rose her most agreeable greeting.

"Good morning, my dear! I have just laid out the tea and scones, so come and warm yourself." Mrs. Wilson pointed to the teapot in its cozy, set on a tray with two china cups. A blue plate held fresh scones, wisps of steam rising from each golden pastry. A small pot of strawberry jam and a dish of clotted cream finished out the offering.

Rose's mouth watered at the sight and scents of the delectable repast. She removed her coat and hat and stored them with her reticule behind the counter. As she returned to the small table, she noticed the small red plaid bonnet still sitting where she had left it before Christmas.

"Have you heard any word of how little Sofie is faring? The poor little darling has been sick for so long." Rose sat in the chair beside the table, picked up the teapot and poured the fragrant oolong tea into both cups. She handed a cup to Mrs. Wilson. Rose took a hot scone and placed it upon a small plate, placing a smear of strawberry jam and a dollop of clotted cream on the scone as Mrs. Wilson smiled and shook her head.

"No. Mrs. King said to wait and deliver the bonnet later as Sofie was too ill to even stay awake for her Christmas dinner. It's been over a week since Christmas and there still has not been any word. I have been so concerned for the poor wee soul." Mrs. Wilson stirred her tea then reached for one of the scones. "I can tell you were not raised in Scotland as you put the jam on your scone before the cream. Every genuine Scot knows the cream goes first." Mrs. Wilson chuckled good-naturedly and winked as she demonstrated correct form by buttering her scone with the clotted cream and placing a small glob of the strawberry jam in the center.

"We didn't have anything like your heavenly scones when I was growing up on the farm. The only treat my mother made was the Chrusciki or Polish angel wings and those were very rare. I would love to travel to Scotland and other countries around the world to learn about the cultures and traditions. There are so many places I wish to see." Rose bit into the scone and wiped the sides of her mouth with her handkerchief.

"My parents brought us from Scotland when I was just a little girl, but I can tell you I never wish to take an ocean voyage again. We were crammed in tight quarters with so many of the passengers very ill with seasickness and the like. My mother fought so hard to protect my brother and me from getting sick that she fell ill herself and though she did not die she never quite recovered physically. I could not wait to get on land again and vowed I would always stay away from the sea. When my father took us inland towards Wisconsin territory, I took it as a sign I would never have to worry about it." Mrs. Wilson rocked back and forth quietly for a few minutes, caught up in the memory of her family emigrating to Wisconsin.

"My mother mentioned coming from Poland only a couple of times. She made it sound like one of the worst things that ever happened to her." Rose took another sip of her tea before she proceeded. "I intend to travel first class instead of steerage when I go abroad. I think it will be important for Freddie and Lotte to see Europe. I am sure Laura would have wished for me to take them."

Mrs. Wilson stopped rocking in her chair to stare at Rose. "Rose, I know you have ideas about marrying the doctor, but don't you think you may have to change them? I would hate to see you devastated again because your plans did not work as you thought they should. Believe me when I say it might be for your best interests if you get as far away as possible from Dr. Mitchell and this town.

I will miss you very much, but I am willing to see you situated somewhere else away from here. My brother and his family settled in Iowa, and they would welcome you as one of the family while you find a new position. I might even be persuaded to move there as well if the right opportunity presented itself. We could build a new millinery business there together."

The teacup in Rose's hand rattled slightly as she held it. She set it down on the tray before turning to look at Mrs. Wilson's earnest face. There was a look of pleading in the gentle lady's eyes Rose found difficult to resist. She would do anything for her dear friend, but she could not release the promises that she made to Laura.

"As much as I would love to continue our work together, I feel my situation may change next year. Dr. Mitchell has been very agreeable towards me lately and it leads me to believe he has heeded the advice of some notable citizens who advised him to marry me and allow me to continue to raise his children. I know Ella was attracted to him, as many other women have been in the past, but I think she will understand when I explain it to her." Rose smiled as she related her happy news, pondering why Mrs. Wilson's face portrayed sentiments that this was not happy news.

"Exactly when do you plan to explain this to Ella? She may not react the way you expect. I would hate to see the two of you at odds." Mrs. Wilson shook her head as she placed her hand to her brow and closed her eyes in consternation at Rose's revelation.

"I have devised a plan for it. I am asking her and her sister to join me for a dinner party this Thursday. I will lead them all to believe it is a going away party for Mae, but I will seek out some time to have a private conversation with Ella. She is less likely to react in a disagreeable manner if the other girls are in another room. The invitations are in my reticule, I am handing them out this afternoon."

Rose's well-constructed plan only increased Mrs. Wilson's consternation. It reminded her of a spider spinning an intricate web, then lying-in-wait.

"Rose, even if Ella is agreeable to this plan, I think it would still be ill advised. You seem to be basing your entire marriage to this man on the raising of these children. What happens when both are grown, and you are left in a marriage that was never based on love and trust? You deserve to wait until you find someone who will love and cherish you as his wife instead of someone who is looking for a nanny while he takes the attention that belongs to you and gives it to others. Even if he remains physically faithful to your marriage, if he gives his time and attention to other women, he is unfaithful and does not deserve you." Mrs. Wilson stood from her chair and approached Rose, placing her hand on Rose's shoulder in entreaty.

Rose felt heat in her face as the color of anger tinged her cheeks. She knew Mrs. Wilson was a very kind woman and did not wish to hurt her by telling her what the rest of the town believed. Rose was not good enough to marry into the Mitchell family. She was only the hired help, like Annie and Mrs. Hendy. Ella would be considered acceptable in the town's standards to become the new Mrs. Mitchell.

"People marry every day for reasons less honorable or idyllic than the ones I have chosen. While it is not a storybook romance, I will have advantages of position and wealth I would never have if I married a poor farmer like my own father. I have witnessed what it's like to live in poverty and raise a passel of children while losing one's health and all of one's dreams. It is exactly what happened to my own mother, and I'll be hanged if I follow suit." Angry tears coursed down Rose's face. She swiped at them with the back of her hand, refusing to look back into her employer's face after her tirade. No one was going to stop her from seeking this arranged marriage to George Mitchell, not even Mrs. Wilson.

Mrs. Wilson kept her hand on Rose's shoulder, a gentle presence of acceptance rather than her initial entreaty for Rose to relent. She handed Rose a hat form with fabric to be stitched and returned to the counter to gather materials for their next order. The two women worked in an uneasy silence for the next hour until the jangling of the bell on the shop door caused both to look up from their labors.

Mrs. King, her eyes brimming with tears, entered the shop, causing both women to hold their breath with trepidation. Rose stood and felt dizzy as though a black fog was about to envelop her and cast her down into its depths. She gripped the counter next to her, knuckles turning white at the effort while she waited for the pleasant lady to speak. Rose did not realize she was murmuring a prayer out loud until she saw the surprised look on Mrs. King's face.

"Rose, are you unwell? You look as though you may pass out where you stand. Do you need a glass of water?" Mrs. King glanced at Rose with concern. When Rose shook her head no, Mrs. King continued, "I came to pick up Sofie's bonnet. After being wretchedly ill for so many weeks, she sat up in her bed this morning and asked for toast with jam and her new bonnet from Mrs. Wilson and her friend, Princess Irene! It is nothing short of miraculous."

Rose sat down in Mrs. Wilson's rocking chair with a thud, the relief that Sofie had not been lost draining all the energy from her limbs. Mrs. King paid Mrs. Wilson for the bonnet and came to pat Rose's shoulder in sympathy, glancing at the milliner with a look of curiosity about Rose's bizarre behavior. Mrs. Wilson quietly nodded her head in return while wrapping the bonnet in tissue paper. Both women watched as Rose sat rocking and humming to herself with her hands covering her eyes.

Finally, Mrs. King wished both women a good day and left the shop. She passed Mrs. Lovering on her walk home and shared her wonderful news about little Sofie's recovery as well as her concern over Rose's peculiar conduct in the shop.

Before nightfall, the entire town heard the glad tidings about Sofie King and the account of Rose Zoldoske's erratic demeanor, the latter news traveling even faster than the former. It was a small town after all.

CHAPTER 42

WEDNESDAY, JANUARY 7, 1891

The bitter January wind pushed against the front display windows of the Bailey Dry Goods Store, causing the movement in the glass panes to emit a sound like that of a person sighing. Ella sat at her desk in the small alcove at the side of the room, leaning her face against her hands while rubbing her temples in a circular motion.

Ella felt homogeneous with the window's sighing sounds; she had tossed and turned all night and rose before dawn, rumpled and feeling out of sorts with the world. She burnt the bread she was toasting for breakfast and spilled her tea on her mother's braided rug, leaving an ugly brown stain on the cream-colored surface.

Even her customary walk to work, which usually made her refreshed and cheerful, left her irritable with the warning signs of a nagging headache. Uncle Charlie greeted her at the door and, after being rebuffed with her aloof silence, had quietly gone to work in the back storeroom, leaving Ella alone in her dark mood.

The sudden jangling of the bell on the shop door sent sharp pains clawing up Ella's spine to the base of her skull. She lifted her head from her hands to see George approaching her private alcove from the doorway and felt a mixture of excitement and annoyance warring with one another. Ella attempted her brightest smile as she stood to greet him.

"Ella, are you feeling alright?" George noted the dark circles under her eyes and the wincing as she attempted to open her eyes widely and smile. "You look as though you are in pain, my dear."

"I didn't sleep well last night so I am feeling a bit peaky today. I am sure it will go away soon." Ella attempted to answer in a light conversational tone that belied the throbbing pain in her temples.

George placed his hand on Ella's arm, feeling her wrist for a pulse as she stood swaying slightly beside him. He guided her back into her chair and stood close to her for support.

"You don't have to be brave for my sake, Sweetheart. Is your head hurting terribly?" George leaned in close to touch the side of Ella's face and then moved his hand to her forehead. His touch felt cool and smooth. Ella attempted to nod in the affirmative but winced from the pain the motion caused.

"I was taking a bottle of headache medicine to one of my patients after I stopped here to see you, but it looks as though you could use it more readily. Let me get you a glass of water and we will mix some of it in". George left Ella's side to cross over to the other side of the store where a barrel of water was kept. He picked up a clean glass jar from behind the counter and turned the spigot in the barrel to partially fill the jar. He returned to Ella holding the glass jar of water and took a small brown bottle from his coat pocket.

"I will have you feeling your usual bright and beautiful self in no time." George uncorked the small brown bottle and poured a few drops of the liquid into the water. He swirled the liquid into the water by making a circular motion with the jar, mixing the two liquids together into a solution with a lovely dark purple hue. George sniffed the liquid and took a small sip before handing the jar to Ella.

"What is this? I have always been quite careful with remedies as I react strongly to them." Ella sniffed at the liquid; it had a sweet, pungent odor that was pleasant.

"It is a tincture of belladonna. I use it frequently for my lady patients' ailments. Not to worry, my dear. In Italian it means 'beautiful woman', as the Venetian women took it as a beauty aid in ancient Italy. It will help with your pain although you do not need any beauty treatments in my estimation." George chuckled in an intimate fashion as he nodded his encouragement.

The warmth caused by George's compliments seeped into the coldness surrounding Ella's thoughts. She smiled at him as she lifted the jar to her lips and sipped the sweet berry concoction. Ella closed her eyes and felt an almost immediate relief from her pain. She felt as though she were lifted upon a cloud, light and airy, as the darkness was banished from her body and soul.

When Ella opened her eyes again, George was kneeling next to her, watching her with an appreciative, knowing, smile playing about his lips. He leaned forward and kissed the tip of her nose. Ella knew she should object to such a public display of affection. Even though they were alone in the store, absolutely anyone could waltz through the door at any time. Instead, Ella grasped George's face between her palms and kissed him soundly on the lips. George returned the kiss with a passion Ella had never experienced.

Ella gasped in breathlessness as she pulled herself away from the embrace. She longed to continue exploring these newfound sensations but knew they had already encroached the boundaries of what was considered decent by highly moral, small-town standards. Her face transformed from a pale, wretched visage of pain to a dewy, translucent glow, beautiful to behold. Even the pupils of her eyes widened, causing her hazel eyes to form voluminous liquid pools that seemed endless in their depths.

"Belladonna, beautiful woman", George whispered in a breath against Ella's neck as he attempted to pull her close again. Ella's heart began to beat in a staccato rhythm at the sound of longing in George's voice.

Ella attempted to stand from her chair. She knew she needed to distance herself from George's nearness to her. She was not concerned about what George might do at this point; he had always been a gentleman in her presence. Ella feared what she might do if she allowed herself to proceed without restraint. She wanted to blame the belladonna, but she knew it was unlikely the drug would have taken effect so swiftly.

"Dr. Mitchell, you are a miracle worker! I find myself completely cured in your capable hands." Ella's hands still trembled as she walked to the corner of the desk, placing the piece of furniture between them.

George stood, understanding Ella's intentions of placing the physical barrier between them and thereby dispelling the intensity of the passionate embrace. His eyes were downcast, and his face was somber as he reached for his hat upon the desk.

"Forever your servant, my dear. Please advise me when you have further need of my capable hands." The last part of the sentence was said as he lifted his eyes to meet Ella's, pulling her in with just a look of rakishness.

George turned to exit the alcove with Ella following a short distance behind him. Both stopped in their tracks as they entered the main store. Just a few feet away from the alcove stood Rile Smith, Mae Hyndman, and Annie McClaren staring at the couple as they made their entrance.

All three people had made their way into the store without Ella and George noticing and all three people had obviously overheard the last part of Ella and George's conversation by the looks of shock on their faces. Rile looked disappointed, Mae looked jealous, and Annie looked angry and horrified to find her employer in such a compromising situation.

Uncle Charlie took this moment to return from his seclusion in the back storeroom to find all of them staring at each other in awkward silence. He watched as George took his leave quickly, leaving Ella to deal with the embarrassment alone.

Ella kept her head up high and patiently waited on each of the customers as if nothing out of the ordinary had occurred. Annie was last, and especially brutal, refusing to speak to Ella, merely pointing at the objects she wished to purchase and signing the ledger under Dr. Mitchell's account.

"And not even a year since his poor dear wife passed. For shame." Annie muttered the scolding under her breath but just loud enough for Ella to hear. "I am thinking other parties will be very distressed to hear about this when I get home."

Annie's threat was clear. She was going home to tell Rose about the scandal. Ella realized that Rose's party for Mae was tomorrow night and she and Lillie promised to bring the cake so she could not back out of the plans without causing even more harm to her reputation. She would have to face them all in George's house.

Ella returned to her desk in the alcove. She noticed George had left the small brown bottle of belladonna on her desk for her future use. Ella realized she might need more of the belladonna to help her brave the future discomfort of facing Rose and the others the following night.

Ella went back to her bookwork without the pain of the nagging headache but with a heavy feeling of trepidation. At the end of the day, she placed the small brown bottle in her reticule and headed for home. She was so distracted by the events of the day and the coming events of the following day she never thought of reading the label on the small brown bottle. It had originally been prepared by old Dr. Lovering and sold to George.

The handwriting on the bottle was the almost illegible spidery script of Mrs. Lovering. It simply read, "Belladonna, Deadly nightshade, Use with utmost caution."

CHAPTER 43

LATER THAT EVENING

The tantalizing aroma of beef stew greeted George as he entered the house from the front door. Rose, Freddie, Lotte, and Mrs. Hendy all sat around the dining room table as Annie served the rich brown stew with steaming biscuits she had just pulled from the oven. Happy chatter and clinking silverware added to the warmth of the scene before him as he paused in the doorway to watch the family at dinner.

Freddie laughed as Rose teased him about the way he tossed the too hot biscuit back and forth in his hands as though it were a toy. Freddie responded by taking a huge bite of the biscuit followed by a gulp of milk to cool his mouth from the scorching morsel, then proceeded to shove the rest of the biscuit in his mouth as he reached for another. Annie playfully swatted at his hands as he grabbed two more of the biscuits from the platter she held, causing Lotte to laugh and clap her little hands at her brother's antics.

Mrs. Hendy cleared her throat loudly as she was the first to notice George standing in the doorway. Most of the happy chatter ceased immediately except for Lotte, who was not old enough to realize that the sudden presence of her father changed the jovial atmosphere. Lotte continued to chatter and laugh, waving at her father when she noticed him standing there in the now silent room.

"Good evening, everyone. I see dinner is just being served, which is fortunate as I find myself quite famished." George walked to the head of the table and pulled out his chair, seating himself as the others continued to eat quietly, glancing at one another surreptitiously.

"Annie, the stew, and the biscuits smell divine. The scent made my mouth water as soon as I opened the door." George graciously held the bowl from the place setting in front of him so that Annie could serve him. He was trying to placate the housekeeper so she would forget her anger towards him and Ella earlier.

Annie's response was a curt nod as she served the stew into his bowl and set the platter of biscuits on the table next to George with a hard thump. Rose and Freddie looked up from their meals in surprise as they watched Annie glare at George and whirl herself to face little Lotte sitting in her highchair at George's left side. Annie smiled at the baby as she smoothed the curls on the top of Lotte's head.

"That's right, sweet girl. Do you like Annie's biscuits? Such a beautiful child you are. I swear she looks more and more like her dear mama every day." Annie handed Lotte another bite of biscuit slathered in butter as the baby cooed her appreciation for the tasty morsel. She opened her tiny mouth, resembling a baby bird, as Annie popped the biscuit into it. Everyone at the table, including George, smiled at the sight. Annie turned to exit through the kitchen door with a loud "humph", clearly indicating she was not placated by George's attempts at complimenting her.

George took a bite of the stew; the beef and vegetables were tender without being soggy and the rich brown broth was savory. George took several more bites before he reached for one of the biscuits on the platter. The biscuit was light and fluffy, the airy crevices baked within it were perfect for soaking up the brown broth of the stew. George tore the biscuit in half and dunked one half into the bowl of stew, savoring the combination.

George finished half of the biscuit and reached for the other half when he noticed all the others gathered around the table had ceased eating to stare at him. He brought the second half of the biscuit to his mouth and smiled at the assemblage as he popped the entire half into his mouth at once.

Freddie's mouth dropped open in surprise. George was constantly correcting him on his table manners, so the use of the biscuit as a spoon for the stew and the cramming of the biscuit into the mouth made Freddie wonder who the man sitting in front of them might be. Freddie glanced at Rose, seated next to him, to see what her reaction to this extraordinary break in deportment was. Rose continued to stare at George with her eyebrows raised but a slight smile playing at the corner of her lips.

"When I was only a boy in the Battle of Hancock there was a kind lady who made some fresh biscuits for us out of the last of her supplies. She was so grateful we showed up to protect the town. She baked them by the dozens, and we stopped at her doorway to take several each. They were steaming hot, but we ate them quickly, burning our mouths. I didn't think I would ever enjoy a biscuit as much as I enjoyed those, but Annie has made a close second." George held a biscuit up and handed it with a wink to Freddie at his right side. "There are just some things in life that should be appreciated to the fullest."

Freddie accepted the biscuit from George and, after a moment's hesitation, broke it in two to dunk it in his stew broth, following his father's example. He brought the biscuit to his mouth and took a bite, closing his eyes in appreciation of the savory combination. George chuckled as Freddie crammed the rest of the half into his mouth and continued to eat his stew and biscuits together.

Annie returned from the kitchen holding a dish of tapioca pudding. She spooned the creamy treat into the small dessert bowls, handing it to each person around the table, giving an extra serving to Mrs. Hendy for Lotte. As they ate their dessert, the cheerful conversation returned along with the clinking of the dessert spoons against the dessert bowls.

George savored the tapioca pudding, one of his favorites, but he refrained from complimenting Annie any further as he realized the housekeeper needed time to calm down. He caught snatches of the conversation between Rose, Freddie, and Annie as he sat quietly.

"I will bring the oysters home early in the day so you will have plenty of time to make the oyster stew, Annie. I appreciate your help with our little soiree for Mae. I will also pick up some fresh oranges and Ella and Lillie are bringing a cake." Rose was smiling at Annie but stopped suddenly at the look of sheer disapproval she received from the housekeeper. "Is there something amiss with the plans? I thought we worked them out last week?" Rose looked confused at Annie's reaction.

"You are having a party here tomorrow night?" George's question flew out of his mouth before he was aware he had asked it. He heard Ella's name along with Mae's and the churning thoughts of the awkward situation from earlier in the day disrupted his enjoyment of his dessert. The creamy concoction turned sour in his mouth immediately. George reached for his glass of water to wash it down.

Rose, Freddie, and Annie all turned to stare at him once again. Rose and Freddie looked confused while Annie remained openly hostile, glaring at George with her hands placed upon her hips and her head cocked to one side in defiance. George knew he needed to diffuse the situation before it grew out of his control.

"Frederick, close your mouth. You still have food in it." George didn't recognize himself as he barked the order at his son. George resorted to his usual pattern of behavior, finding a perceived fault in his son so he could divert any real fault away from himself. He watched as Freddie's soul crumpled in front of him. The boy shut his mouth and turned his eyes to look at the table while the red coloring of humiliation crept up his neck, face, and ears.

"I am going to find my paper in the parlor." George rose from his chair and made his way out of the room. His enjoyable meal had been ruined by the unfortunate mention of Rose's party and Annie's reaction to the parties attending. He did not understand why he could not just enjoy his children and his home without someone else causing trouble.

By the time George found his evening paper and settled in his chair in the parlor, he made up his mind to begin instituting some much-needed changes in his household. George determined the best way forward was to remove those who caused the turbulence, mainly Rose and possibly even Annie, if she did not acquiesce.

No one would be able to pay the housekeeper what she was currently making in the Mitchell household and George knew he could use this fact in his favor to regain Annie's compliance. There might be a reason to remove Mrs. Hendy as well if Ella decided she would accept the role of mother to Lotte and Frederick. Lotte would be easy enough to handle as she was too young to object and Frederick was old enough for military school if he would not accept the new changes.

There was a slight tap on the door as Rose and Freddie entered the parlor. George ignored them as they walked to the small table where their game of checkers was set up, sitting down to their nightly match. George looked up to see Rose remove a paper bag filled with chocolate creams from the desk and offer it to Freddie. The boy shook his head in refusal of the treat and Rose placed the bag back in the desk. The two whispered back and forth as they played the game, each whisper grating on George's nerves.

"I have decided it is high time to make some changes in the household." George snapped his paper shut and looked at Rose and Freddie seated by his side. "Lotte is in need of more than a caregiver and it is time for Frederick to make some decisions regarding his future. I think we shall sit down and have a discussion, but I will wait until after your party tomorrow night so there aren't additional distractions." George knew he could convince Ella to marry him if he had another opportunity like the delightful tryst that morning. She would give in to him soon and he would make an honest woman of her afterwards.

George was so wrapped up in his own guilty thoughts, he did not notice the two very different reactions to his proclamation from Rose and his son. One looked as though her dreams had just come true and the other looked as though his life was about to end.

CHAPTER 44

THURSDAY, JANUARY 8, 1891

Ella looked up from her bookwork as the bell on the front door of Bailey's Dry Goods jangled once again. There had been numerous customers that morning keeping Uncle Charlie and Liza McCay, the counter girl, very busy.

More than once, Ella left her alcove to go and assist them, wishing she could remain in the private area away from the prying eyes of the customers. She caught various townsfolk staring openly at her and several had been bold enough to whisper in her presence. She heard the louder whispers and each one mentioned Dr. Mitchell and herself.

Uncle Charlie was quick to rescue Ella from the gawkers, making small talk in his jovial style while distracting them from her. Ella's cheeks burned with humiliation from the forwardness of the town gossips. None of them asked for correct information about what had occurred, they only repeated the more sordid details they heard from others and added extra tidbits that were outright falsehoods.

During one of many of Ella's escapes to the back storeroom, the store's owner, Mr. Bailey himself, noticed Ella had been excusing herself frequently and expressed his concern for her health. Mr. Bailey was not among the gossip circles, so he had not heard the malicious stories being circulated.

"Ella, are you feeling poorly today? I would understand if you needed to leave early." Mr. Bailey expressed a genuine concern, making Ella grateful to her kind employer.

"Thank you, Mr. Bailey. I am feeling quite well. It has just been very busy today and I have been trying to help Uncle Charlie by fetching things the customers requested from the storeroom. He and Liza have been helping customers almost non-stop since this morning." Ella made several trips to fetch items, so she felt telling the partial truth was better than having to explain why she was hiding from the town's gossips to her employer.

"Well, see that we add an extra dollar to your wages for the extra help today. You should not have to come and wait on the customers." Mr. Bailey was well known in the town as a miserly person, so Ella knew he was being very gracious towards her. She determined she would stay and finish her bookwork for the day even if she were late for Rose's party later.

As though she were summoned by the mere mention of her name in Ella's thoughts, Rose entered Bailey's and walked past Uncle Charlie and Liza straight towards Ella. A hard knot formed in Ella's stomach. She was unsure if Annie had gone home to tell Rose about what she thought she had witnessed yesterday.

Rose was a kind girl, but she had the tendency to be very dramatic and Ella could not stand the thought of Rose creating a huge scene in the store. Ella considered another escape but saw that Rose already approached her desk, blocking the exit to the backroom. Ella would just have to try and keep Rose in a good mood.

"Hello Rose! You look pretty with your new hat." Ella rarely used a compliment as anything but a genuine statement, but she felt desperate and wanted to place Rose's focus on herself instead of Ella.

"Thank you. I made it myself." Rose's face held a slight smile as she placed several bundles on the edge of Ella's desk. Rose did not seem angry. She put a hand to her hat and adjusted it slightly, making Ella hope her idea had worked. "I stopped by to tell you that Mae, Rena, and Alice will all be arriving by 5:30 if you and Lillie can make it by then as well, we shall have supper at 6:00."

"I have quite a bit of work to finish so it may be closer to 6:00 before I can arrive. Lillie has the cake frosted and she can bring it from home and meet me here so we can come straight away." Ella omitted the words 'to your house' as she didn't wish to draw attention to the strange fact that Rose still lived in a house not her own with a family not her own.

"Yes, of course. I understand. I was lucky to have Mrs. Wilson's permission to leave early so I could buy the oysters and some oranges and get them home to Annie right away." Rose contemplated Ella with a mild interest, but she seemed very calm.

Ella drew a sigh of relief. Rose had not come to confront her and create an ugly scene. In fact, Rose was being very gracious. After the morning she endured, Ella was more than grateful for this reprieve.

"I wonder if it would be appropriate to invite Liza for supper too. I didn't think of it before, but I would not wish for her to feel left out. Would she feel offended by being invited at the last minute? What do you think?" Rose stood beside Ella glancing out of the doorway to the alcove at the group of onlookers gathered at the counter staring in their direction. Liza McCay was among the group of whisperers looking in their direction.

Suddenly Ella felt as if her reprieve was over. The same group of gossips from earlier congregated again, having heard that Rose had entered the store. They were waiting for Rose's reaction to Ella as though they were watching a play on the stage. If Rose were still innocent of hearing the circulating gossip she would soon be enlightened if Ella allowed her to remain much longer.

"I am quite sure I heard Liza discussing prior plans for this evening with Uncle Charlie. I know a few of the girls are going to church as well." Ella was amazed at the way the lie seemed to flow from her lips without effort. She realized Liza was standing among the group of gossips, and she did not wish to add Liza to the group gathered that evening. It would be all Ella could do to keep one of the other girls from mentioning it to Rose. Ella realized she must have been frowning as she saw Rose studying her with her own brows knit together in perplexity.

"You know better than I do, Ella. I just know you were always kind enough to try and include me when I first arrived and didn't know many of the girls yet. I will always remember you for that." Rose patted Ella's shoulder and turned back to the desk to pick up her bundles to leave. "I will see you and Lillie at 6:00."

Rose exited the alcove and walked past the group of onlookers that seemed to be growing by the moment. The only sound Ella could hear was the click of Rose's heels on the wooden floor as she passed the silent group and then the jangle of the bell as she made her exit.

As soon as the door closed on Rose, the loud whispers began in earnest again. Ella sat down hard in her chair, overcome with relief and more than a little guilt for her deception. She did not like this version of herself, and she knew what she would have to do to correct the situation and make things right again.

She would have to sit down and explain things to Rose, explain how she and George had come to develop feelings for each other, and ask for Rose's understanding of the matter. Ella knew she must do this very soon so she would not hurt Rose unnecessarily, but she decided to wait until after the supper was over to avoid the awkwardness of Rose's possible feelings about George ruining the party for Mae. She would hope Annie and the other girls had the good sense not to introduce the subject in the presence of Rose and the Mitchell children.

Ella picked up her pencil to resume her work so she could finish by the designated time. She grinned as she noticed Uncle Charlie shooing the group of onlookers out the door with his shop broom. She was glad she had taken a small dose of the belladonna first thing that morning.

As she felt the pangs of another headache beginning, the medicine had done its work keeping the headache at bay. Ella put down her pencil, took the small bottle from her reticule, opened it, and took another dose. She had felt enormous pressure in her head when she encountered Rose earlier, so she wanted to stay ahead of a possible headache. Feeling satisfied that she could remedy the current situation with Rose, Ella picked up her pencil and began her work in earnest.

Ella concentrated on the figures in the ledger before her until Lillie appeared at her side holding the cake they baked for the party. Ella noticed the old clock on the far wall showed 5:45 p.m. She had finished her work with a few minutes to spare. Ella closed the ledger and placed it in her desk drawer. She decided not to take the time to clean her desk off so that she would be on time. She could always arrive a little early in the morning to make certain things were neat and tidy.

"Let's go to supper." Ella laughed at the unenthusiastic expression on her sister's face as she put on her coat and hat and grabbed her reticule. They walked towards the door and waved goodbye to Uncle Charlie as they exited the store.

Ella felt rather like a Roman gladiator about to face an arena of hungry lions. There was a moment's temptation to turn left towards home when she reached the end of Court Street, but she and Lillie turned right and headed down Church Street towards the Mitchell house and the party of girls awaiting their arrival.

CHAPTER 45

THE MITCHELL HOUSE

The clanging of metal pots and pans was ringing in Rose's ears as she entered the house through the kitchen door. Annie's dark mood of the previous night had not abated by the indication of the torturing of the kitchen cooking utensils. The big black cook stove was heated to a high temperature, leaving the windowpanes with a thick layer of condensation on the inside, entombing the kitchen's occupants.

This added to the impression one had stepped up to the gate of Hades complete with intense heat, a small puddle on the floor which represented the river Styx, and the chief occupant having the disposition of Cerberus (without the two extra heads).

Rose entered the kitchen cautiously carrying the parcels of oysters and oranges plus a few more chocolate creams she purchased to replenish her supply in the parlor desk. After placing the parcels on the side counter, Rose removed her coat and hat, the perspiration from the stuffy room already forming at the back of her neck.

Annie had her back turned to Rose, vigorously stirring a kettle bubbling on the top of the cookstove. It seemed to glow almost red from the heat of the huge fire Annie built within. She did not turn to acknowledge Rose, so Rose felt it was best to leave Annie alone with her thoughts and the beating of the pans.

Rose picked up the small bag of chocolate creams from the counter and brought them with her coat and hat to the front hallway where she hung the coat on the coat tree. She proceeded to the main stairs and stealthily climbed the stairs to the second floor, knowing it was Lotte's naptime. She did not wish to wake the baby if she was able to sleep through the tumultuous sounds emanating from the kitchen.

Rose reached her bedroom door, noticing it was slightly ajar. She was almost certain she had closed the door firmly this morning trying to keep the cold draft of the hallway from robbing the small bedroom of its heat. Her room was located just above the kitchen, so the heat from below had risen through her floorboards, causing the same condensation on her small window by the dresser. Rose entered the room and noted that nothing seemed out of order. She must have been mistaken about shutting the door.

Rose placed her hat on the top of her dresser, then opened the dresser drawer looking for a bag of chocolate creams she had stashed there a week ago. The small brown paper bag of chocolates stood upright and open in the corner of the drawer. Rose frowned in consternation. She was certain she had neatly folded the top of the bag over itself so that it was closed and would not spill.

Rose picked the bag up to examine the contents. She wondered if Freddie had been in her room because he knew she kept the chocolate creams there. He might have helped himself without closing the bag. She didn't mind the boy taking the treats, but she would try to remember to ask him to close the bag again so it would not spill out onto her clothes. Rose took several of the chocolate creams and popped them in her mouth, folding the bag over itself again and closing the drawer.

The loud crashes continued in the kitchen below. Rose did not know how long the cookware could withstand the rough treatment from Annie, but she decided it was better that Annie's aggression be taken out on the inanimate objects than on innocent members of the household, herself included. She picked up the new bag of chocolates from the top of the dresser and headed downstairs using the main steps again to avoid Annie's domain.

Rose was part of the way across the parlor floor before she noticed George sitting in a chair near the desk. His expression of momentary surprise was quickly covered over with a mask of calm smugness until he saw Rose approaching the desk with a new bag of chocolate creams in her hand. He stood from the chair and stepped between her and the desk, bringing himself into proximity in the process.

"Have you just come in from outside? Your cheeks are bright and rosy. Very fetching indeed." George reached for her hand, taking the small bag from her, placing it on the top of the desk, then turning back to cover her hand with both of his own.

"Yes, your poor hand is still cold from being outside. Why don't you sit down with me for a few minutes and tell me about your dinner party?" George slid one hand to Rose's elbow, guiding her to the settee by the fireplace.

The intoxicating scent of his cologne and hair pomade mingled with the scent of the wood burning in the fireplace, creating an intense longing in Rose to be near him if only for a few minutes. She allowed him to seat her on the settee and was thrilled when he took the place right next to her instead of his usual chair across from the settee.

"I think I have a few minutes to spare but there are so many last-minute preparations to be made. I appreciate your understanding of my using the dining room and the parlor for hosting the other girls. It will be the last time Mae is here with us before she is married. Once a girl gets married, life is just never the same." Rose stared down at her hands folded in her lap. She could almost envision George getting down on one knee and placing a ring on her left ring finger. The thought made her shiver in excitement and anticipation.

"I brought you over to the fire, but you are still shivering. Here, let me help you." George had mistaken the shivering for coldness, but Rose refused to correct him as he gathered her in his arms and held her tightly against his chest. Rose could feel the warmth of his breath against her temple. He nuzzled the side of her face with his lips whispering something so lightly that Rose could not hear it over the sound of her heart drumming in her ears. She knew all she needed to do was to turn her head ever so slightly and accept his kiss.

The crash of porcelain shattering on the floor in the dining room alarmed both of them. George stood up too rapidly, causing Rose to slide off the settee onto the floor, narrowly missing striking her head on the fireplace hearth. The moment they shared was demolished and, like the porcelain in the other room, the passion was shattered into a million little shards that could not be recovered.

Rose turned until she was on her knees, using the settee as a ballast to pull herself into a standing position. George moved away from the settee until he stood in the parlor doorway looking down the hall towards the dining room. His face was contorted in anger. He completely forgot about Rose's presence.

"I have already warned that harridan about her anger this morning. I won't have her acting like this. She can be replaced and go begging on the street for a living for all I care!" George shouted angry words at the dining room door. He was greeted with deadly silence which infuriated him even more.

"I know you are listening, Annie. You are always eavesdropping on everyone in this house and all over the town. And what you don't overhear by your eavesdropping you just make up in your deceitful little tales. Just remember who you are in this town and who I am. I can ruin you!" George's anger got the best of him as he shouted his threats, raising his fist in the air against the unseen housekeeper.

The blood drained from Rose's face as she heard the malevolent tone of his voice. George's intent to do harm was genuine and not the result of a mere temper tantrum. Rose realized she needed to escape the room. She walked briskly to the doorway where George stood, pressed herself against the trim as much as possible to get around him, and walked across the hall, opening the dining room door, and closing it on the other side.

The first thing Rose noticed was Annie on her hands and knees cleaning the shards scattered on the floor with a small broom. The porcelain was sharp and had cut Annie's hands in multiple places, but she continued to clean the mess, ignoring the soft pattering sound of her blood dripping onto the floor, leaving brilliant red smears among the white shards.

Rose ran through the swinging kitchen door to grab clean rags, soaking a rag in water and wringing it out. She returned to the dining room and knelt beside Annie, taking the broom from

Annie's bloody hands and pressing the wet cloth against it. Rose sat there keeping a firm pressure on the cloth and Annie's hands.

Annie opened her mouth to speak but Rose quickly shook her head to discourage any discussion. She knew George would be listening on the other side of the door, doing exactly what he had accused Annie only a few minutes prior. In her moments of reflection while sitting in silence with Annie, Rose thought it was ironic that in so many situations the accuser is often the perpetrator of the accusations.

After a few minutes, the blood stopped enough for the two girls to help each other up from kneeling positions on the floor. Rose gently pushed Annie through the door into the kitchen and turned to clean the rest of the mess. The clock in the hall chimed as half past five. Mae, Alice, and Rena would be arriving any moment. Rose took the mess to dump into the drop bucket in the kitchen.

Annie had rags wrapped around her hands, but she stood at her post at the stove stirring the milk into the boiled oysters to create the creamy base of the soup. The scent of the fragrant soup which normally made Rose's mouth water now turned her stomach sour, churning with the turbulent emotions that assailed her mind.

"There is something I need to tell you and I have already waited too long for the saying," Annie whispered quietly without turning from her task at the stove. "I was worried I would lose my job, but I guess that is a foregone conclusion now."

"You won't lose your job. He doesn't mean what he said." Rose interrupted Annie's confession with what both girls knew was a lie. "Let's just get through this supper and then we will sit down and find a way to work all of this out."

"But that's just the thing. You won't be able to…" The ring of the bell on the front door, announcing the arrival of several guests, interrupted Annie's second attempt to apprise Rose of what appeared to be an immense burden to her. Annie closed her eyes and shook her head as she heard Rose exit the kitchen.

Rose noticed George had vacated the parlor as she made her way to the front door. Mae, Alice, and Rena stood waiting for Rose to open the door. Her stomach suddenly lurched again, causing her to gasp and throw her hand over her mouth as she closed the door behind them. She leaned against it for a moment, relishing the cold air in her face. Rose felt as if her cheeks had been set on fire. Putting the back of her hand against one side of her face, she could feel the heat emanating from it.

Rose followed the other girls into the parlor where they were removing their outer garments. She gathered them from each girl and carried them to the small anteroom just off the parlor, placing them on the bench just inside. When she turned back into the parlor, she found all three girls staring after her with looks of pity on their faces. Rose assumed she must look as bad as she felt to garner such pity from the usually unmerciful trio.

"Dinner is almost ready. I thought we could visit here until Ella and Lillie arrive. Ella told me this morning she might be delayed for a bit." Rose gestured for the three to make themselves comfortable on the parlor furniture as she leaned against the parlor doorway. Her head spun, making her blink rapidly as she felt for the chair just in front of her. Her stomach was churning wildly.

"Ella is still coming tonight. I thought she would cancel." Mae looked genuinely shocked. Rose glanced at Rena, who made a soft clucking sound with her tongue, and Alice, who awkwardly stared at the floor in front of her. Rose tried to focus on the baffling responses about Ella, but her angry stomach was taking front stage, causing her to focus all her energy on refraining from emptying its contents right there in front of everyone.

"I brought a special visitor to your gathering, Ladies." George entered through the parlor door carrying Lotte in his arms, followed by Freddie and Mrs. Hendy, who looked as bad as Rose felt. The nanny's eyes were red-rimmed and puffy as though she had been crying.

Rose noticed that Mae and the other girls ignored George completely, an uncustomary female response to the physician. They smiled brilliantly at the curly-haired little girl who blew kisses at them and laughed. Lotte reached for Rose as soon as she saw her sitting to the side. She happily settled in Rose's lap, smiling and playing peek-a-boo with the guests who cooed at her.

Freddie entered the room quietly and walked towards the small table where he and Rose played checkers. He paused at the desk and reached for the small bag of chocolate creams still standing on the top of the desk. Rose smiled her encouragement at him but mentally took note to remind him about closing the bags when he was finished.

"Frederick, put those down. You will ruin your dinner." George's command sounded like the crack of a whip in the quiet room. All the women except Rose turned to glare at the speaker, causing George to quit the room without another word.

Rose winked at Freddie to encourage him to help himself to the candies despite the admonition from his father. Freddie selected three of the creams and offered the rest to the young ladies seated around him. Rena selected one, but Mae, Alice, and Mrs. Hendy politely refused. Freddie brought the bag over towards Rose, but she shook her head quickly to keep him from getting near with the fragrance of the chocolates. Freddie took the bag back, folded it over itself, and placed it in the desk drawer.

Lotte shifted her position on Rose's lap, causing a sharp pain in Rose's side. She signaled for Mrs. Hendy to take the baby and the two soon quit the room for the nursery upstairs.

The front doorbell rang again just as the hall clock struck six o'clock. Rose started to rise, but Mae stayed her with one hand and marched towards the door herself, throwing it open with more than a little force, surprising Ella and Lillie, who stood waiting on the other side.

Rose stood from her chair; her legs felt numb and tingling. Rena took Rose's arm as they walked to the hallway to greet the newcomers and Alice flanked Rose on the other side. By now Rose was suffering so much from whatever had taken her over she failed to notice the tense reactions of the other girls in the hallway.

"Come in, Ella and Lillie. I think Annie is just about ready to serve supper, so we can just go in and sit in the dining room." Rose progressed from the hallway into the dining room, leaving the others to follow her. She seated herself at the near end of the table and waited for the other girls to choose seats around the table.

Ella smiled as she sat down in the chair on Rose's right. "The dinner smells wonderful! I love a good oyster stew." Lillie placed the cake they brought in the middle of the table and sat down beside her sister. The other girls chose seats on the opposite side of the table and Freddie sat in his father's usual seat at the end.

Rose could hear her stomach growling in protest over the tense silence in the room. She knew she would lose her stomach if she waited for Annie to enter with the oyster soup. She needed fresh air and the chance to empty her stomach. She stood back up, swaying as she gripped the edge of the table for support.

"I must apologize to all of you. I find that I am feeling unwell, and I need to excuse myself. Please go on without me. Freddie, will you be a dear and act as a gracious host in my absence?" Rose noticed the looks of pity from Mae, Alice, and Rena and the look of horror from Ella as she watched the other girls' reactions.

Rose left the dining room quickly and headed down the hallway to the front door. She knew she did not wish her dinner guests to hear her retching as they were being served their meal. The ice-cold air hit her in the face like a slap, but it relieved the severe nausea momentarily. Rose ran around the corner of the house before she lost her stomach.

Rose stood in the snow waiting for the sickness to pass. She made her way to the kitchen door and opened it quietly, the unoiled hinges creaking noisily announcing her entrance to her guests in the other room. Annie entered the kitchen again, took note of Rose's pallor and led her up the back stairs towards Rose's bedroom. Annie helped Rose lay down on the bed and handed her a bucket she brought up with them from downstairs.

Rose passed out. She woke again an hour later when the clock chimed seven o'clock, feeling shaky but better. She was embarrassed. Her first opportunity to act as a hostess had been a dismal failure, but even worse, she had almost given in to George and allowed him to compromise her.

George had shown his true colors in his reaction to Annie. There was a part of him that was ruthless in his determination to get his own way in all things. He would demolish anyone in his path, including her and the children, if it suited his purposes. At the same time, George had the uncanny ability to convince others he was a man of great honor. He was correct when he told Annie that the whole town would believe him over the housekeeper, no matter what the circumstance.

A light knock sounded on the bedroom door and Rose attempted to lift her head and sit upright in her bed. Mae entered the darkened room and approached Rose with a light tread so as not to disturb her if she was still asleep.

"I came to check on you and tell you that we are going to leave soon for church. I hope you will be feeling better soon, Rose. I am sorry for all the circumstances that surrounded this evening. None of them were your fault." Mae sat on the bed beside Rose and patted her hand lightly.

"I am not sure what you mean by circumstances, Mae. The only thing I am aware of is a rift between Dr. Mitchell and Annie, but I am certain we can get it remedied soon. I apologize if that casts an uneasiness over the gathering. Truly, Annie means well. Please don't think ill of her, Mae." Rose sat up further, attempting to gauge Mae's reaction to Annie. She knew Mae had been very fond of Dr. Mitchell at one point, and she didn't want George to start turning the town against Annie by starting with the very outspoken Mae.

"Rose, I hate to say something that will make you more upset, but Annie is not the problem here as I see it. She was standing in Bailey's store yesterday with me when we heard the doctor making an amorous advance to Ella and she responded in kind. Their shocking behavior in public only indicates what is certainly also happening in private. I know you have been hoping that he was interested in marrying you, but please let me advise you to remove yourself from his advances and from his household before you are ruined by him as well." Mae held Rose's hand gently as she spoke. Rose was amazed this was the same young woman she met several years earlier. Mae had developed a compassion Rose would have thought was impossible for her. Rose nodded her agreement without the deep sense of loss she would have expected at this news.

Rose surprised herself further by not having a shred of malice towards Ella. In fact, she was concerned that her friend would end up marrying George and share the same fate as Laura. Suddenly, the desire to speak with Ella transformed from asking the girl to step aside to imploring her to reconsider the relationship with George for her own sake.

"Thank you for telling me, Mae. I know it was difficult for you. I wonder if you could tell Ella to come up and see me before she leaves? I think it is necessary to pass on the same precautions to her." Rose regarded the obvious surprised reaction on Mae's face even in the dimly lit room. "You have become a true friend to me. Mae and it means the world to me."

"And you to me, Rose. I will tell her you wish to see her, but I doubt she has the nerve to come up here after her behavior yesterday. Although I never expected her to show her face this evening." Mae stood and crossed to the door. Both girls noticed the shadow of someone moving down the hallway quickly, as if to prevent detection by Mae heading downstairs.

As Rose waited for Ella to appear she stood and walked to her door to peer down the hallway. She began to reconsider having this important conversation with Ella when George might overhear them and cause more trouble between the two girls. Rose had her plan formulated when Ella appeared in the doorway looking apprehensive.

"Ella, thank you for coming up here to check on me. I am feeling better, and I wonder if you might help me downstairs to see the others off. I am afraid I have been a terrible hostess." Rose reached for Ella's hand and saw the relief wash over Ella's countenance as the two made their way to the stairs. Lillie was seated at the bottom of the stairs staring up at her sister and Rose as they began their descent. Rose knew she only had a moment to say something of importance to her friend.

"It seems there have been many stories circulating today." Rose felt the jolt of alarm from Ella as she froze in place on the stairs. "You have always protected me from the gossip of others, and I want you to know I will do the same for you." Rose's whisper was only for Ella's ears, but she knew the girl heard by the tears forming in her beautiful hazel eyes gazing at Rose in gratitude.

Rose and Ella met Lillie at the bottom of the stairs and the three girls joined Freddie in the parlor. The clock was just chiming eight o'clock when Ella and Lillie started to take their leave. Freddie went to the dining room to bring back a bag of leftover oranges for the girls to take home to their siblings.

Rose went to the anteroom to get their coats and hats. She handed them to Ella and Lillie when she thought of the chocolate creams in the desk drawer. Rose knew the candy was a particular favorite of Ella's. It was the perfect peace offering to end the evening.

Rose opened the drawer to find two bags of the creams sitting side by side. One was shut and the other sat open in the drawer. Rose reminded herself again to tell Freddie to close the bags when he took a piece. She picked up the open bag and took it to Ella and Lillie with a smile.

"Hold out your hands, girls. These will make the cold walk home more enjoyable." Rose poured a share of the chocolates left in the bag into their hands. Both girls tucked the treats into their pockets as they walked with Rose to the front door and took their leave. Ella hugged Rose before she joined her sister waiting below on the sidewalk.

Rose closed the door. The stomach distress seemed to have passed as quickly as it appeared. Rose returned to join Freddie in the parlor. He had the small table set to play dominoes instead of their usual checkers game and Rose joined him at the table feeling a great sense of relief.

It was then Rose noticed the still open bag of chocolate creams still sitting on the top of the desk where she had left them. She knew she needed to ask Freddie about closing the bag before she was distracted by something else and forgot it entirely.

"I am wondering if you could help me by making sure that the bags of chocolate creams in my room and down here are closed when you help yourself to them. You know you are always welcome to them. I just don't want them to spill, especially in my bedroom dresser, all over my clothes." Rose smiled as she played her domino and waited for Freddie to take his turn.

Freddie looked up from his dominoes. Looking thoroughly confused by Rose's request, his statement quelled all her newfound relief.

"Rose, I don't know what you mean. I haven't eaten any chocolates from your room in weeks and the only two I had today were the ones I ate in front of you, and I know I closed the bag again."

CHAPTER 46

THE WALK HOME

The snow crunched underfoot as Ella joined Lillie on the sidewalk in front of the Mitchell home. Lillie sighed as Ella stopped near the gate and took off her woolen mittens long enough to take one of the chocolate creams from her pocket.

"Lands sake, I would think you would be as full as I am from all the oyster stew, bread and butter, oranges, and cake we ate. I think I will regret eating such a rich soup this time of the evening later." Lillie chuckled at Ella's lack of response to her statement as her sister's mouth was full of candy. "It looks like I should give you those candies more often. You are less inclined to argue with me since your mouth is full."

Both girls laughed as Ella grasped Lillie's arm and they walked along Church Street towards the Bailey Store. The night was crystal clear with many stars, but the sky was dark; the moon was just a tiny crescent causing each constellation to shine against the velvety blackness of the sky. Ella pointed at several constellations as they walked along the sidewalk.

"Orion the hunter shines brightly tonight and there is Taurus just above and at his side." Ella stopped as she pointed above their heads into the winter night sky. "And, over there are the Pleiades, the seven sisters watching over us from above." Ella's eyes were luminous as she gazed overhead while Lillie shook her head impatiently and pulled at her sister's arm.

"Lillie, did you ever imagine what it might be like to be up among the stars? To see the millions of galaxies that are beyond what we might know? Ella paused long enough to pull off her mitten again and take out another chocolate cream from her pocket. She popped the candy in her mouth as she sighed and took her sister's arm again. They resumed their walk, passing Bailey's store and making their way further down Church Street.

"Really, Ella. Sometimes you have the most fanciful notions. I have never thought about what might be out there beyond what we already see. I doubt there is anything at all and I doubt anyone will ever find it if it is there. To think of a soul flying about in the sky among the stars seems impossible but if anyone can manage it, I expect it is you." Lillie leaned her head against her sister's shoulder, feeling a slight shudder run through Ella's body. "Are you getting cold? I can feel you shivering."

"No, I feel rather odd. My legs feel numb." Ella shifted her head from gazing above to looking down at the ground, closing her eyes briefly and putting her free hand to her forehead.

"Do you feel sick in your stomach? I am always worried about getting a bad oyster when we eat them." Lillie stopped their progression to look into Ella's eyes and feel her face. The pupils in her sister's eyes appeared larger than normal, but Lillie couldn't tell in the darkness if they were out of the ordinary.

"My stomach hurts but I don't feel sick. I don't know what is wrong, even the chocolates tasted bitter when I ate them and there is still a terrible taste in my mouth." Ella shuddered again, bending slightly at her knees as though she might fall forward.

Lillie put her arms around Ella, trying to keep her from falling as they progressed another block towards the corner of Union Street where they turned right and came to the corner of Park Street. It was now only a turn to the left and part of the block, but Ella was failing rapidly. She began to cry as she staggered forward.

"Lillie, what is the matter with me? I feel so queer. I don't think I can walk any farther." Ella's plaintive wail pierced the stillness of the darkness around them and went straight through Lillie's heart. Lillie tried to gather Ella into her arms again to keep her from tumbling forward onto the frozen ground.

"Please don't touch me. It hurts so badly when you do. Please Lillie, go and get Mama." Ella gagged and coughed violently as she started to choke. Suddenly, she pitched forward, hitting the ground with a violent thud; she had not been able to use her hands to break her fall.

Lillie screamed as she ran part of the way towards Maly's house, "Mama! Mama! Come quick! Something is wrong with Ella!" Tears coursed down Lillie's cheeks as she screamed again, "Please! Will someone come to help us? My sister is hurt!"

Lillie watched as her mother emerged from their kitchen side door with an oil lamp in her hand. She waved wildly with both hands in the air to get her mother's attention in the darkness. "Over here, Mama! Ella is over here!"

Catherine Maly ran across the side yard as Lillie led her towards the barn, located near the spot where Ella had fallen. She could hear thrashing sounds and gurgling as though her daughter were being held under water. She found Ella's crumpled body on the sidewalk, her face downward into a snow drift. Catherine landed on her knees hard and reached to flip Ella's body, bringing her head up out of the snow.

The gurgling sound was replaced by a blood curdling scream as Ella's body, bloated and stiff, repelled her mother's touch.

"Don't touch me!" Ella shrieked. Her body seized violently as a convulsion wracked her tiny frame. The body tremors and gurgling and thrashing sounds escalated again, followed by a lengthy period of deadly silence as Ella's body grew rigid, arching her back up off the ground.

Catherine knew they needed help immediately. A group of neighbors assembled in the street around them, so Catherine pleaded for assistance.

"Lillie, run for Dr. Mitchell as fast as you can." Catherine glanced into the concerned faces gathered around them. She saw her neighbor, Charles Knobel, standing there and asked, "Can you run for Dr. Haskell to see if he's at home?"

"Yah. Sure, I will." The German man spoke broken English, but he understood his mission and set out running towards Park Street and the home of Dr. Haskell. The physician lived a mere two blocks from where they stood but he was one of the most sought after in his profession and Catherine had great doubts that Dr. Haskell would be readily available.

"What can we do for her? Won't she freeze out here?" Caroline Wrightman, another neighbor, knelt beside Catherine in the snow watching Ella's deathly still body. "Isn't it best to have someone carry her inside? Is there someone here who can do that?" Caroline searched the group of people for the best person to carry Ella into the house without dropping her.

"I will carry her. I can manage. Please let me help Ella." Rile Smith stepped forward, his long, angular face contorted in anguish. "Just go out ahead and get the doors open so we can move as quickly as possible." Rile bent his long body to kneel in the snow beside Ella.

Catherine watched as the stiffness in Ella's limbs and back started to wane slightly. She knew Caroline was right about moving Ella inside the house and decided it would be better if Ella was still in the tonic form of the seizure. They needed to move fast before Ella came to again.

Before Catherine could ask, Charlie and Amelia ran towards the house to hold the outer side door and the inner door to the small bedroom downstairs in readiness for Rile's approach with Ella. Catherine glanced down at Ella's still form, placing her trembling hand lightly upon Ella's chest to make certain she was still breathing. She nodded quickly at Rile across from her, and in a moment's time he scooped Ella up into his arms.

During the brief trip to the house, Ella regained consciousness. She cried out in pain and sobbed, her breath coming in shallow, short pants. Rile's heart broke to cause her pain, but he continued into the house and into the small bedroom, setting Ella gently on the bed. He backed away to allow Ella's mother and Caroline more room to attend her. The lamplighter seated himself on a chair in the kitchen, buried his head in his hands and sobbed loudly.

Mrs. Haskell arrived on the scene with the bad news that Dr. Haskell had been called out of town hours before and had not yet returned. She left Charles sitting in her kitchen so he could alert her husband as soon as he returned and went to see what she could do for Ella.

"Charles said it looked like poisoning. How on earth could that have happened to her?" Mrs. Haskell whispered to Catherine as they hovered over Ella, who was slowly coming to after another seizure.

"I am sure I don't know. She is probably the healthiest of my brood and always so careful with medicine." Catherine looked at Mrs. Haskell in confusion. How could it be poison? How would Ella have taken it? Who gave it to her?" The seeds of possible connivance had been sowed into fertile ground, the heart of a loving, protective, and terrified mother.

"What has happened here?" George Mitchell rushed into the room with Lillie at his heels. George approached Ella's bedside and took in the wretched sight. Ella's beautiful face was bloated with a tinge of blue, her closed eyes protruded from their sockets, and her lips curled back, baring her teeth in a grimace. There was a noisy rattling rasp to her breathing that was apparent before George even used his stethoscope to listen to her lungs.

Ella tried to open her eyes when she heard George's voice. George's heart sank when he saw the hugely dilated pupils that almost eclipsed Ella's hazel irises, even in a room filled with several lamps to add light. He took Ella's hand and noted her clammy skin and purplish nail beds on each finger as he checked her pulse; it was barely perceptible and rapid. Each consecutive seizure seemed to be ebbing the life away from her. What had she done to cause this?

George's mind reeled at the memory of the previous day when he had given Ella the belladonna; he left the bottle with her but there wasn't a way for it to cause this reaction unless she had consumed the entire bottle. George had a moment of real fear for Ella's wellbeing. It was soon pushed aside by his own sense of self-preservation.

"I need everyone to leave the room for a few minutes. There are too many of you and it isn't good for Ella." George looked at Catherine with a silent plea for her assistance. "I will call for you in a few moments when I have things in hand."

George's lie placated Catherine and she stood from the chair nearest to Ella. Catherine motioned for the others to leave the room and walked to the door, herself watching her daughter over her shoulder as she exited.

George crossed to the door and closed it, then crossed back over to Ella's bed. He had only a few moments to gather whatever indications he could find and form a plausible reason for Ella's convulsive state. Instead of assessing Ella, he walked to where her coat and reticule had been placed on top of a small bureau. Without a single hesitation, George opened the reticule and searched for the brown bottle he had given to her. He found the vial and uncorked it to see what remained of the belladonna inside.

It was still half full, meaning that while Ella may have taken multiple doses, it was not enough to cause an overdose. Relieved of his culpability, George recorked the bottle and slid it into his pants pocket to avoid detection by anyone else. Having found what he was looking for, George did not continue in his search for other possible causes.

George crossed back to Ella's bedside and took her hand once again. Ella began to writhe in pain, whimpering as she no longer had the strength to scream. George opened his bag, selected a vial of Nux Vomica, and selected a hypodermic syringe.

"George" The one word was barely distinguishable over the sound of the fluid rattling in Ella's lungs. Ella opened her eyes momentarily as George administered the injection. He patted her shoulder as he placed the syringe back in his bag and sat down beside her.

"Don't worry, Darling. I am here now, and you will be fine. Ella?" George called her name as the strong tremors began to shake her body and the gurgling sound of choking began. "Mrs. Maly, you may come back in." George called to the anxious mother who waited on the other side of the door.

Mrs. Haskell gasped as she reentered the room with Caroline and Catherine. Ella's tiny body seemed almost suspended in midair as the convulsions caused her to rise off the bed from the point of her head down to her heels. The girl sounded as though she were drowning, followed by periods of stillness so quiet they were unsure if she was still breathing.

But it was not Ella's state that caused the astonishment in the doctor's good wife; she had been with Dr. Haskell through numerous patients with seizures and had seen them before. It was the dandy of a doctor who sat beside Ella adjusting his tie and cleaning his fingernails as Ella struggled to breathe that caused Mrs. Haskell to catch her breath in horror.

Dr. Haskell arrived by midnight. Ella fell into a deep sleep interrupted by brief periods of semi-consciousness and stupor. He looked at the girl and would have admitted he would have had a difficult time determining her identity if he had not been told it was Ella.

"The worst seems to have passed. She is sleeping peacefully and should recover." George made his proclamation to Catherine and Dr. Haskell. "We shall have to look carefully at what caused this, so it does not reoccur in the future. What did Ella have for dinner?"

Catherine looked at George in amazement. "Why, Dr. Mitchell, you know very well Ella ate at your house this evening for supper with Rose and a few other girls, including her sister. None of the other girls seem to have been stricken, so how could this happen?

Catherine walked over to the bureau and picked up Ella's coat where George placed it. She stuck her hand in the pocket and drew out three chocolate creams, holding them in her hand for both doctors to see.

"I don't think anyone gets sick from eating too much chocolate." Dr. Haskell observed, dismissing the evidence with a wave of his hand. George's face had a fixed stare at the candies she still held out to them. George looked back at Ella's form, still struggling to breathe, and nodded his head in agreement.

"Yes, I am sure Dr. Haskell is correct about the candy. It is best thrown out before it melts in the heat of the room. I am willing to stay on through the night so you can rest, Dr. Haskell." George sat back down in his chair beside Ella.

"Thank you, Dr. Mitchell, but I think it is best if we both stay the night. I am not as convinced that the worst may have passed us just yet. Perhaps you should go and lie down, Mrs. Maly. We will call you if there are any changes." Dr. Haskell sat down on the chair by the door.

It was arranged for Mrs. Maly to be taken upstairs to rest by Caroline while Mrs. Haskell sat with Ella and the two doctors sat with the family and Rile Smith, who had not moved from his chair in the kitchen.

Ella woke an hour later and began to say a few sentences to Mrs. Haskell. She looked improved; Mrs. Haskell called for her husband to note the improvements in the patient.

The improvements were unfortunately short-lived, as by the time the clock struck three in the morning, Ella's convulsions began again with relentless force. They came one after another, each one causing more of her life to ebb away until the clock struck seven and the family and friends gathered to say their goodbyes as Ella breathed her last.

The grief in the house was palpable as Dr. Haskell and his wife made their way to the door for the short walk home. Dr Haskell attended many people in their final moments, but it was never more heartbreaking than when a woman so young and sweet had been suddenly taken from them. He held his wife's hand tenderly as they walked in silence.

They were on their front steps when Mrs. Haskell addressed what was troubling her the most. Her hands trembled in his as she told him her story.

"My dear, in the middle of the night when we thought Ella was improving, she awoke and asked me the oddest question, something I will never forget as long as I live. She looked straight at me and simply said, 'Is this how Mrs. Mitchell died?' Whatever could she have been thinking about, asking that question?"

CHAPTER 47

FRIDAY, JANUARY 9, 1891

The sound of barren tree branches tapping against her window woke Rose from a fitful night's sleep. She looked out her window at the gray, sullen sky and heard the wind whistling as it sought entrance through the gaps in the sill. When she turned her back to the window to return to sleep, the incessant tapping grated her nerves until, in sheer frustration, Rose threw her legs over the side of the bed and made contact with the icy wood floor below.

The house was unusually quiet, most of the occupants still asleep in their beds, as Rose tiptoed down the hallway towards the front stairs. Even Annie seemed to be missing as Rose entered the kitchen looking for a hot cup of tea to calm herself from her rude awakening. The kettle at the back of the stove was hot, and a pot of oatmeal was slowly bubbling on the front burner, so Rose made a cup of tea and helped herself to a bowl of oatmeal, adding some maple syrup from the pantry.

Rose knew Annie would have scolded her about the maple syrup, as the ascetic housekeeper felt the addition of sweeteners was far too luxurious for daily meals. She grinned as she reflected that what Annie didn't know would not hurt her and added an extra dollop of the syrup.

Rose carried her bowl and teacup to the dining room table. She sat and mulled over the events of the dinner party the previous evening. While she had intended to have a private discussion with Ella as to why she should step aside, Rose had changed her mind completely and decided to step aside herself.

If Ella was determined to marry George, then Rose would not stop them, but she hoped Ella would be agreeable to allowing Rose to remain a special aunt to the children. Rose was certain Ella would be a wonderful mother to Freddie and Lotte, loving them like her own children that she and George would most likely have in the future. In a way, Rose would have fulfilled her promise to Laura of having a good mother for the children without being that mother herself.

This allowed Rose to begin imagining what her own future might look like. She realized she might need to rethink Mrs. Wilson's offer of traveling to Iowa and setting up a business there. Ella would need some time to take her place in the Mitchell house without Rose present, for if she remained, Freddie and Lotte would not accept Ella as their new mother. Freddie had made threats in that general direction.

Rose heard the back door open, and the wind banged it against the wall. She assumed Annie had returned from an early morning errand but when she returned her dishes to the kitchen, Annie was still nowhere to be found. There was hot, soapy water in the basin, so Rose washed her teacup, bowl, and spoon and rinsed and dried them, putting them back in the cupboard.

Part of the cake that Ella and Lillie brought last night sat on a plate covered by a bowl on the counter side. Rose was tempted to snitch a small piece of the cake, but she decided to wait until later as she had eaten the maple syrup in her oatmeal. She left the silent kitchen and returned upstairs by the back stairs to her bedroom.

After completing her morning ablutions and dressing in a bright blue wool dress, Rose picked up her hat and reticule from the dresser and made her way back downstairs to the front hallway to fetch her coat. The loud ticking sound of the clock in the hall echoed in the unusually quiet house. It was just after seven-thirty.

Rose shivered against the harsh wind as she walked down the street. The clouds overhead were heavy with snow, they looked angry and turbulent. Rose hastened her steps as she turned down Court Street. Bailey's store was alight with several customers standing on the walk outside, huddled in a group around Rile Smith.

The wind pushed at the door to the millinery shop as Rose entered. She braced herself against the door, using both hands to shut it. Her cheeks were red and chapped from the brief exposure to the blustery wind and her hat had been knocked askew to the side of her head as Rose looked ahead of her into the empty shop. A small concern that something had befallen the always present Mrs. Wilson niggled against the oatmeal in the pit of Rose's stomach.

"Mrs. Wilson! Are you here?" Rose called out to her employer as she walked to the small stove at the side of the room. She removed her woolen mittens and held her icy hands out to the stove to warm them. Rose heard footsteps coming towards her from the doorway leading to Mrs. Wilson's house. She assumed some errand had brought the older woman back to her house instead of the shop. Rose began to converse as she heard the footsteps draw nearer.

"Wait until I tell you about all the goings-on last night!" said Rose. "It was a comedy of errors, to be certain. I fell sick suddenly, and couldn't be at my own dinner party, but I did get a chance to speak with Ella and there are changes I have made in my thinking about our situation."

"I now realize you gave me very good advice before, and I should have listened to you right away. Do you think you could still contact your brother about my staying with them in Iowa? I think it will be best with the changes I have made to leave sooner rather than later, and I would love it if we could talk about both of us moving. Are you surprised that I finally came around to your way of thinking?" Rose laughed as she spun around to see Mrs. Wilson standing behind her.

Rose's laughter died on her lips as she saw the pale, stricken look on Mrs. Wilson's face and the incredulous look on Mrs. Hyndman's face, who was standing beside Mrs. Wilson. Both women stared at Rose in shock, her jovial conversation now ending in abrupt silence at the sight of their countenances.

"Rose," Mrs. Wilson took several steps towards her, the tears stood in her eyes as though they would spill over at any second. "Rose, something terrible has happened." The elderly woman's hands shook as she grasped Rose's hands in her own. "Rose, Ella is gone." Tears cascaded down her cheeks at the statement.

"Gone. What do you mean 'gone'? Is Ella missing?" Rose was startled at the news, then immediately wondered if Ella had run off with George to elope. If the story of the scandal Mae had told her the night before were true, perhaps they ran off into the night to get married to try and salvage Ella's reputation. Rose would have to plan her own departure right away.

Mrs. Wilson blinked in shock at Rose's question. She tried to form the words as she shook her head. Mrs. Hyndman was not as delicate.

"No, she isn't missing you, ridiculous girl. She is dead. She died this morning after a night filled with painful convulsions. Charles Knoble was right there when Ella fell on her way home from your party. He told my husband that it looked like poisoning." Mrs. Hyndman blurted out the terrible news, including the suspicions of the neighbor, Charles Knoble. His suspicion had already circulated with the news of Ella's passing throughout the town.

"Rose!" Mrs. Wilson calling her name was the last thing Rose heard before the overwhelming darkness came to claim her and she crashed in a heap on the floor. Only one thought repeated in Rose's mind in the dim, remote world beyond consciousness.

Ella was gone. Ella was gone. Ella was gone.

"Rose, can you hear me? Open your eyes." Mrs. Wilson's voice broke through the thick fog of unconsciousness that covered Rose like a blanket. "Dear girl, you have given me such a scare. I think I see her eyelids moving, Doctor." Mrs. Wilson spoke to someone else present in the room with them while Rose searched her mind for why she was in a lying down position when she had been certain she was standing only moments before.

Rose's eyes batted as she willed herself to open them and reclaim her sensibility. Her own mind and body seemed to wage a war against her, struggling to keep her in the dim mist of oblivion.

Rose slowly forced her eyes open. She was lying down upon her own bed with Mrs. Wilson sitting next to her, shaking her shoulder. The bedroom was dark. A small opening of the bedroom door emitted light from the hallway, casting shadows on the far wall that seemed disproportionately large.

The shadow of a person standing in profile loomed over her as though he would stoop over and snatch her up like the Erlking of

German and Polish myths. The mythical villain made famous by Goethe and later by Grimm possessed the power to kill his victims with a single touch. Rose shuddered and closed her eyes to block the thoughts of the evil surrounding her. She knew she needed to escape his grasp, but she did not know how.

"Open your eyes, Rose. I have something for you to swallow. Here, let me help you." Rose felt a strong hand slide underneath her shoulders and lift her so that she was sitting up against the headboard of the bed. The other hand lifted a glass to her lips and urged her to open her mouth and drink. The contents of the glass smelled potent and yet strangely familiar.

Rose opened her lips to drink just as she opened her eyes again. George was standing over her, giving her a heavy dose of laudanum. Rose wanted to protest, to spit the concoction out, to order George to leave her room, but she was paralyzed with fear. Her mind screamed but she made no sound until the entire glass was empty and the waves of lethargy began to creep in to claim her once again.

It was in this stupefied state that a moment of clarity came to Rose, piercing the numbness pervading all her senses. Ella was taken and the Erlking returned for her.

CHAPTER 48

SATURDAY, JANUARY 10, 1891

The news of Ella's death staggered the small town as the word passed to each resident, young and old. Already the conjecture about poisoning followed the sad news, gaining credence with each telling.

The story of the evening's events; the dinner party, Rose requesting to see Ella upstairs, and most importantly, the chocolate creams, was told and retold with embellishments added for emphasis by those who were convinced they possessed the facts of the case even though they had not witnessed any of the events.

It was early in the morning as Dr. Haskell made his way back to the Maly home. He had been summoned by Ella's father, Anton, who was away from home during Ella's sudden collapse and death, along with his son Anthony. Mr. Maly wished to get to the bottom of what had occurred and trusted the physician's version of the events.

A black wreath adorned the front door as Dr. Haskell knocked and waited for entrance. Lillie, pale-faced with red-rimmed eyes, answered the door and bid the doctor to enter. He followed the girl to the parlor where Ella had been laid out and the family, minus Catherine, gathered. The grief crashed against his senses like a tide as he took in the scene of the family members in mourning.

"Thank you for coming." Anton rose from his chair to shake the doctor's hand. His hands trembled slightly but he maintained his composure as he led Dr. Haskell to the settee and motioned for him to sit. He took the place beside the doctor and spoke in a low tone.

"As you can see, things are very hard for us right now. I cannot believe I returned from my trip to Madison to find one of my daughters." Anton paused as though he could not form the next word. "I found her gone. How did this happen, Doctor? What do you know?" There was a note of pleading in Anton's voice as he wiped his eyes and looked at Dr. Haskell in earnest. "How did this happen to a very healthy young girl like my Ella?"

Dr. Haskell looked at the carpet as he thought carefully about how to answer the grieving father. He was a man of science. He believed in the validation of cold, hard facts and not in the distortion of half-truths told to misrepresent his expertise. The most difficult answer he had to give was the most honest one.

"This isn't easy to say, but I honestly don't know what caused Ella's convulsions. I do think it was so many convulsions in a row that caused Ella to aspirate fluid into her lungs and caused her to drown in those fluids even after the convulsions seemed to have subsided. Ella was able to speak to us in brief moments in the middle of the night. She professed her love for Jesus and her love for her family during those moments." Dr. Haskell paused at the memory of the young woman stating clearly as her final words, "if I had a thousand lives, I would live them all for Jesus."

Anton nodded his head as he closed his eyes. A single sob shook the man's body, bearing the hard truth about what had taken Ella's life while treasuring the precious last words of his child. The two men sat in silence while the father regained control over his emotions. The whispers and tears of the rest of the family saturated the room, their loss was beyond estimation.

The recollection of the words Ella spoke to his wife pricked at the good doctor's conscience. Ella had been intentional in asking her question of Mrs. Haskell and who was he to withhold it from her father? Against his better judgment and against his normal requirements for empirical evidence, Dr. Haskell began what would become a maelstrom of accusations in the ripe atmosphere of speculation by the townspeople.

"Ella did ask a question of my wife which I feel you may need to know. Ella asked if her current affliction was of the same manner as that which killed the former Mrs. Mitchell." Dr. Haskell cleared his throat as he saw the shock register on Anton's face and the faces of the family members gathered around the room, all of them realizing Laura Mitchell also died of similar convulsions in the prime of life.

"It may have been induced by the chloroform administered but she asked the question nonetheless and my wife is bewildered as to why." Dr. Haskell scrambled in an attempt to correct what might have been a hallucination of Ella's into appearing as something far more sinister, but the damage had been done as Anton's son, Anthony, stood from his seat nearby and stormed from the room.

Dr. Haskell took his leave an hour later after checking on Catherine, who had taken to her bed. He made his way down the walk as the group of women who would watch over Ella's body that night came towards him. It was hard for him to miss that Rose Zoldoske was in the small group, walking silently as the women whispered incessantly around her.

Rose paused when she saw the doctor staring at her. Her eyes were glazed as she stared back at him. She opened her mouth as if to speak, then shut it again and cast her eyes downward, passing him by and following the other women into the house.

The doctor stood in the path watching Rose as she walked away from him. The expression in her eyes, locked with his own, gave him the briefest sense of an animal caught in a trap. Dr. Haskell attempted to dismiss the abject ridiculousness of his observation from his mind.

He knew his sentimentality had been heightened by the seeds of speculation placed there by Ella's question. By the same token, Dr Haskell also knew that any creature caught in a trap was at its most desperate and deadliest point.

CHAPTER 49

SUNDAY, JANUARY 11, 1891

A somber mood that matched the dull-colored, leaden gray skies
blanketed the town as the pews of the Methodist church filled to
beyond capacity. The doors and more than one window were opened
to allow the mourners gathered outside to hear the funeral services
for Ella Maly.

An oak coffin with extravagant brass handles was positioned at
the altar, wreaths and bouquets of fragrant flowers surrounding it to
the point of almost obscuring it from view. There had been a line of
those wishing to pay their final respects formed since before daybreak;
each person moving through the queue until they reached the closed
coffin and Ella's parents and siblings waiting on the other side.

Anton stood with one of his hands placed tenderly on the coffin
and the other hand on the shoulder of his wife seated next to him.
Catherine had taken to her bed until that morning, insisting she must
be present to say goodbye to her precious girl. She did not speak to

those who filed past, merely nodding her head and dabbing her eyes with her handkerchief as she accepted the condolences of the entire town and county.

"I was told Mr. Bailey himself picked out the coffin, insisting on the expensive brass handles and a silk ruffle lining. The Pratt brothers ordered the handles from Chicago, and they just came in on the last train in the middle of the night." Alice Berryman whispered as she waited in the long line with Annie German, Mae Hyndman, and Rose. "My father said that the handles would have been over a week's wages for Ella or the other clerks in his store."

"I am certain Mr. Bailey is just trying to express his sentiments for Ella like everyone else. It has been such a shock for us all." Mae glanced at Rose who was staring off in the distance towards the doors of the church. "None of us realized the other night that it would be the last time we were all together. Things might have been different if we had." Mae swept at her eyes with her handkerchief, her tears forming tiny crystals on her eyelashes from the frigid temperature.

"Has anyone questioned any of you about what happened that night? Rena said Anthony Maly came to her house yesterday with Marshal Chandler to ask her about what happened at the dinner party." Alice looked at the other girls around her, nodding her head for emphasis. She glanced at Rose, who seemed to be ignoring their conversation entirely. "Rena also mentioned that Dr. Mitchell was called over to the house and asked if he thought it could have been poisoning."

"My mother said lots of people are saying Ella was poisoned because she told Mrs. Haskell she was before she died. I posed the question of who in the world would want to hurt Ella? She was kindness itself to everyone. Mrs. Brewer told us they would probably do an autopsy in the next few days to find out more. They just couldn't mention that to Mrs. Maly as she took all this so hard and couldn't bear the thoughts of an autopsy." Annie German repeated all the buzzing she had gleaned over the past two days to the other girls as though each morsel were a solid fact.

"They should just leave Ella alone. She has already been through so much. There is nothing of value to be gained from it as no two doctors will agree on the findings." Rose's voice sounded as icy as the bitter wind pushing against the huddled group. "No one would have hurt Ella intentionally." Rose added quickly, watching the dubious expressions on the girls' faces.

Mrs. Wilson beckoned Rose from the front porch of the parsonage next door. Rose seemed to look right past her until Mae nudged her and led her towards the parsonage and away from the condemnatory glances that Alice and Annie now sent her way.

"Rose, I called for you at the house and Mrs. Hendy said you left before dawn. Weren't you one of the watchers at the Maly house last night? It isn't good for you to go so long without sleeping. We don't need anyone else taking ill." Mrs. Wilson put her hand to Rose's forehead in concern. "Then, you are standing out there in the freezing cold looking as if you have been frozen in place."

"Have you heard they are doing an autopsy? Why would they do that?" The questions spilled from Rose's lips in a panic, she felt the waves of nausea, the staccato rhythm of her racing heart. She reached for Mrs. Wilson's hand to steady herself as she heard the familiar buzzing in her ears get louder and her peripheral vision start to flicker with tiny pinpoints of light and dark intermixed.

"Rose, come here and sit down. Dr. Ludwig is standing in the next room, and I am going to fetch him." Mrs. Wilson sat Rose in the chair, propping her against the wall to prevent Rose from crashing onto the floor. Rose could hear the hushed voices of Mrs. Wilson and the doctor, but the buzzing noise in her ears was so loud she could not make out what they said.

Kindly Dr. Ludwig, the county coroner, returned with Mrs. Wilson and took Rose's hand in his own.

"What's this Rose? You have frightened poor Mrs. Wilson. She said you have barely slept for two days and have been standing outside in the cold for several hours. That is enough to make anyone feel indisposed." Dr. Ludwig spoke softly to Rose as he felt the pulse in her wrist and looked closely into her eyes.

"Dr. Ludwig, do you know why they are doing an autopsy on Ella? She wouldn't want that done. Is there anything you can do to stop them?" Rose felt her breath come in short pants as the anxiety grew within her breast. "Don't let them hurt her!"

Dr. Ludwig exchanged concerned glances with Mrs. Wilson as he knelt in front of Rose and whispered, "Rose, don't concern yourself with this. Ella is with the angels where no one can harm her anymore. As for findings, they will only find what I have said since I did my examination last night. Ella succumbed to uremic convulsions because her kidneys failed. All this other conjecture about poisoning is utter nonsense."

Rose nodded and tried to calm herself using the deep breaths Lou taught her. The effects of exhaustion mixed with the side effects of the laudanum she had been consuming had her mind spinning in a million different directions. Her hands still trembled as she tidied her hair and tried to stand with the doctor's assistance. She knew she needed to return to the group of girls waiting to give their condolences before she was missed.

Mae was waiting for Rose at the front door of the church when she returned with Mrs. Wilson and Dr. Ludwig. Mae linked her arm through Rose's and the two proceeded inside the church.

The scent of flowers was overwhelming, the press of bodies standing close together in the space made Rose feel as though she was suffocating. She stood with her head down and her eyes closed as she inched forward in the line with Mae and Mrs. Wilson.

Rose dreaded seeing the coffin with her own eyes; although she had been a watcher overnight, she refused to go into the parlor where Ella lay. She knew she needed to continue to press forward and refused to show her absolute terror at being present with a dead body nearby. This had been one of her nightmares since her brother Willie died.

Mae squeezed her arm gently in encouragement and Rose lifted her head to see she was standing only a few feet from the coffin. Rose blinked as she stared ahead, not turning her head to the left or right.

It was as she stood there in the front of the church that the buzzing in her ears quieted enough for Rose to hear the buzzing of the whispers around her.

"Imagine that she has the nerve to be here."

"You can tell she is guilty by just looking at her."

"They are saying it was poison in the chocolate creams."

Rose did not have time to react as she crashed to the church floor right in front of Ella's coffin; right in front of Ella's family, right in front of a whole town watching her with judgment in their eyes.

CHAPTER 50

WEDNESDAY, JANUARY 14, 1891

The days following Ella's funeral were filled with speculation by the residents of Richland Center. Dr. Ludwig finally consented to consulting a specialist from Chicago, sending only Ella's stomach and a few other samples in glass jars to the renowned physician Dr. Haines instead of an entire autopsy.

Anthony Maly obtained the chocolate creams his mother found in Ella's coat pocket and insisted that the candies be sent for testing as well. He asked George and a family friend, Robert Burns, to assist Dr. Ludwig, in preparing the samples to be sent for testing, and told everyone who would listen to him. "We need Dr. Mitchell to help them get this right."

No one seemed to question that Dr. Mitchell's involvement with the evidence could be a conflict of interest in finding the cause of Ella's death, since he had treated her at her bedside. Most of the town began to herald him as a form of hero in his earnestness to prove that Ella was indeed poisoned with strychnine.

The whispers about Rose's involvement in Ella's death began as faint murmurs increased in intensity by the day. There were a few who believed in Rose's innocence; Mrs. Wilson, Mae Hyndman, Mrs. King, Lou and Isaac Newkirk, A.A. Ghastin, Uncle Charlie, Emma Brewer, and Dr. Ludwig, but most of the town had been drawn to the tale of murder by poisoning spun by George and Anthony Maly.

Mrs. Wilson kept Rose sheltered in the back of her millinery shop during the day, insisting Rose be spared the gossip of the townspeople. The entire town seemed to be holding its breath in anticipation of the findings that would be dispatched from Chicago. Most of the people felt it would prove Rose's guilt and a few clinging to the hope that poison would not be found.

Dr. Haskell regretted his involvement in the sordid business. He sought to bring solace to Mr. Maly by sharing Ella's thoughts during her final hours, but his words spurred the Malys into believing Ella had been murdered. More than once he tried to convince the concerned citizens of Richland County it was highly unlikely that Ella could have been poisoned by anyone. Soon the populace began condemning Dr. Haskell for his stand against popular opinion. They did not wish to hear information contrary to their school of thought and any dissension was dismissed as lies.

Annie and Mrs. Hendy remained silent. Rose initially looked to both women to help exonerate her in the community by telling what they knew of the Mitchell household and George in particular, but the sudden decision by George to retain both women when he had formerly decided to dismiss them kept them particularly quiet. While neither spoke out against Rose, their refusal to speak on her behalf made Rose appear even more guilty.

Rose was treated to a deafening silence in the house. The children were both kept from her company. Meals were brought to her room; she was no longer welcome in the common areas of the house. George was the only person to address her, giving Rose notice that she would have to vacate the premises by the end of the week, even though he knew she had nowhere else to go. George had seen that most of the doors in the town were closed on Rose.

Mrs. Wilson made a space for Rose and welcomed her with open arms. Rose's things were gathered from her room by Annie and unceremoniously dumped in the alley behind the millinery shop by several young men hired by George. The locket given to Rose by Laura was missing from the pile, as well as the beautiful music box George gave to her only weeks ago at Christmastime. Added to the pile was the ragdoll Rose made for Lotte, one of the little girl's favorite toys, now discarded by her father.

One of the oddest things absent from her belongings were sheets of Rose's personal stationery, stenciled with her initials R.Z in a flowery script at the top of each page, her wood pen with its steel nib, and her bottle of ink. Rose could not imagine why George would have any interest in them, but she realized she was not in the position to ask him to return them to her.

Rose sat in Mrs. Wilson's small parlor, a piece of fancy embroidery in her hands. She sewed almost non-stop during her waking moments, attempting to repay her employer for her generosity and succor, though no repayment was requested. She heard the shop bell ring and the voices of Mrs. Wilson and Mrs. Hyndman in discussion, then the footsteps leading to the portion of the house where she sat by the fireplace.

The door adjoining the house to the shop opened and Mrs. Wilson entered, beckoning Mrs. Hyndman to follow. Rose noted the looks on both ladies' faces as they stared at her, one of disbelief and one of indignation.

"Rose, Mrs. Hyndman has come with something rather distressing. Mae received this letter by post this afternoon asking her to lie to the authorities on your behalf. Understandably, both Mae and her mother are very upset by this request." Mrs. Wilson's hands trembled as she held a sheet of stationery in her hands.

"My Mae has been a good friend to you, Rose. However, she would not ever think of spreading falsehoods, especially swearing to such things as the truth. She has been asked to say that she requested Ella come upstairs to you and that candy was never given out. Both are bold-faced lies, as you well know" Mrs. Hyndman shook her head vigorously at Rose in disapproval.

"Yes, of course. Mae shouldn't say things that are not true, and no one should ask her to do so. I guess someone thinks I need help but lying will not help at all. I am sorry this happened to her." Rose looked at the incensed Mrs. Hyndman with curiosity as she held her hand out to Mrs. Wilson to receive the missive.

Rose recognized the stationery with the familiar R.Z. in flowery script at the top of the handwritten note. The ink was her own and the handwriting even very close, close enough to convince most that Rose wrote the note herself.

Now she understood why her stationery had been missing. She glanced up into the face of Mrs. Wilson and thought she detected the slightest seed of doubt beginning to form in her friend's eyes. George threatened Annie only a week ago with turning the entire town against her and Rose realized she was now the one George intended to ruin.

There was little Rose could do in the face of the storm brewing around her, but she needed to do something to try and save herself from complete ruin. She would need help. She would need a lawyer soon.

It was dusk by five o'clock that evening. Rose assured Mrs. Wilson she would only go on a short walk, and she would stay away from very public places. Rose hurried through the alley behind the millinery shop towards Park Street and the courthouse. She had formulated a plan that afternoon and had very little time to accomplish it.

Levi Bancroft, an attractive young attorney, stepped from the back door of the courthouse and descended the steep stone stairs rapidly. He had been delayed in court, and now he would be late for dinner. His young bride of a year, Myrtle, was expecting their first child and events like the ruination of a carefully planned meal caused her great distress, which in turn caused Levi great distress after she had finished chastising him.

"Excuse me, Mr. Bancroft. Do you have a moment?" Rose stepped out from the side of the courthouse that was sheltered from the street by a small group of trees.

Levi wanted to respond; he certainly did not have a moment to spare, but his good manners bred from a beginning as a farm lad in Bear Valley told him he could not respond to a young lady asking for help that way. Levi was born and raised in Richland County, only leaving to attend law school in Madison, then returning to his childhood home.

"How may I help you, Miss Zoldoske?" Levi recognized the young woman who had helped at so many church and charity events and even assisted Myrtle with the decorating of the church for their wedding. He heard the horrible news of Ella's death and some of the gossip concerning Rose's involvement, but Levi was a person who chose ethical behavior over popular opinion.

"I don't really know where to begin. I find myself in a very difficult circumstance. Several prominent community members have all but accused me of harming Ella Maly, something I would never do as she was a dear friend to me. With the amount of speculation building, I am wondering if I will need to hire an attorney to defend me against the hearsay." Rose spoke softly, her voice trembling when she spoke Ella's name. Her eyes filled with tears that threatened to spill down her cheeks.

"Yes, unfortunately, I have heard some of the scuttlebutt, but you must remember you are not on trial, and you cannot be convicted by hearsay. That being said, if there are people harming your reputation by spreading malicious gossip, you may have the recourse to take them to court for defamation of character." Levi looked towards his carriage and back at the frightened girl in front of him. He knew Myrtle was waiting for him, but he refused to leave Rose standing alone on the sidewalk as he rushed away.

"I don't wish to take anyone to court. This is a good town full of good people. I just want everyone to understand I would never hurt Ella, especially her family. They have been so very kind to me ever since I arrived. I don't wish to cause them to be hurt any more than they have already endured by losing Ella." Rose swiped at her cheek, the unbidden tears streaming down her face.

"I would advise you to wait a few weeks and allow things to simmer down. Most of the talk will abate when people find something else to talk about. It is unfortunate they feel the desire to discuss supposed problems instead of possible solutions as it is a very base part of human nature. Until then, please let me know if I can be of more assistance to you." Levi removed a fine linen handkerchief from his vest pocket and handed it to Rose. Myrtle had folded the handkerchief for him that morning, but he knew she would understand and appreciate his gesture on Rose's behalf.

"Thank you for your help and understanding. Please give Myrtle my greetings. I won't detain you any further." Rose wiped her face with the handkerchief and handed it back to him. She turned to walk back across the street towards the alley and Court Street.

Levi stood to watch her cross the street safely, then turned towards his own carriage and home. He hitched the horse to the carriage and jumped onto the seat. He chose to drive down Haseltine Street towards his home further down on Sheldon Street. He only hoped Myrtle's dinner would still be servable and that his expectant wife would understand his delays.

As Levi paused to turn the carriage onto Church Street, he noticed that the Mitchell house on the corner was teeming with people, many were standing on the sidewalks and on the steps. George Mitchell and Anthony Maly addressed the crowd from the open front door. Levi frowned as he heard the words Anthony Maly shouted over the angry, noisy mob.

"We will have justice for Ella's murder! Richland County's Lucretia Borgia is going to pay!"

CHAPTER 51

SATURDAY, JANUARY 17, 1891

The sun shone brightly, sparkling off the icicles that hung from the edges of each building as Rose walked along Court Street. She felt an urgent need to take in the fresh air and sunshine, so despite Mrs. Wilson's misgivings about being seen in public, Rose ventured outside.

Rose knew Mrs. Wilson had her best interests in mind when she cautioned her about going out in public, as many of the townspeople had become openly hostile in the last week.

It was as if the wind carried the tale of the "murder by poisoning" and the "Borgia of Richland County" who had committed it to every home and farm in the county. Rose complied with her employer's wishes; she understood that Mrs. Wilson faced censure from some of her wealthiest customers for supporting Rose and giving her refuge in her home.

But, when the morning dawned bright and fair for a winter's day, Rose could not resist the temptation to leave her refuge for a short walk. Her decision to stay in Mrs. Wilson's house only made her look even more guilty to the suspicious townsfolk. As a conciliatory gesture, Rose took a path down Court Street away from the Bailey Dry Goods Store where half the town held a daily tribunal concerning her and Ella.

Rose noticed that the street seemed very quiet for a Saturday morning. None of the usual families were gathered in front of the shops, and the farmers who were almost continually present in front of the feed mill were conspicuously absent. She was relieved by the silence except for the occasional yapping of a stray dog that lived in the adjacent alley.

Working her way down the street towards the river, Rose saw the ice floe formed by the frigid temperatures and the rising of the river. The floe looked deceptively beautiful, dazzling white with shimmers of sunlight, forming the appearance of a field of diamonds. Many a novice to the river had been lured out onto the floe only to fall through the ice and have the floe close, trapping them underwater until they perished. Mothers of the town warned their sons not to play near the ice floes, but a few boys had not listened only to be lost.

Rose knew Freddie was very fond of the river. She worried he would be more careless now that she was not there to keep track of him and his playmates. She had not seen Freddie or Lotte since she left the Mitchell home. She wondered what the children were told about her sudden departure from their daily lives. Her heart constricted when she thought that either one of the children might believe the lies about her since Ella's death.

Freddie had been extremely withdrawn since the night of the dinner party. He played his usual game with Rose that evening and seemed in good spirits despite his father's foul mood, but by the time the news of Ella's death reached them the following morning, Freddie sequestered himself in his room and in his treehouse.

Freddie returned to the morose behavior that occurred after his mother's death. His behavior struck Rose as odd, since he had not known Ella well and at one time considered her a threat to the happiness of his home. Rose shuddered as she recalled Freddie's threat after they followed his father and Ella downtown.

"I don't want a new mother, Rose, and I will do whatever I need to prevent it from happening" Freddie's words spoken then slapped Rose now with their jolting, reification. The look of desperation in Freddie's eyes had prompted Rose's decision to pursue a loveless marriage with George to prevent the boy from making good on his threat.

Rose stood frozen in place, staring at the river. How could she suspect her sweet little Freddie would have brought anyone else harm? She knew Freddie might try a prank that would embarrass Ella, but he did not have a mean bone in his body. She was certain Freddie would never intentionally harm Ella or anyone else.

As she stared at the ice floe, another thought came with a sudden undeniable clarity, as clear as the crystals sparkling on the sheet of ice before her: what if Freddie put something in the candies that were supposed to make Ella embarrassingly indisposed in front of everyone?

Rose had eaten some of the candy without Freddie's knowledge and became so wretchedly ill that she had to leave the dinner party. If Ella ate more of the candy, she could have had a much more serious reaction leading to her death. In that case, it would have been a complete accident prompted by the prank of a boy, but who in this town would believe it was an accident?

Rose realized how she needed to proceed in the coming days. She would hope and pray the autopsy showed no form of poison in Ella's stomach at the time of her death, but if there was something found she would have to defend Freddie at all costs, even if it meant she would have to deflect the blame onto herself until they could find proof that Freddie did not mean to harm anyone.

She returned to the millinery shop with a new sense of purpose; the "mother" who defended her "son" at all costs.

The sun was setting when Rose heard the loud rap on the door of the closed shop. She followed Mrs. Wilson, carrying the oil lamp to light the way through the darkened room.

The town marshal, Austin Chandler, stood waiting on the sidewalk as Mrs. Wilson unlocked the door, allowing him to enter the room. Rose noticed Marshal Chandler did not look at her as he held out a piece of paper towards her. She received the missive with trembling hands.

"A dispatch has just arrived from Chicago. A finding of three-fourths of a gram of strychnine was found during Ella Maly's autopsy. Her brother Anthony has made a formal charge and Justice Wulfing has signed the warrant you hold in your hands." Marshal Chandler paused, clearing his throat.

Rose glanced at the document she held in her hands. It was a blur of words with the clear signature of Justice Wulfing at the bottom. Rose felt the black void start to envelop her, but she fought against it for the first time. She must hold out. She had to protect Freddie. She heard a loud gasp from Mrs. Wilson and felt the kind woman's arms surround her.

Everything seemed to be occurring in slow motion. The marshal reached forward to grasp Rose's arm, turning her as he brought her other arm behind her back to meet it. The manacle felt icy cold against her wrists, seeming to pierce her skin with its squeezing tightness. It matched the tightness in Rose's chest, constricting her breathing to small gasps, but she continued to fight against the haze of unconsciousness still threatening to overtake her.

"Rose Zoldoske, you are under arrest for the murder of Ella Maly. I am taking you to the county jail at the courthouse where you will be held until the time of your preliminary hearing. Do you understand?" The older man with a graying beard looked at his prisoner with the semblance of sympathy for her plight. "Mrs. Wilson can gather some of your personal things and bring them to you."

Rose nodded her appreciation at the marshal for his compassion towards her. The black fog which threatened her was now retreating to an unknown place in her mind. Rose felt a small sense of victory in overcoming one of her strongest adversaries. She would need that sense of victory for the days to come.

Tears formed in Rose's eyes and cascaded down her face as she nodded at Mrs. Wilson in encouragement. While the marshal and Mrs. Wilson misunderstood Rose's tears to be originated by her fear, only she knew their true origin. Rose looked in the face of an enemy and had not wavered or succumbed to it. In a moment that held some of Rose's greatest fears, she found her ability to press on. She found her courage came not as a lack of fear, but a willingness to proceed despite it.

CHAPTER 52

MONDAY, JANUARY 19, 1891

The bitter cold stung Levi Bancroft's eyes as he looked at the old stone jail located on the southeast corner of the Richland County Courthouse. The weather-darkened edifice stood in bold contrast to the foggy gray sky above. Sizable icicles protruded down from the roof, evoking the sense of a formidable dungeon.

Levi stepped to the side door and knocked, the sound on the massive wooden door echoing into the air, as he waited for Sheriff Snyder to admit him. He held his leather satchel under one arm and a freshly baked loaf of cinnamon bread under the other arm.

Myrtle, upon hearing of Rose's arrest, insisted on sending something to offer the poor girl comfort. He knew it was highly irregular to bring a gift to an accused murderer, but he also knew the entire business surrounding Rose's arrest for murder was highly irregular.

It was the sheriff's wife, Jane, who answered the door and bid Levi to enter and follow her into the family living quarters situated on the first floor. Jane paused in the dim corridor to retrieve the key from a ring of keys on her waist. She unlocked another massive wood door and the warmth from the woodstove in the family's small sitting room caused the spectacles Levi wore to fog over.

Sheriff George Snyder sat in a chair beside the woodstove finishing his morning cup of coffee. He looked up from the copy of the *Republican and Observer* balanced on his knees. Levi noticed the headlines in bold print, "**Richland County Borgia**" and grimaced.

"This was a special edition put out to try and scoop the *Richland Rustic* who moved their print date up from next Saturday to today. The boy who delivered it said they sold all their papers in less than an hour." George indicated the paper he was holding as he motioned for Levi to sit in the chair opposite him. "I would say that you may have your work cut out for you with this one."

"It amazes me the townsfolk and the papers have so much information that I have not been made aware of as the defense attorney for the accused." Levi perched on the edge of the chair, holding his hands towards the stove to warm them, the satchel and the loaf of cinnamon bread placed on a small table beside him.

Jane reappeared from the kitchen bringing a cup of hot coffee, placing it in Levi's grateful hands. The rich scent of the strong black coffee mingled with the scents of eggs and bacon in the kitchen, causing Levi's stomach to rumble with hunger. He had been so hurried in arriving early to meet with Rose he had gone without his own breakfast despite Myrtle's admonitions.

Jane smiled at the noise. "I sent Belle in with a basin of water so she could have some morning ablutions as Mrs. Wilson brought fresh clothing for her yesterday. I will come and fetch you when she is washed and dressed and ready for visitors. I'll also ask Charlotte to dish up an extra plate of breakfast when she brings Rose's."

"Thank you." Levi expressed his gratitude as Jane bustled off again to the kitchen. "Has it been fairly quiet since the arrest?" Levi directed his question to the top of George's head, bent over reading the newspaper in front of him.

"She has been very quiet and appreciative of the small comforts Jane has offered her. We set her up in the small spare bedroom down here as it has been so cold upstairs and there are several unsavory fellows in the cells above. Jane felt it was indecent to put her where she could hear the coarse talk of the drunks as they sobered up." George lifted his eyes to the ceiling overhead, indicating the upper level of the jail which housed inmates in cells with rough cut stone walls and iron bars.

"As far as anyone else, there were some curious folks milling about the courthouse lawn yesterday. I guess they thought they might get a glimpse of her somehow through a window, but she has not ventured near the small window in her room as it has bars over it, and she seemed repulsed by the thought." George took a pipe from his vest pocket and reached for a tin of tobacco placed nearby. He put three pinches of tobacco leaves in the bowl of the pipe, tamping them down, picked up a matchstick and lit the leaves while drawing on the mouthpiece with long draws until a pleasant curling smoke emanated. "So far, it is my opinion that my obligation lies in protecting her from them rather than the other way around."

Levi nodded in agreement. "Yes, I was besieged by "well-meaning" parishioners yesterday morning at church. There is an alarming amount of gossip about what happened and what should happen from now on. People tend to forget that everyone has the right to be considered innocent until proven guilty in a court of law and if something cannot be proved in the law it is as if it did not exist."

"There must be a source for all this gossip, and I refuse to believe it is Ella's family. They are good, solid people who only want to find out how this happened to their child. There isn't a bad one of them among the bunch." George put his pipe aside and picked up the coffee cup. My heart goes out to them but accusing this girl of murder doesn't add up to me. There isn't any evidence against her except a bunch of hearsay."

"I agree that Ella's family is not at fault. Hopefully, this will be cleared up in the preliminary hearing and never make it to trial with the utter lack of evidence." Levi placed his empty coffee cup on the table and picked up his satchel and the cinnamon bread as he noticed that Jane had come back into the room.

"Even if it does happen that way, I feel sorry for her trying to live in this town afterwards. You and I have both witnessed what small town justice can do to a person." George's voice followed Levi as he stood and left the room with Jane.

Jane led him down another corridor to a small bedroom at the end. The door stood slightly ajar, and Levi could hear the faint lilt of a child's laughter emanating from within the bedroom. Jane and Levi entered to find Rose sitting in a small rocking chair with a table beside her.

Two chairs were situated at the table as well as place settings and a small vase of fragrant pine sprigs and holly. A bright braided rag rug had been placed on the floor at Rose's feet, making the room look more like a guest room than a prison cell. Snyder's seven-year-old daughter, Belle, stood beside Rose watching as Rose folded scraps of paper into little animals.

Rose stood up when she saw Levi enter the room with Jane. She put a nervous hand to her hair and then smoothed out the clean apron over her dress. She looked pale but cheerful as she offered her hand to Levi in greeting. Her handshake was firm, and she looked Levi straight in the eye; two things only the innocent did, according to his past experiences with both the guilty and the innocent.

Charlotte, the hired girl, entered the room bearing two plates laden with scrambled eggs, bacon, and toast. She walked to the table, placed the plates on the table settings, then turned and smiled shyly at Rose.

"I brewed some of the Oolong tea Mrs. Wilson sent over and I added a dollop of milk and honey for you. I will go and fetch it and bring back another cup of coffee for Mr. Bancroft." Charlotte turned to leave. "Would you care for some marmalade for your toast?"

"My gracious, no. You have done so much, Charlotte. Thank you." Rose reached out to touch Charlotte's arm as she passed by. "Charlotte and I are both teachers in the same Sunday School class." Rose explained to Levi as he pulled her chair out and then seated himself in the other chair. Jane took Belle by the hand and led the reluctant child from the room, leaving the door open for the sake of propriety.

"I apologize for the delay in coming because of the Sabbath. I came as soon as my business day began this morning. It is good to see you have been treated well by the sheriff and his family." Levi marveled at how composed Rose looked although she picked at the food in front of her, moving it around the plate without eating it. Her fingers trembled slightly when she held the fork and knife.

Charlotte returned with the tea and coffee, placing the beverages before them with care. "The Sunday school class said a special prayer for you yesterday and some of the ladies wish to come and sing hymns outside each day so that you will be encouraged, Rose." Charlotte gave a small curtsey to Levi and exited the room leaving Rose with the one person who would defend her in the court of law and, more importantly, in the court of public opinion.

Levi looked at the young woman sitting before him and was encouraged by her calm demeanor and gentle grace. He hoped the citizens of Richland County would see Rose as he saw her at that moment instead of seeing the depiction portrayed by her revilers, an impression of a cold-blooded killer they had nicknamed 'Borgia Rose'.

CHAPTER 53

MONDAY, JANUARY 26, 1891

The howling wind and blinding snow of near-blizzard conditions did not keep the citizens of Richland County from filling the courtroom to beyond its capacity. People lined the hallways on both sides and spilled out onto the courthouse lawn, standing in the knee-deep snow to hear the updates as they were passed along in whispers. Everyone wished to witness the preliminary hearing of the State of Wisconsin vs. Rose Zoldoske.

The quiet chatter among those who arrived before daybreak and were lucky enough to be seated in the courtroom, hushed as Rose was brought in through a side door by Sheriff Snyder and placed at the defense table beside Levi Bancroft. Rose looked pale and thin but demure in her best black dress with a matching black hat and black silk gloves.

Sheriff Snyder patted Rose's shoulder in encouragement after sitting her in the chair Levi pulled out for her. Rose could feel all the eyes in the room on her; some in friendly rallying and others in open hostility. She felt someone press her shoulder and moved her eyes from the table before her to see a freshly pressed handkerchief handed to her by Mrs. Wilson.

Rose's breath caught in her throat and tears rimmed her eyes as she saw the love and concern in her friend's eyes. Rose managed to nod her thanks and place her hand over Dora's for a moment before the older woman was asked to seat herself by the bailiff.

Rose was exhausted. Although she had been given many comforts by her jailers, she spent a sleepless night tossing and turning. Every time she closed her eyes, she could see an angry crowd amassing outside the jail with a rope to lynch her in the tree just outside her window. She recalled the story Anthony Hellar told her; of the young man who murdered poor Mrs. Coleman, how the crowd came to get him from the jail and used the pile of stones used to build the courthouse to hang him.

At times, in her moments of light sleep throughout the long night, Rose could feel the rough fibers of the rope abrade her neck; she would sit up in the darkness clutching her throat in terror. She put her hand to the high lace collar of her dress in memory of the anxiety that caused her heart to hammer in her chest until she thought it would burst.

Rose looked up as Levi touched her hand gently. She had not realized she was breathing audibly, each rasping breath sounding out in the eerily quiet courtroom. She nodded at Levi and shut her eyes while focusing on her breathing and counting as Lou taught her to do in moments of panic.

"Look! She's praying. As if that can help her now." The disgusted voice had a distinct German accent. Rose realized with a shudder the same Anthony Hellar who told her the ghoulish tale of the lynching, was nearby, watching with morbid curiosity what would befall her. He was surrounded by a massive contingent that resembled the angry lynch mob from her dreams.

The door to the judge's chamber opened and everyone stood as Justice Wulfing entered the courtroom. Rose felt dizzy as she stood with assistance from Levi, but she willed herself to remain standing.

The judge's gavel sounded like the rat-tat-tat of a gun. Rose resisted the urge to cover her head with her arms and kneel beneath the table to take cover. She sat back down in her chair and stared straight ahead, choosing a picture of President Washington on the wall to focus her attention on. She did her best to put a serene look on her face as her heart continued to beat like a hammer.

Rose was grateful to Levi. He took charge of their portion of the proceedings and signaled for her to reply as they had rehearsed. During their meetings, Levi had been so certain the case would be dismissed due to the lack of evidence against her that he had not discussed other possibilities.

Rose sat and listened to the tale of deceit and murder spun by District Attorney Burnham. He cited the testimony of numerous individuals that pointed towards Rose's infatuation with Dr. Mitchell and her jealousy of Ella. He presented the evidence from the coroner in Chicago stating that Ella's stomach contained strychnine. He quoted witness statements of things Rose said to others when Rose had never thought of such things. Rose realized that if the District Attorney were to be believed, she looked very guilty even to herself.

But then it was Levi's turn to address the judge. He spoke so eloquently and earnestly on Rose's behalf, summing up the argument in one statement: there was no proof whatsoever that Rose had murdered Ella Maly.

"It is at this point, your Honor, that I request a dismissal of this charge as the state has no physical evidence and only very limited circumstantial evidence, most of which is built on hearsay and not admissible in a court of law. The great tragedy of Ella Maly's death is felt by everyone in this courtroom but adding another tragedy to it by wrongfully accusing Rose Zoldoske of murder is beyond reprehensible in my humble opinion." Levi finished his argument by nodding to the judge in respect and turning to face the crowded courtroom of onlookers.

"Everyone is presumed innocent until proven guilty by undeniable evidence of law and not by public opinion no matter how strong." Levi's statement to the courtroom fell upon ears deaf to logic and eyes blind to justice as the onlookers glared at the young attorney.

"I find the evidence presented in this case is strong enough for the defendant, Rose Zoldoske, to be tried on the charge of murder." Justice Wulfing's simple statement brought an enthusiastic response from the onlookers, who were immediately silenced by his gavel.

"Your honor, I request a change of venue for my client." Levi's request came as the word had been passed along the corridors and reached the outside masses where the blizzard was now raging. Loud cheers could be heard through the closed windows and over the howling winds.

"Obviously, you have been tried before we began in this town," Levi muttered to Rose as she stood with the sheriff's assistance. "We shall get you moved to Lancaster, Rose, and hope for cooler heads and justice to prevail."

CHAPTER 54

MONDAY, JUNE 1, 1891

The arctic blizzard winds of January that saw Rose held over for trial gave way to the gentle breezes of June, but the emotional climate of the county seat of Richland County had grown much more turbulent in the passing months. Each citizen seemed to know all the pertinent "facts" of the case against Rose and with each public discussion the people grew more intense in their wish to see her prosecuted for the murder of Ella.

By the time Levi convinced Justice Wulfing that a fair trial for Rose could not exist within the county and had her change of venue completed, the coterie of elite citizens pressed for Rose to be charged with a second murder, the intentional poisoning of Laura Mitchell.

While Anthony Maly gave the impression of being the ringleader of the partisan faction, Levi understood the inner workings of the societal structure of their small town all too well. Anthony Maly was being used as a symbol of moral justification by those who had a larger interest in seeing Rose prosecuted than anyone else. It sickened Levi to see Ella's brother thus exploited, due largely to his overwhelming grief at the loss of his beloved sister.

While the group of supporters for Rose reduced by the week, those who remained were fiercely loyal. The Sunday school class led by Charlotte came several times each week to sing hymns outside Rose's window so she could sing with them. Mrs. King brought Sofie at the little girl's insistence, holding her up to the window so Rose could see that her little friend had regained most of her health again.

Even Uncle Charlie, though very grieved at the loss of Ella, refused to take the stance against Rose when there was nothing but conjecture to accuse her. He would play his guitar outside her window so Rose could listen and enjoy his music as she rocked in the rocking chair, tapping her foot to the beat.

Mrs. Wilson visited Rose every day, bringing food and tea, scraps of material to sew, and paper and pencils so Rose could sketch. Her business had suffered from the blacklisting she received as Rose's main supporter. The once busy shop was often very quiet as the dust collected on the fabrics that sat in the unused piles on the worktable.

There were still those who sought Dora out to create their hats and some who created extra work to help the elderly woman pay her bills, but it was inevitable that the millinery shop could not sustain the lack of usual clientele for an extended period. This did not diminish the loyalty Mrs. Wilson expressed for Rose to anyone who would listen to her. She would not be swayed by the coercive tactics employed by those who claimed to clamor for justice.

It was early morning as Levi pulled his carriage as close to the side door of the jail as possible. It was time to move Rose to Lancaster by train so she could be present at the first day of jury selection the following day. Though Levi and Sheriff Snyder kept their plans for moving Rose as quiet as possible, there were curious onlookers gathering in groups at the corner of Central Street.

Levi was not surprised that a crowd was gathering as the whole town seemed to scrutinize Rose's every movement and it only took one person to realize the sheriff had called deputies into work early that day for the purpose of moving Richland County's most notorious resident.

Sheriff Snyder opened the side door before Levi reached the top step. He stood surveying the perimeter from the top step before stepping aside to assist Rose down the steep stone stairs. Levi could hear the gasps of the collected throngs from across the street. He knew they only had precious minutes to get Rose to the depot before an unruly crowd gathered to block their progress.

Rose was in her best black dress; the same one she wore for her preliminary hearing. She donned a small black straw hat with a veil in the front, shielding her eyes from the onlookers and giving her a mysterious air. Her black silk gloves were neatly fitted to her slender hands as she held a freshly pressed white cotton handkerchief and a small reticule.

Rose followed Levi down the stairs, the heels on her shoes clicking against the stone. She seemed to understand the necessity of making haste; soon she was seated in the small carriage between Levi and Sheriff Snyder. Two other deputies arrived on horseback flanking the carriage on both sides. Levi had no choice but to drive the carriage forward towards Central Street and the waiting crowd that was growing quickly.

"Isn't that nice though? Looks like she is just out for a Sunday drive! Where are her handcuffs, Sheriff?" The angry words, hurled like a stone, caused the others gathering to shout similar sentiments.

"She has to run away like the coward that she is. She knows what will happen if she stays here for her trial, she will get the justice she deserves." A woman shouted the ugly words and shook her fist towards the passing carriage.

"Not so brave now are you, Borgia Rose? Why should you be allowed to live when you poisoned two innocent women?" The nickname that originated in the newspapers was used frequently by the townspeople.

"Urge the horse to go faster." Sheriff Snyder urged Levi on to the depot. The beginning rumbles of a riot threatened like the thunder that sounds before a storm. The three blocks down Seminary Street flashed by the carriage in a blur. Rose kept her head down, hidden between her hands to muffle the nasty slurs and threats hurled at her. The morning train was being stoked for the trip to Lancaster via Avoca and Montfort.

Levi pulled up to the depot platform, handing the reins to a waiting liveryman who would drive the carriage back to Levi's home. Levi stepped out onto the platform and reached out his hand to help Rose from the carriage. He noticed that Sheriff Snyder stood up in the carriage, facing back down Seminary Street, with his hand on the revolver in the holster at his hip. He motioned with a nod of his head for Levi to take Rose to the last car on the train and help her aboard.

Levi walked swiftly down the platform. Rose was nearly running at his side as she clung to his arm for stability. He could not slow the pace for her as he could hear angry voices getting closer from at least two different directions. He momentarily wished he had put on a sidearm himself, but he could see Sheriff Snyder and his deputies surrounding the platform on three sides blocking entrance to the train.

Levi was steps from the train door when he noticed the elderly man approaching them from the train. The man looked disheveled and exhausted, his beard at least a few days grown. His gray hair stood up in peaks as though he had run his fingers through it repeatedly. He froze in place when he saw Rose approach, so Levi assumed he was just one more of the morbid curiosity seekers wishing to see his client up close.

"Stand aside please, Sir." Exasperated and hurried, Levi barked the command at the man, watching as the man winced at the acerbity in his tone. Levi put his hand outward to push the old man out of the way when Rose came to a screeching halt beside him.

"Papa? What are you doing here?" Rose's voice cracked with emotion as she looked at her father. "How did you know?"

"Mrs. Wilson sent me word of the trial date and I came as soon as I could get the money for my fare. I cannot let you face this alone, Rose." Andrew stood only a foot away from his daughter, tears streaming down his face. "I have only just arrived, and you are leaving?"

At the mention of leaving, Levi recovered from the shock of finding Rose's father on the depot platform only moments before they were to depart. He nodded at Andrew and grasped his arm to turn him back towards the train door. He helped Rose up the steps and through the door, then turned to beckon for her father to follow them. Sheriff Snyder was close behind them, shutting the door firmly and pulling down the shades on the windows. The two deputies stationed themselves at the two entrances to the train car, their rifles poised on the train car railing.

Within moments, the train lurched forward, belching smoke, and drowning out the noise of the angry crowds gathered on the platform. The conductor, realizing the dire situation, decided to leave the depot before the designated time, abandoning several employees who ran to catch a hold of the train car ahead of the one Levi had designated for Rose.

There was silence except for the occasional sniffle from Rose's father, who was still crying openly at the sight of his daughter under arrest. Rose sat beside him on the seat and patted his bent shoulders in a comforting way.

The rest of the trip was uneventful as the train only stopped briefly in Avoca and Montfort without allowing people to gather at the end of the train where Rose and her father sat hand in hand, waiting for the stop in Lancaster and the trial that would commence the next day.

By the end of a long day, they reached the depot in Lancaster. The Grant County Sheriff was waiting for them to take custody of Rose. Levi noticed that the new sheriff held handcuffs and hoped Rose's new location would not make her regret the request for the change of venue.

One thing was certain to Levi; the only justice for Rose would be found outside Richland County.

CHAPTER 55

FRIDAY, JUNE 5, 1891, LANCASTER, WISCONSIN

Every seat in the Fifth Circuit Courtroom of Grant County was taken with an overflow of onlookers spilling out the doorway into the halls. The honorable Judge George Clementson made a wise decision regarding the public viewing of the State of Wisconsin v Rose Zoldoske.

He ordered tickets of admission be given out to waiting spectators each morning so no single group could monopolize the courtroom seats and cause a disturbance in his courtroom. Once the tickets were dispensed, everyone else would be escorted outside the courthouse and made to wait for an update. Anyone who caused a disturbance would be thrown out of the courtroom and barred from returning for the remainder of the trial.

Judge Clementson was known for his decorum. He had emigrated to the United States from England and kept many of the more formal practices that had been instilled in him in Yorkshire. He detested dramatic performances from the attorneys or from those called upon as witnesses. Levi felt relieved to see Judge Clementson presiding as it was less likely that the overemotional public sentiment built upon in Richland County would be allowed in this courtroom.

The only exceptions Judge Clementson allowed for persons being admitted into the courtroom daily were for Ella's parents and for Rose's father. Judge Clementson had the bailiff seat Andrew Zoldoske next to his daughter at the defense table. Likewise, Anton and Catherine Maly were given reserved seats directly behind the prosecution's table. All other parties were expected to abide by the judge's rules or risk being charged with contempt of court.

It was a warm and humid morning. The air inside the courtroom was stale. The rank smell assailed Levi's nostrils as soon as he stepped inside the courtroom with Rose's father and seated himself at the defense table. Levi's friend, Herbert Chynoweth, an impressive attorney, and a former state assistant attorney general, greeted Levi at the table.

H.W. (as Levi referred to him) had become aware of Rose's case and offered his assistance to Levi at no charge to Rose. Like Levi, H.W. had been appalled at the lack of physical evidence against Rose; he was also an aficionado of a "good fight". Neither Levi nor H.W. had ever lost a courtroom case due to their argumentative skills, and Levi did not intend to lose this case.

Jury selection had begun three days prior. Twelve men sat in the jury box awaiting instructions from the judge for the testimony portion of the trial to begin. Levi and H.W. had done their best to choose jurors that were removed from the influences of the powerful people behind Rose's prosecution, but he could not help feeling that the young milliner still did not have a "jury of her peers" in the twelve men.

Young George Darrah, at age 23 was the only juror under the age of 40, most of them being farmers. The jury foreman, Charles H. Baxter, was an honored veteran of the Civil War and the mayor of Lancaster. Levi could see H.W. studying the jurors to determine which ones might be the most sympathetic to Rose, twirling his well-groomed mustache as he sat in deep concentration.

It was 10:30 before the door opened and Rose was brought into the courtroom. She wore her black silk dress which had been freshly laundered by Mrs. Wilson, her black silk gloves, and a new black hat with a wide-open brim. Levi silently congratulated Mrs. Wilson in changing the hat with the veil for this hat, which made Rose appear more like an innocent young schoolgirl. Rose held a red geranium in her hand, a gift sent from Sofie King and her mother. The red accent of the flower was a striking visual contrast against the black silk of the dress.

The sheriff, MV Burris, led Rose to her seat between Levi and her father. It had been many months since the sheriff stopped employing handcuffs when he took Rose from her room in the jailhouse. He learned through experience of the past few months that Rose was not a threat to the public. Instead, it was Rose who seemed to need protection.

Rose hugged her father, who stood to pull out her chair. Andrew wiped away tears as he saw Rose in her chair and sank down into his own again. While Levi wrote a few notes, he could sense H.W. still watching the jurors to see which ones had been affected by Rose's father's embrace. Young Mr. Darrah seemed to be showing the most interest, while several more looked sympathetically at the elderly father weeping next to his daughter.

As soon as Judge Clementson appeared, the trial was underway in earnest. Richland County District Attorney Burnham gave his opening remarks, informing the jury that while much of the evidence presented might be considered implausible by some, when pieced together it told the story of a cold-blooded murderer who made more than one blunder along the way.

Levi was next to make his opening remarks. He focused on the main point of the defense's entire case.

"Gentlemen, a tragedy occurred on the evening of January 8th. A beautiful young woman who was beloved by the entire community died suddenly for unknown reasons. While the state tries to make the case that my client is a murderer because everyone feels the grief of losing Ella Maly, we cannot allow a person to be convicted of a crime when there is no actual evidence against them. Please focus on the fact that all the pieces that will be presented are not actual physical evidence against Rose, only the strong sentiment wishing to find an answer to this tragedy."

The first witness called by the state was Anton Maly, Ella's father. The bespectacled older man answered the District Attorney's questions with a wavering voice full of emotion. Levi noticed the jurors leaning forward as they listened, not usually a good sign, as they were showing interest and possible sympathy. He needed to decide how to proceed.

H.W. scribbled a word on the paper in front of them and pushed it towards Levi. "Sympathy" was the communication. Levi nodded his agreement as he rose from his chair to question Ella's father.

"Mr. Maly, I think I can speak for everyone when I say how very sorry, I am for the loss of your daughter. It is a tragedy that goes beyond words and can make anyone feel as though it is unjust. Were you a witness at any time to Ella's collapse, her sudden illness, and her untimely death?" Levi eased into his line of questioning using a sympathetic approach.

"No, I wasn't at home. I was in Madison when it happened." Anton Maly looked down at his feet as he admitted he had not been present and had not witnessed anything firsthand. His testimony was his own opinion or hearsay from others.

"Thank you for your honest reply. You have my sympathy for your loss. No further questions, your Honor." Levi returned to the defense table. He noticed the look of sympathy written clearly across Rose's face as she watched Ella's father stand and leave the witness chair.

The next witness would be more difficult. Catherine Maly came forward after having to leave the courtroom during her husband's testimony. She wore full black mourning clothes, customary of a mother to wear for as long as she felt disposed of, but it was an emotional trigger for the jury that was difficult for the defense to overcome.

The jury was more inclined to listen to Catherine's testimony because she was Ella's mother and had suffered a great loss rather than because she had clear-cut evidence. H.W. signaled to Levi he would take on the questioning so that Levi would not question both bereaved parents, causing him to appear as a villain to the jurors.

District Attorney Burnham guided the bereaved mother through her story; beginning with finding Ella lying in the snow writhing in pain and ending in watching her beloved daughter die the next morning.

"Her last words were, 'If I lived a thousand lives, I would give them all to Jesus.' My Ella was a good girl." Catherine's voice trembled. She looked down at her clenched hands in her lap, summoning the courage to continue her testimony. Every eye upon her, including the rather stoic Judge Clementson, was filled with sympathy.

When it was H.W.'s turn, he rose slowly and came to stand near the witness chair and Catherine Maly. He noticed the tears still stood in her eyes and offered his fresh white linen handkerchief from his vest pocket. Catherine received the handkerchief and dabbed her eyes as she waited for him to speak.

"It is very brave of you to come and share this painful story with the court today, Mrs. Maly. I know you do this to ensure that your daughter receives the fullest amount of justice that is due her. I assure you; I am interested in the same thing. My questions to you are not meant to upset you or cast aspersions on Ella's memory in any way. My purpose is to get to the bottom of what really happened to Ella so we can all give her the fullest amount of justice due her."

"Mrs. Maly in your testimony you mentioned the chocolate creams you found in Ella's coat pocket after her collapse. Can you tell me what happened to those chocolate creams?" H.W. gently led Catherine towards the subject of the candy she found.

"When I found the chocolate creams it was because Dr. Mitchell asked me what Ella had eaten and I reminded him that Ella had eaten dinner at his house. I looked in her coat to see what might be there and found the candy inside."

"Yes, I see. Can you recall how many candies you found and what you did with them?" H.W. looked towards the jury box to make certain he had not lost their attention.

"There were three candies. I threw them out at first because Dr. Haskell and Dr. Mitchell said they couldn't be the cause of Ella's sickness and it might melt in her coat pocket." Catherine recalled with clarity the instructions given by both doctors.

"So, you followed their instructions and threw them out? Where did they end up?" H.W. was clearly focusing on the candy's progression after being found in Ella's coat.

"Yes, they were in the slop bucket that had been brought in to use for the vomit." Catherine stalled, recalling the violent fits that wracked Ella's body.

"Were the candies taken back out of the slop bucket and by whom?"

"Yes, once we were sure Ella was poisoned and Lillie said that Rose gave them the chocolates, then they were taken back out to be sent in for testing for poison. I think it was either my son Anthony or Dr. Mitchell that took them, though I can't be sure which one because I had taken to my bed with grief." Catherine dabbed at the tears in her eyes again.

"So, the evidence of the candy was removed from the waste where it had been left with other waste for an undetermined amount of time and was retrieved only after someone thought the candies were given to Ella by Rose? No one suspected the candy until they thought it came from Rose. Is that correct?" H.W. was now at the main point in his line of questioning; the candy was not considered evidence by two physicians until someone decided Rose had poisoned Ella and needed to prove how she had done it. The candy sat with other waste and could have been tampered with at any time after Ella's death by one of two individuals' intent on proving Rose's guilt.

"We all thought afterwards it might be the candy and I thought it was poison like strychnine. I read a book that described the symptoms of strychnine poisoning and Ella had nearly all the symptoms." Catherine nodded her head in emphasis over her findings.

"I see. I am unsure why the candy would be thrown out if anyone suspected it as evidence, but odd things happen sometimes. Mrs.

Maly, when did you read the book about strychnine poisoning and where did you get the book?" The young attorney continued to be gentle and calm, as though he were questioning his own mother.

"I read the book after Ella died because I needed to know more about what happened to her. Dr. Mitchell loaned the book to me." Catherine did not realize her testimony alluded to the possible tampering with a witness, but Levi and H.W. were suspicious as to what had happened to bring Rose forward as suspect versus anyone else. The look on District Attorney Burnham's face showed he realized the same thing.

"Very interesting. Thank you, Mrs. Maly. No more questions at this time, Your Honor." H.W. had effectively taken away the "smoking gun" that had been put forward by the prosecution.

Rose stood with the bailiff when the judge announced a recess until the following day. She hugged her father and turned to follow the sheriff when Levi stopped her.

"Get some sleep Rose. Things went well today and hopefully we will continue the process tomorrow." Levi patted Rose's arm and nodded at her father, who rose from his chair.

"Do you know who will testify tomorrow?" Rose had difficulty watching Ella's parents cry as they talked about their daughter.

"I am expecting the state to call several doctors, including Dr. Haskell and Dr. DeLap. They will also call Dr. Haines from Chicago about the strychnine found in the autopsy." Levi picked up the papers on the table before him and straightened them out to place in his satchel. His next statement made Rose turn pale immediately.

"Rose, they will also call Dr. George Mitchell."

CHAPTER 56

SATURDAY, JUNE 6, 1891

The sun had just risen as Rose opened her eyes. Her shift clung to her, the heat and humidity of the June weather making sleep difficult. Rose rolled from her side to her back, watching the faint light of day appear through her small window.

As Rose attempted to throw her legs over the side of the bed and sit up, she was assaulted by the pain in her body. The lack of mobility and small space she had been kept in caused arthritis to settle in a few of her joints. Sheriff Burris had been very accommodating to her, but they couldn't allow her outside to exercise for any period without attracting groups of onlookers that could easily turn into a riot or possible lynch mob.

Mrs. Burris, a kindly older woman who reminded Rose of her Grandmother Gottschall, arrived with water in a basin and a towel and comb.

"I freshened your dress up a bit from yesterday. It's a shame what we women must endure to be considered proper in this kind of heat.

I will leave you to it and come back to help you with your hair when I bring a tray for breakfast. I have some nice eggs and sausages ready." Mrs. Burris bustled about the room, reminding Rose of a plump robin that would flit and flutter from place to place.

"Thank you, Mrs. Burris. Don't trouble yourself with a lot for breakfast. I am not hungry. A slice of toast and a cup of tea would do." Rose accepted the heavy black silk dress from the woman's outstretched arms. She dreaded having to put all the undergarments and the heavy dress on again and sit in the sweltering courtroom again today. Most of all, she dreaded seeing George again.

"My dear, you must eat to keep your strength up. I will see if there is a berry or two to add to the fixings on your tray. You are wasting away right in front of our eyes, Rose. The defense attorneys will accuse the sheriff and I of starving you to death." Mrs. Burris patted Rose's shoulder, giving Rose some much needed human contact. Anyone who knew the generous Mrs. Burris would know she would never starve anyone, much less her favorite "guest" as she had begun calling Rose.

"I will try to eat just for you. I don't know what I would do without your kindness." Rose spoke as the older lady bustled from the room. Rose climbed into her undergarments. She put a light wrapper over the undergarments and sat in the solitary chair provided for her use. Rose picked up the bible she had been given by Mrs. Wilson and returned to her reading the book of Proverbs.

"Trust in the Lord with all thine heart; and lean not unto thine own understanding." The third chapter and fifth verse of Proverbs seem to leap off the page as Rose read the words over and over, trying to commit them to memory.

Mrs. Burris soon returned with a tray including some fresh, sweet strawberries in a small dish. Rose tried to eat some of the eggs while avoiding the heavy sausage and delighted in the sweet taste of the ripe red berries. She finished her breakfast and dressed with assistance from Mrs. Burris.

Rose followed Sheriff Burris outside into the brilliant sunlight. Her eyes burned from the intense light as she had been housed inside for months without reprieve. She could feel what seemed like hundreds of pairs of eyes upon her as she walked slowly, leaning on the Sheriff for assistance.

Occasionally a shout rang out, random people cursing Rose and calling her names. Without exception, someone always called her Borgia Rose, as others jeered in agreement. This morning, Rose was startled for a moment when her Sunday School class from Richland Center gathered to sing as she passed on the way to the courthouse. Rose was not amazed by the group's presence as much as by what they chose to sing; it was in complete harmony with her bible reading that morning. The chorus of the new hymn, written by Anthony Showalter, filtered across the courtyard to Rose.

"Leaning, leaning, safe and secure from all alarms. Leaning, leaning. Leaning on the Everlasting arms."

Levi and H.W. were waiting with Rose's father as she entered the courtroom with Sheriff Burris. Rose looked at the onlookers gathered, there were familiar faces and those of curious strangers. Rose sank into the chair offered to her by Levi.

When Judge Clementson appeared, District Attorney Burnham called Dr. Haskell as his first witness. Rose watched as the kindly doctor was sworn in. He had aged in the few months since she had seen him. DA Burnham began his questioning.

"In my opinion, Ella Maly died of asphyxia produced by spasms of the respiratory muscles. It has not been proven this was due to

poisoning by strychnine or anything else." Dr. Haskell's firm statement could not be dissuaded by DA Burnham's attempt to contribute
to the seizures as a symptom of poisoning.

"I have said it was uremic convulsions and I will continue to say
that no matter what anyone else says. There was a massive amount
of albumin in the urine of the deceased when I conducted the initial
autopsy. Dr. Mitchell was not satisfied with my findings so he went
on to find others who would support his theory, but it does not
change what I found." Dr. DeLap's testimony was just as firm in
conviction as Dr. Haskell's.

Both doctors nodded towards Rose as they left the witness chair.
It reminded her that while the most vocal citizens of Richland
County wanted to see her prosecuted for Ella's murder, there was
still a group who wanted to see the truth of what happened to Ella
be discovered and told.

Mrs. Haskell was called as the next witness for the prosecution.
She looked in sympathy at Rose while she answered the District
Attorney's questions. The ultimate question made Mrs. Haskell falter
for a moment before she answered. When asked what Ella had said
to her in her last hours she responded quietly,

"She asked me if this was how Mrs. Mitchell died."

The gasps could be heard in the quiet courtroom, causing Judge
Clementson to pound his gavel. Rose felt numb as she heard Ella's
words spoken aloud. What did Ella realize that would cause her to
ask about Laura's death?

A conversation with Freddie flitted into her mind; Freddie had
openly threatened to prevent George from marrying Ella. Freddie
had been one of the last people to sit with Laura before she died and

if the medical expert from Chicago was to be believed, both Laura and Ella had died in similar ways.

The next loud gasp came from Rose as a stark new realization struck her with force. Had Freddie been involved in harming Ella and his mother? She refused to believe Freddie would do anything intentionally harmful to anyone, much less his own mother whom he adored, but had he done something accidentally?

Just as he might have wished to make Ella sick to embarrass her at the dinner party, he might have given an accidental overdose to his mother while he watched over her that last morning. Everything happening to her might be to cover up what he did unintentionally.

Rose looked up to see her attorneys and the judge staring at her. She blushed deeply, realizing she had gasped aloud, breaking the judge's rules about decorum. She glanced at the judge who returned her gaze with a stern air, raising his bushy eyebrows in question.

"I beg your pardon. I was not aware of what Ella said and I found it meaningful, but not in the way everyone else does. Please forgive my outburst." Rose spoke with a genuine frankness that seemed to appease the judge as he nodded curtly in her direction and turned back to Mrs. Haskell in the witness chair.

It was four o'clock when DA Burnham called George to the witness stand. Rose noted that George seemed his usual self; with an air of arrogance and dressed to perfection. George began answering the questions about Ella and soon he answered the more probing questions about Rose.

"Dr. Mitchell, did you ever have the occasion to use strychnine in your household? Did you place it in cheese to kill mice and was Rose Zoldoske present to witness this?" District Attorney Burnham's questions led George exactly to the accusation the prosecution intended to make against Rose.

"Yes." George barely spoke the word before Levi raised an objection.

"I object. The Prosecution is leading the witness rather than asking the witness to state his testimony. I ask that the response be taken from the record." Levi needed the jury to understand George had not witnessed Rose using strychnine nor was there any strychnine missing from the bottle he kept in his office.

"Sustained. Strike the response of the witness from the record." Judge Clementson agreed, but not before the jury had been heavily influenced by the damaging one-word answer from George. It was just as District Attorney Burnhan intended.

George continued with his testimony about Laura's death, "My wife died in very similar circumstances when Rose would have been one of the only people present in the room with her. It was after Ella's death I became concerned that both women might have been poisoned. I had my wife's body exhumed in early February and sent samples to Dr. Haines in Chicago. He found strychnine present in my wife's stomach just as it had been in Ella's." George's testimony was damaging but Rose knew parts of it were outright lies. She scribbled the word 'lies' on the paper in front of her and pushed it towards Levi and H.W.

It was just before six o'clock when Levi took over questioning George. He knew an overnight recess would be called soon, but he needed to make an impression on the jury before resuming his questioning the following morning.

"Dr. Mitchell, in your testimony you have referred to your late wife's death being very similar in nature to Ella Maly's. Is that the case?" Levi wanted George to trip over his own arrogance in front of the jury.

"Yes, there were striking similarities between the two that could not be ignored." George smiled smugly at the defense attorney, thinking he had made an impression on Levi.

"And yet, you claimed you recognized Ella Maly's symptoms as the result of poisoning almost immediately upon seeing her. Why didn't you recognize the 'striking similarities' to strychnine poisoning in your late wife's symptoms at the time of her death? In fact, didn't it take over ten months for you to make that assumption on behalf of your wife? I would think, of all the people that you would seek justice for, your wife Laura Mitchell would lead the list if she had been murdered as well?" Levi leaned towards George for the first few questions but turned out towards the jury as he asked the final one. George had stepped squarely into either admitting falsehoods in his testimony or admitting he was an incompetent doctor and uncaring husband. Levi suspected all the above.

"I object!" District Attorney Burnham's voice boomed in the courtroom, attempting to rescue his arrogant witness's blunder. "This witness is not on trial here!"

"Not yet." Levi stared George straight in the eye. "Perjury is a serious offense."

"Overruled. The defense has the right to ask questions about Mrs. Mitchell's death since the prosecution introduced it as part of their case in the testimony of this witness." Judge Clementson glowered at George in the witness chair. "I will call a recess for the night and Mr. Bancroft may resume questioning this witness in the morning."

Levi walked back to where Rose sat staring in shock at George. It was obvious Rose would never have believed that George might lie to make the case against her.

Rose stood when Deputy McGonigle came to get her to escort her back to her cell. Her legs were shaking, but not from her weakened condition. At that moment, Rose realized just how far George would go to incriminate her and have her convicted of not one murder, but two.

As they passed back through the courtyard, passing the shouts and jeers of the crowds, Rose heard the same words from the hymn the Sunday School class sang to her that morning.

"Leaning, leaning, safe and secure from all alarms. Leaning, leaning. Leaning on the Everlasting arms."

CHAPTER 57

MONDAY, JUNE 8, 1891

The line to enter the courtroom wound around several blocks before dawn. The word spread that George was testifying about both Ella's and Laura's deaths. Again, Rose was brought from the jail past the jeering crowds who called out to her as she walked slowly between Sheriff Burris and Deputy McGonigle. Extra guards had been brought from neighboring Iowa County so that there were six men on duty around the clock.

Levi stayed up into the wee hours of the morning consulting with H.W. on how to proceed with the questioning of George. They were convinced that DA Burnham would redirect and advise George about the way he answered certain questions. H.W. sent telegrams to several people overnight, keeping the local telegraph operator awake until almost dawn. H.W. was convinced the sacrifice of sleep would be a small price to pay for gaining some of his information.

George entered the courtroom with a bevy of young ladies from Richland Center. He looked every part the dandy, including a wide-brimmed straw boater hat with a bright blue band. Judge Clementson grimaced when he saw George take the witness stand. He did not appreciate George's vibrant apparel at such a solemn occasion.

It had been agreed upon by the two lawyers, in the wee hours of the morning, that H.W. would take over the questioning. His vest pocket held several telegrams that he received in response to the ones he had sent in the middle of the night. He took them from his pocket and laid them on the defense table.

H.W. began by asking several summary questions of George, to remind the jury of George's testimony from the previous day so he could allude to several discrepancies. George gave very short answers with limited details, trying to recover from his blunders with Levi. The more trivial questions H.W. asked, the more confident George became in answering, until some of the swagger from the previous day was present again.

"As the physician for both Laura Mitchell and Ella Maly, can you tell the jury all the medications you administered to them? For instance, what did you administer to Mrs. Mitchell?" H.W. carefully framed the question so George would feel confident as a physician.

"As I recall, I gave her alternate doses of Belladonna for her persistent headaches and female maladies and Nux Vomica for the prior seizures she had experienced. Both are used widely and are safe enough to be used for infants." George immediately took on the demeanor of the experienced doctor who had to explain medical practice to an inexperienced layman.

"And what did you administer to Ella Maly?" H.W. asked patiently.

"I gave her the Nux Vomica for the seizures, and I believe Dr. Haskell gave her chloroform later on after he arrived." George looked slightly bored at H.W.'s questions.

"I only need to hear what you administered, Dr. Mitchell. We can recall Dr. Haskell to see what he administered to Ella. Did Ella take any Belladonna that you are aware of? Was there any evidence she had taken Belladonna prior to the 8th of January?" H.W. leaned one hand against the jury box railing as he watched George carefully.

"Not that I am aware of, no." George glanced at his hands as he answered the question. An almost invisible sheen of sweat appeared on his upper lip just above his mustache. It was unnoticeable to the casual observer, but H.W. was far from a casual observer. He had hit his mark.

"If both patients had such similar symptoms, why would the same medications not be used for both? Your testimony yesterday said the symptoms were, as I quote, 'strikingly similar'. If they were alike, why were they not treated alike?"

"Not every symptom was an exact match. My wife had given birth only a month before and was still recovering from it." George lost his patience with the questions and was now becoming more reckless in his answers.

"I see. So, you are saying your wife could have had complications from a difficult birth that Ella Maly did not have and so they were treated differently. If they were treated differently, couldn't the causes of the symptoms be different as well?" H.W. continued to press on slowly, knowing he was prodding George into a state of anger.

"Well, as the autopsies showed, they both had strychnine in their stomachs, so there is your common denominator. You don't have to medicate both the same if they both die of strychnine poisoning. One has nothing to do with the other. It isn't what I gave them afterwards, it is what she poisoned them with in the beginning." George pointed angrily at Rose, causing a buzz of whispers in the gallery.

"Dr. Mitchell, do you prepare your own medications, or do you buy them already prepared?" H.W. walked back to the defense table and picked up the telegrams he laid there.

"I have my medications prepared locally by Dr. Lovering, as do several of the other physicians in the county. He has the oldest practice in Richland Center and is above reproach in his reputation as a physician." George almost spit the answer back in H.W.'s face, his contempt for the defense attorney now evident.

"Yes, well, I have a telegram here from Dr. Lovering who prepared your Nux Vomica, and another telegram from a Dr. Allen from the same Rush Medical College as Dr. Haines who conducted the autopsy that found the presence of strychnine. Both doctors concur one of the main ingredients in the Nux Vomica that you administered to both patients before their deaths is strychnine. Is the strychnine therefore found by Dr. Haines in both stomachs from an intentional poisoning or from the Nux Vomica that both patients were given?" H.W. watched calmly as George gripped the railing in front of him until his knuckles were white. George did not have an answer and they both knew it.

"No more questions Your Honor." H.W. stepped aside so that George could leave the witness chair and the courtroom in a rage.

As Judge Clementson called for a noon recess, the people in the gallery started to mill about and the whispering buzz grew louder. Levi stared into the gallery and then back at a list he held in his hand. Rose leaned forward to see a list of the witnesses that were still to be called by the prosecution. The list included Alice Berryman, Rena Allen, Mae Hyndman, and Lillie Maly.

Rose followed Levi's gaze at the people milling about in the gallery; all the girls on the list had entered the courtroom with George

Mitchell and sat and listened to his testimony that day. They had apparently stayed up from the previous night to obtain tickets for the courtroom proceedings without anyone questioning whether they were witnesses themselves and therefore not allowed to hear the testimony of other witnesses.

"We have all the makings of a mistrial already." Levi whispered to H.W. as they stood to acknowledge Judge Clementson's reappearance for the afternoon session.

H.W. shook his head, "We aren't going to need a mistrial. We have established reasonable doubt. We can bring this up in a sidebar with Clementson if Burnham proceeds to try and put them on the stand. Some of this trial has the making of a penny dreadful, except parts of it are so bizarre, no one would believe this story is true."

The witnesses called by the prosecution in the afternoon session seemed to prove H.W.'s point; a butcher, a baker, and a candymaker were all called upon to testify Rose had purchased oysters, oranges, and chocolate creams on the morning of June 8th.

None of them could answer that they saw Rose put anything additional such as poison in the aforementioned items. The defense did not argue that Rose had not made the purchases since she had bought each for the dinner party. All the dinner guests ate the oysters and the oranges and both Ella and Lillie Maly had eaten the chocolate creams.

The prosecution also called Anthony Hellar to testify about seeing Rose with a small package of oysters that morning in Constantine's mercantile.

"She was acting suspicious-like, so I watched her while hiding behind the cookstove in the store. She took out a vial and sprinkled it on the oysters and then took out a knitting needle and pierced the chocolate cream with it, pouring more from the vial inside it. I followed her as she left the mercantile and walked straight to Bailey's store and Ella. I watched her offer Ella an oyster to eat but Ella refused it, so Rose left the store and threw the oysters down by the curb in the street. I went and smelled the oysters, and something was very bad for them. Later, when I ate my lunch, there must have been something from the oysters on my fingers still because there was a bitter taste and I got so awful sick I could hardly make it home."

Rose sat shaking her head at the outrageous lies. "This never happened." She whispered to Levi, who nodded in acknowledgment.

Levi approached Anthony Hellar with only a couple of questions to punch holes in his testimony, showing it to be fabricated.

"Mr. Hellar, you were at Constantine's at what time of the day? Obviously, it was before your lunchtime." Levi helped Anthony recall his testimony about eating lunch after seeing Rose.

"Yah, I guess it would have been about eleven o'clock in the morning or so." Anthony took a stab in the dark at a reasonable time.

"And you followed the defendant to Bailey's store after witnessing her put a substance in raw oysters?" Levi sounded dubious. "If you witnessed Rose putting something in the oysters and the candy, why would you let her offer it to Ella Maly knowing it could harm Ella?"

"Yah, I followed her right over and I didn't know she was going to do that. I tried to warn Ella that I seen it, but she didn't listen to me." Anthony was stumbling and faltering.

"So, you spoke to Ella Maly after this occurred? Did you get the oysters and come back, or did you speak to her right after Rose left the store?"

"Um, I spoke to Ella right after Rose left the store." Anthony nodded his head.

"Well then, I have two more questions for you. How did you see Rose enter Constantine's at eleven o'clock with oysters when the butcher just testified this morning that Rose bought the oysters from him at two o'clock in the afternoon? How did you see where Rose disposed of the oysters after she left Bailey's if you stayed behind to talk with Ella? Wouldn't you agree this is very confusing?"

"I might have remembered something wrong." Anthony began to back pedal out of his testimony, but it was too late. He had left far too much reasonable doubt.

"Yes, I would agree that something was remembered wrong." Levi shook his head in disgust as he walked back to the defense table and seated himself beside Rose.

Rose wrote a brief note for Levi to read on his return, "I refused to attend a dance with him last year. He told me I thought I was too good for him." Levi handed the note to H.W. as Judge Clementson called the court into recess until Monday morning.

H.W. shook his head as he read Rose's note, "This is a fine piece of irony, isn't it? She is accused of a crime because of unrequited love, and he seems to have no problem with committing a crime because of unrequited love. I told you this story would make a penny dreadful except it would be too ludicrous to believe."

CHAPTER 58

THURSDAY, JUNE 11, 1891

The morning sun sent beams of brilliant light through the courtroom windows as Rose sat with her father, Levi, and H.W. at the defense table. The two prior days had been filled with the testimony of the townspeople, most of whom had decided Rose's guilt without the inconvenience of her trial.

Rose sat in the stuffy courtroom sweating profusely under all the garments she was required to wear as a "lady of good repute". She had been surrounded by men for the last several days; Judge Clementson responded to the appeal by Levi and H.W. regarding the young women who were witnesses attending the daily hearings, by removing them from the proceedings but still allowing them to testify after hearing several days of testimony.

"The girls" as H.W. called them, Mae, Alice, Rena, and Lillie, each testified, recounting the days prior to the party, the night of the party, and the day of Ella's funeral. While each one told her own version, many of the phrases they used in their testimonies were strikingly similar, as if the girls had rehearsed their testimonies together. All of them focused on the candy given to Ella by Rose as a theme. Lillie went as far as to say she was certain the candy had contained poison, even though she had eaten some of it herself without dire consequences.

Lillie also testified that she heard Rose talking about people who died from seizures the night of the party, though no one else could corroborate hearing Rose say this. Rose shuddered as she watched her companions build the state's case against her. None of the girls would look at Rose, though she sat in a chair just a few feet from the witness stand with tears coursing down her cheeks at the loss of what she had considered her friends.

Mae's testimony was the most damaging against Rose as it included the letter. She claimed Rose had sent the letter to her after Ella's death asking Mae to give false testimony about the night of the party.

Levi asked the state to produce the letter as it had not been given to the defense prior to Mae's testimony, but somehow the letter had been misplaced and could not be relocated. DA Burnham produced several witnesses who had seen the letter, including one witness who claimed even Mrs. Wilson had stated it was in Rose's handwriting.

Levi and H.W. both objected that the testimony concerning the letter should not be admitted as evidence since the actual physical proof could not be given over for the defense to examine, but Judge Clementson overruled it, stating that too many of the witnesses had seen the letter for it not to have existed.

H.W. angered the judge by asking if the girls would also be permitted to produce spectral evidence much like the young girls of the Salem Witch trials in the 1600's. He was given a warning that he would soon stand in contempt of court. It would match the contempt H.W. felt for this "evidence".

Rose sat mute through the assassinations of her character, her mind reeling from the outright lies her supposed friends told about her. Everything in her wanted to stand up and protest, to defend herself, but both Levi and H.W. decided it might not be necessary for her to testify.

The past several days had worn Rose to the point of exhaustion. Each day she was taken from her tiny room in the sheriff's quarters to the stuffy, hot, smelly courtroom where she listened to countless versions of how she plotted to kill Ella in cold blood. She didn't think anything could be worse than what she had already endured.

Rose looked up from her silk fan she had placed in her lap to see Freddie being brought into the courtroom by George. Her heart froze as she saw how pale and thin Freddie had become in the last few months. Tears welled in Rose's eyes as she watched the bailiff swear Freddie in and seat him in the witness stand.

Freddie's voice was thin and reedy as he answered a few of DA Burnham's initial questions. Rose noticed his red-rimmed eyes and the tell-tale redness on the tips of his ears as signs of his distress. She tried to smile her encouragement at him when he glanced her way, but he turned in his seat so he could not glance her way again. That was when Rose understood she had not endured the worst of her trial yet.

"Yes, my father kept a bottle of strychnine in his office. He used it to poison mice by stuffing them into bits of cheese." Freddie answered the DA's question about the strychnine in the house with an honest account of its use. Rose nodded her head gently at Freddie, encouraging him to continue.

"Did Rose Zoldoske ever watch your father use the strychnine for this purpose? Did she know where the strychnine was kept?" DA Burnham led Freddie towards placing Rose with the strychnine.

"Yes, everyone in the house knew what it was for and where it was kept. Except for Lotte, of course, but she is only a baby." Freddie nodded while looking at his hands twisted together in his lap. Rose could tell Freddie was under duress by the way he pinched his own skin on his hands until they were bright red.

"Did Rose ever speak to you about becoming your stepmother or about Ella Maly becoming your stepmother?" The DA asked the question and allowed Freddie to sit quietly while everyone waited eagerly for his answer. Rose feared Freddie would incriminate himself by telling of the threats he had made against Ella to her. Freddie sat for a long time staring at his hands, then he glanced at George and blurted out the answer.

"Rose asked me about my father giving her a ring once. She wanted one. She told me Ella Maly liked my father too. Rose said if her own father ever tried to remarry, she would shoot or poison the woman. I guess that is what she wanted me to do but I didn't, so she did." Freddie stuttered slightly over the last few words, the clear sign to those who knew him well he was lying. He cleared his throat several times, trying to catch his breath.

The dagger of his lies pierced deep into Rose's heart and shattered it to pieces. Rose had given everything for Freddie and Lotte to keep her promise to Laura. Betrayal crashed down upon her in huge waves. She felt as though she were drowning, unable to take her next breath and unwilling to go on. Rose slumped forward onto the table, cracking her head against the hardwood.

Judge Clementson called a brief recess. Rose was picked up by Levi and carried from the courtroom with Deputy McGonigle leading the way. Mrs. Burris followed them as they took Rose to a nearby room to revive her.

"Rose, can you hear me?" Levi spoke loudly as he sat Rose in a chair and knelt beside her. Mrs. Burris splashed cold water on Rose's face and held her handkerchief with smelling salts near Rose's nose. The acrid smell of ammonia revived Rose enough to open her eyes. Her throat still felt closed, and a massive weight sat upon her chest. Rose recognized the initial pangs of grief she had suffered after hearing of her mother's death, but this new, strange grief seemed even more piercing in nature.

"He lied." The two words were pushed out of her closed throat with great exertion before the torrent of tears assailed her.

Levi looked up to see Dr. Haskell entered the room carrying his satchel. He laid the satchel on the table next to Rose and extracted a small vial from the bottom.

"She was overcome last year by the deaths of half of her family, and this looks like the reaction she had then. This will help calm her until we can think of something else." Dr Haskell poured the liquid into a cup of water Mrs. Burris held out for him. He held the cup to Rose's lips and encouraged her to drink the contents.

Rose opened her mouth to refuse, and the warm liquid rushed in over her teeth and tongue. The familiarity of the smell and taste of the laudanum soothed Rose before the medicine took effect. Soon, a hazy cloud covered her pain; she welcomed the relief.

Rose stood with help from Levi and walked back into the packed courtroom. H.W. was finishing the defense's questioning of Freddie, who still sat forlornly in the witness stand.

"So, to recap, you are saying Rose took excellent care of both you and your infant sister after your mother passed away?" H.W. tried to lessen the damage that Freddie's initial testimony incurred. "Do you recall who gave the medicine to your mother before she passed away? Was it Rose?"

"No, Rose wasn't in the room. It was my father. I was the only other person there with her." Freddie's eyes filled with tears at the memory of Laura's death. "I gave her the Nux Vomica, but he gave her something else along with it. She had a seizure and she died." Freddie's voice broke. He wiped the tears on his face with his sleeve.

Rose listened and was not certain she had heard Freddie correctly. She had never been told that George entered Laura's room and was there with Freddie when Laura died. She just remembered Annie shaking her awake at the dining room table and screaming that poor Freddie was with his mother when she died.

As though Rose's thoughts of Annie produced a sudden vision of the housekeeper herself, Annie stood at the witness stand as soon as Freddie exited it. Rose blinked her eyes several times, trying to decide if Annie was present or if she was seeing things. The strong smell of Annie's Lemon Verbena scent wafted through the air and mixed with the fetid body odors of the men gathered around her in the stuffy room. Rose felt the bile rise in her throat and forced it back down with a gulp.

Annie answered the DA's preliminary questions and went straight to the heart of her testimony against Rose.

"After the party, I saw Rose bring down a small paper bag and throw it on the cookstove fire. She asked me if the law could tell how a person had been poisoned after they died, and I told her I supposed they could. She then asked me if God forgives murderers, and I said I believed He most certainly wouldn't if it was someone as innocent as Miss Ella. Rose stormed from the kitchen and returned to her room where she paced back and forth the entire night. I asked what she was doing, and she told me she was praying. I then told her to be quiet about her praying." Annie blurted out her story quickly while staring at George in the gallery.

The familiar pangs of betrayal tripped about in Rose's chest, but the heavy dose of laudanum held the piercing grief at bay. Rose tried to shake her head in disagreement, but it felt too heavy to keep upright. Rose leaned her head in her hands with her elbows on the table. Her father sat close by, trying to help her remain upright in her chair.

Levi approached Annie on the witness stand with a grim look on his face. Annie told her story in a way that indicated she had memorized parts of it. Annie watched Levi warily from her seat and immediately looked at George in the gallery again. Levi noted the slight nod from George as he smiled smugly at the defense attorney.

"Miss McClaren, I noted from your testimony that Rose was noticeably upset the night of the dinner party after her guests had left. You stated that she threw away a paper bag into the cookstove and asked you about murderers going to heaven. Do I understand you correctly?" Levi read from the notes he had written of Annie's own words.

"Yes, Sir. That is correct. I also told her they could search the house and if anyone had anything to find they should get rid of it. Then Rose came back down with the paper bag." Annie nodded as she added the part of her story she had forgotten in her initial testimony.

"Hmm. I see. And as you stated, this was the evening of the party?" Levi remained calm as he pressed his question.

"Yes, Rose was up all night carrying on as I said." Annie twisted her handkerchief in her hands, nodding her head vehemently.

"Miss McClaren, if this occurred at the time as you have just testified, can you explain why Rose would be so upset about the murder when Ella Maly was still alive at the time? When, in fact, her own physicians, including Doctor Mitchell, thought Ella would live? Ella did not die until the following morning, so why would Rose react in such a way to you alone the night before Ella's passing? We have asked Mrs. Hendy and young Freddie who were both present with you and Rose and neither one can confirm your testimony." Levi watched Annie's eyes open wide with alarm as she glanced yet again at George.

"I might have got the time wrong. I was really upset. It was probably the night after Ella died. It all seemed like the same time." Annie's face was flushed, and her breath came in little pants. "It all seemed like the same time." She repeated to herself, another sign of false testimony.

"I would think such damaging testimony against Rose would be very easy to remember. You seemed to remember her words very well, but you can't recall when she said them?" Levi turned to the jury with an incredulous look, allowing them to see the discrepancies in Annie's memorized testimony.

Annie burst into tears on the stand and was promptly dismissed by Judge Clementson, who called both DA Burnham and Levi to his bench.

"I am calling a recess until tomorrow, when I expect to see a calm return to my courtroom and less frantic females. Don't disappoint me, gentlemen, or there will be hades to pay."

Rose was escorted from the courtroom in a haze of delirium. Mrs. Burris helped her lie down on her bed in the tiny bedroom, leaving her clothing on to speed the process for the following day. Dr. Haskell left a small amount of laudanum with Mrs. Burris along with instructions for ministration.

Levi walked from Rose's room in the jailhouse to the tavern down the street where H.W. was waiting in the private backroom. H.W. had an open bottle of whiskey with two glasses, he handed a glass to Levi as he downed his own.

"Looks like it will be another long night. We need to decide what to do about Rose and the witness stand." H.W. poured another drink from the bottle for himself before offering the bottle to Levi.

Levi poured another drink. He was not accustomed to strong spirits, but he needed something to help him face the outrageousness they had experienced from the opinions of the girls to the outright lies of the housekeeper. It seemed the entire community of Richland Center found Rose guilty first and then found the evidence they needed to prove it, whether it was true or not.

"After Judge Clementson's warning about frantic females, I don't see as though we have any choices left." Levi took another drink to assuage the strong feelings of doubt about his decision. He hoped it was the right decision; the rest of Rose's life depended on it.

CHAPTER 59

FRIDAY, JUNE 12, 1891

Rose sat in her chair in the Lancaster courtroom for what felt like the one-hundredth day of testimony against her, when it had been only seven days. Dr. Haskell adjusted the amount of laudanum he gave in each dose to help Rose remain alert without having an emotional breakdown in front of Judge Clementson. So, here Rose sat, numb and mute, wondering if she had died and been sent to her own personal version of hell.

DA Burnham finally concluded the state's case after calling fifty-two witnesses, many of whom Rose had never even met. There were medical doctors explaining what could have happened if Rose had poisoned Ella, townspeople who overheard Rose saying incriminating things about herself and Ella's death, and even Laura's sister who testified that "she never liked the girl."

Each witness for the state was carefully cross-examined by Levi and H.W. to make certain no one had seen Rose poison Ella, and no one heard Rose admit she had done anything to Ella or Laura.

Levi, on the other hand, was very succinct. The burden of proof was on the prosecution, who in his estimation failed to make any case of substantial proof against Rose. He called Mrs. Dora Wilson to the stand to testify on Rose's behalf. The elderly milliner sat in the witness chair and faced the jury with a determined look on her face. Her gray dress was immaculate with a darker gray hat to match it, framing her silver hair to perfection.

"Mrs. Wilson, you have been called as a witness on behalf of the accused, Rose Zoldoske. Can you give the jury an idea of your relationship with her?" Levi smiled gently as Mrs. Wilson straightened her back and nodded her head emphatically.

"Yes, Sir, I can. I am one of the only people who have known Rose from the first day that she came to our city. She was sent by her parents to work in my milliner's shop to help them financially. I set up the boarding arrangement at the Mitchell home with the late Mrs. Laura Mitchell who was so happy to have Rose as a boarder and later as one of her closest friends." Dora Wilson spoke clearly as she looked at the men of the jury.

"Did you ever experience any problems with Rose as an employee? Was she dishonest or untrustworthy as the prosecution has claimed?"

"No. Rose was an honest girl and an excellent employee. She always stayed up late if she thought I needed extra help. I came to count on her and trusted her completely. Rose helped at the Mitchell home as well, for no extra monetary benefit. She helped to care for Mrs. Mitchell who was often ill and for the Mitchell children." Mrs. Wilson glanced up to see George staring at her from his seat in the gallery. She stared back at him momentarily, making him look away.

"The prosecution brought testimony that Mrs. Mitchell was only sick after her second child was born and after Rose entered their home. Is that the case?" Levi knew Mrs. Wilson had strong feelings about what happened to Laura Mitchell.

"It is not true. Laura Mitchell's health declined after the sudden death of their daughter, Nellie, in 1887. Many thought Laura would fade away and pass on, but Rose brought Laura back from her despondency when she came to stay with them. Laura had a very difficult childbirth with the baby, Lotte, in February of last year and never recovered from it. I was present at the birthing and can attest to the fact that we almost lost Laura Mitchell at that time. Dr. Haskell had to be called in to try and save Laura's life as well as the baby's. Rose had nothing to do with Laura's death just as she had nothing to do with Ella's."

"You mentioned Ella's death. Did you ever hear Rose say anything bad about Ella Maly? Did Rose behave unkindly towards her?" Levi knew that, as one of the people closest to Rose, Dora was the most likely to hear or see something.

"Ella was kindness itself. She was friendly to Rose when several of the other girls who testified in this trial were very unkind to her and left her out. Ella included Rose in activities with the young folks so Rose would not be a stranger in a new place. Rose acted grateful towards Ella and counted her as her friend. I never heard a mean word about Ella uttered by Rose, and I spent more time with Rose than anyone else." Dora told the truth about the relationship between the two girls, dispelling the conjecture of jealousy and rage.

"Did Rose ever mention wanting to marry Dr. Mitchell? Was she jealous of Ella Maly?" Levi went to the heart of the argument against Rose.

"The only time Rose mentioned a relationship with him was when she talked about the Mitchell children. Rose was devoted to

Freddie and Lotte. She promised Laura Mitchell she would always look out for them. At one point she spoke of marrying Dr. Mitchell in a type of arranged marriage so she could be a mother to the children, but I told her that she deserved a marriage based on mutual love and respect. Rose would not have been jealous of someone she did not even love." Dora glanced at where George sat again to find that his chair was empty.

"Then this was not a case of unrequited love as the prosecution would have us believe?" Levi turned to the men of the jury as he asked the question. Without a clear motive, the circumstantial evidence gathered by the prosecution was of little use.

"Rose did not love Dr. Mitchell. No one could love Dr. Mitchell as much as Dr. Mitchell." Dora's blue eyes snapped with her response as several of the jury members chuckled out loud.

"I see. I have only one more question for you. It is about the testimony concerning the letter sent to Mae Hyndman asking her to give false testimony. Several of the state's witnesses testified that you saw the letter and proclaimed it was Rose's handwriting. Is that the case?"

"No, it is not. There was a note that Mac's mother brought to my house. This note asked Mae to state Rose had not asked Ella to come upstairs and that there was not any candy. It was supposedly written and signed by Rose on her personal stationery. I did not state that it was Rose's handwriting to anyone because I knew it wasn't Rose's handwriting. Rose wrote out customer orders for me every day and I know what her handwriting looks like. All of Rose's stationery was missing from the pile of her belongings that were dumped by George Mitchell's hired hands behind my shop. Rose did not have access to her stationery to write that note to Mae. That is what I stated to Mae's mother and to anyone else who may have overheard it. I find it is odd that Mae supported Rose's innocence until she received that note, as did all the other girls who testified against Rose." Dora Wilson's clear voice carried through the silent courtroom.

Levi noticed several of the jury members nod and lean forward during the last part; signs that they believed Dora Wilson as a witness. He smiled at Mrs. Wilson as he walked back to the defense table. DA Burnham asked Mrs. Wilson several questions about the letter and its existence, using her to verify that the letter had existed but failing to get her to verify Rose was the writer of the letter.

"Rose is a good girl. Some people have gotten an idea in their heads that someone must pay for Ella's tragic death, but Rose has done nothing to show she did anything to Ella. There are several other people in town who would be just as likely or more likely to have hurt Ella than Rose. Why don't we see their good names dragged through the mud as they have done to Rose? Is it because she is a woman, from a poor family, who has no power or prestige?" Dora Wilson finished her testimony with questions that would linger.

"The defense rests its case." Levi stood as Mrs. Wilson was helped from the witness stand by the bailiff. She paused for a moment in front of the defense table to touch Rose's hand as she passed by, a moment of warm human contact.

H.W. nodded his appreciation for Mrs. Wilson's efforts in defending Rose. The elderly woman nodded back and continued to follow the bailiff back to the ante room where witnesses were kept.

"One witness, and she says the whole thing in a nutshell," H.W. whispered to Levi as they stood for Judge Clementson's departure. They both knew they would face redirect testimony of the prosecution's witnesses and then the closing statement by DA Burnham the next morning, but they were ready.

"Once it has been exposed, a lie loses all of its acceptability." Levi encouraged Rose as he helped her from her chair and walked with her towards the jailhouse. Mrs. Burris nodded in agreement as she and Rose's father followed them through the throngs of people gathered on the courthouse lawn.

Rose braced herself for the customary jeers from the crowds, including the name she had come to dread, "Borgia Rose". She put her head down, covered her ears, and closed her eyes to shut out the taunts. Rose was startled when Levi paused in the mass of people and leaned to whisper in her ear.

"Rose, look up. Listen to what they are saying." Levi pulled one of Rose's hands away from her ear as she lifted her face. Scores of women and girls were gathered in small groups along the way, all of them chanting the same thing.

"Save Rose Zoldoske! Set the innocent free!" The gentle lilt of the voices together rose through the air, building each time the phrases were repeated until it echoed off the old stone walls of the massive courthouse. Rose was certain she was hearing a chorus of angels and she was in hell no longer.

CHAPTER 60

SATURDAY, JUNE 13, 1891

Rose returned to the courtroom with Levi, heartened by the support of the gathered groups of women and girls along their morning route to the courthouse. The bright pastels of the crinoline dresses and parasols they wore reminded Rose of a vibrant bouquet.

Many of the ladies handed Rose nosegays fashioned of daisies and violets bound together with ribbons. Mrs. Burris collected the individual nosegays into a colorful bouquet that dispelled the more unpleasant odors emitted from the inhabitants inside the stuffy courtroom.

It was time for each side to give their closing comments to the jury before they retired to decide their verdict, sealing Rose's fate. DA Burnham stood before the jury box leaning on the balustrade to emphasize his unity with the members of the jury.

"This is a simple matter of a woman's jealousy. Rose Zoldoske realized she was not the recipient of Dr. Mitchell's attention, so she did what she thought necessary to remove any competition for those attentions. In fact, this time was easier because she had removed Dr. Mitchell's wife, the unfortunate Laura Mitchell, from her place in Dr. Mitchell's affections."

"While Mr. Bancroft would like you to believe the state does not have a case, this is anything but the truth of the matter. Rose Zoldoske herself is the most damaging witness to her bizarre conduct before and after Ella Maly's murder. *She* gave the party, *she* bought the food, *she* gave candy poisoned with strychnine to Ella Maly, because *she* alone had the ultimate reason; *she* wanted Dr. George Mitchell for herself. This was a cold-blooded murder. Gentlemen, *she* did it. Do not let the murder of so bright a star as Ella go unpunished. Give her justice."

Levi placed his hand over Rose's hand momentarily before rising from his seat to face the jury. He had put a single daisy from Rose's bouquet in the buttonhole of his lapel as a reminder to the male jury of the substantial female population amassing outside proclaiming Rose's innocence. Though they were not allowed to serve as members of the jury, they wished for their collective voices to be heard.

"Gentlemen of the Jury, what has been presented to you by the prosecution has not been evidence that would convict a person of any given crime. It has been the opinion of those who did not see Rose Zoldoske commit any crime, let alone murder, but the presumption she must be guilty because they think she is."

"It was only by means of an outrageous public sentiment that Rose was held over for trial in the first place. While here in this courtroom, Rose has been made to endure the cutting, humiliating remarks of a bunch of vinegary old maids who took it upon themselves to besmirch her character, which until that time had been spotless in the community. Has anyone dared to ask themselves the question if Rose had been guilty of murdering Mrs. Mitchell why no one had, including the good Dr. Mitchell, made accusations for nearly a year? Why would Rose be allowed to remain in their home caring for their defenseless children if she was a cold-blooded murderer? That accusation concerning Laura Mitchell was only made because it was then easier to believe that Rose would also murder Ella Maly in a similar fashion."

"Evidence, fueled by public opinion, does not provide the burden of proof necessary to convict Rose Zoldoske of murder. It is now up to you as the members of the jury to decide whether hearsay and sentiment will be allowed to convict my client of murder as you are not deciding about her innocence or guilt. The prosecution failed to present anything to you to convict her."

"A tragedy has occurred in our small town. A beautiful young woman died, leaving all who knew her shocked and devastated at such a loss. While my sympathy continues for Ella's parents and her family, I find myself devastated that another life could be completely ruined on the basis that the popular feeling is, 'she did this'. We cannot bring Ella back with this verdict, but we still have the capacity to rescue Rose from the tragedy that has befallen her by declaring her innocent of all charges."

It was four-thirty in the afternoon before Judge Clementson began his instructions to the jury. Upon reminding them of their sworn duty, he dismissed them to deliberate in the attached jury room.

H.W. watched the men selected as the jury members file out after being dismissed. He knew he and Levi had done their job; they had defended Rose to the best of their abilities against the tide of public sentiment against her. Now came the most helpless feeling endured by any attorney in a trial when their job was complete, leaving the entire decision in the hands of twelve people.

CHAPTER 61

SUNDAY, JUNE 14, 1891

The remnants of a home-cooked fried chicken dinner were still on Rose's small dining table when Sheriff Burris arrived with Mrs. Burris following close behind. Rose stood by the small rocker and automatically smoothed her hair and dress to receive her visitors.

"The jury has reached a verdict. We must get you ready to appear before Judge Clementson in the next hour. I apologize for interrupting your Sunday meditations, Rose. It is very rare the court will convene on the Lord's Day, but it must when the verdict has come back." Sheriff Burris's large form took up a great deal of the space in the small room as he looked sympathetically at Rose.

"Thank you, Sheriff. I will change my clothes and be ready to leave shortly. I am sorry this interrupts your time with your family." Rose knew from her time spent in the home of the Lancaster sheriff that Sunday afternoons were set aside for the Burris family to gather in the parlor of their home. She could hear the faint giggles from the grandchildren drifting down the hallway towards her room.

"Hopefully this will mean you get to return to your home and family, Rose. Soon it will be something of the past to put behind you." Mrs. Burris stepped forward to embrace Rose. She noted the slender form in her arms shaking slightly. Mrs. Burris realized Rose was terrified of facing her fate that was in the hands of the jurors.

"I am not certain where I will go next or what I will do when this matter is finished. I realize it would not be prudent to return to my home in Richland County but to return to Oklahoma with my father when my mother and siblings are gone seems just as bleak. I guess I will have to make those decisions after I hear what decision the jury has made." Rose walked to where the black dress she wore each day of the trial hung from a nail in the wall. The dress looked as limp and lifeless as Rose felt. "Wherever I go, I think I will spend days and days outside in the sun and fresh air."

Sheriff Burris left his wife in the room to assist Rose with dressing herself and combing her hair into a tidy bun at the nape. Soon Rose was ready to leave her room and cross the courtyard towards the courthouse. She hoped this would be her final trip to a courtroom or a jail.

Levi and H.W. were waiting for Rose at the courthouse door. Crowds of people had begun to gather in mass as the word spread through the small town that the verdict had been reached. Many of the town's inhabitants waited on the courthouse lawn overnight, eager to gain access to the limited seats in the courtroom when the verdict was read.

The tickets for the seats had been dispensed in less than ten minutes to the fortunate few who waited and slept on benches and the ground. The rest of those gathered drew near the main doors, understanding that word of the verdict would be called out from the front stairs.

There was a nervous hum in the courtroom as Rose entered. Her father had been summoned by Levi from a nearby boarding house. He hugged Rose tightly as she approached the defense table.

"Steady now, my girl." Andrew Zoldoske whispered in his daughter's ear. "Mr. Bancroft says a quick verdict is usually a good thing for the defendant." He nodded his encouragement as though he were trying to convince himself as well as Rose.

"That is often the case. This jury only took twenty-one hours to reach their verdict. It means their minds were set on their decision from the beginning. With the lack of evidence that bodes well for us." H.W. added his vast experience with juries as encouragement for Rose.

Everyone stood as Judge Clementson entered the courtroom, followed by the members of the jury. The hum in the room grew louder as the anticipation grew to a frenzied pitch. Judge Clementson glared at the gallery as he pounded his gavel for silence.

"There will be quiet in this courtroom. I want to caution everyone to not succumb to dramatics when hearing the verdict read by the foreman. I will not abide by outbursts of any kind. Mr. Bancroft, is your client ready to stand and hear the verdict?"

"She is ready, your Honor." Levi and H.W. stood, helping Rose to her feet, and bolstering her on both sides. Rose watched as the jury foreman stood and faced the judge, waiting to read the verdict, being prompted by the judge's question.

"Foreman Baxter, in the case of the State of Wisconsin vs. Rose Zoldoske, how do you find the defendant? Guilty or not guilty?

"We find Rose Zoldoske guilty of murder in the first degree." The jury foreman's voice crackled slightly, his hand holding the paper before him trembled.

There was a slight whoosh as though the air in the room were being sucked out in a vacuum. Rose closed her eyes and bowed her head, trembling at her knees but staying upright with help from Levi and H.W. She felt as if the small amount of life that had been left within her was suddenly gone.

"Rose Zoldoske, you have been found guilty of murder in the first degree. This holds a mandatory life sentence. Henceforth you will be remanded to the state penitentiary in Waupun to begin your sentence." Judge Clementson's low voice resembled a growl to the listeners. Everyone was so shocked at the verdict that no one noticed the momentary look of surprise displayed on the magistrate's features before he gathered his composure.

"This is not over, Rose. We will appeal this ruling." Levi whispered in Rose's ear, hoping she would hear him. She had not made a sound. Her reaction seemed almost supernatural in quality.

"Your honor, we would like to request the application for appeal. I request the motion for a new trial." Levi's voice carried through the courtroom like a command.

"Yes, I had no doubt that you would, Mr. Bancroft. I will set a date for a hearing for the twenty-first of July and keep the defendant here in Lancaster until that date. Court is dismissed." Judge Clementson studied Rose as he spoke. She had not uttered a single cry nor shown any emotion save for a flush of color in her face.

A sorrowful Deputy McGonigal came to escort Rose back to her room in the jailhouse. He held one of Rose's arms firmly and Levi held the other. Both men prepared to carry Rose, if necessary, but Rose proceeded forward, walking on her own powered by sheer determination. She promised herself that those who wished to see her downfall would not get the luxury of seeing her collapse.

The courthouse bells were ringing as the silent procession made its way out of the courthouse. The crowds watched in awe as Rose proceeded forward, flanked by Levi and Deputy McGonigal and followed by H.W. and Andrew Zoldoske. She stared straight forward and did not flinch at the taunts of "Borgia Rose" flung at her; the words used as weapons of hatred.

They reached the sidewalk of the jailhouse when Andrew fell to the ground, sobbing with grief for his daughter. The crowd hushed to watch the grizzled old man writhe on the ground. H.W. stopped to help Andrew, lifting him, and placing him on his feet, guiding him along the pathway.

They ascended the stairs leading into the main part of the jailhouse, their normal route to the side door blocked by the massive crowd gathered. Sheriff Burris and Mrs. Burris met them at the doors, throwing them wide open for Rose to pass through with Levi and the deputy on both sides. H.W. followed, carrying Andrew up the stairs and into the jailhouse.

Sheriff Burris closed the heavy doors behind them, blocking out the noise of the crowds. The coolness of the stone walls kissed Rose's cheeks as the silence of the empty hallways seemed almost deafening in comparison to the tumult outside.Rose took several steps then threw herself forward onto the stone floor. She lay prostrate, the coldness of the stone seeping through her garments matching the icy cold that surrounded her heart. Mrs. Burris and Levi knelt beside her, allowing her to lie there, hidden at last from the prying crowds.

The first wracking sobs bubbled up in her throat. She had held her peace until she could no more and now the grief of her reality assailed her body and soul. The keening grew in intensity, echoing off the walls until it sounded as though a multitude mourned with her. A life sentence.

The small group of supporters surrounded Rose and quietly waited for her crying to subside. No one told her to hush or tried to stop Rose in her mourning process. Their consolation for Rose came in the simple act of being quiet, patient, and present.

Those gathered around Rose traded glances imparting the mutual feeling they shared; Ella had lost her young life and now Rose, in turn, had lost her own.

CHAPTER 62

TUESDAY, JULY 21, 1891

The sultry July heat caused crystal beads of condensation to form on the cold glass of iced tea that sat untouched in front of Levi. He and H.W. met at their usual spot in the back of the tavern on Madison Street after Rose's appeal hearing that morning.

H.W. swirled the whiskey in his glass before taking another sip. He wiped the perspiration from his brow with a white silk handkerchief, then returned the wadded handkerchief to his inner vest pocket. His linen suit coat lay over the chair next to him. He had removed it due to the sweltering heat.

H.W. watched his law partner carefully. Since returning from the courthouse, Levi had not said a word. Like Rose, the young attorney was struck mute by the incredible outcome of the original trial and now the written motion for a new trial. H.W. knew he needed to get Levi to talk; even if that speech involved yelling, cursing, crying, and a complete paroxysm.

"There have been plenty of rumors about town that the jury stood at six and six originally. This paper says it went to eight and four by Saturday evening but then stuck there until the wee hours of Sunday morning when it turned to ten and two. The final juror is quoted as stating that he changed his vote because his family was in town to fetch him, and he wanted to return home with them. So, you don't have any evidence to convict Rose, but you condemn her with a life sentence because it fits in your timeline to get home before dark?" H.W. balled up the copy of the *Lancaster Teller* and threw it at the wall.

Levi stared at the glass in front of him, seemingly unaware H.W. had spoken. The separate beads of condensation now joined to form rivulets of water that flowed off the smooth surface of the glass and pooled on the oak table beneath it. Myrtle would have scolded him for allowing the water to make a ring on the table. His thoughts shifted from the water stains to his wife and newborn daughter Carolyn.

Carolyn had been born that May and Levi spent little time with his first child and her mother. He had been so preoccupied with Rose's trial he had not realized how many times he left their home in Richland Center to stay in the boarding house in Lancaster so that he could prepare their case with H.W.

Myrtle seemed to understand and yet lately there was a tension each time Levi prepared to leave for Lancaster since the trial in June. He convinced himself that all their sacrifices would be worth it when Rose was acquitted in a second trial.

Myrtle told Levi about the public sentiment in Richland County upon hearing the verdict. There were cheers and well wishes; someone mentioned getting together for a town picnic, but a few felt that might be in bad taste. Myrtle had been ostracized by a few of the more prominent families except for Julia Bowen and Laura Briggs James. This powerful duo helped to form the brigade of women and girls that kept a vigil on behalf of Rose at the Lancaster courthouse. Laura's fifteen-year-old daughter, Ada, had been at her side during their vigils.

"I was satisfied to hear that the jurors faced a mob of angry women when they left the courthouse." H.W. commented as though he had been reading Levi's thoughts; it seemed to be one of H.W.'s particular skills. "Those jurors weren't so high and mighty when set upon by a huge group of very irate women. One fellow even commented, 'I do not claim that she was guilty,' to try and escape the wrath. If you don't claim that she was guilty, how in the world do you vote that she was guilty?"

H.W. poured more whiskey into his empty glass. "Then, we arrived at a hearing today to appeal for a new trial amid several errors that would cause a mistrial in any other venue and the honorable Judge Clementson has surrounded himself with a group of cronies who have convinced him the verdict is correct, and no new trial is needed. So, we have a murder conviction based on no real evidence and a denial of the motion for a new trial because he 'feels it was right the first time'. I was ready to claim a kangaroo court today."

Deep pain stabbed through Levi's chest at H.W.'s reminder of the denial of the motion for a new trial. All the sacrifices he had made were for nothing. Rose was due on tomorrow morning's train to Waupun where she would begin her life sentence without parole.

He needed to ask himself honestly, how had this happened? He knew from the moment he met with Rose on the street that cold morning she had been the victim of public outrage and there wasn't enough evidence to convict her beyond a reasonable doubt. He had never lost a case prior to this one; many of those cases had far more evidence against the defendants. How could an innocent person spend the rest of her life in jail because there were enough people who "felt" she did it?

"Well, I guess it's time to pull up shop and go home. I mean, we did everything we could to help her, right?" H.W. paused to study Levi. This was his final tactic. If he knew anything about Levi H Bancroft, this tactic would work, telling him to give up.

Suddenly, with a clarity that cut through the mental haze of his thoughts, Levi knew with certainty this case was not about the number of sacrifices he made, it was not about losing his first trial. It was about defending an innocent person against extreme measures of bias and injustice. It was the reason he had chosen law over all other professions.

Levi stood from his chair, scooped up the still full glass and threw it hard against the opposite wall. Shards of glass flew as the glass disintegrated from the force, sending the amber-colored liquid cascading down the wall.

"No. We don't go home. We get ready to go to the Wisconsin Supreme Court." Levi glared at H.W. and turned on his heel, leaving the room.

H.W, smiled broadly to himself as he reached in his vest pocket for money to recompense the tavern owner for the mess they had created. He picked up his suit coat and his hat from the nearby chair, remembering to pick up Levi's hat from where Levi had left it during his hasty exit.

"Yes, indeed, Mr. Bancroft. The Wisconsin Supreme Court it is."

CHAPTER 63

APRIL 6, 1892, WAUPUN STATE PENITENTIARY

"Visitors." The single word was barked through the early morning gray that surrounded Rose as she lay on her cot. Her eyes remained closed; she did not need to see what surrounded her as she had memorized every square inch of her cell in the past nine months. Rose shivered and pulled the scratchy wool blanket tighter against her body. She learned through the freezing cold winter that she would rather suffer the intense chafing than suffer hypothermia from the lack of the blanket's meager protection.

"I said get up!" the guard demanded as a rod, thrust through the cell bars, poked Rose hard in the small of her back. She looked over her shoulder to see the guard watching her with a lewd expression that conveyed his salacious intentions. Rose rolled over quickly and scrambled to her feet, grasping the wall to keep herself upright. She knew she had moved too quickly but she did not want the guard to have a reason to enter her cell. She witnessed what happened when the guards entered the female prisoners' cells alone.

Rose leaned her head against the filthy cement wall as she tried to clear her vision. She had been experiencing dizzy spells frequently. Her black hair hung in limp strands across her face. She tried to push it back, but it clung there.

"Please. I need some water to wash." Rose knew her request would fall on deaf ears. Most of the prisoners were given a basin of cloudy water once a week if they were lucky, and many had given up on taking care of personal hygiene altogether.

The smell of body odor mixed with stale urine pervaded the cell block. Rose tried to keep herself clean with what little she had available to her disposal, but she had been doing less and less as of late to try and dissuade the interest of her guards.

Rose was surprised to hear the clang of a basin coming through the slot in the door and looked to see a chipped white enamel basin with an inch of clean water in it. Rose stooped over to pick up the basin, carrying it to her cot. She reached for the old rags she kept from a prison laundry pile and dipped a rag into the water. It was frigid, with small chips of ice floating in it, but Rose did not care.

Rose bathed her face with the rag and turned her back to the cell door. She unbuttoned the top of her dress, giving her just enough room to slide the rag inside her dress. She attempted to be as modest and quick as possible because she knew for a fact the guard still stood there watching her. She unbuttoned the dress further to reach below her waist, knowing that was the better option than trying to lift her skirts. A lifted skirt was an automatic open invitation for undesired attention.

Rose wanted to take her time with the unexpected bath, but she knew the guard would grow impatient. She soon finished her scrubbing. Rebuttoning her gray prison dress, she reached under the cot for one of her prized possessions; the hairbrush sent by Mrs. Wilson. Rose tried to brush her oily hair into a semblance of order. She finally placed the required gray scarf over her hair to cover it and hide the entrenched snarls.

"You're a pretty gal, if only you were nicer." The guard's blatant suggestion made Rose shudder inwardly. She knew many of the female prisoners traded their bodies for the favor of the guards. It seemed to be an accepted part of the penitentiary's existence, but Rose had kept herself distant, still hoping for the reprieve from the Supreme Court that Levi promised her.

She went to the cell door and held her hands with her wrists touching through the upper bars. The clink of the iron shackles biting down on her wrists rattled in the silence around them. Rose pulled her hands back towards herself as the door began to rattle, announcing that her guard would fling it open whether or not she had pulled free of the door.

Rose followed the guard several steps before a second guard stepped out of one of the nearby cells and followed her down the corridor. She had learned to walk quickly, keep her head down, and her eyes on the floor in front of her as they traversed through several locked doors and into a separate section of the prison.

The hallway walls in this section were a bright white in color and the windows allowed the rays of the morning sun to shine through, illuminating the brilliance. Rose winced, as her eyes adjusted to the bright light. She wanted to pause in front of a window to feel the warmth of the sun on her face, but she knew a hard shove would be the response of the guards if she faltered.

The guard in front of her paused at a door and opened it, stepping aside to allow Rose to enter the small visiting room. Rose entered in her customary stance, with her head down, her eyes on the floor, and her hands shackled in front of her.

"Blimey!" H.W. spoke the word in shock at seeing Rose in her current state. Rose lifted her head to see him standing beside Levi and another man she did not recognize. H.W.'s face turned beet red as he ran his hand through his hair in frustration.

"Take those things off her." H.W. turned to the guard, pointing at the shackles on Rose's wrists. The guard found his key and stepped over to unlock the restraints. Rose shied from the guard's touch, momentarily causing a look of alarm on Levi's face and a murderous look on H.W.'s. As soon as Rose was freed from the shackles, Levi led her to a chair by the table in the center of the room.

"You can leave now." Levi instructed the guards. H.W. stepped towards the guard who entered the room with Rose, clenching his fists in a threatening manner.

"We ain't allowed to leave the prisoner alone." The young man knew he had made a mistake as soon as he uttered the words. H.W. stepped closer until he was inches from the guard's face.

"We are her legal counsel so we can be alone with her. You will leave this room now. In fact, don't come back. Send someone else for her if you know what's good for you." H.W. had an illustrious college career as a pugilist, having never lost a boxing match. He was silently daring the young bully to step out of line. The guard left the room, quickly closing the door behind him.

Levi picked up his satchel and pulled out an apple, sandwiches, and several cookies. "Myrtle always sends too much for me to eat.

Please help yourself." Levi placed the food on his handkerchief in front of Rose. "We will go and get you something to drink as well."

Rose wanted to refuse the offer of the food, but her stomach growled, and her mouth watered at the sight of the repast. She nodded at Levi and picked up half of a sandwich. The fresh bread and salty ham melted in her mouth and before she knew it, she devoured the entire thing. Levi pushed the other half of the sandwich towards her along with the second sandwich.

"Please have all of it. I get tired of the same thing, and it will give me a chance to get something else for a change." Levi's lie was obvious, but he knew Rose might refuse the offering otherwise. "Just take it slowly so that you don't make yourself sick."

"We have been working to get your case scheduled with the Wisconsin Supreme Court, Rose. We are on the docket for the end of May. Levi has filed a writ of error and it has been accepted for consideration by the high court." H.W. sat beside Rose watching her inhale the food in front of her as she nodded at him. It was obvious from her nonverbal responses that she was out of the habit of social conversation. His heart broke at the sight before him; the once vibrant, social, meticulous young woman was reduced to a mute, ravaged shell of her former self.

Rose lifted her eyes from the food she consumed to the man who sat quietly observing her from the other side of the table. She looked back at Levi with a questioning expression on her face.

"Please forgive my manners, Rose. I failed to introduce Mr. Chamberlin. He is an attorney from northern Wisconsin. He has experience in arguing cases before the state Supreme Court, so we have asked him to join us on your defense team." Levi gestured towards the older man who continued to study Rose quietly.

"I am pleased to meet you, Rose. Please call me Frank. Hopefully, I will be able to assist Levi and H.W. in getting your verdict over-turned. I think there may be a couple of ways I can aid you regarding your current circumstances as well." Frank stood and crossed to the closed door, opening it, and calling for the guard stationed down the hallway.

"Please inform the warden that F.C. Chamberlin is waiting for a word. I will expect him in a few minutes." Frank shut the door in the guard's face and turned back to the table. Rose looked at the older man. He was short and wiry; his full gray mustache and beard reminded her of a goat. It was obvious Frank was a prestigious attorney and expected other people to listen to him, but there was a gentler side he reserved for a few.

Within minutes, the prison warden appeared in the doorway looking nervously at the lawyers gathered around their bedraggled client. Frank stood and came to shake the warden's hand in introduc-tion. He wasted no time getting to the point of the matter; Rose liked that.

"Can you tell me which cell block Miss Zoldoske is currently housed in and who her overseer is?" Frank spoke with a direct authority that was polite but authoritative.

"Yes. The prisoner is in Cell Block B. There isn't a female over-seer." The warden shifted his weight from one foot to another. He knew female prisoners were supposed to have female overseers to prevent violations against them.

"That won't do at all. I want to see Miss Zoldoske moved to Cell Block A this morning. I believe Edna Barnett is the overseer there. Am I correct?" Frank's eyes pierced the warden's glances at his hands grasped in front of him.

"Yes, Edna is in charge of Cell Block A, but I don't think there is room for the prisoner in that cell block." The warden gave one attempt at asserting his meager authority but soon crumbled at the withering looks he received from Frank and H.W.

"Then you will go and make room for her right now. I don't want to see her in the sole company of male guards again or I will be forced to call for an investigation by the commission. We will wait here while you go and make those arrangements and send Mrs. Barnett back to collect Miss Zoldoske, who will not be referred to as 'the prisoner' by you or your staff henceforth. Please make certain those arrangements are permanent as I will be checking on our client personally, with unscheduled visits. You can send this helpful fellow back to collect Miss Zoldoske's possessions from her other cell so she can account for everything in my presence." Frank pointed at the young guard who had brought Rose from her cell that morning.

Both men departed and within an hour, Rose's bag with all her possessions arrived, as well as the overseer of prison block A, Edna Barnett, who greeted Frank with a smile and a handshake.

"I can see you have received a less than satisfactory welcome, Rose." Edna Barnett spoke directly to Rose with a calm demeanor. "Let's go get you settled and perhaps look into getting a bath and some new clothes for you. All my girls are respectable and conduct themselves with decorum and, in return, they receive the respect they deserve. I will also find a job for you, perhaps with the seamstresses, as it helps each one of us to have an occupation. If you will excuse us gentlemen, Rose and I have a lot to do." Edna helped Rose to her feet. When Rose held out her hands for the shackles, Edna shook her head and patted Rose's shoulder.

"There won't be any need for those. I can already tell you are going to be just fine with me." Edna nodded at Frank as she led Rose out of the room.

Rose was given not only the promised bath in a private room but the opportunity to wash her hair and braid it. Edna brought a new gray prison dress along with new undergarments for Rose to don. She also brought a small needle and thread for Rose to keep in her cell with her belongings.

"I find keeping a needle and thread on hand helps my girls to keep their own dresses mended and tidy. I will leave you to settle here and get a place ready for you to join in the mending room after lunch." Edna stepped from Rose's cell and closed the door with a clank.

Rose could not believe her change in circumstances. In one morning, she went from a dismal place void of hope to a place of promise and optimism. She was still in prison, but she was going to be treated as a respectable person with a purpose instead of a primal animal that needed to be locked in a cage. Edna Barnett was one of the pioneers of rehabilitation in the penitentiary system.

Rose used her time to embroider a small design on the inside cuff of her dress to mark the day her life began again. She would work, she would wait, and she would hope Levi, H.W., and Frank would get her conviction overturned in the coming month.

Hope had returned in the darkest of places.

CHAPTER 64

SATURDAY, MAY 28, 1892, STATE CAPITOL. MADISON, WISCONSIN

Levi sat waiting in the hallway leading to the north wing of the Wisconsin State Capitol. He had come to sit on the bench outside the Supreme Court hearing room before dawn as he had not been able to sleep in his comfortable hotel room located down the street.

"How long have you been waiting here?" Frank approached Levi's bench from the staircase leading to the ground floor. "I thought I was too early, but you have me beat. What time is H.W. arriving with Rose?" Frank took a seat on the bench and removed a cigar from his vest pocket. He clenched the stogie between his teeth without lighting it, an obvious sign to Levi the veteran attorney was nervous despite his calm façade.

"They are due on the eight o'clock train. H.W. sent a telegram this morning. He said Rose was waiting and ready to leave when he arrived." Levi's voice carried through the silent hallway even though he attempted to lower his volume. The dome of the building carried the slightest sounds and echoed them throughout the structure.

"That doesn't surprise me one bit. Edna Barnett will be accompanying Rose and she doesn't stand for tardiness. I guess that makes us a flock of early birds." Frank chuckled at his own pun. Levi grimaced slightly.

"I have gone over every argument in the case again and again. It still galls me to believe a jury could come to a guilty verdict with no actual physical evidence against Rose. From the first day of law school, we are taught things that are not proved in law are the same as things that have no existence." Levi gripped the stack of documents in his hand, pointing them at the courtroom door down the corridor.

"Unfortunately, the farmers who composed the jury never attended law school. We both understand a trial is a civil procedure and not a religious one. It appears to me that the emotional sensationalism created by a few powerful and upstanding citizens became a moral judgment that didn't require legal evidence." Frank took the cigar from his mouth and studied it, rolling it between his fingers.

"Which makes Rose's trial more of an inquisition than a legal criminal trial. There were people in Richland Center who compared the twelve members of her jury to the twelve apostles after the verdict was returned!" Levi relived the complete astonishment he had experienced to the town's reaction.

"This is why we can set this straight beginning today. I wish the recently retired Justice Cole was still presiding over the court. He has always been a vehement defender of the poor and the downtrodden. He adamantly refused to uphold the fugitive slave act when it was still enforced." Frank stood as he saw H.W. approaching them, escorting Rose and Mrs. Barnett.

Rose looked demure in a modest navy-blue dress with a small matching hat. The brief time under Mrs. Barnett's care and supervision transformed her until she appeared more than a remnant of her previous semblance. Her face, which had been gaunt and haggard with soulless, empty eyes, now flourished; an elegant, angular visage with her former piercing, dark eyes full of life.

"Quite a transformation, isn't it?" H.W. whispered to Levi as he passed. "At first I didn't believe she was the same girl we saw last month."

"The credit belongs to Mrs. Barnett," Rose smiled at her attorneys' hushed conversation concerning her. "I owe all of you so much, more than I will ever be able to repay. Most people had given up on me, including myself."

"There will be nothing to repay, Rose. I told you from that first day I would help you and I intend to keep my word." Levi offered Rose his arm as he led her towards the wooden doors of the courtroom. "Today I get a second chance to make good on that promise."

The small party made their way down the corridor to the doors leading to the room where the three Supreme Court Justices now waited. As the doors were opened for them, Rose paused for a moment, taking in the sight of the three men who sat high above her head on the bench. All three justices were older men with varying shades of gray hair, their countenances somber and impassive as they watched her approach.

Rose felt in her pocket for the small piece of paper she placed there. Mrs. Barnett had written the words of Micah 6:8 to remind Rose of her purpose that day.

"He hath shewed thee, O man, what is good; and what doth the Lord require of thee, but to do justly, and to love mercy, and to walk humbly with thy God?"

CHAPTER 65

WEDNESDAY, JUNE 15, 1892, WAUPUN, WISCONSIN

The wooden floor echoed each step Rose took down the hallway as she followed Mrs. Barnett to the day visitor's room. A small window located high on a wall showed the gray, overcast sky outside as she passed by it. Dark clouds, heavy with the coming storm, loomed in the distance, making Rose shiver involuntarily.

Seventeen long days had passed since Rose appeared before the Wisconsin State Supreme Court, hoping for an overturn of her conviction by the jury in Grant County. She had been sent back to the prison in Waupun while Levi, Frank, and H.W. argued her case before the high court. Several encouraging telegrams sent by Levi helped Rose to remain optimistic this ordeal might soon be over.

The heavy metal door swung open, and Rose entered the visiting room. Levi, H.W. and Frank were gathered around the small table in the center of the room. Their overcoats and hats, sodden with rain, had been set aside but all three still appeared as though they endured a deluge on their way to the prison. Rose caught herself in a lopsided grin at the sight and corrected her unladylike response to their disheveled state.

She had been so distracted by their drenched appearances she had not bothered to note their countenances until she sat in the chair Levi held out to her. When she lifted her eyes to meet Levi's, she was suddenly chilled by the troubled look in his eyes and the lack of his usual smile in greeting.

"We need to get right to the point for you, Rose." H.W. was the first to speak. "The news we bring is not good. The high court handed down their ruling this morning to uphold the lower court's verdict. This has been the most confounding case I have ever seen; the decision was given over to public sentiment without direct evidence against you."

Rose sat, expressionless, staring into the faces of the three dejected men. The highest court in the state had spoken; she was guilty of murdering Ella, and she would spend the rest of her life in this prison. A numbness coursed through her blood like ice water. Rose wanted to be angry; to scream, to cry, but she felt nothing.

"In all my experience, I have never tried a case like this." Frank broke the silence that weighed heavy around the table. "I have read every word of the transcript recorded in the trial, seen every piece of evidence, and interviewed the jurors myself. Six of them now admit they were ready to acquit you right away but were heavily influenced by the more outspoken members into changing their votes. When they finally acquiesced, they thought you would receive a light sentence because Judge Clementson brought up a prior case that held a precedent in his jury instructions. The defendant of that case received a mere two years of prison time and so they assumed the same for you. All of it is an egregious comedy of errors." Frank stood from his chair and paced back and forth in the small room as he spoke.

Rose sat looking at her hands in her lap. She heard the words H.W. and Frank spoke, but she felt as if she were a million miles away from them. She understood their elucidations but could not make herself respond to their commentaries. She heard that when a person dies, they can see themselves as they depart from their mortal body, but they cannot respond to those around them. Rose wondered if she had just died.

Levi's face had been buried in his hands as he listened to his colleagues explain to Rose that her life was now bound to this prison without a possibility of parole. He lifted his head and turned to face Rose directly. She deserved respect and courage in the face of what she had endured and was about to endure.

He could agree with the others that the verdicts were unfair, he could make an excuse or offer a platitude that lessened his sense of responsibility towards her. He would be able to walk out of this room and return to his home a free person. Rose would not.

"We have failed you, Rose. More importantly, the system of justice based on a fair trial has failed you. We stand without excuse and ask for your forgiveness though it is not deserved." Levi's voice broke as he uttered the final few words. He closed his eyes and waited in the silence.

The piercing pain of recognition stabbed Rose's heart violently. She was not dead; she was very much alive and bound to remain a prisoner for the rest of her natural life. She was able to build a solid wall within herself against anger, fear, and pain, but she had no such defense against the sincere loving kindness offered by her humble friend. Rose raised her hand from her lap and reached to place it over Levi's hand resting on the table beside her.

"You have my forgiveness, though you did not need to ask for it. You have been my defender when I had very few others and I will not forget your sacrifices on my behalf. I appreciate your honesty and your integrity when others who opposed you lacked it. You have done nothing wrong. You have only told me the truth when I needed to hear it." Rose looked into the eyes of each man as she spoke and rested her gaze at length upon Levi.

"Faithful are the wounds of a friend…" Edna Barnett placed her hand upon Rose's shoulder in comfort. "In our morning meditations, the girls and I were reading Proverbs. Rose read this one aloud the other day and asked me what it meant. I told her our truest friends will tell us not what we want to hear, but what we need to hear, because they are directed by truth and discriminating affection. While difficult to hear, it is much better than the flattering lies of those who would manipulate us for their own purposes and our detriment. It seems this rings very true in her situation."

Rose smiled and nodded at Edna in agreement as she stood and shook the hand of each of the gentlemen in front of her. She followed Edna out the door and down the hallway towards her cell. A singular thought remained with her; the rest of the proverb Edna had quoted.

"Faithful are the wounds of a friend, but the kisses of an enemy are deceitful." Rose realized she had experienced the kisses of the enemy and she would pay the price for it for the rest of her life.

CHAPTER 66

TUESDAY, JANUARY 23, 1894, WAUPUN PENITENTIARY

Rose walked down the corridor following Mrs. Barnett to the visitor's wing. She could hear the January winter wind howling outside as it battered against the prison walls, increasing the frigidity of the usually cold cells. Rose had been pleased about the heat emanating from the prison laundry area where she sat mending garments near the boilers full of steaming water.

When Mrs. Barnett arrived to collect her, the matron told Rose she had important visitors waiting and Rose reluctantly followed the kind woman out of the laundry room. Rose shuddered to think who might be waiting to see her this time. Since her arrival over two years before, Rose had been one of the more notorious prisoners held in the penitentiary.

The warden had often made a spectacle of her by calling her to appear so the rich and prestigious visitors could look at the "Borgia Rose of Wisconsin". These visitors, in turn, made generous donations to the funds of the prison that ended up lining the warden's pockets while making Rose feel like an animal on exhibit at a zoo.

Mrs. Barnett tried to stop the warden from exploiting "one of her girls" as she referred to Rose, but she had been threatened with dismissal. Rose had intervened, stating she was willing to endure the humiliation if it meant that Edna would stay in her protective position supervising Rose and the girls in Cell Block A. Rose knew there would be worse calamities to befall her if she was out from under Edna's protection and she had grown to respect and like the prison matron.

When they reached the door of the visitor's room, Rose paused, breathing slowly to compose herself before facing the forthcoming condescension. She nodded at Edna, who opened the door and waited for Rose to enter the room. Rose adjusted her eyes to the brighter lights of the room, now unaccustomed to the normal amount of light in her cell and work area. The two gentlemen seated at the table made Rose stop to stare.

H.W. and Frank were seated at the table, and both stood when Rose entered the room. The customary politeness of their greeting gesture made Rose wince. She did not know how long it had been since a man stood out of respect for her. It was hard to remember in this place that there was still a world of civility beyond the walls of the prison.

Rose sat in the chair Frank held out for her and studied her red, chapped, workworn hands folded in her lap. She had once been so proud of her delicate hands, even slathering them with Hind's honey and almond cream and wearing mittens to bed to keep them soft and smooth. The trivial things she had done that seemed so important at the time now mocked her in her new reality.

"It is good to see you again, Rose. It looks as though Mrs. Barnett has kept you in good health." Frank nodded at Edna as he spoke to Rose. "We came to update you on your appeals process. Levi is scheduled to meet with Governor Peck this afternoon. He will be asking the Governor for a full pardon."

"I don't understand. I thought when the Supreme Court handed down their decision that my appeals process was over. How can he appeal to the Governor?" Rose felt a slight increase of heart rate at the thought of having her verdict overturned, but she would not allow herself to anticipate any measure of success on her behalf.

"Each Governor is allowed by state law to look at certain cases and pardon the person if they feel that the person did not receive justice in their trial and verdict. Levi has not let this rest and has called on Governor Peck countless times to pardon you. He even started a petition for the people of Wisconsin to sign that he could present it to the Governor on your behalf. Thousands of people have signed it, Rose. It might feel as though you have been forgotten, but I assure you that you are not." Frank smiled as he watched Rose take in the information.

"But why would this Governor Peck disagree with the original verdict and the decision of the Supreme Court justices?" Rose refused to allow the sprig of hope that pressed in her heart. "Nothing has changed."

"That is where you are wrong, my dear girl. There have been several developments since you were incarcerated. I think the most telling is that good, upstanding Dr. Mitchell sold everything and ran off to Washington state for a period. Who would leave a promising practice unless they needed to get away? I have always had my own suspicions about him." Frank slapped the hat he held in his hands upon his knees while H.W. cleared his throat to gain Frank's attention.

"George left Richland County? What about Freddie and Lotte? Did they go with him?" Rose felt a familiar panic arise about Laura's innocent children. They were already without a mother. Did their father abandon them as well?

"Frank is correct in saying that Dr. Mitchell left Richland County for a period, but he came back to Richland Center." H.W. paused before continuing, "In fact, Dr. Mitchell married a local woman last spring and returned to buy a house in town and resume his medical practice." H.W. studied Rose's countenance to gauge her reaction to the news of George's marriage. He was relieved to find Rose did not seem upset in the least about the man she supposedly killed someone over in a fit of jealousy, remarrying.

"But what about the children? Where are they?" Rose's focus was solely based on the welfare of the Mitchell children and not upon some fancy of unrequited love on her part.

"Dr. Mitchell married Minnie German. They say she is a very kind woman and has been good to both Freddie and Lotte. She comes from a rather affluent family, but she seems shy and humble. I think the children are flourishing under her care." H.W. spoke the words Rose needed to hear most; Freddie and Lotte were well cared for and loved by their stepmother. Rose put a finger to the corner of her eye to keep a single tear from escaping. Frank immediately handed Rose his fine linen handkerchief. It smelled of bergamot.

"There has been another more significant development in my estimation," H.W. continued the conversation while Rose recovered her composure. "A young newspaper editor from Wausau named Mark Barnum has championed your cause. He printed a letter in the newspaper mysteriously sent to him by a young woman who had made some shocking claims about what happened and about your innocence. I brought a copy along with me for you to read if you like." He handed the newspaper with the letter in it circled to Rose.

Rose squinted at the page before her. Her eyes had failed drastically since she arrived at the prison. She looked at Edna and handed the newspaper to her to read aloud.

"To whom it may concern, it is with a heavy heart but a great feeling of relief that I now unburden my mind. I can no longer carry my secret. I speak now of Ella Maly, Dr. Mitchell, and myself. I was once an intimate friend of Ella and also of the doctor; although she is dead, I must relieve my mind-may a merciful Savior witness my words. The doctor was intimate with us both. He promised to make Ella his wife, but alas, those vows were broken. She told me a week or so before her death that the doctor and her would never be married. He had ruined her, and she said her life would be forever blighted. She said that she wished that she could go to sleep and never wake up again. I will say now that Dr. Mitchell had poisoned her virtue and she herself poisoned her body. I, too, am a fallen woman due to Dr. Mitchell. I wish I might have done what Ella did, but I could not, so I fled up North with my shame. I cannot be known. I would rather die, but if you disbelieve me, take only the child I gave up for adoption and place it face to face with the doctor. You will see him written in every feature. The doctor will try to say this was only written by someone trying to injure him, but why could good Ella not injure him herself? She could not open her mouth against him, and he knew it well as she would have left a disgrace on her name and family. I write this for a feeling that haunts me night and day; an innocent woman sits in a cell and pays for that she did not do. Ere this reaches you I will be far away as I live by aliases as Isabel Shields and others known only to myself. My fate is sealed and the life I lead is short. I will soon go down and fill an unknown grave. My lawful name will never be known. Yours. Respectfully, Minnie Braddock." Edna gasped as she finished reading the letter to the others.

"This young editor, Barnum, has taken a lot of anger from the citizens of Richland Center. They are asking Ella's mother to sue him for defamation of character on Ella's behalf." Frank nodded his head emphatically. "Richland County seems to inspire unusual court cases."

"What about Ella's father? Isn't he suing Mr. Barnum as well?" Rose knew Ella's father had been very protective of his daughter.

"Unfortunately, that is one of the other developments. Mr. Maly died suddenly of heart complications. The doctor said his heart just gave out on him." H.W. noticed the sympathetic look on Rose's face at the news. "Poor Mrs. Maly lost both in a short time. I know that you can sympathize, having suffered a similar loss."

"I am so sorry to hear that. Mr. Maly was a good person and will be missed by everyone, including me." Rose's voice was quiet as she spoke of Ella's family. "Most likely he died of a broken heart."

A short knock at the door interrupted Rose's private thoughts about broken hearts. Edna crossed to the door and opened it. A guard standing in the hall handed her a telegram which she carried to the table and handed to Frank. Frank opened the telegram quickly, all of them understood it was from Levi and held the latest news of Rose's fate. Frank paused and then read the telegram aloud.

"Met with the Governor (stop). Pardon denied (stop). Will never give up (stop) – Levi" Frank's rasping voice broke with the news he read. He looked to see Rose standing from her chair and offering him her hand to shake.

"Thank you for your many efforts, gentlemen. Please tell Levi that he can stop now. I will bid you goodbye." Rose straightened her weary back and shoulders and held her head high as she crossed to Edna and followed her out the door and down the corridor towards the laundry room.

Rose was not surprised their attempts had failed again. Instead, she focused on the one vague thing she did recall, the Halloween night a few years ago and a young gypsy who had called herself Minnie Braddock.

CHAPTER 67

SATURDAY, JUNE 13, 1896, WAUPUN PENITENTIARY

The warm rays of the summer sun shone brightly through the ornate windowpanes, catching the small dust motes dancing lazily in the slant of sunlight. Mark Barnum sat in a horsehide covered chair in the parlor of the prison warden, James Murray. He was offered a cold glass of lemonade by Mrs. Murray, upon his arrival, the ice chips clinking against the side of the glass as he lifted it to his lips and sipped.

Mark sat in his best gray suit with a starched white shirt and a pale blue tie. His wife helped him choose the tie earlier that morning before he made his way from Wausau to Waupun, over one hundred and thirty miles away. He had left in the predawn darkness and completed his journey by train in the late afternoon. He glanced at the closed door across the room, his anticipation was building by the moment.

The clock on the parlor wall chimed at four o'clock just as the door latch clicked and the door opened. Edna Barnett entered, accessing Mark with a cautious gaze before turning back towards the doorway and gesturing for Rose to follow her into the room. Mark stood as the women entered the room with Warden Murray following behind them.

Mark had read so many accounts of Rose's history, he felt as if he knew her personally even though they had not made a personal acquaintance. The pictures Mark had seen of "The Wisconsin Borgia" did not do her justice. They did not portray her shiny black hair, her luminous dark eyes, and a pert nose that was slightly upturned at the end.

Mark realized with a start that she had been caricatured by those who opposed her to keep the public from being mesmerized by her natural beauty. It was only when Mrs. Barnett made a sharp sound in her throat and Mark also realized he had been staring at Rose for several minutes without speaking.

Rose sat in a matching chair opposite where Mark sat and watched him blush like a schoolboy after he had been caught staring at her entrance. Her mouth upturned slightly in one corner as though she found his discomfiture amusing, but her eyes showed no mirth, only a serious, steady gaze.

She looked away long enough to accept a glass of lemonade from Mrs. Murray, whispering a soft reply to the prison warden's wife's gesture of hospitality towards her. She then returned her gaze to Mark's face as she took one sip of the lemonade and set the glass on the small table beside her.

"Excuse my rudeness, Miss Zoldoske. I was very anxious to meet you and talk to you myself, but I don't wish to make you uncomfortable." Mark began his apology with a genuine frankness that had been a trademark of his career as a writer and newspaper editor. He was honest to the point of being blunt and appreciated others who treated him in kind.

"I am accustomed to people staring at me, Mr. Barnum. It used to make me uncomfortable, but I have grown quite used to it. The former prison warden often required me to give an audience to visitors who had come just to stare at me and ask intimate questions of a complete stranger, but Warden Murray has not required that of me since he began his term. I agreed to meet with you today because my attorney, Mr. Bancroft asked it of me, but I must caution you that I will not answer any questions that I deem intimate or inappropriate." Rose sat with her slender hands folded demurely in her lap, her back straight, not touching the back of the chair behind her.

"Your terms are very agreeable to me. I would rather you view this as a conversation between us rather than an interview for publication in the newspaper. In fact, I will not print anything you have not given prior approval. As I mentioned, I have anticipated meeting you in person for several years after reading of your trial and subsequent research I have done regarding your case." Mark reached for the lemonade beside him. His mouth was suddenly dry. He chided himself over his reactions; they were not indicative of a veteran newspaper man.

"I am surprised at your continued interest in my trial. It was five years ago. Most people have forgotten about me, and I prefer it that way to be very honest. I have resigned myself to living a simple life without malice or resentment about the past. I do my work and mind my own business; a lesson I wish I had learned when I first came to Richland Center." Rose's words were matter of fact without a trace of self-pity.

"I have not been able to forget what has happened to you because I am convinced it is an utter travesty of justice. As a newspaperman, I have reported on famous crimes, including the Whitechapel murders of Jack the Ripper. None of the other cases have garnered my attention the way your case has, because you were convicted on the sentimentalism of an entire town rather than on reason. I find that I tend to speak out when I find such an injustice done; to stay silent would make me complicit. I don't see you as a notorious criminal or as an interesting news story. I see you as the innocent victim yourself." Mark stood as he spoke and paced back and forth behind his chair until he came to stop beside an oval picture window overlooking a lush lawn outside. White wrought iron chairs graced a veranda beside a small pond. A sudden thought overtook him.

"Could we possibly sit outside? I find I can do better in the out-of-doors myself if Miss Zoldoske is willing?" Mark turned to Mrs. Barnett and Warden Murray who sat in chairs across the room. The warden stood and nodded his agreement, leading them out the door of the parlor, down a back hallway to the backdoor.

Mark led the way outside and gathered several of the chairs in a semi-circle. Mrs. Barnett followed the party carrying a tray with their lemonade. Mark offered a chair to Rose and sat in one beside it. He noticed Rose close her eyes for a moment and lift her face towards the summer sun, basking in the rays before returning her gaze to him. Mark thought he noticed a touch of gratitude in her glance for the rare opportunity.

"You might as well call me Rose. I know that is how you already refer to me in your mind." There was a hint of a smile as Rose lifted the glass of lemonade placed beside her for another small sip. Mark understood she had just given him a modicum of trust, something she did not give readily to anyone outside her small circle. He allowed her to enjoy the sun's warmth for a few more moments before continuing their conversation,

"Then please call me Mark. I was supposed to give you greetings from some friends in Richland Center if ever I met with you, Sheriff Snyder, his wife, and their daughter Belle all spoke very highly of you, Rose. I made their acquaintance while serving time in the jail myself, after being found guilty of libel."

"Sheriff Snyder and his family are wonderful people. Richland Center is filled with wonderful people, many of them were so kind to me throughout my time there. I realize many of them feel differently about me after all that has happened, but I look back fondly on so many memories and friends." Rose did not look at Mark as she spoke, she kept her eyes on the trees in the distant horizon. A wistful expression played about her face as the gentle breeze pulled small tendrils of hair at her temples from the severe bun at the nape.

"I did not find many kind expressions towards myself during my incarceration. It seems that the townspeople took the publishing of the letter by Minnie Braddock as a personal affront to Ella, her family, and the entire town. I assure you there was not a shred of malice intended towards any of them, I only wanted the truth about what happened to come to the surface as I felt they had blamed the wrong person for Ella's death." Mark leaned forward as he spoke, his hands spread out in front of him in a gesture of entreaty. He could hear the small sigh that escaped Rose before she turned her head to look at him again.

"I read the letter that you published as my attorney brought it here for me. To state that Ella was ruined and possibly took her own life is more than her family would be able to bear. Their response to you was not personal. They were defending her memory against anyone who might attempt to tarnish it. The Maly family has been through so much already." Rose's voice softened as she uttered the last sentence; it was unbelievable to Mark she could show sympathy to the people who had helped ruin her own life.

"While I understand their feelings, it is imperative that the truth be brought forward no matter how inconvenient or uncomfortable it might be to hear. It is my opinion Dr. Mitchell should be claiming libel if this letter were untrue, and yet he was completely silent on this matter." Mark voiced his suspicions about the real person behind all the conspiracy he had uncovered.

"George Mitchell will never acknowledge this letter, nor will he admit to any wrongdoing, purposeful or accidental, on his part in the events that led to Ella's death or Laura's death, for that matter. To do so would be against his very nature. He must believe he is infallible or face the darkness of his soul that he keeps carefully concealed from everyone, especially himself. He will never do the latter; it would ruin him." Rose's statement was matter of fact, spoken with resignation but without the anger Mark would have expected.

"So, in not seeing his own ruin, is he willing to ruin countless others? How many people must be ruined before it is enough? I, for one, cannot abide this. I have continued gathering signatures for a petition for Governor Upham concerning your pardon. I can't help Ella Maly, but I will not rest until I see justice for you, Rose. I am also continuing to help in the search for Minnie Braddock. If we could find her, she could set everything straight for you. Do you have any idea who she is and where we could find her?" Mark finally arrived at his main objective; to see if Rose might know anything about the mysterious Minnie Braddock.

"I don't know Minnie Braddock. I told you I would not answer anything that was inappropriate. What happened to that woman is beyond unseemly and indelicate." The deeply troubled cast of Rose's countenance indicated that Mark had gone too far. Rose stood from her seat and looked around for Edna Barnett, who came to her side within moments.

"I have asked my attorneys not to pursue any more appeals. Each one is only a reminder of the utter void of hope I must face each day. I will ask you to stop trying as well; it is futile. Goodbye, Mr. Barnum." Without allowing Mark to reply, Rose turned and walked back across the veranda between the matron and the prison warden. Her bearing resembled a lady of fine repute rather than a notorious murderer known to everyone as Borgia Rose.

CHAPTER 68

MONDAY, JANUARY 4, 1897, WAUPUN, WISCONSIN

The winter sun had just won its struggle against the foreboding gray clouds when the clock on the wall chimed ten o'clock. Beams of brilliant light pierced the haze, illuminating the small room where Rose and Edna still sat. Rose winced as she attempted to stretch her fatigued legs and arms; she had sat in the wooden chair for hours while ruminating over her story and waiting for the possibility of a next chapter.

Rose did not even attempt to believe that the reason she had been called this morning was for something positive on her behalf. She had rid herself of any vestiges of hope long ago after being taunted with the possibility of freedom only to have it ripped away again and again. Very likely, it had something to do with important visitors to the prison requesting to gape at one of Waupun's most notorious killers, as she was now known.

Rose reached for the cup Edna handed her; both women were tired of waiting for the unknown. The hot tea emitted wisps of steam curling from its surface. Rose wrapped her cold fingers around the cup rather than holding the handle as she normally did. The fragrant scent of Oolong tickled her nostrils and she smiled, thinking of her time with Mrs. Wilson.

There was a vague memory of a story Mrs. Wilson told her about the tea's history, but she couldn't quite get it to materialize in her mind again. Her days were like that; sometimes she had clear thoughts and sharp, vivid memories and other times she felt as though everything was in a haze. At least her terrible nightmares of the past had ceased, when she saw things in her sleep that she could never utter out loud.

Rose had just finished her tea and placed the cup on the window-sill when the door opened, admitting Warden Murray along with all of her attorneys. It had been a long time since she had seen Levi, Frank, and H.W. She noticed that all three men had aged considerably from the first time she met them. The fleeting thought that she had aged considerably as well made her grimace slightly. Rose stood to greet the men, shaking each one's hand in turn. Levi was the first to speak.

"Rose, we came as soon as we had certain news. Governor Upham declared a pardon on your behalf just minutes prior to leaving the office this morning. I guess he wanted to wait until the final moments of his tenure before proceeding with it to avoid any public outcry from Richland County."

She stared at Levi, unable to comprehend what he said. She blinked then frowned. Certainly, these men had not joined those who made a jest of her, especially Levi, who had been the most compassionate to her plight. Rose shook her head lightly. She could feel the darkness trying to come back to claim her as it had so many times in the past during moments of great distress.

H.W. stepped forward to help her, placing his hand under her forearm for support. Rose withdrew from his grasp immediately, feeling a scorching burn from his touch. She backed several steps away from him until she was pressed against the freezing glass of the windowpane. H.W. looked stunned at her reaction.

"Rose, I understand this may be disorienting for you. We did not prepare you for it in any way because you had requested not to know, but I want to assure you that this wonderful news is real. You are pardoned and can leave this prison today." Frank spoke in a slow and steady voice while gently ushering Rose into the wooden chair next to her. Rose sat with an unladylike plop upon the seat and put her hands to her face. Could it be true? She had been pardoned.

Rose heard the buzz of excited voices around her, but she still could not fully grasp the extent of what she had just been told. After serving nearly six years of a life sentence, she would be able to walk out of the Waupun penitentiary and never return. Tears began to stream down her face. She finally lifted her eyes to look at Levi and saw the tears on his cheeks as he continued to smile and nod at her.

"I told you we would never give up and I meant it, even when you had given up. Rose, I have waited for so long to say this: you are a free woman."

A rush of emotion tore through Rose, overwhelming her with its intensity. She opened her mouth to speak but no words would come to her lips, only a gut-wrenching sob from deep within her soul. Edna was weeping while patting her back in comfort.

The small group stood closely gathered around Rose for several minutes, allowing her to give way to the tears that, once unleashed, came so freely. There was not a dry eye in the room, including the usually austere Frank, who simply sniffed a few times and turned away to wipe his eyes on his sleeve. He was the first to regain control of his emotions and proceeded to explain the details of Rose's release.

"We have brought clothes for you from Mrs. Wilson and have booked tickets on the next train. There may be the necessity to be careful and expedient; not everyone will take this news as joyfully as those gathered here. It is important that you leave the state today and live somewhere quietly to protect you from vigilantes and those who would take advantage of your circumstances. Mark Barnum has agreed to publish the story in a delayed manner to give us a head start. Are you able to stand and walk out with us?"

Rose nodded and stood. She turned to Edna Barnett and hugged the matron goodbye. She felt Edna's arms around her in a firm embrace as Rose's body trembled.

"I will have the guard go and fetch your belongings while I help you change your clothing." The matron was matter of fact, but Rose could feel the unspoken emotion behind her words. Edna proceeded outside to speak to the guard as the men left the room to give her privacy. She returned and assisted the former prisoner in changing from the drab gray uniform into a modest dark blue dress and coat with a matching hat. When they were done Edna stepped back to inspect Rose carefully before hugging her one more time.

"Go forward from this day and don't ever look back. Live a good life. I wish you some joy in place of all the despair." Edna nodded her approval at Rose's appearance and led her to the door. She opened the door to find Levi, Frank, and H.W. waiting just outside in the hallway.

And just like that, Rose walked out of the prison.

The sun was just setting when Levi stepped off his train at Richland Center. A lone figure with several satchels awaited his arrival. He hurried to where Mrs. Wilson stood to help her with the bags at her feet.

"I am grateful that you can accompany Rose and Frank. We left H.W. in Waupun to board a train heading for Oklahoma with a young woman who resembles Rose in his company. Mr. Barnum was told that Rose would go to a location there and that is what he will publish in the newspaper. If anyone goes to look for her, they will start in Oklahoma and not Iowa. God forgive us for our subterfuge, but it was necessary." Levi led Dora towards the train car carrying her bags as they walked.

"I closed the millinery shop indefinitely and told my customers I was needed by my family in Iowa. Since I have traveled there quite frequently, no one should be any the wiser. I will decide whether it will be a permanent move for me at a later date; it was one of the things Rose and I had dreamed of doing. I find it amusing she is here in Richland Center before anyone in the town even realizes that she has left the prison." Mrs. Wilson's laugh sounded like tiny bells ringing, making Levi smile.

Minutes later, the train pulled from the station as the rose-pink hue of sunset deepened over the quiet town. The only person to raise their head at the train's whistle was Rile Smith, as he went about his way checking the new streetlamps. He would tell people later that he was certain he had caught a glimpse of Rose Zoldoske through the train window as she pressed her hand to the glass pane in a gesture of farewell.

The town would later claim that the old lamplighter had been mistaken, the shadows of the evening could deceive one into seeing things that didn't exist.

CHAPTER 69

OCTOBER 24, 1912, ESTHERVILLE, IOWA

It was a crisp fall morning as Mark Barnum stepped from the driver's door of his Renault town car into the tree-lined street of the picturesque Iowa hamlet. The brilliant red, orange, and gold leaves on the trees reminded him of the hills of southwest Wisconsin, where he had stayed as an inmate in Richland County nearly seventeen years past.

Mark made the journey from his home in Wausau, stopping for a rest in Minneapolis before continuing to the far west side of Iowa. His wife Phoebe begged him not to make the trip, claiming Mark had been away from home too often in the last several years. His work as a Wisconsin State Assemblyman and his law practice had kept him traveling to Madison, the state capitol, frequently. He was ready to retire from public service and find some new hobbies after he completed this trip to Iowa.

He wanted to acquiesce to Phoebe's requests to travel less, but he knew he must make this journey after receiving a letter in the mail the week before. The mysterious letter, much like the one he had received from Minnie Braddock all those years ago, asked Mark to meet the author in this small town in Iowa on this date.

The author, a person named G. Fuller promised to enlighten him about the identity of the elusive Minnie Braddock with certain specified conditions: Mark would never reveal the information to anyone else, and he would lend his aid as an attorney.

Mark had searched for Minnie Braddock for years, even after Rose's pardon in 1897. He felt strongly that the young woman could lay all doubts about Rose's guilt to rest even among the citizens of Richland County who had not received the news of the pardon by Governor Upham with the same zeal as the rest of the state. Every one of Mark's attempts to locate Minnie had come to a dead end. Mark could not resist the opportunity given to him by the mysterious letter.

As Mark walked towards a modest white house at the end of the block, the door of the house opened, a middle-aged man exited the house and approached him on the sidewalk. The man looked like a burly lumberjack from one of the logging camps in the Northwoods of Wisconsin; tall, dark curly hair with a long beard and a muscular build. Mark began to rethink the wisdom of meeting this stranger in a remote place, but all his concerns were brushed aside at the friendliness of the man's greeting.

"Mr. Barnum, I recognize you from the pictures in the newspaper clippings my aunt, Dora Wilson, saved. You will probably remember that my Aunt Dora owned a millinery shop in Richland Center and employed Rose Zoldoske." Gustav Fuller smiled broadly as he shook Mark's hand.

"Yes, I recall your aunt. She is a very nice lady. Is she here to meet with me? I could readily believe that Mrs. Wilson might know the identity of Minnie Braddock as she had been a lifelong resident of Richland Center. It would be wonderful to finally make her acquaintance." Mark looked at the house while calculating how old Mrs. Wilson might be after all these years.

"No, sadly my Aunt Dora passed away recently. She left much of her estate to a trust, and I am the trustee. I have been trying to carry out her final wishes, which included a matter that concerns you. If I have your agreement with the conditions set forth, then we can proceed into the house and get underway." Gustav gestured towards the front door.

"I am so sorry for your loss. As I said, Mrs. Wilson was a very kind lady. I have come all this way to meet with you, so I do agree with your conditions. I will promise not to reveal Minnie's identity to anyone else and I will give legal aid if possible." Mark nodded his agreement as he followed him to the door.

Gustav opened the door and allowed him to enter while closing the door behind them. He led Mark up a small staircase to the second floor and down another hallway to the back of the house. Gustav pulled a set of keys from his pocket and paused in front of the locked door.

"Minnie is inside. I will ask you not to ask too many questions of her as her health is very delicate. I think once we sit down altogether, many of the questions you may have will already be answered. I keep the door locked for her protection." Gustav reached for the doorknob and inserted the key into the lock. Mark's heart was beating rapidly with anticipation. He would finally meet Minnie Braddock.

Mark followed Gustav into the room, which was a combination of a bedroom and a sitting room. It was appointed with beautiful oak furniture in ornate designs. The walls were covered with striped wallpaper in a pale rose color with a green ivy border at the ceiling level. The sitting room had chairs upholstered in a gold fleur-de-lis fabric and bookcases filled with books, as well as a cheery fireplace in the center. Everything about the rooms stated comfort and a modest sense of luxury.

Mark noticed that even though it was a cool morning, the many windows were open, allowing the fresh air and sunshine to flood the room. He removed his hat and waited behind Gustav respectfully for Minnie to appear in the sitting room from her bedroom.

The bedroom door opened, and the young woman walked through it, heading straight to the chairs on the other side of the room. Mark stood still, staring at the familiar figure before him.

"Come and sit down, Mr. Barnum. You seem to have a continual problem with staring at women." Rose sat in one of the gold chairs and indicated the other chair opposite of her. She had aged minimally since the last time Mark had seen her at Waupun. She was still a natural beauty.

Mark walked woodenly to the chair she indicated, confusion clouding his vision momentarily. He looked at Gustav in surprise and was answered with a slight shake of the head as the other man approached Rose and seated himself in another chair on her opposite side.

"Minnie, I see that you recall Mr. Barnum. I didn't know if the two of you had ever met." Gustav spoke in a calm, soothing tone while Mark shook his head in disbelief.

"I was present when he met Rose back in Waupun. He obviously didn't know I was there, but then, neither did Rose. I found it amusing that he asked Rose if she knew me when I was sitting right there with her. As I recall, it upset Rose because she had some inkling of who I was even then." While the woman before Mark looked just like Rose, her attitude and mannerisms had changed drastically.

This woman had more of a sharp edge to her voice, bordering on flirtatious as she gave Mark a seductive grin. He watched as she lifted a cigarette from a case on the side table and waited for Gustav to light it. She leaned back in her chair languorously and crossed her legs. She looked at Mark's bewildered face and laughed out loud at his lack of understanding.

"I thought that you told him he would be meeting with me. Why is he staring at me with his mouth open like a flounder?" Minnie turned to Gustav, pointing at Mark while still holding the smoldering cigarette. She looked at Mark again with a look of sheer disdain.

"I did explain that he was meeting Minnie. I think he may be confused because you and Rose look alike. Perhaps you could explain to him what happened. He looks reasonably intelligent." Gustav used the same soft tone he began with despite the condescension in Minnie's voice. Gustav glanced at Mark momentarily, sympathy written across his features.

"Explain what happened? How do these things usually happen? Rose had a lot of bad occurrences, starting early on with her younger brother, Willie, dying in her arms. Rose couldn't deal with all the emotions so she would faint, and I would just take over. I have always been the one to get things done and the one to enjoy life while Rose was too busy being a good little girl. She didn't realize I was even there other than a few memories we shared that she thought were dreams." Minnie spoke between drags on her cigarette, the smoke curling around her head like a cloud.

Mark was in disbelief. He had read a few legal reports of individuals who possessed more than one personality, often ones that were polar opposites of the other, but he had never witnessed anything like this himself. His curiosity sprang into action with a flood of questions in his mind, but he remembered Gustav's admonition about asking too many questions. He decided to follow the gentle man's lead in dealing with Rose, who was now Minnie.

"Were the two of you together when Rose lived at the Mitchells' house? I would think she probably needed your help as so much tragedy seemed to happen there." Mark tried to phrase the question in an agreeable way.

"Of course, I was there. Rose would not be able to handle any of that on her own. Do you understand that silly Laura Mitchell asked us to keep her husband distracted while she was with child? The woman knew what a womanizer he was. There was no way Rose was able to distract him with her prim and proper ways, so I needed to take over at times. Those ridiculous townspeople accused Rose of being infatuated with George when it was clear that George was infatuated with me. He was confused at the difference between the two of us, however, and he grew tired of Rose, unfortunately, so he made up stories about her." Minnie's pragmatic tone held no anger, which surprised Mark.

"So, did you write the letter to me? How did you send it from Rhinelander when Rose was in prison in Waupun?" Mark needed to know the origins of the letter that had caused him to be convicted of libel before being pardoned by Governor Upham.

Minnie laughed again, a gravelly, sultry sound.

"All of these curiosity seekers came to see Rose at Waupun from all over the state. The warden would let anyone who donated the correct

amount of money gape at her. One of those spectators happened to be
Mrs. Spooner from Rhinelander. This same Mrs. Spooner mentioned
to Rose that she had given shelter to a beautiful red-headed housekeeper from Richland Center who had been in a family way without
a husband. Rose, being very naïve, didn't recognize the circumstances,
but I certainly did. I asked Mrs. Spooner to take a letter I wrote back
to Rhinelander and mail it from there. I also asked her to call the
young woman, Minnie Braddock, if anyone asked about her in the
future and she was only too happy to comply. That is how you arrived
in the situation, Mr. Barnum." Minnie smiled smugly at what she
considered a coup de grace in Rose's release from prison.

"I can see that you have taken good care of Rose throughout the
years. Did you see Laura Mitchell and Ella Maly as threats to Rose?"
Mark asked the question carefully, dreading the answer. He had
played a key role in Rose's pardon.

"Do you mean did I kill them? No, I did not. I don't have the
stomach for it. I think poor Laura died of bad doctoring and a broken
heart. Rose certainly didn't kill her or the Maly girl. She was ready to
leave George, but that upset Isabel, who liked our arrangements and
didn't want anything to change." Minnie's brash voice had dropped
to almost a whisper when mentioning the name Isabel.

Mark recalled from the letter that she had also mentioned the
alias, Isabel Shields. He looked quickly at Gustav, who gave him a
look of concern at Minnie's mention of the name.

"Minnie, I believe that you didn't hurt anyone. Do you think
Isabel was upset enough to harm Ella?" Mark's mind was reeling at
the thought of another personality emerging.

Minnie's brazen countenance changed instantly to one of reserve
and timorousness. She leaned forward to extinguish her cigarette in a

small ashtray, then stuck her pointer finger in her mouth and began to chew her fingernail.

"I can't say Isabel did anything, but I can't say she didn't. She will do whatever it takes to anyone who gets in her way. She always put large doses of laudanum in the candy but that was meant for Rose not anyone else. I don't like talking about her because she punishes Rose and me when we do. It isn't a good idea to ask about her."

Mark nodded his understanding as a lead weight settled in his stomach. Had he been a chief proponent in releasing a murderer? What was his responsibility now?

"We won't talk about that anymore, Minnie. You have been a good friend to Rose, just like Mr. Barnum has been and it was time for the two of you to meet." Gustav patted Minnie's shoulder as he stood and motioned for Mark to follow him from the room. Mark looked back to see Minnie leaning back in the chair again with her eyes closed.

Mark was silent as he followed Gustav from the room, watching as the man relocked the door and led him down the hallway and down the stairs. His thoughts were turbulent by the time they reached the parlor on the first floor.

"What in the world are we supposed to do with this? I can't leave her here with you in good conscience, knowing what I know!" The urgency in Mark's voice caused Gustav to put up his hands in defense.

"No one knew about Isabel until my aunt died. Aunt Dora suspected that Minnie was present in some sense, but she just referred to it as 'Rose's oddity'. She left a small fortune to take care of Rose for the rest of her life, but I agree it is not safe to have her here. From all I understand, she had no part in harming Ella, nor does she have any knowledge of what might have happened, so in truth, she is innocent." Gustav's explanation produced a strong reaction in Mark.

"While 'Rose' may be innocent, we have no idea what this 'Isabel' can do! Was it your aunt's death that caused this change in her?"

"She acted odd after Aunt Dora's passing, but it wasn't until we received a telegram a week ago that the transformation occurred. Rose found out her father had just died, and she fainted dead away. When she awoke, Minnie was in her place. I have not seen Rose since. I fear she may be gone forever." Gustav produced the telegram and handed it to Mark to read.

The two words were painfully stark. "Father dead" was the extent of the message. Mark felt an overwhelming sympathy for the young girl who had lost so much and now had probably lost herself.

"I contacted an old friend of Rose's; one of the only people she kept in contact with. She was a matron at the Waupun prison, Edna Barnett. She has retired from her position there, but she suggested a plan that involved you, Mr. Barnum."

"Edna said Rose must be incarcerated, but her special circumstances make it so we could commit her to an institution for the incurably insane. She is willing to leave her home and come to be Rose's caretaker at Edinburgh Manor near Stock Grove. Rose or Minnie will not feel as though they have been put back in prison, but everyone, including them, will be protected from Isabel. You are needed for your legal work on the documents to change her identity, commit her to the hospital, and for your complete confidentiality." Gustav explained the plan carefully. It made sense to Mark.

"After all these years of searching for Minnie, it is hard to believe she was here all along. I will escort you to Stock Grove and assist you with all the documents. Is there a date set?" Mark was already assuming the role of attorney, hoping they could transfer Rose sooner rather than later.

"Edna said she could be there as soon as this afternoon if I could get you to agree to come and meet with us today. She has everything ready there and I have told Minnie that we are going to take a short trip to visit Edna. I am sorry if I had to deceive you in any way to get you here." Gustav apologized.

"No apology is necessary. I tried to help Rose from the very beginning because I believed in her innocence. I will do what is essential to protect Rose from herself because she was innocent and continues to be innocent in this."

It was late in the evening when they reached Edinburgh Manor. Minnie had fallen asleep in the backseat while Gustav sat beside her and Mark drove. Edna was as good as her word, waiting for their arrival with hot mugs of cocoa and coffee.

Edna led her friend away towards their new rooms; Gustav made certain no expense was spared in establishing a secure and comfortable home for the two of them. Soon she returned to let the men know that Minnie had been tucked in and was fast asleep. Mark worked into the wee hours of the morning completing the documents necessary to change Rose's name and admit her as a permanent resident of the asylum. At the break of dawn, the three shook hands with each other while Edna promised occasional updates written in vague terms in case they were intercepted by others. No one else would ever know that Rose Zoldoske remained in an institution for the rest of her life.

It wasn't Rose who stayed institutionalized as she never reappeared after suffering the news of her father's death. There were just too many griefs for her to bear in her brief lifetime. As Minnie had stated on behalf of Rose in her famous letter to the editor:

"My fate is sealed and the life I lead is short. I will soon go down and fill an unknown grave. My lawful name will never be known."

EPILOGUE

Life continues, and many of the people involved in Rose's story made a name for themselves in various respects.

Levi Bancroft remained in Richland Center. In the years following the Zoldoske trial, he served as a county judge, a member of the Wisconsin State Assembly, Attorney General of the state of Wisconsin, and a Wisconsin Circuit Judge.

Once he retired to stay at home with Myrtle, he decided to run for Mayor of Richland Center and won the position. Rose turned out to be Levi's second most famous client as he represented famed architect, Frank Lloyd Wright, in his second divorce trial against artist Miriam Noel Wright. Levi always believed in Rose's innocence.

Dr. Marcus Haskell and his wife also remained in Richland Center their entire lives. He maintained his medical practice in an office within the H.B. Allen drugstore located on Court Street. Dr. Haskell was the first Richland Center resident to own an automobile, which he used to make house calls around the town. His name was often associated with both Ella Maly and Rose Zoldoske.

Charles Baxter, the foreman of Rose's jury, became a Wisconsin State Senator. It was later revealed by other members of the jury that Mr. Baxter argued vehemently with all the jurors who believed in Rose's innocence. He even allegedly threatened physical violence against the last two men who held out for a not guilty decision, causing them to reluctantly change their votes, resulting in her conviction.

Van Buren McCollum, the poet-adventurer from Sextonville who had traveled to the Marquesas Islands and lived with the Nuku Hiva tribe fell victim to an influenza outbreak while visiting in the United States. He partially recovered and decided to return to his beloved island in the South Pacific, where he was convinced, he would fully recover.

On his journey, he stopped in California to rest and never made it to his destination. He was buried in a small cemetery there, but when his family came to visit, they were told his remains had been taken from his grave. Everyone was confident that some of the Nuku Hiva tribesmen had come to collect their "brother" and take him back to his final resting place. There is a monument in his memory in the Sextonville Cemetery. He was referred to as Bard McCollum by Robert Louis Stevenson. Rose had first heard from Van who the "real savages" were and lived that hard lesson herself.

Laura Briggs James' young daughter Ada became a well-known activist and suffragette. She had a special heart for disadvantaged women and children. In 1919, Wisconsin became the first state to ratify the Nineteenth Amendment to the U.S. Constitution due largely to Ada's tireless efforts. Women had the right to vote in the 1920 presidential election. It would take until 1968 for women to be called to serve as jury members, giving defendants like Rose the opportunity to have a "jury of their peers".

George Mitchell remained a popular physician in Richland Center until 1917, when he moved to Madison. Current medical studies now show even small doses of the homeopathic remedies, Belladonna and Nux Vomica can cause fatal reactions in patients if used incorrectly. The complications of long-term use of laudanum are also understood.

George's second wife, Minnie German Mitchell, was well known for her kindness and charitable acts in the community. She helped to raise Freddie and Lotte as well as their own three children, providing the love and comfort Laura Mitchell had desired. Minnie's brother, A.D. German, built a building designed by Frank Lloyd Wright on property he purchased from George. The original Mitchell home still stands on Church Street across from the beautifully restored A.D. German Warehouse.

It is Rose Zoldoske alone who seemed to ultimately disappear from all records, including the U.S. census. It was presumed she lived a quiet life in anonymity in parts unknown. No one, especially Mark Barnum, searched for her or Minnie Braddock again. Though she received a complete pardon, in history she would always be referred to as "Wisconsin's Borgia Rose".

ACKNOWLEDGEMENTS

To the many readers of my debut novel, Face Down In Rising Sun; your support and encouragement was beyond compare. Thank you for your patience in waiting for Borgia Rose to become a reality. If only I could write as quickly as many of you can read!

Thank you to the many indie bookstore owners who took a chance on an unknown author and featured my debut novel in your store. Ocooch Books and Libations, Driftless Book Warehouse, Arcadia Books, and the lovely ladies from Paper Moon, (along with their shop cat, Pearl) were among the very first. I encourage everyone to support local indie bookstores.

Thank you to my beta readers, Lorrie, Michelle, and Alyssa for reading Borgia Rose and giving your valuable input. Thank you to my outstanding copy editor, Marilyn, who gives so much of her time and energy for the good of others. All of you deserve so much more than my thanks.

To a wonderful book launch team: Grace, Hayleigh, Annalyn, Melissa, Elaine, Jessie, Sherry, Cheryl A., Laurie, Julie, Ardie, and

Cheryl D. Your enthusiasm made getting the word out about Borgia Rose so much easier.

To Ghislain of Creative Publishing Design, thank you for your artistry in creating the book cover and interior formatting and your patience in listening to my suggestions.

To my mom, Charlotte, and my daughters, Michelle, and Alyssa. I was raised by a strong woman, and I am thrilled to see that my daughters are equally strong women.

To my husband, John, thank you for listening to every chapter as I wrote it and for attending so many book signings, author talks, and public markets to sell books with me. Your love and support keep me going!